UNDERCURRENTS

An Anthology of What Lies Beneath

UNDERCURRENTS

An Anthology of What Lies Beneath

EDITED BY LISA MANGUM

WFP
WORDFIRE PRESS

ISBN: 978-1-61475-676-7

Cover painting by James A. Owen

Cover design by Janet McDonald

Kevin J. Anderson, Art Director

Published by
WordFire Press, an imprint of
WordFire, LLC
PO Box 1840
Monument CO 80132

Kevin J. Anderson & Rebecca Moesta, Publishers

WordFire Press Trade Paperback Edition 2018
Printed in the USA

Join our WordFire Press Readers Group and get free books, sneak previews, updates on new projects, and other giveaways. Sign up for free at wordfirepress.com

CONTENTS

WHAT LIES BENEATH

LISA MANGUM

This anthology almost didn't happen. For three consecutive years, the attendees of the Superstars Writing Seminar have banded together to compile an anthology of original stories inspired by a specific mythological creature and focused on a specific theme. Purple unicorns sparked our imaginations. Red unicorns drove us to conflict. Dragons lifted us up on wings of creativity.

But what to do next? Kevin J. Anderson and I brainstormed some ideas—and discarded them all. Our schedules started getting bogged down with other projects and responsibilities. "Maybe," we said to each other, "we skip the anthology this year." That announcement on the first day of the conference resulted in an audible, disappointed gasp from the audience, and Kevin pointed to me and said, "It was her idea!"

All weekend long, I heard variations on the same question: "Are we *really* not doing an anthology this year?" followed by more disappointed sighs.

The conference ended late Saturday night, and I was in my hotel room—pajamas on, Netflix queued up—when Kevin texted me: *Are you still up and conscious? Can we meet quick for a possible exciting idea? Lobby.*

I didn't even bother to put on my shoes.

1

As soon as the elevator doors opened, Kevin was there. "Sea monsters!" he said. "We should do an anthology about sea monsters, and I have the perfect story for it. Are you interested?"

Yes. Of course, I am, yes.

Turns out, people had hounded Kevin all weekend, telling him their stories of how the anthology had helped them with their writing, their career, their confidence. How they couldn't bear to miss out on the chance to take up another challenge.

How could we say no after that?

Sometimes all a writer needs is a little boost of confidence.

Because part of being a writer is dealing with the fears we feel *all the time:* What if no one wants to publish my story? What if no one reads it—or likes it? Is this the only story I'll ever write? What if I never feel like a success? What if my story isn't good enough? What if *I'm* not good enough?

And just like that, I knew what the theme of this particular anthology would be: fear. Not just fear of the creatures of the deep (though there are plenty of stories about that in this book), and not just fear of the unknown (though there are stories about that, too). But the fear that hides underneath everything else. The fear that creates ripples and currents in our lives that sometimes result in tsunamic waves that threaten to wash us away.

Standing strong in the face of those fears is how we survive.

Compiling and editing the Superstars anthologies is an annual highlight for me, and this year was no different. I have loved reading the submissions, marveling at the boundless creativity and imagination from my fellow Tribe members. I have loved editing their work, giving many of the authors their first experience working with an editor and participating in the publishing process. And I have taken a quiet measure of pride in seeing so many contributors go on to publish other short stories (and even novels) afterward.

Creating something new always carries with it a measure of fear. And each story in this anthology is a testament to an author who stood up, faced their fear, and shared something they created. And that shadow you see over there? Why, it's nothing to be afraid of. Come on in. The water's fine.

SEA WIND

KEVIN J. ANDERSON

T he man held everyone's attention as he shouted into the milling, familiar chaos of the harbor, forcefully waving the stump of his right hand. For reasons I would always regret later, I stopped to listen.

"I have been sent here by the captain of the *Sea Wind*, a three-masted lateener lying at anchor in your beautiful harbor of Lisbon!" His voice was hoarse and gravelly, as if from too much shouting in his life. He stood tall on an old wooden crate, flanked by two burly seamen in fine sailing clothes, canvas trousers, striped shirts. The smell of salt breezes and fish stalls hung heavy around us. Many merchants and dockworkers flowed around the obstacle, wrapped in their own business, but others paused to hear what the man had to say.

"The captain bids me to tell you that the *Sea Wind* is now taking on crewmembers for a voyage of discovery. We need twenty brave young men, and we will pay well."

Francis, my older brother, pulled me with him as he pushed through the loose crowd, weaving our way closer to the man on the crate, our own task forgotten. I held two mended iron hoops in my hand, fresh from the blacksmith, which our father needed for a barrel he was making. I knew we were expected back at the cooper shop promptly, and I tried to tell Francis, but he told me to hold

3

my words. Only a few people were actually listening to the man.

"Where are you sailing?" an unkempt man called out, lounging against an empty cart with a broken wheel.

The man with the stump turned toward the question. "We shall sail westward to the newly discovered island of Madeira, a paradise with jungles, flowers and fruits, and birds the colors of jewels! Then we sail southward along the coast of Africa to rich ports and lands unknown, perhaps even to the kingdom of Prester John himself!" He wobbled on the old crate. "Our own Prince Henry commanded us to discover the world—"

"*Prince Henry* himself commissioned your ship?" Francis scoffed.

The man smiled uncomfortably, turning to gaze down at my brother. The two burly sailors did not seem amused by the challenge. "The prince gave *all* men the task of exploring the seas, boy. Not two years ago, his own Squire Eannes successfully rounded Cape Bojador in Africa—what was once thought to be Hell itself, where men are black as charcoal because they stand so close to the sun, and the ground is a burning lake of sand! Eannes brought back tales of vast lands farther south—and the *Sea Wind* will go *beyond*, mark my words! To lands of untold riches—pearls as big as your fist, more gold than our ship can carry!"

He looked directly at Francis, pointing with the raw pink end of his stump. "Do you remember the stories of Marco Polo? Of the exotic places he visited, the adventures he had? Would you like to see lands never before beheld by the eyes of Christian men?" He paused and lowered his voice, adding fervor to his words. "Would you like to sail with us on the *Sea Wind*?"

The man made me uncomfortable, but Francis's eyes were glittering. He had caught the fever. I tugged on my brother's sleeve, but he stammered out, "How long ... how long do I have to decide?"

"The *Sea Wind* will set sail in four days, but we intend to gather the crew today. Are you interested, boy? Can you write your name?"

"Of course!"

I don't know which question my brother was answering. I was afraid for him, but Francis looked so sure of himself. One of the burly sailors handed him a stained piece of paper and a quill. Francis refused to meet my gaze and carefully wrote his name. Grandfather had shown him how to write it—Grandfather's name was Francis, too—but the old man couldn't show me how to write my name, since he had never seen what "Stefan" looked like.

The man from the *Sea Wind* smiled congratulations at my brother and rested his stump on his hip as if to say he would have shaken Francis's hand had he been able.

The iron barrel hoops in my hand had grown very heavy.

≈≈≈

In the cooper shop, Father turned back to his work, away from Francis, struggling to quell his anger. His voice was gruff. "You can't go. You are my oldest son. I need you here." He began to arrange the staves for the barrel.

Francis wouldn't let his dreams be broken so easily. He gestured to me, even though I wanted no part of this. "Stefan knows how to do the work as well as I do—he can carry on! I *am* going, Father. This is what I want to do, to sail the seas and see the world. I'm old enough now." He paused, still waiting for Father to look at him, to face him. "Don't make me run away from home."

With a tired, defeated sigh, Father let the curved staves fall together with a flat clatter and stood up, abandoning the work. "How long?" He drew a deep breath, looking down at the barrel and then at me as if I were part of a conspiracy. "How long will you be gone?"

Francis seemed to fight back a smile, knowing he had won. "Maybe a year, no more. We'll sail down the coast of Africa, maybe even find a passage to India. I'll bring back more riches than we've ever had!"

Father wasn't as angry as I had thought he would be. Instead, he seemed resigned to the fact, as if he had been expecting this to come any day now, knowing his son's restlessness as well as anyone.

"If you're going to be gone for a year, then you'd better at least help me finish this barrel."

〰〰

Francis breathed in awe as he stared at the *Sea Wind* lying at
anchor in the harbor. "Look at her! Oh, just look at her." We sat on
the wharf as the late afternoon sun turned golden heading toward
the distant watery horizon. The waves brushed against the docks.
The air was heavy with screaming gulls and the salty scent of the
sea.

The masts of all the ships were like a forest on the water. The
city of Lisbon stumbled downward from the surrounding hills like
a staircase into the Tagus River where it met the ocean, forming a
calm, sheltered harbor at its mouth. The *Sea Wind* rocked gently in
the sleepy water, giving us a peek at the line of scum and barnacles
crusted below the waterline. She was a magnificent ship, one of
the largest in port—seventy feet from bow to stern—and could
comfortably hold thirty men on a long voyage.

She had three raked masts, fitted with wide triangular lateen
sails rippling in the wind, brushing against the spiderweb of
rigging that entwined the ship. The *Sea Wind*'s hull was also finely
decorated as an exploring ship should be to bear the pride of
Portugal and Prince Henry the Navigator throughout the oceans.
Her railing was painted gold, as was the stem, embellished with
ornate feathers and curls.

Francis wrapped his arms around his knees as he sat, marveling
at the ship he would call home for the next year, but I could see
that wonder blinded his eyes. I knew my brother didn't notice that
the gold paint on the railing was peeling and scarred by the graffiti
carved there by other sailors. The ship creaked more than it should
have in the gentle wash of waves, and the hull looked as if it might
have shipworm. I squinted against the sun, and I could make out
that the sails had been patched several times. The thick layers of
barnacles at the waterline showed that the *Sea Wind* had been in
the water a long time.

The wind picked up, and the ship creaked. "Francis, what if
you don't come back?"

"I'll come back."

"But you'll be out on the ocean, alone! Everyone knows about the sea monsters just waiting to prey on sailing ships. What if you sail off the edge of the world? You're going where no other vessel has sailed before."

Francis turned away from the ship, looking at me with scorn, but I could see the fear behind his eyes. "Stefan, somebody has to go. Somebody has to show the way, somebody has to dream. I talked to other sailors—the *Sea Wind* has voyaged south once before, but they thought they could never make it past Cape Bojador. They told me terrible stories of the bleak desert that pokes its finger into the sea, making the water dirty brown with sand and so shallow that the keel scrapes the bottom even twenty miles offshore. And they told me of barren cliffs of sandstone without so much as a weed growing on them. That was the edge of the world."

He blinked, then swallowed hard to drive away his anxiety. "Or so they thought. So *we* thought! Until Squire Eannes rounded the Cape, and came back to say there was more of Africa beyond … and more, and more! It wasn't the edge of the world—instead, it might be a gateway to India! Somebody's got to go—you know that."

I saw a strange expression on my brother's face, not just a sadness, but an actual pity for me. "You wouldn't understand. You were always content with the excitement of Lisbon, with helping Father make his barrels, but you know I've always wanted to go to sea, how I've stared at the ships, heard the sailors' stories. I *have* to go. I don't have any choice."

Even though less than a year separated us in age, he seemed infinitely older than me. "I'll miss you, Francis."

"I'll miss you, too."

≈≈≈

One candle in the corner guttered badly, flashing shadows like moths around the room, randomly switching the patches of light and darkness, but it was getting late and we would extinguish the candle soon anyway. Francis wanted to be in bed early, for the next morning he would board the *Sea Wind*, but I didn't see how he could sleep this night of all nights. I would be lying awake myself.

Mother had already tucked our little brother Matteo into his basket of straw, supposedly to sleep, but the toddler could sense the tension in the air, and his bright eyes watched as our family sat together in uncomfortable silence.

Father brooded by himself, not looking at Francis. I honestly didn't know if he approved or disapproved, if he were angry or sad.

Mother stared at Francis, as if she needed to say something but found it impossible to speak. Her fingers played nervously with a loose thread in her faded dress. Her dark hair was drawn back into a braid that was becoming undone, rampant hairs protruding wildly to shine in the uncertain candlelight.

"Francis ..." Her voice sounded uncertain. "We love you."

My brother obviously didn't know how to reply. On the other side of the room, little Matteo began bouncing up and down, shouting in his tiny voice.

"How long until I'm old enough? I want to go on a ship, too! I want to go with Francis!" When Mother ran to the child, she was crying.

After a long moment, Francis met Grandfather's gaze. The old man sat in his chair, the one he rarely left except when he helped Father in the cooper shop. He was not yet too old to work. Grandfather spoke softly, which forced Francis to sit beside him in order to hear his words. I followed my brother, wanting to stay by him for every minute we had left together.

"Francis, you have talked with the other sailors?" the old man said in a raspy voice. "You know what awaits you ... out there? In the unknown?"

Everyone in our family knew the story. As a boy, Grandfather had wanted to embark on a similar voyage, but before the ship had even left Lisbon harbor, he had tangled his hand in one of the winch ropes, crushing it, and was forced to return home without seeing the sea as he had hoped. Perhaps the old man now looked at Francis with envy, because he had a chance to make the voyage Grandfather had never been able to do.

Francis had gotten good at his show of bravery. "I've heard

stories of the abyss at the edge of the world where horrible creatures wait to devour unfortunate sailors. Of the great sea serpents and sirens and—"

"And the kraken? Have you been warned of the kraken?" The fearful look on Grandfather's face said that he would refuse to tell the story, whether or not my brother had heard it.

Francis looked up into the shadows where the walls met the ceiling, lost in his own imagining. "They say that when you are out there, and the sea turns dark, and the sky turns darker—you'll know. You'll know when the kraken has come, veiled in storms. And when the wind whistles through your rigging and tears at the sails, when the water foams and seethes—you'll know."

Grandfather pushed his face closer to Francis's. "And when black tentacles thick as a mainmast rise out of the water to wrap around your ship and *crush* it as if it were straw, and when the kraken drags you under, *screaming*, to feed his children—you'll know. And you won't ever return, Francis, but your bones will keep him company far beneath the sea, alone forever—for the kraken can never die."

Francis looked nervously around the room.

Grandfather sounded forlorn. "And we will wait for you here, a year, maybe two, before we will know what has become of you, Francis."

"Oh, Francis!" I gasped, drawing a breath which was cold with shadows. The candlelight seemed dimmer than before.

A different light came into Grandfather's eyes. "But I know that no stories can change your mind. When that sea wind blows, you must follow it. You must go to the sea, answer your dreams. I know. There is no other way."

Francis smiled, undeterred. "You understand." He turned to look at Father, then back at the old man. "You understand."

≈≈≈

Life was lonely without Francis.

He had left the morning before, looking both excited and afraid waving from the side rails as the *Sea Wind* set sail away from

Lisbon and out to sea. My older brother had been by me ever since I could remember, to talk with, to dream with.

And now I was alone.

Our small bedroom was dark, and the air was humid and filled with the raw scent of the wood slats Father soaked for his barrels. Light rain trickled against the whitewashed walls of our house overlooking the harbor. Faint echoes of thunder rumbled in the distance.

Francis was gone, in distant waters.

Little Matteo cried in the corner, frightened by the storm. I heard Mother comforting him, whispering, "It's just rain. The storm won't hurt you—it's far away. The storm is far, far out at sea."

The storm was out at sea.

I lay on my straw tick mattress, damp with sweat and rain mist, and I knew I would waste my time trying to sleep for a while yet. Silently, I crept to the window and moved aside the canvas curtain, cut from an old sail, so I could peer into the night. Ricocheting raindrops glistened on my face.

The cobblestoned streets were wet, reflecting distant flashes of lightning. The other buildings, every one of them a white box with narrow windows decked with flowers, perched on the steep levels of the city. I could barely make out the dark water of the harbor, and I certainly couldn't see the ocean. But the storm was out there, and so was Francis.

Is the sea dark now, Francis? And is the sky filled with storm clouds even darker? Does the wind sing through the rigging and tear at the sails? Does the white foam boil against the side of the ship and crash on the deck? Is that roar of thunder your cry for help?

I could picture him standing at the rail, his knuckles white and his fingers gripping the peeling gold carvings scarred by graffiti, trying to hold himself steady against the screaming wind and crashing waves, peering down into the dark sea, pale with terror and waiting for the black tentacles of the kraken to reach up and smash the *Sea Wind*.

Francis!

Will you ever return to us?

~~~~~

Days later I walked alone on the beach, far from the harbor. As if the storm had never been, the sun beat down to strike away my sweat. I wandered down the shore, looking for shells, for flotsam, for treasure. By myself.

The greatest loneliness was past now, and I was learning to be Stefan, instead of "Francis's brother." Father had begun to teach me what I needed to know as a cooper, and I was already becoming more independent. When Francis came back from his voyage, I might even be ready to embark on an adventure of my own.

But I would wait for my brother. I would wait to hear his stories, the sights he had seen and the perils he had survived. Mother was already asking sailors from newly arrived ships if they had any news of the *Sea Wind* and when it would return. I could be patient and wait for Francis, though I would miss him.

The sun glared on the water, but I shaded my eyes and saw a dark shape floating toward the beach, a piece of driftwood. I watched it bob along for a few moments and finally, when patience deserted me, I waded out to retrieve it.

I stood with warm water lapping about my waist, soaking into my coarse shirt. I looked at the wood.

It was a piece of wreckage, part of a ship, probably the splintered remnant of a rail. I turned it over, but in my heart, I already knew.

Peeling gold paint, scratched and obscured by sailors' graffiti.

The ocean made soft rushing noises, and I stared at the rail for a long time. Many ships had the same design, many ships could have shed that piece of wood—but I had no doubt.

Mother would continue to wait, day after day, for some word, watching for the *Sea Wind* to return. How long would she wait?

I let the driftwood slip back into the water, and I pushed it away from shore. I knew I wouldn't tell her. For all she knew, all any of us knew, the *Sea Wind* was still out sailing to marvelous, unknown places.

I turned and walked back toward the beach, washing the flecks of gold paint from my hands.

~~~

Kevin J. Anderson is the author of 140 novels, fifty-six of which have appeared on national or international bestseller lists; he has over twenty-three million books in print in thirty languages. Anderson has coauthored fourteen books in the Dune saga with Brian Herbert; he and Herbert have also written an original SF trilogy, Hellhole. Anderson's popular epic SF series, The Saga of Seven Suns, as well as its sequel trilogy, The Saga of Shadows, are among his most ambitious works. He has also written a sweeping nautical fantasy trilogy, Terra Incognita, accompanied by two rock CDs (which he wrote and produced). He has written two steampunk novels, *Clockwork Angels* and *Clockwork Lives*, with legendary Rush drummer and lyricist Neil Peart. He also created the popular humorous horror series featuring Dan Shamble, Zombie P.I., and has written eight high-tech thrillers with Colonel Doug Beason.

He holds a physics/astronomy degree and spent fourteen years working as a technical writer for the Lawrence Livermore National Laboratory. He is now the publisher of Colorado-based WordFire Press. He and his wife, bestselling author Rebecca Moesta, have lived in Colorado for twenty years. Anderson has climbed all of the mountains over 14,000 feet in the state, and he has also hiked the 500-mile Colorado Trail.

THE KRAKEN'S STORY

ROBERT J. MCCARTER

The school of fish is close. I can feel them and taste them, and although I hunger, it is not time to feed. My mother is beside me, her mind closed to me as we wait. I hate waiting, but I am nearly a full cycle past my time as an egg, and I must learn to control my impulses.

We float, my mother and I, in deep waters, but near the boundary of the shallows. There are other beings near us—some common fish, some predators—but they all give us a wide berth. Even though I am not mature yet, I am larger than anything in the sea except for my own kind.

The dolphins visited recently, and since then my mother has been tense and quiet. She has not told me what tales they shared, but they could not have been good. I think it is why we are here.

Something is coming, I can hear it, but it is not a familiar sound. It is coming from the direction of the shallows, from the place where the rock rises out of the water. Mother tells me there are creatures there, strange creatures that live in the no-water and are somehow able to breathe.

Watch, daughter. Taste, feel. Tell me what you think it is, Mother says to me, her mind a comfort to mine.

I watch and I taste and both are foul. The thing slices though the surface of the water in a smooth, straight line. Its shape is long, narrow, and unnatural, and what I feel ... I cannot describe it. There are beings on this thing in the no-water, and their minds are chaotic and troubled, worse than the surface of the sea when it is whipped up by the no-water when the lights stab down in bolts that shake.

And the thing is large, larger than some of my kind, larger than me. I feel something I have not felt since I became larger than the other predators. Fear.

I do not understand, I tell my mother.

They are enemy. You must destroy them. My mother is tense and worried.

How? It is large—larger than me, almost as large as you.

Follow, she tells me, diving down and swimming rapidly along the shelf of rock.

I follow, pushing water from my mantle and letting my tentacles relax and lengthen so that I move fast and catch up with Mother. We glide down into deeper, darker waters, passing several sharks and a school of large fish with yellow tails. It is still not time to feed, so I keep moving until we come to the floor of the ocean. There is something there I do not recognize. It is large, as large as my mother, covered with algae and sand. It is long, its shape unnatural, and has stiff, straight things, like tentacles that stick straight up. I can taste it; it is made of trees, which my mother has told me grow above in the no-water.

What is it? I ask.

Look at the bottom.

I swim down and look. It is shaped like the horrible thing that passed above us.

It is called ship, *and this is what the Great Mother wants us to do with them. She wants us to bring them down. They are terrible; they destroy. You must learn to defeat them.*

〜〜〜

We live as masters of the sea, prey to none, but we are servants to the Great Mother. We do her bidding even if that means our bodies will be destroyed and our spirits released back to Her. Mother tells me that the ship and the beings on it prey on us. That they are wrong-spirited and kill more than they eat, that they always expand their territory even if there is room for all, that now that they are here, in our ocean, we must fight them back, not let their ships on the deep water.

She tells me stories that make me feel small and afraid, and then she has me attack the ship that lies on the bottom of the ocean. Biting at it with my beak, learning to hold it so my tentacles do not leave the water where they will be vulnerable.

I don't like this at all, but I do as she instructs. I attack and attack, eat through the wood to make a hole, expand the hole with my tentacles. I do this until I am exhausted and hungry and what is left does not look like a ship, just a jumble of dead trees.

The creatures on the ships do not breathe water like right-spirited creatures. If we create holes in their ships, those ships will sink and the monsters will die.

Mother tells me tomorrow I will sink my first ship, but that now I can go feed and rest.

She swims away, but I stay looking at the pile of no-longer-ship and am afraid.

〜〜〜

We watch, our eyes just above the water, as the ship skims past. It has great white membranes that catch the wind. Mother has taught me that word—*wind*—to describe the restless no-water. The wind in the white membranes push the ship along. We watch because Mother wants me to understand our enemy.

I do not like the wind. It makes my skin feel strange and my eyes hurt. I cannot breathe wind, nor can I swim through it. I can't imagine what it must be like to live above the water in the wind. I do like birds, though. I should be watching the ship, but I am watching them instead. They swim in the wind much as we swim in the water. For a moment, I feel bad for the terrible creatures on the ship. They breathe the wind, but they cannot swim in it like the birds. They are stuck to the ship and cannot soar.

There is noise aboard the ship, strange sounds I don't understand, and the ship turns, its white membranes snapping as the beings on it point their stiff arms at us.

They have seen us, Mother tells me. Her mantle enlarges as she pulls in water, getting ready to move. I feel such fear, I am unable to do anything. I stare at the ship, the thing made of dead trees, as it groans and slowly turns towards us. It is clumsy, but it is so big. I feel the minds aboard the ship; they are eager for their prey. We are their prey.

Dive, Mother tells me as she sinks below the surface, but I cannot move. I cannot think. We, the chosen of the Great Mother, are not prey. A school of sharks working in concert can challenge us, but they rarely do so. Sometimes an overambitious whale might attack, but despite their size, it's not much of a problem. But these tiny creatures long for a fight; they long to kill us.

The ship grows closer, and I can see the beings more clearly. They have skin that ranges in color from pink to brown, and strangely flexible and oddly colored shells. They have four stiff arms. They move around on the bottom two, and the top two have strange claws that end in stiff little tentacles that they use to manipulate things. They have no fins, no tail, no antennae, but some kind of fur grows on their heads and faces. Their shells are all different colors in white, brown, and blue. There are three of them at the front of the ship, their top arms busy with something I can't fathom.

Dive, now! Mother tells me, her thoughts urgent. But still I stare.

There is a loud noise, and something flies from the ship towards me. It is long and narrow. My mother rises out of the ocean, the sharp thing piercing her mantle. From the ship, the creatures make rough, inelegant noises, and in their minds, I sense joy. This thing, this stinger they hurled, has pierced my mother. I feel her pain in my mind.

She releases her ink and sinks below the surface and tries to swim away, but the stinger is attached to the ship and it begins to pull her in, the stinger doing more damage to her. She is in horrible pain. I can feel it, and it makes me more afraid.

Do as I taught you, she tells me. *Do the will of the Great Mother.*

I am below the water, my tentacles entwined with hers. I taste her blood and feel her pain. These creatures are cruel. If they truly are our predators, they should afford us the dignity of a clean, quick death so we may return to the Great Mother in joy to serve again.

Mother has been pulled close to the ship and is being drawn up into the no-water, into the wind. As her mind fades, I feel the creatures' minds become stronger, more joyful. I sense their hunger. They want to eat my mother. This, at least, is a right-spirited thing to do with your prey. But they are few, and the waste will be tremendous. It will not honor my mother.

I am below the water and, though I cannot see it, I feel my mother's pain as they pierce her with more of their long, sharp stingers. The water fills with her blood, and her tentacles go limp.

To the Great Mother I go, she tells me, and then I can't feel her mind anymore. I let go of her tentacles and sink into the deep, dark ocean.

~~~

The wind dwellers are enemy. I know this. I grieve for the loss of my mother, but I know that she was right-spirited, that the Great Mother will take her and use her again, finding her another noble vessel for her spirit.

But what of me?

My mind in chaos, a current pulls me out into deeper waters, and I slowly sink. My will is gone, my spirit is damaged by what I have seen. Mother wanted me to attack these ships, but how can I when they so easily defeated her? The ships are so large, the stingers so sharp. I am so afraid.

As I float, I am surrounded by a small school of sharks. They sense my grief and fear, and they keep close to me as I drift, as I sink, as my mind despairs.

Over time, more sharks join, and they swim all around me. I am trapped. There are enough of them to defeat me, enough of them to honor my death by eating my flesh. If they do, I will return to the Great Mother. Perhaps I will be reunited with my mother.

The sharks have grown excited, their minds focused on me. They are going to attack. It would not be a bad death, but so confused am I that my spirit is not right. My mother died defending her child and doing the Great Mother's bidding. There is no more right-spirited way to die than that. But me, I will die from my grief. Will the Great Mother even welcome me then?

That stirs something in me, the will to survive. I slowly pull water into my mantle, not wanting the sharks to attack quite yet. I study them as they circle me. There are only a few below.

I listen carefully; I watch them closely. When they move in to attack, I swim straight down, brushing past several sharks. The water expelled from my mantle is my main source of propulsion, but I also use my tentacles, holding them together as one and moving them as if they were a long tail. I guide my path with the fin on my mantle.

The burst of speed catches the sharks by surprise, and I put a little distance between us, but sharks can swim faster than I can over the long run. That is why I head down, straight down.

I had drifted quite deep in my lethargy, down to where the light is dim, but now I swim as fast as I can, deeper and deeper. Relying on my tentacles to keep me moving, I draw water into my mantle, feeling the sharks grow close, and then I expel the water and gain more distance.

This goes on, for how long I could not say. The sharks snapping at my tentacles, but their numbers thinning out. Some because they thought I could be taken without a fight, more because they were not fast enough, and yet more because of the depth.

I swim until I am exhausted, until there is no light, until I can feel the great ocean pressing on me from all sides, until I am alone.

≈≈≈

There are strange things down here. Fish that glow with their own light, fish with giant eyes, strangely shaped fish that look like rocks, and, distant cousins of mine, small, pale squid. The water presses hard against me, along with my exhaustion and grief. I continue to sink. Down into the depths of the great ocean, deeper than I have ever been, deeper than the stories my kind tell.

The world was once just water without fish or shark or crab. The only being in its vastness was the Great Mother, and she was lonely. She created ocean dwellers one by one to keep her from being so lonely, to fill the ocean with life and spirit. And it was good, but not quite complete. In the end, she created one final species to watch over the ocean when she was away creating more oceans and more right-spirited creatures. She created my species, the Kraken. We were not created in her image, for the Great Mother's majesty cannot be captured in mere flesh, but we were created so that all others swimming in the ocean would recognize us as her emissary.

As I drift deeper and the swimmers become less frequent and the ocean presses harder, I can't help but think of the Great Mother. Was this dark, cold, lonely place what it was like before she created all of us? Before she imagined the ocean as a world full of life and not just darkness?

And then I can see her. She is a light in the darkness, so bright, so brilliant. And she is nothing more than light, my eyes hurting at her brilliance.

Do not give up, my child, she tells me, and the sound of her is joy in my mind. *Do as your mother bade you. Know your enemy. Let them have the land, but keep them out of my ocean.*

My mother, I begin, trying to tell her of my great shame and sorrow.

She is with me, my child. All is well. Now go. And she shows me things, but not in words. Things that I don't fully understand. I see the world as a drop of water, perfectly round, surrounded by darkness that is only broken by tiny bits of light. She shows me there are many of these in the darkness and that this world is not the only world. That the Great Mother has seeded oceans on many worlds and has lost them to the strange wind-breathing creatures. That this world is young and there is still a chance that the oceans can remain pure and right-spirited.

The water is so heavy on me that I can barely move. I draw a small amount of water into my mantle and swim up. The light of the Great Mother is gone, but my spirit is right now. I must do her bidding. I must guard the oceans against the wrong-spirited. I must find a mate and have children to carry on the work. I must honor my mother and her great sacrifice.

~~~

The sun and the wind burn my eyes as I watch them. There are two of them in a very small ship made of dead trees. One is the size of the other wind-breathing creatures I have seen with bits of fur on his head and face. The other one is much smaller with long fur on her head; she stares at me.

I have entered the shallow waters as far as is safe for me to come. I have looked on the land and the strange, upright creatures crawling on it, using their odd claws to build things. I do not understand them or what they are doing, but I do see that they are changing the land, dramatically. Many trees are gone, there are brown gashes on the land, and they build strange things out of dead trees that are shaped unnaturally and have a purpose beyond me.

In the very small ship, the larger creature has a stick in his claws and is dangling it over the water with a thread that is tipped with a tiny hook. I watched from below for quite some time. They have used this stick and thread and hook to catch some fish, but in a right-spirited way. Just enough so they can live.

The small creature must be new from the egg, not yet mature. That one has seen me and her eyes look into mine and I see that there is spirit there. Did the Great Mother create them, too? If so, why have they destroyed other oceans? It would be so easy to lash out with one of my longer tentacles, wrap it around the very small ship and crush it, pulling them under, feeding on their flesh to honor their spirits.

But I don't.

I sink below the surface and swim out to deeper seas.

~~~

This ship is large, larger than the one that killed my mother. I am far below it, watching its strange form slice through the surface of the water, driven by the wind. I feel for their minds, and there are many and their disorderly thoughts hurt me. They are hunters. They are not right-spirited.

I have a duty to the Great Mother, to my mother, to my fellow creatures of the ocean. There are not many of my kind, each female having her own territory. The males die after mating so it is we who must guard and protect.

But I fear the stingers of the ship, so sharp, so strong. I watch, but still cannot act, visions of my mother's death plaguing me.

~~~~

The two wind-breathing creatures are in their very small ship again as they use their stick and thread and hook to capture fish. It is the same two, the normal-sized creature with fur on its face and the small, new-from-the-egg creature with eyes that show spirit.

If the Great Mother did not create them, who did? They cannot see me, and I can feel their minds. They are calm minds, simple minds. They fish to live. They feel love toward one another. There is another creature on the shore in one of the things they built that they love, too. A family, like me and my mother once were.

I rise up slowly, at a distance, and the little one sees me right away. Her mouth opens and sounds come out, her claw pointing at me. The bigger one is afraid; the smaller one is delighted.

I move slowly towards them, and the big one is now paralyzed in fear while the small one makes more sounds with her mouth. They fish for their family in a right-spirited way. With one of my longer, hooked tentacles, I snag a fish—small for me, but large for them—and drop it into their very small ship. The larger creature is even more afraid, but the small one is very, very happy. I watch as the large creature uses his claws and some sticks to clumsily move the very small ship towards the shore.

~~~~

Not all wind-breathing creatures are wrong-spirited.

This confuses me. I wish my mother was here. She could help

me. I think of going back into the depths and seeing if the Great Mother would appear again, but I doubt it. She was clear, she wants me to stop the great ships, keep the wind-breathing creatures to the land.

Above me, another ship slices through the ocean, driven by its great white membranes that catch the wind. I am still afraid of it and its great stingers, but I decide to try something. After it has passed, I rise to the surface and watch it, the wind hurting my eyes, the sun so very bright above.

I feel their many minds, but more carefully now, trying to visit one at a time. Some are proud, some are scared, some are lustful, some calm. They are not as one as a pod of dolphins would be. Their minds are scattered, lacking unity. They are well past me when I hear the noises they make from their mouths. The ship slowly turns and their minds change. Fear, anticipation, hunger. They are predators. They mean to kill me.

I freeze again, just like with my mother. Their stinger will spear me, and I will feel pain like my mother did. They will put all their stingers in me and pull me up into the wind. They will honor my flesh by eating it, but surely, they are too few to truly honor it.

And what do they gain? The shallows are full of fish, enough fish to feed all of them, so why do they hunt a creature such as I?

The ship grows closer, moving from side to side, the wind not blowing in my direction, forcing the ship to move in a most awkward way.

I feel their minds again, and they all feel fear, some of them pure fear, some mixed with lust, a few with anger. I can see their stinger as a group of the wind-breathing creatures attend to the thing that hurls it forth. I no longer believe they have shells, but rather cover their soft bodies with colorful membranes, the same kind that they use to catch the wind. How can such a delicate creature be so bold?

The oceans are mine; the Great Mother has said so. The ship grows closer, their minds grow tense, they are about to release their stinger.

Visions of my mother's death, memories of her pain in my mind, assault me. I will not fall to them.

I sink below the surface just as they release their stinger. I feel it pierce the water above me. I dive down and watch as the ship passes over where I was and turns around. They are seeking me, but they are trapped in the wind, and I am in the water, the bottom of their dead-tree ship exposed to me.

I rise up out of the water again, behind them. I must know my enemy. They turn their ship, this time with the wind blowing in my direction, and they move toward me, fast. Again, I dive right before they release their stinger.

Hunters they may be, but they are ill-equipped to hunt my kind. My mother fell prey to them only because she was protecting me.

That thought is like a rock in my beak, hard and painful. She is gone because of me. These wind-breathing creatures are monsters, hunting what they don't need, lusting after the kill.

Above, they are still seeking me, their desire still there, but also their fear. They fear me just as I fear them.

This thought brings me to motion as I do as my mother wanted me to do, as the Great Mother wants me to do. I come up underneath the ship and touch my tentacles to it, the suckers latching on. I am careful to keep completely under the water. I pull my beak close, and just as I did with the ship at the bottom of the ocean, I bite it. I let my anger at these wrong-spirited creatures out as I rapidly chew.

I can feel the vibration of my chewing through the dead wood, and so can the creatures, their minds moving from fear to terror. For this, I am grateful. After I chew through, wind escapes from the ship in great bubbles. This surprises me, and I let go of my grip, and the ship slides past as a great stream of wind bubbles up through the water.

I swim down far below the ship and feel the panic in the creatures' minds. I watch the ship slowly sink, see the wind-breathing creatures put small ships into the water and get into them.

The small ships remind me of the right-spirited creatures I met in the shallows. I swim below the small ships as the big ship falls onto its side and begins to sink rapidly. I could easily lash out with a tentacle and break these small ships, but I think of the new-from-the-egg, wind-breathing creature and hold my wrath. The Great Mother said the land was for them. Let them return to the land.

~~~~~

The grown wind-breathing creature is the younger one's father, and it is their mother that stays on shore in the place they sleep. Their males do not die after mating, which is why there are so many of them. For these creatures, the males are the warriors and protectors and are larger than the females. This seems backwards to me, but the mysteries of the Great Mother are not mine to solve.

Now when I come to visit, when I deposit a still-flapping fish in their very small ship, they do not panic. They greet me with joy.

Both my mother and the Great Mother told me to understand my enemy. I can't say that I do, but as I have come to know them better, I have come to fear them less.

These two wind-breathing creatures are not like those in the ships who still fear me and hunt me. They understand me better than the others. I am hoping they will tell stories of our meetings to help the others understand.

The sailing ships still try to leave this island that I guard. When they head out to the deep seas, I show myself. If they attack or if they don't turn around, I sink their wooden ships. If they turn back toward the shallows, I leave them be. Let them have the land and the restless wind.

Their minds are slow, but I feel them starting to understand.

I have told my story to the dolphins, and they are sharing this story to my kind throughout the great ocean. If you are one of us, if you are Kraken, this is the Great Mother's bidding. The ocean is ours, and we will protect it. You know what to do.

~~~~~

Robert J. McCarter is the author of six novels, three novellas, and dozens of short stories. He has been a finalist in the *Writers of the Future* contest, and his stories have appeared in *Andromeda Spaceways Inflight Magazine*, *Everyday Fiction*, and numerous anthologies. His short stories have been published alongside such luminaries as Brandon Sanderson, Peter S. Beagle, Jody Lynn Nye, and David Farland.

He lives in the mountains of Arizona with his amazing wife and his ridiculously adorable dog. Find out more at RobertJMcCarter. com.

A Marsh Called Solitude

Gregory D. Little

The marsh lay south of the Faithwall's edge. Kitt stood just inside the wall's golden, glowing dome, watching as rippling fingers of gray water gathered, then periodically darted forward before springing back from the Faithwall as if shocked. The unnatural effect kept most decent folk far away from the south side of the Faithwall and the marsh beyond. Most decent folk would never even consider entering.

But if Kitt didn't enter the marsh, her entire town might die.

"Kitt!" Pip's pealing voice called. Kitt's little brother believed the decent folk. If he saw what she intended to do, he'd run straight to Ma and Pa. So Kitt stepped through the Faithwall and entered the marsh called Solitude.

Her first step sank her ankle-deep in slimy water. Uttering a strangled cry of disgust, she splashed up onto a small island of loamy peat humped around a tree. Seized by fear, she looked longingly back at the Faithwall and the cheery lights of Faith's Hollow beyond.

The unconscious pooling of the entire town's Belief—the physical manifestation of their souls—maintained the dome, shielding the town of Faith's Hollow. Within it, Kitt saw a small, familiar-looking Belief sphere, innocent blue dwarfed by the Faithwall's golden sheen. At the center of that sphere Kitt saw Pip's small, pudgy form.

She had to clamp a hand over her mouth to avoid crying out as she ducked behind the tree. Until recently, the marsh had been the scariest thing in her life. But news from the north had arrived with the last peddler. The Army of Conviction, the all-conquering force that had already swallowed a dozen towns like Faith's Hollow, was on the march south. And the marsh might hold the secrets needed to stop them.

~~~~

"Nothing out there in that marsh can help us, Kitt. You know why it's called Solitude. No one who goes out there comes back."

Pa's words echoed in Kitt's memory. And she'd believed him, at first. *Everyone* feared the marsh. But there were always people with strange ideas, people other adults warned you away from.

Neither Dell Cattarack's pa nor the widow Grannit had been quite right since the marsh claimed their sons—the Cattarack boy two years gone and the town bully, Till Grannit, a year before that. But both bereaved parents had told her—separately, yet with the same fervent eyes—that some nights they went to the marsh's edge and spoke to things that never came close enough to see. During such talks, they learned new names for things, even for the Army of Conviction.

The Liars' Army.

Both said the marsh called Solitude once held a different name as well: Truth. Kitt didn't want her town to be overrun like all the others. And if there was a better weapon against an army of liars than truth, she couldn't imagine it.

But Kitt's own conviction almost faltered before the reality of the marsh.

Air and water both rippled around her in a pulse. She felt it in her chest wall, like the crack of boomers at Festival, but fainter. Then it happened again. Her little tuft of land swayed with it. *Ripple.* Like a beckoning finger being curled in her direction.

Kitt moved deeper into the marsh.

~~~~

Travel through Solitude demanded island-hopping more than proper walking. The islands were little more than clumps of accumulated peat occupying the hollows at the roots of the gnarled willow trees that draped curtained leaves toward the surface of the strange water.

Sometimes so hot it looked set to boil, sometimes so cold that fog curled along its surface, the water's only constant was that Kitt feared to touch it. In some places, bubbles rose for no discernible reason, often circling particular islands she avoided.

Ripple. She forged ahead. *Ripple.* They grew stronger with each beat, as though the marsh's heart was waking from long sleep. The thought frightened her, but not as much as the ripples enticed. Something powerful lay out there, something that could help her village. When she finally reached the heaped mound of spongy earth towering above the churning, gray water, she was certain she'd located the ripples' source.

A squat tree with limbs grown up into the shape of an oval frame jutted from the island's peak. Dirty shards of something jagged and sharp lined the frame's inner rim, like teeth ringing a yawning mouth.

Horror seized Kitt as she saw a body lying to the frame's right. The bone of its skull looked soft and crumbly. Its lower jaw hung askew. A gaping hole lay where the eyes should have been. Something had opened up the face of the skull, and Kitt could see right through to the back of it.

Someone or something had lodged a jagged shape between the neck and the lower jaw of the corpse. The shape matched one of the remaining shards in the strange oval frame, like it had bitten the body's neck and lost a tooth in the process. The gloom of the marsh chose that moment to shift, and a tiny sliver of the jagged shape gleamed reflective silver. The glimmer subsided, but not before Kitt felt another ripple.

Could it be a shard from a mirror? The frame reminded Kitt of a large, free-standing mirror. She crept closer on shaking legs and had just glimpsed another gleam when a shiver raced through her and her sphere of Belief puffed away as on a stiff breeze. Shock stilled her. Her body went cold all over, a chill that sucked the breath from her as a dreadful emptiness rushed in to fill the void of her lost Belief.

My soul.

She could not even muster fear, just a desperate animal craving. *Give it back.* There was a terrible scrabbling in the back of her mind as black and grasping things clawed for purchase in the newly empty spaces. Then thoughts of home and Pip and Ma and Pa flooded her, as though summoned in defense. Though it was a struggle, her Belief locked back into place, her sphere reigniting its sea-green glow around her.

Nearby splashing startled her.

"Woke when it entered," a voice said. The words were both resonant and rasping, the first syllable stuttered out dozens of times. Each attempt sounded like a different voice trying to speak, as though thousands competed to vomit the same words. "And here it is."

"Who's there?" Kitt cried out, darting back from the shard of mirror lodged in the corpse as though she had done the deed. Something splashed again at the island's edge, the water disgorging a figure covered in drenched, rotting sackcloth. It was human-shaped, but a hood covered its head and face, cinched at the neck with a length of frayed twine tied tight enough to strangle. Dripping, the shape lurched to unsteady feet and that cloth-covered face turned to regard Kitt.

"It speaks," the sackcloth monster said, many voices still battling over its words. Its head tilted like a quizzical dog. "It fears."

"I'm no 'it'!" Kitt cried before she could stop herself. The creature loomed two paces away and was easily that tall.

The head tilted the other way. "Perhaps so," it said. "A near thing, but you are still ... *you*. For the moment. See the shape of your fear. The army comes to swallow all that differ from it."

"The Army of Conviction," Kitt whispered.

"The Liars' Army," the creature said slyly.

Kitt's heart spared a single beat in its terrified percussion for a thrill of hope. "I need to protect the town from the army. I've heard this place has powers."

"Only one power here," the thing's manifold voice replied,

gesturing at the frame and the shards of mirror. "And you found it on your own."

Kitt's heart sank. "But it's all broken. What did it do?"

"Here," the creature said in a hiss. Its eagerness chilled Kitt's blood. "Can show you." As it spoke, it reached its hands up to the hood covering its face, fingers curled as though to tear into the soft, wet cloth. Kitt's blood froze the rest of the way at the sight of its hands.

Its skin was corpse-gray, patched with green mold and laced with swollen, red-black lines bearing corrupted blood.

Kitt's paralysis broke, and she ran.

〰〰

Despite her long wandering on the way in, after only seconds of sprinting, Kitt splashed through tepid water and breached the Faithwall, landing hard. She rose and ran, not stopping until she'd reached the pooled light of streetlamps. When she finally turned back, the sackcloth monster stood just beyond the Faithwall, staring in, one hand raised as if in farewell.

For the first time, Kitt realized the creature possessed no Belief sphere of its own. She blinked back tears at the memory of her own such experience. When her eyes cleared, the monster was gone.

〰〰

"Kitt, be careful," Ma said, her voice a gentle chiding layered over concern.

Kitt shook away the memory of the marsh, realizing she'd almost knocked Mrs. Choya's pyramid of apples to the ground. She blinked in embarrassment and murmured apologies, moving to a broader part of the market avenue.

"Usually it's your little brother I have to worry about," Ma said. "Your head's been in the clouds all week, my darling. What's bothering you?"

"Nothing, Ma," Kitt said, trying not to sound sullen.

"Well, I need to get some eggs," Ma said. Watching Ma quash her worries only made Kitt feel worse. "Stay here and watch your brother."

As Ma wandered off, Kitt turned a false smile on Pip. But Pip watched her with a suspicious glower.

"What's eating you?" she asked.

"You've been strange since that night I was looking for you. Where were you?" Pip asked, eyes narrowing.

"Looking for snakes by the crick with Jinny and Marston," Kitt replied smoothly. She'd practiced the lie all week.

Pip squinted harder. *Faith, he's guessed something.* Kitt forced down her nerves. He had no proof, and it wasn't like she was going back.

"I want some candied berries," Pip said, all sly eagerness. He wasn't allowed candied berries and didn't have any money besides, but his message was clear. *Candied berries or I start asking questions where Ma and Pa can hear.*

"Here you go, you little cow pie," Kitt grumbled, stuffing a few dented coppers into Pip's grasping fingers. "Don't you dare tell Ma." But he was already off and running.

Kitt drifted to the market's edge. Slow hoofbeats on rutted cobblestones pricked her ears as a peddler's wagon rounded the last bend into town, driven by a haggard man and pulled by exhausted nags. Kitt gasped. It was the same peddler as before, the one who had brought news of the army.

Bent with weariness, the man dismounted his wagon, leaving it and his blown horses. He staggered up to Kitt and slumped, hovering briefly as their Belief spheres touched. Then his burnt orange sphere dimmed, and he sagged into Kitt's waiting grasp, exhausted. Kitt had never felt that much resistance from another's sphere and wondered what strange beliefs and convictions moved this peddler's soul.

"Run get your elders, girl," the man wheezed after regaining his footing.

"What's wrong?" Kitt asked, feeling a rime of frost on her bones.

"The Army of Conviction's overrun Surety's Bluff, and not peaceably. This little hamlet is next. Now go!"

Kitt ran, thoughts whirling. She'd been to Surety's Bluff, just north of Faith's Hollow, several times. She imagined an army of thousands of souls projecting conviction so strong it could overwhelm any Faithwall opposing it. She pictured that impossible power swooping down upon the sleepy clutch of houses nestled atop its namesake bluff. Had they burned Surety's Bluff? Had they killed everyone?

Faith's Hollow was a simple place with a solid Faithwall. It protected the town from wolves and bandits well enough, but it could never stand up to an army. And once through that meager defense, the soldiers could do whatever they liked to the townsfolk.

Her breath grew ragged as she ran. Another thought intruded over and over again, a memory of her Belief sphere guttering out like a candle flame as she peered into that tiny sliver of visible mirror.

〰〰〰

Tobacco smoke hung thick in the tap house air. The ebb and flow of the meeting went by in a blur. Belief spheres flared bright and dimmed as arguments were advanced and then dismantled. The town could be abandoned. No, where would they go, and what if the townsfolk themselves were the targets? The town could surrender peaceably. No, argued the peddler, for Surety's Bluff had reached the same conclusion and had been told in tones of false sorrow that "purity of conviction" would not allow it.

"Did you see them killed?" old Choya asked the peddler.

"I fled in the night," the peddler responded without shame. "The army's Lord-General promised a reckoning at dawn. It was not a claim made lightly," he said, sounding shaken.

"But that proves nothing," Choya shot back. Others agreed. The goal might be to frighten each town into submission without bloodshed.

Harlin the woodcutter spoke as his gilded sphere flared bright. "We should stand and fight!"

"You'd die a bigger fool than you lived, woodcutter," the peddler shot back. "The Bluff's Faithwall collapsed even as I fled.

That, I *did* see. You can't hope to stand against such conviction."

The meeting lapsed into fretful silence, spheres dimming and plunging the room into gloom. Kitt almost spoke up, but she was new to town meetings, and those speaking were all older, wiser, experienced, and strong of Belief. Most of all, set. The people of Faith's Hollow *did not go* into the marsh called Solitude.

For any reason.

Neither the widow Grannit nor old man Cattarack had come. Neither could back Kitt's tale of having spoken to something in the marsh. So she remained silent, thinking about a mere sliver of mirror swallowing a sphere of Belief.

The meeting adjourned with nothing decided. The Army of Conviction was at least two days' march to the north. The town would discuss matters with their families and meet again to make their decision.

But Kitt had reached her decision. She was going back.

≈≈≈

For her second trip to the marsh, Kitt carried a lit torch like a ward against evil. She hoped the thing would be wary of fire, even wet as it was.

Once past the Faithwall, she picked up the trail of ripples, making her way back to the island of the shattered mirror. The rotted corpse was still there, but she saw no sign of the sackcloth monster.

She had a choice. She had no desire to look into the shards of mirror herself. But how could she know what kind of weapon she held without doing so? How could she be sure it would be powerful enough?

Idiot. Do you test a sword's edge by stabbing yourself? But a sword could be pushed through a beam of wood. *How do I test a mirror that eats Belief?*

"By asking," said the legion voice of the sackcloth monster from right behind her.

Kitt squawked, tripping as she spun and sprawling on the wet humus.

The dripping monster, risen silently from the water, made no move to approach. Kitt rose, jerked the torch from the soft earth before it guttered out, and brandished it at the creature.

"You keep back!" she said. Her voice climbed with each word. The creature neither moved nor spoke. "Tell me about that mirror," she said, emboldened. "What does it do?"

"It first speaks a lie," the thing said in its manifold voice. "Then the truth."

"The other day, it swallowed my Belief, just for a second." Kitt paused. The creature had no Belief sphere and might not understand. *Or remember.* "You know Belief?"

"Recall it," the creature said, sounding sarcastic across the majority of its voices.

"How did it do that?"

"You caught a glimpse."

Kitt didn't understand. "A glimpse of what?"

The thing tilted its head. "Truth," it finally said.

A sudden urge seized Kitt. "I want to see this truth." She turned toward the frame with its toothy shards.

"Once fully seen," the creature said, "can't be unseen."

"You saw it?" Kitt asked. The creature nodded. "Why warn me? I thought you wanted to show me."

The monster hesitated. "Was lonely," it said at last, gesturing to the corpse. "Marsh is called Solitude for a reason."

"Which were you?" Kitt whispered. "Cattarack or Grannit?"

Another pause. "Am neither now."

Kitt made up her mind. "I need a piece of the mirror."

It tilted its head. "The Liars' Army comes."

"Yes," Kitt said. "Will it work? Can I bring the shard into the town safely?"

Another head tilt. "Wrapped carefully, perhaps. Must get it inside their Belief. Get their leaders to gaze into it."

"It's said their Belief can't be withstood," Kitt said, but her heart thrummed with hope. Could this actually work?

"Greatest lie is still just a lie," it said with grim satisfaction.

The creature started forward, and Kitt tensed, but it angled toward the mirror. Tearing a piece of rotted cloth from beneath the corpse with a wet ripping noise, it pulled the shard of mirror from the neck of the corpse and scrubbed at the fragment with the cloth. After wrapping the shard in the cloth, the monster approached Kitt, holding out the bundle.

Kitt reached out warily, then snatched her hand back as a thought occurred to her. "How do I know you aren't lying right now?"

The thing's many voices laughed in unison, beautiful and terrible, before abruptly falling silent.

"Can't lie any longer," it said, all its voices fused into perfect harmony for one brief moment.

How can I trust it? But Kitt had no choice. She steeled herself and reached for the bundle, but this time the creature snatched it back.

"Do not look into it," it said. Its vocal unity shattered as it spoke, the words barely comprehensible. Many voices protested, apparently reluctant to speak this warning. "You will *believe* yourself strong enough to withstand it," it continued. "You will yearn to *know*. Resist." Then it pushed the bundle into Kitt's hand.

Kitt walked away, troubled. At the edge of the island, she paused one last time.

"Why are you helping me?" she asked.

"An awful thing you do," it said, and Kitt didn't know if that was an answer or not.

"I'll do anything to save my village," she said angrily, but the monster neither moved nor spoke again.

～～～

The Liars' Army arrived early. Kitt returned to see the north end of town aglow with the light of hundreds of campfires. In the cooling air of early evening, a soupy fog blanketed the village, as though she'd dragged it with her from Solitude.

Fearing she was too late, she made for the lights, skulking behind buildings as she approached the Faithwall's northern edge. In the rising mists, she heard the voices before she saw anyone.

"Please believe us, Lord-General." Pa's voice. Squinting, Kitt found him, his bronze Belief as dim as she'd ever seen it. "We have nothing to do with that awful marsh. We'd love it gone, but we don't know how to remove it!"

"I've heard such pleas before," the Lord-General boomed in an imperious voice. "Here it's a festering marsh, but we've seen similar horrors bordering villages. A lifeless desert. Caves no light can penetrate. The villagers always claim innocence, swearing their pathetic Faithwall holds the abomination at bay, but I know vile heresy when I hear it."

The tall, regal man was on the other side of the Faithwall, but to Kitt's shock, the wall bowed inward from the blindingly white Belief the Lord-General projected.

Just one man, but his Belief is so strong. The small bundle Kitt cradled seemed a flimsy thing.

"These blights do not spring up from nowhere," the Lord-General continued, overriding Pa's protests. "Why do you imagine we began this cleansing? We sweep these blighted lands away before our Belief. I've no intention of letting some backward village corrupt this entire continent. You've been told what will happen on the morrow. I suggest you retire to your homes and families to ponder it. Now go. Everything about you offends me."

The Lord-General began striding back north.

"Wait!" Pa cried with a strangled gasp that shamed Kitt a little. "We are putting together a basket of gifts, the best our village has to offer." The Lord-General was still striding away, the Faithwall struggling to reassert itself in his wake. "We make a very fine apple brandy!" Pa called in desperation, and at that, the Lord-General stopped. When he turned back, Kitt saw the greedy gleam in his eyes.

"Have this basket brought to the edge of town, but know it will change nothing," the Lord-General said. "And I will have each and every item within tested for poison," he added wryly. "Three of your fellow villages already tried that trick." Then he turned and was gone.

Pa looked lost. Kitt rushed up to him and threw her arms around him in a hug.

"Pa!" she said. "I want to be the one to deliver the basket."

"Kitt," Pa said, his surprise unable to overcome his weariness. "How long ... never mind. You can, if you're careful," he said, sounding emptied. "The basket is at the taproom. It should be ready by now. Leave it here then come straight home. I want to see my family a good long while before morning."

≈≈≈

Kitt kept expecting it to go wrong somehow. She retrieved the basket filled with brandy, wheels of cheese, and the finest cured meats Faith's Hollow had to offer. Once, Kitt would have goggled at so many fine foods gathered together. Now they looked pathetic.

Still, there was plenty of room in the bottom to slip in the tightly wrapped bundle. Kitt hoped the filthy sackcloth would not discourage the Lord-General from unwrapping it, but she wasn't about to risk switching the cloth herself.

The campfires north of the market lit the fog a baleful orange. Each warmed soldiers eager to see her town ground to dust. And why?

For a lie.

"Oy," said a gruff voice. A soldier emerged from the gloom, armor clattering and shining in the light of his Belief. "Bring that basket here."

"I'm to leave it, m'lord," Kitt said, not wanting to get too close to the man. She put the basket down and took a step back at his approach. The man's smile below his steel helm was predatory. He bent to root in the basket.

Breath catching, Kitt lied without thought. "My father told the Lord-General exactly what to expect. If you pilfer, he'll know it!" Her voice trembled.

The soldier stopped his search, turning cold, reptilian eyes upon Kitt. He smiled again.

"Have it your way, girl," he said. "But I'll be the one killing you tomorrow. Sleep tight while you think about that." Then he strode off into the gloom, the basket at his side.

≈≈≈

"Kitt!" Pip's voice came from far away. Vigorous shaking followed.

Gray light poured through Kitt's cracked eyelids. Morning. Why did that seem so important?

She rose so swiftly she knocked Pip over, earning a startled cry and a small fist under her ribs.

"What happened?" Kitt asked, ignoring his temper. The family had stayed up late, playing games and reminiscing, filling the hours with laughter for Pip's sake. Kitt couldn't remember falling asleep.

But the village was apparently still standing.

"Kitt," Pip whined. "Ma and Pa went out, and they said I can't go outside without someone watching me. There's just *you* now." His tone held such disgust that Kitt almost smiled. But not yet.

"What's the hurry?" she asked warily.

"Something strange happened last night, and I want to see!" Pip's eyes were wide with pure eagerness and just a hint of fear. Kitt felt the exact opposite. Could it have worked?

"Okay," she said. "But get dressed first," she added after Pip stopped whooping.

Their house stood near the town's northern edge, so Kitt did not have to wait long for answers. The people of Faith's Hollow stood in a large clump at the Faithwall's edge. They should have been locking eyes with an army ready to exterminate them.

Instead, they stared into a marsh that had not been there the night before.

〰〰〰

Kitt pawned a protesting Pip off on the first adult she found. She jogged a quick circuit of the Faithwall to confirm her fear. *The marsh surrounds the whole town. It grew in the night.*

Twenty paces in, Kitt understood her plan had worked when she saw the first members of the Liars' Army. Or rather, what was left of them.

A dozen men stood in scattered clumps, knee-deep in what looked like scalding water. Their armor dangled loose from their shoulders. Their heads hung in their hands, fingers laced together and covering as much of their faces as possible. They didn't stir at all as Kitt island-hopped past them.

Not one of the soldiers possessed a Belief sphere. The mark of a person's soul, theirs had been snuffed out. It was far more awful than she'd expected.

I didn't do this, did I?

The imagined voice of the sackcloth monster answered. *What did you expect?*

She followed the ripples without thought, navigating by instinct, her mind pondering the hundreds of soldiers standing in the same pose, bereft of Belief.

It ate *the soldiers' Belief and grew more marsh out of it.* A sick feeling churned in Kitt's gut, solidifying into a weight that grew heavier with each step. She had saved the town from one threat and doomed it in one fell swoop. All their farms and crops lay outside the Faithwall … if they even still existed in this new world.

Kitt had only seen a fraction of the men she'd condemned to this fate before she found the shard of mirror. A man held it up before his face, just a common soldier she had no way of recognizing. Kitt approached the shard's non-reflective side, so her first view of the truth was in the man's face.

The soldier's eyes no longer existed. His face now matched the corpse near the mirror, a gaping hole where his eyes and most of his nose should be. But instead of bone or brain or the fierce glow of his soul, within that rough oval of puckered flesh was an infinite blackness more profound than any she had ever seen.

Voices emerged from that gaping emptiness. Howling, arguing voices.

Kitt reached up and plucked the mirror shard from the man's grasp, holding it facing away from her. The man's hands immediately closed around his face, covering the hole and muffling the voices. She knew they lurked still.

Splashing behind her. "So many new brothers," said the sackcloth monster's voices. "The Liars' Army, liars no more."

"You did this," Kitt said, turning to face the creature. "You tricked me."

"*Warned* you," it said. "Can't lie any longer. Must spread truth if given the chance. You made the choice."

"They'd have killed us all!" Kitt replied around tears. "Because of you!"

"Because of truth," the creature corrected.

"And what is this truth?" Kitt cried.

"Certain?" it asked softly, and Kitt's whole body shuddered. *What have I done? My village. My family. Pip. I can't face them. Not until I know what I've done.*

"Yes," she said.

"A lie affects the world only so long as someone believes it. Once belief stops, the lie is gone, yes?"

"Stop riddling!" Kitt roared around her sobs. "Tell me the truth!"

The creature tilted its head.

"The *soul* is the lie," it said softly. "So long as you believe, it can exist. The moment you stop ..."

"No!" Kitt said. "No, *you* are lying! Lying to get me to do *your* dirty work!"

"You have to believe such," the creature whispered in its chorus voice. "The soul's lie unites the warring voices that make up you. Gives them direction. Purpose. It makes you ... *you.* Thought of losing that, too much to bear or believe."

"You're lying!" It was all Kitt could say. Every fiber of her being told her it must be so, told her the same thing: *I am me. I exist.* If she didn't, what was she?

"Look and see," the sackcloth monster said genially. "Look and see."

Kitt did. Turning the mirror in her hands, she stared down into its bright surface. She saw herself, her face tear-streaked, reddened with guilt and grief. She was Kitt, and Kitt, frightened and defiant and guilty, stared back at her.

That's right, she thought in savage triumph. *I am me! You are the liar!*

Then something minute shifted in her reflection's dark eyes. Her pupils lost their sheen. That was all, but it was everything.

Kitt saw. She really *saw.*

The wave of terrible truth rippled out from those reflected

pupils and consumed everything she could see. She tried to turn away, to see something that still contained the lie—*no not a lie can't be a lie can't be can't be!*—to rebuild a bulwark she could hide behind. But everything rippled. Everything dissolved. *She* dissolved.

A sea-green sphere of Belief puffed out, and this time it did not relight.

A loose amalgam of howling demands and desires spilled forth from the ruins of what used to be a person. They called out in confusion, hearing one another for the first time, each fighting for control.

They shared only one imperative.

More.

〜〜〜

Rocket scientist by day, fantasy and science fiction author by night, Gregory D. Little is the author of *Unwilling Souls* and *Ungrateful God*, the first two volumes of the Unwilling Souls series. His short fiction can also be found in the anthologies *A Game of Horns* and *Dragon Writers*. When not writing, he can generally be found traveling or planted in front of a gaming console. He lives in Virginia with his wife and their yellow Labrador.

You can visit him at www.gregorydlittle.com.

THE SIRENS' SONG

AUBREY PRATT

The anticipation of the hunt thrummed through my veins. I detested the sensation. It wasn't something I had become accustomed to, and I hoped I never would. But the others, my sisters, as I was supposed to think of them now, relished the feeling. The pulse of power that bled through the Sirens, heightening our strength, vision, smell, also sent swells of venom through our saliva.

My sisters swam next to me, their bloodlust palpable, waves of it rippling through the black sea. They swarmed in circles, clustered and waiting, twenty feet below the surface which raged with a storm the king had created, his power strong enough to control the weather of the human realm. A ship was near, and with our Siren instincts, we could all sense it.

Siren. The word still rattled inside my mind, the final, cutting word of the king's decree. His curse had stripped away everything that I was, everything that I held dear. For I had been born Fae, one of the race of ethereal Faerie created by the Gods. The Fae looked like humans, only stronger, more powerful, and more beautiful in every way. Divided into four kingdoms, the Fae realm had been my home. I had been born a noble into the Water Kingdom, and blessed with the gifts of the Goddess of Water.

It had been eight months since I had been *Changed.* Eight months since I had been banished from the Fae realm into the flat, faded world of the humans. Eight months since I'd spoken my last words. I wish I had fully realized at the time they would be my last.

Such empty, useless, naïve words.

I didn't say goodbye to my parents, or tell them I loved them. I wasn't brave enough to be honest, to tell the king exactly who had convinced me to break his command, who had promised me protection from consequences. Instead I had begged Rhion to save me, to defy the king—his father. The entire court heard the plea I shouted across the throne room as I was hauled away by the High Guards of the Water King's forces.

Rhion didn't answer my plea. He didn't do anything except watch, surprised and perhaps angry at the decision of his father. But that anger wasn't enough to persuade him to act in defense of his lover. My parents watched in horror as their only daughter was stripped of her title, her immense power, and cursed from being Fae nobility to a Siren—a lower race of Fae regarded as little more than intelligent animals or sexual conquests for bored Fae males.

Now I lived among the Siren who were tasked to guard the borders outside the realm, but we were no guardians. We were *huntresses.* No human had ever breached the shield of the Fae realm, and if they had, they would have met the higher Siren, our sisters inside the realm who were the real guardians. No, we were dumped outside and left to hunt stray humans for our king and his *experiments.*

Nihala, our leader, motioned for me as she swam for the surface. I followed, grateful her tail was pale blue and her hair almost white, allowing me to see her through the darkness. Slowly, Nihala and I breached the surface of the water, keeping low, out of sight. The promised ship sailed across the black water, glinting silver in the moonlight. The rain and wind had died, leaving only the chop of the waves as evidence of the storm. A storm that had brought the ship a hundred miles off course and right into our hunting grounds.

Nihala turned to me, her pupils dilated. She fought off the beast within her, looking to me to help her stay anchored. I didn't succumb to the feeding frenzy the way natural-born Siren did. The blood of the sailors called to me, singing its song of temptation on the breeze, but not in a way that made me half-crazed with need. It was why Nihala had put up with my sulking demeanor since my banishment to Siren Island. She learned on my very first hunt how useful I would be. It took great effort on her part not to feed on the humans she needed to capture; for the other Siren, it was nearly impossible.

The sailors called to one another, haggard, but relieved the storm had finally calmed. If only they knew the true storm that was about to descend. On Nihala's command, a dozen Siren silently sped to the hull of the ship, pressing their hands against it, their tails beating against the rough waters. The ship began to slow, then seconds later, ghosted to a stop.

The remaining Siren spread through the water, their swarming circle unfurling up toward the ship. One by one, twenty heads appeared above the surface of the water, each more striking and deadly than the last. Hair of so many hues—white, black, blonde, green, flaming red—floated across the water, tresses decorated with shells and pearls, clipped back with the bones of small fish. The Sirens' parted lips and clever eyes were accentuated by high cheekbones and pert noses. Beautiful. Even in my distaste for what they were—what *I* was—I couldn't deny the primal, sensual allure they held. Both their beauty and their exquisite melody were their weapons.

Nihala rose higher out of the water and began the song.

My body convulsed as I fought against the song, hating this part of my new self. I didn't want to sing; I wanted to *speak*. I wanted to be Fae again. I wanted the last eight months to be a horrible dream. But my curse didn't care what I wanted. Unbidden, my mouth opened, and the song poured out, the melody interlacing with my sisters' as our web was woven.

The song drifted across the salty breeze to the ship, layered with harmonies to entrance and entrap. High, feminine notes to prick the ears of males and lure them away from reason. Sweet, midrange notes to soothe their suspicions and fears. Rich, low notes to lull them into submission.

The sailors wandered from their posts toward the ship's railing, their eyes wide, their ears filled with song. With each step, the song assaulted their senses, their reason, pulling them farther and farther into a trance.

Some of the men climbed down the rope ladders, while others stood frozen, too addled to do anything but stare into the stunning faces of death. The captain of the ship seemed to be the only one of them who had not fully succumbed to the Sirens' song. He gripped a post of the ship, his eyes half-vacant, refusing to let himself wander from it.

Nihala waited until most of the sailors had drifted into our trap before she let out a last, haunting note, and the song ended. She smiled at a sailor dangling from a rope ladder only a foot from her. Death's smile. He smiled back, beguiled and utterly at her mercy. She lunged forward faster than the mortal could comprehend, and sank her fangs into his neck. The tang of blood burst into the air, and I could almost taste it. Venom surged through my throat, lengthening my canines into fangs.

The remaining Siren darted forward, and all of the sailors near the water were snatched within seconds. Their cries pierced the air as venom-coated fangs bit into the soft flesh of their necks. The venom took almost thirty seconds to tranquilize, and for those thirty seconds, the males thrashed and screamed and fought, but none were strong enough to break free of the Sirens' grips. The Siren greedily drank up the humans' blood, hardly noticing the writhing of their prey.

The sailors still on the ship began to stir, their trance fading, pierced by the screams of their shipmates. Nihala looked to me and passed off the unconscious male she had bitten. She had bitten him only to tranquilize him; she would feed later, after her mission was completed. I reached for the male and held him, taking care to keep his face above the water.

Nihala grabbed onto the rope ladder and hauled herself out of the water. With a flash of magic, the only magic Siren possessed, she exchanged her tail for legs and climbed up the hull of the ship. A wisp of pale, iridescent blue cloth hung from her waist to her knees, the exact shade of her tail. As she climbed, she began her song again. I joined her, our voices sounding flat compared the choir that sang just moments ago. But it was enough. By the time Nihala reached the railing of the ship, the song had cast its spell once more.

The males' faces lit with lust as she slid over the railing, graceful as a cat. Seconds later, two of them were tossed over the side, their necks bloody, their bodies useless until her venom left their system, which wouldn't be for several hours. The limp bodies splashed into the water, and I grabbed them. It was my task to hold the humans until they were ready to be transported.

I looked around the watery carnage for Iska, Nihala's second, who was to transport the humans with her into the Fae realm. Iska should have already been by my side, but she loved the hunt too much. She wasn't content to wait and watch the humans be fed upon as I always did.

I finally spotted her near the rear of the ship, her orange hair bright, even in the dark. She fed on a human as two other bodies she had already feasted on floated near her. But that was her way— she only had a sliver of self-control after she had devoured a few humans first.

"Ready?" Nihala called out in the Siren's language from the railing of the ship. The Siren's language was rudimentary, with only a few hundred words that didn't sound like words so much as yowls and caws above the water. Beneath the waves, the language was a bit more graceful, but still so, so limited. That was another reason for the loneliness I had endured since becoming a Siren. There was no discussion of complex thoughts or emotions; there simply weren't words for them.

Iska either didn't hear Nihala's call or ignored it.

Nihala plunged into the water next to me, another male tucked beneath her arm. Her tail bloomed from her legs, and she reached for one of the males I held. I pushed him toward her, my heart pausing as I saw his face illuminated by the moonlight. His head hung at an unnatural angle. I pulled him back and pressed my fingers to his throat, searching for a pulse.

Nothing.

He was useless to us now. The king only wanted *live* humans.

Nihala grabbed the two remaining males from me, then waved at me to return to the ship. I hesitated. I had never hunted. I had never been the one to make the kill, to sink my teeth into a human, to taste the blood the Siren savored so much. But I knew Nihala's self-control was waning. She wouldn't be able to bite again and not feed.

I pushed my unease aside and grabbed the rope ladder to climb up the ship. Just as I did, one of the last sailors splashed into the water only feet from me. I jutted toward him and grabbed him before he could escape. But I hadn't needed to worry. The sailor hadn't jumped from the ship to flee; he was so drugged on the song he must have fallen in by mistake.

I held him close, studying his face. He had a mop of mousy-brown hair, overly large eyebrows, a crooked nose. His dazed, watery eyes beheld my own, and widened a fraction. I shuddered at his utter *humanness*. Why any Gods bothered to create humans was a mystery to me.

I leaned in for his throat, but hesitation pulled me back. I looked at him once more, brushing my thumb along his lips, feeling a twinge of pity for the helpless male. He sucked in a breath at the contact, eager for more. The instinct to bite, to consume, raged through me, and I couldn't help but feel that maybe I should follow it. Killing him now would certainly be a mercy. The king's priestesses were searching for some answer they couldn't find, and they had taken to testing their powers and experiments on humans. I could think of no worse way to die than *slowly*, a subject of study and regarded as nothing more than a beast. There would be no sympathy for the human's pain or fear. He would be butchered bit by bit, week after week, until his body gave out.

But whatever pity I felt in that moment was gone in the next. Nihala had been given a command by the king, and we would follow it, or we would all face his wrath. I had already suffered enough for disobedience.

Before I could stop myself again, I shoved my mouth against his throat. A *pop* thundered through my ears as my fangs punctured his skin. Hot blood flooded my mouth and poured down my throat. I tore my mouth away, overwhelmed by the taste. I couldn't tell if

I loved it or hated it, or if I was simply too disgusted to be so near a human. In all my lifetime as a Fae, I never thought I would see a human, let alone bite one.

I looked for Iska, ready to pass her this last human, but she was still lost in her bloodlust. Panic slithered through me. Time was wasting, and the king was not a patient man.

You must come with me, Nihala said into my mind. Communicating mind-to-mind was another gift of the Siren that I had yet to get used to. I shook my head.

I can't. I wasn't allowed. If the king saw me in his realm after he had banished me, I didn't know what would happen.

You must, she said, her voice almost frantic. *There is no one else. If we fail, we may all be slaughtered.*

She shoved one of the humans toward me, dismissing any more discussion. She turned onto her back and swam for the Fae realm, resting the heads of the two remaining males against either side of her neck. I warred with myself, searching for a solution, but couldn't find any. Nihala was not exaggerating about the king's reaction if we failed to deliver to him what he so desired.

I pulled the humans to me as Nihala did and swam after her, shuddering at the closeness of them. The legends I had heard were true—humans did indeed smell like beasts.

≈≈≈

A crackle of electricity hummed through me as we neared the shields. They were invisible but thrummed with a potent magic that surrounded the Fae realm, a thousand miles in circumference. No humans or Fae could cross through the shields, except for through a tiny portal at the seam, a small chink in the armor that had gone unnoticed when the shields were created.

My stomach clenched as I dove under the surface. I was going back into the Fae realm, back to my *home.* I panicked, not sure if I could do it. When I was first banished, all I wanted was a way back to my life. I had tried swimming through the portal again and again, until finally I had turned away, defeated. The portal only opened when the king allowed, and so now, months later, I would return, but not to the life I desired. That life was gone, taken from me, and now lost forever. I would return, parading into the throne room where my world had been torn away, towing two filthy humans in my wake.

Even worse, it was the month of the Goddess. There would be celebrations and nobility gathered for the occasion, and all there would see me as a Siren. The girl that had been dragged from the throne room had been Fae. The girl returning was a creature of ridicule.

A hundred feet below the surface, the water was black, impossible to see through, even with my Siren's eyesight. The magic of the shield pressed down, squeezing me as I swam through it. Just when I thought the pressure would crush me, I shot through the other side. I sped upward, afraid I had taken too long and the humans would have drowned.

When I broke the surface, a balmy breeze kissed my cheeks, so much softer here than in the human world. The pulse of magic from the Fae realm coursed over me, a heady sensation. I dashed forward, swimming almost twice as fast as normal under its caress.

Light danced in the water ahead, illuminating an underwater staircase. We had reached the cavern at the base of the palace. I joined Nihala at the staircase and hoisted my humans out of the water, resting them next to hers. We pressed down on their chests, leeching the water from their lungs, and let out breaths of relief when we found them still alive.

I willed my magic, a weak echo of the power I had once wielded, and shifted my tail into legs, wrapping my waist and thighs in violet fabric to cover my sudden nakedness. The fabric was made of the same fiber as my tail, and the magic it took to keep it, and my legs, in place wouldn't hold for more than a few hours. I stood on the rough limestone steps, my new legs shaking as they supported my weight plus the weight of the two humans I held.

Nihala led the way up the staircase, which crept from beneath the water up along the rough-hewn wall of the cavern to the servants' entrance of the palace. She carried her humans under her arms on either side, an awkward and wide bulk. I followed suit, grateful for the magic of the realm strengthening me.

Jeers and stares followed Nihala and me as we neared the servants' entrance. Fae males were not so easily entranced by the Siren as humans were, but their attraction to them—*us*—was just as potent. Fae males often sought to dally with a Siren as a rite of passage. The challenge of convincing a Siren to trade her tail for legs had become almost a sport for Fae males. And because the Siren usually tried to kill the male first, it made the challenge, and the success of it, all the more thrilling.

I turned my eyes away from the blatant stares. I recognized some of the guards. I had once relished the wanton looks they had given me as I strolled the palace grounds with Rhion. Now I silently prayed they wouldn't recognize me. But I knew that hope was futile. The rare color of my tail, and thus my fabric covering me, would give me away if my face didn't. Still, I lowered my eyes.

One of the guards stepped in Nihala's path. She held her ground, lifting her chin to meet his eyes. He slid the back of his hand across her chin and down her neck. She hissed and jerked out of his reach. He bellowed out a laugh, which was shared by his fellow guardsmen, but he stepped aside, allowing Nihala to pass. She hurried for the doorway and didn't pause to look back to make sure I followed.

When I reached the guard, his eyebrows lifted in surprise. He did indeed recognize me. A blush crept up my cheeks.

"Lady Sintus," he said, then catching himself, smiled. "But you're no lady anymore. Valyria, wasn't it? You look damn fine as a Siren, Valyria."

He reached for my hair, twirling the strands between his fingers. Before I could think, I dropped one of the humans I held and slapped his arm away. The words I couldn't utter beat against the back of my throat, roaring for release. I wanted to yell, to fight, to scream at this guard that if he touched me again he would lose his arm. Eight months ago, I could have rendered him prone with half a thought. A ghost of my power shivered through me, calling to me as if it remembered me, as if it wanted me to wield it once more.

"Beroths!" the head guard called from across the cavern.

"Enough! Let her pass, or I will tell the king exactly who delayed her delivery."

Beroths smirked at me before stepping aside with an obnoxious bow. I picked up the human I'd dropped, anger coursing through me as I walked past him to the servants' corridor. How dare that male touch me! How dare he think that because I was now Siren, he had any right to assert himself. For the first time since I'd become a Siren, I felt angered on their behalf.

But in truth, I realized with a twinge of guilt, it wasn't only the Siren who suffered. Most high-ranking Fae tormented lesser Fae because they could. Memories of screaming at maids for wrinkling my fine clothing, jeering at lesser Fae who could barely control droplets of water, stealing a bracelet of pearls then blaming it on a servant, buzzed through my mind.

I had been awful. Horribly, truly, awful. My time among the Siren had made me question the corruption of the royals and nobility in the Water Kingdom, but this somehow made it more real, made me truly understand the depth of it. I no longer felt simply guilty for my past behavior, I felt *ashamed*.

~~~

Voices rose through the vast entrance hall that led to the throne room.

My stomach fell as I paused beside Nihala outside the massive double doors of the throne room. I had seen them hundreds of times, but I had never truly noticed them. I had never appreciated the color, a subtle sea-green hue blended into the limestone, never wondered at the gold filigree that outlined the doors, shaped like waves to sing the stories of the seas. It was almost as if I had always lived asleep, but now, finally, I was awake.

The doors opened of their own accord, the king sensing our presence, no doubt. I trembled with nerves as I took in the familiar faces of those I had once called equals, and those who I had spent a lifetime looking down upon. I couldn't do it. A dozen thoughts of fleeing danced through my thoughts.

Nihala stepped onto the dusky-pink velvet carpet that divided the throne room and led up to the steps of the throne itself. I tried to follow, but my legs wouldn't move. I stood shaking, frozen, the eyes of the court slowly turning to me as the nobles realized the entertainment of the evening had arrived.

Nihala was halfway to the throne when the sensation I had felt earlier shivered through me again, ever so faintly. The ghost of my power, rising in me like a mist.

The familiarity of that power gave me the surge of strength I needed. And something stronger than the instinct to run gained power and told me to hold my head high. I was no less than these nobles. They might think so, but in truth, they were wrong, just I had been so wrong. I couldn't completely stopper the embarrassment of being on display, but I could choose how I would stand while on display. I wouldn't cower or hide.

Just as Nihala reached the throne, I began to walk toward it. Whispers and occasional laughter broke out among the courtiers, but I paid them no heed. When I reached the throne and noticed Prince Rhion standing a few feet away, gawking at me, I held his stare.

He was still handsome, with his sun-kissed skin and sea-green eyes, but even with all his allure, I still found him wanting. I knew too well the heart beneath the beauty was weak and fickle and had only love for itself.

"Greetings," the king said, the deep timbre of his voice radiating with power. A hush fell upon the guests. "I thank you, my Siren, for your service to our kingdom."

Nihala and I gently laid the humans before the king and bowed in humility.

"*Although,*" the king growled, "I thought I was quite clear the last time we saw one another."

His hard gaze landed on me.

I almost crumbled with fear from the anger held in that gaze.

Nihala, to her credit, interceded quickly, speaking to the priestess standing next to the throne, the only Fae able to understand the language of the Siren. She told the priestess of the other Siren who were so lost in their bloodlust they were unable to deliver the humans. She assured her, in all the words available to her, that I had been the only viable option.

The priestess conveyed the message to the king, and once again, all the eyes of the courtiers landed on me. The king listened, though his face held no trace of his thoughts. When the priestess finished, she crept forward to inspect the humans, and when she was satisfied, she nodded to the king.

"Your delivery of the humans is most timely, and for that, I am pleased," the king said, his eyes alight with something I couldn't discern.

Relief flooded through me. He would be merciful. I rose from my bow, ready to depart as soon as he gave the command.

"But ..."

Ice flooded my veins.

"Adhering to your king's command is law for all our kingdom's citizens. You have done nothing more than obey that law, and it does not negate your insolence in completing your command. You"—he spat at Nihala—"were appointed the leader of the Siren outside of my realm. Yet you cannot control those you were tasked to lead. I do not hold with such shortcomings in my forces."

Nihala shrank, her eyes wide with fear.

"And you"—the king's cold eyes held no mercy—"*you*, it seems, have trouble comprehending any commands given to you."

I opened my mouth to beg for forgiveness, only to remember my bound and useless tongue.

"Twenty lashes each. Now. And I never want to see either of you in my kingdom again."

The crowd gasped, then muttered to one another. The High Guard of the king strode forward, pulling a whip from his belt. Panic seized me. Four other guards surrounded us, grabbing our arms, forcing us to kneel.

I heard the crack of the whip before I felt the bite of its teeth. Stars flooded my vision. Again and again, the sound pierced my ears, followed by the slash of the whip that fileted my flesh. I counted the first five, but soon lost all coherent thought.

At some point, in between the flashes of pain, a song crept

through my thoughts. A song I had heard the Siren sing amongst themselves. But this time, it was Nihala who sang it into my mind, a gift of strength from someone I hadn't realized until this moment was my friend. The song told of a legend of a Fae girl who had been changed into a Siren by her king. She was said to be the first of the *Changed*. She was said to have been blessed by the Goddess herself, and had found a way back to her Fae form, defying her king.

The song lilted, holding my mind in a place where it could survive the pain. Where it forgot the humiliation. It sang a melody for me to follow, and for a brief moment, I was beyond the king's grasp.

Then I knew nothing.

〰〰〰

I woke, riding the calm waves of the sea, only feet from the shields, but still inside the Fae realm. Nihala floated next to me, her skin deathly pale. Searing pain lanced through my back as I raised my hand to her cheek, grateful to find she was still breathing.

The hate I already harbored for the king bubbled and festered until it filled the whole of me. Twice now he had stripped me bare and left me for naught. I promised myself there wouldn't be a third.

The legend the Siren sung sounded through me again, but this time, I didn't cling to it to keep myself from falling—I clung to it because somehow, between those bursts of red-hot pain, I had found clarity. I knew for certain that the song, and the legend it spoke of, was true. There had once been a Siren like me. A Siren made from Fae, who had somehow returned to her former body.

I had no idea how she could have done it, but I knew I had to find out. Because I would be Fae again. Not because being a Siren was terrible; I had learned better than that. But because being a Siren wasn't who I was. Forcing me to change forms didn't change the person inside me. I was Fae. I had always been Fae. Binding my tongue and stripping my powers didn't change that.

I vowed to myself that I would find the legend of the Siren; I would find a way back to my body. And then I would come before the king again, but this time, I had no intention of kneeling.

An impossible task—but if anyone was capable of hunting down a legend, it was a *huntress*. Exactly what the king had made me.

~~~

Aubrey Pratt is a dance instructor/choreographer from South Jordan, Utah. She was a winner of a Superstars Writing Seminars scholarship in 2017, and has worked as a guest coach for Calliope Writing Courses. Aubrey is unapologetic about her obsession with YA books, even if she is a legitimate adult and mother of two crazy girls. When she is not mothering, or cleaning the house that is never clean, she can be found writing YA novels, reading, singing, and Netflixing. Learn more at www.facebook.com/Aubrey-Pratt-Books-258102247704314.

THE SEA DRAGON'S TALE

NANCY D. DIMAURO

Wan light from the ocean's surface filtered down to my green eyes and filled me with the remembered warmth of sunshine. A shadow flickered overhead. I unwound my body from the wreck. Had it been last week or last century that I'd dragged the ship into my trench? Her shredded sails were a mockery of what I'd loved her for. I let her go. The ship broke apart, its timbers settling on the ocean bottom.

The world brightened as I rose. A giant squid scuttled by. Its long pale tentacles undulated behind it. When its yellow eye fell on me, it pushed backward in a cloud of ink, trying to escape. A twitch of my tail, and I pursued.

The light sputtered.

Ah, yes. The ship.

I let the squid vanish into the deep ocean's murk.

Fish clustered on the border between twilight and true day, between the cold depths and the warmth of the shallows. Schools shimmered like chips of precious gems as they flitted through the reef. Drawn by the prey and emboldened by its fine rows of teeth, a white shape approached. Coming under my scrutiny, the shark veered away. I undulated past the coral reef.

White sails snapped in the breeze. Sleek shapes danced in the ship's wake. Dolphins desired nothing more than to frolic. The boldest—a young bull with a shark-bitten dorsal fin—rubbed against my flank.

"Come and play," the bull sang.

Dolphins would sport until they saw my true nature. Then they'd turn on those very talented tails and leave me. Alone. Without a word. I'd had my heart broken too many times to trust dolphins.

I flattened my whiskers, but made no aggressive moves. "Not today, little one," I said in his tongue.

The bull rubbed against me. I hissed. As I expected, he turned away.

I scanned for my ship. She'd skimmed further into my domain. My keen eyes picked out details lost when I'd spied her from the bottom of my trench. The bone-white keel was a third my length. My forked tongue snaked out to taste the planks. A bitter tang reminiscent of blood flooded my mouth before fading into cinnamon and burned oak. The second lick revealed the boards' slickness. The wood was finer grained than what men had used for their vessels last time they dared my waters.

Half in love with the ship, I broke the surface. Five masts each bore multiple sails. A reflection dazzled my eyes. Insubstantial sailcloth shimmered in the light. A shiver ran down my spine as if I'd suddenly swum into a cold current. A cry rang out from the crow's nest on the third, and tallest, mast.

I brought myself level with the sailor. Light brown, sun-streaked hair shone in the morning light. His brown, slanted eyes opened wide. I hooted in surprise. This one was no more than a cub. My neck rills flattened and then unfurled. I gripped the rigging with one clawed hand and nudged the crow's nest. The boy gripped the mast and let flow a torrent of words. Answering shouts rang from the deck. Men held harpoons but stood frozen.

I looped a coil around the heart of the ship.

The galley door slammed open. A man dressed in a white shirt and black breeches ran out, his hand on the hilt of a thin, sword. I bent to get a better look. The ship creaked. Sailors hefted spears. The man bellowed and held his hand outstretched, palm up, in a halting gesture. The crew lowered their weapons.

I hooted softly. The force of my breath drove him back a step. The ship rolled on a wave and he regained his footing. He took a deep breath, and his fingers clenched the hilt of his sword. The acrid stink of fear oozed from him. He barked another command.

Mage stones warmed in my gullet. The man's language washed over me, and I understood. I turned to the crew members who'd hoped to get above me and drop a heavy barrel on my head. They froze in the rigging. I blew. Ropes creaked. I wrapped another coil around the ship.

"Don't," the man I was sure was the captain said. "She seems curious. Not harmful."

"Captain." The speaker, a pale-faced man, clutched a spear and a short club that smelled of metal, oil, and smoke.

"Hold." A note of awe crept into the captain's voice. "Have you ever seen anything as magnificent? Besides, if she wants to destroy us, I suspect there's naught we can do to stop her."

I slithered closer. He reached a hand out, palm extended, but not in the halt gesture he'd used before. Almost as if he wanted to touch me. I pulled back. The last male I'd allowed to pet me had been Rikka. No puny human would stroke my sides. I reared, ready to drag the ship to my trench. The sharks could dispose of the crew. I tightened my coils. Hands flew to weapons.

The quarterdeck door banged open. A piping voice shrilled, "Papa."

My rills extended to frame my face and I arched my neck to get a better view of the new speaker. My hand, positioned on the gunwale to assist in capsizing the vessel, loosened its grip.

A human pup with long, bright red hair dashed out. A swath of fabric ballooned around its legs, much like how sails billowed on masts.

Firmly, the captain pushed the child behind him. His fingers tightened on his sword. Muscles corded in his neck.

With a curiosity my children would have envied, the pup peered around the captain's back.

"Cordie," he snapped. "Get back to the cabin."

I cocked my head. That name belonged to a female. I looked over his head at the child. Sticky fingers clutched his coattails, but for balance, not from fear. The child giggled. She reached out to brush my whiskers. The man swatted her hand away. Tears glittered in her eyes. I moved closer to her other hand and allowed her to stroke my yellow whisker. A shiver ran through me at the contact. It had been years since someone touched me. My breath huffed out. A grin stretched muscles I hadn't worked in centuries. With a sigh, I slid back under the waves.

The crew cheered as I subsided. I followed in the ship's wake, drawn by the memory of laughter and something that made me ache all over.

I'd swum with the pod for years. When I was young—barely larger than the mature sea mammals—Rikka had convinced me to love him. But neither my love nor my protection mattered the day the sorcerer came.

~~~~

The crimson-robed human rode a ship with blood-red sails. Shallow in draft, the vessel was nearly as fast as my dolphins. Magic spread like whale oil over the water. Bathed in its foul tar, my scales flashed the bright blue of a tang. Cries rang out from the ship. I'd been spotted.

I told the pod to swim for the shallows. I surfaced to lure the sorcerer over the depths. My half-dragon, half-dolphin children glowed in the mage's violet light. The coward chased them. Lightning flashed from his fingertips. My children screamed.

Their pain rippled through the water, igniting every inch of my flesh. The sound wormed its way through my impenetrable scales and stabbed my heart. My children were dying for my folly. Living with the pod had made me forget what being a dragon meant.

I was vengeance.

I was death on sleek wings with sharp teeth.

The mage would pay for harming what was mine.

I vaulted into the sky and unfurled my silver-rose wings. I swam the sky as I had the currents. The mage's blood would coat my teeth.

My gold horns had just started to curve away from my head.

Not yet large enough to gut a whale, they'd gored enough sharks. I whistled and clicked before finding my true voice and bellowing my rage.

My children's blue-and-silver-scaled bodies bobbed on the waves. I thundered. The sound wave rippled the vessel's sails and pushed the ship from the pod. Rage seared my heart and burned up my gullet. Flame blossomed from my mouth. The ship's crimson sails transformed to wreaths of fire.

Blood drained from the mage's features, giving him the cast of a water-soaked corpse. He hadn't expected me. Winged death. *His death.*

"Attack," he shrieked in a high-pitched voice.

Hitching his robes around his hips, he scurried to the stern. Rats on a sinking ship conducted themselves with more dignity.

A quick snap of wing, and I banked.

Iron-tipped spears bounced off my scales.

The mage flailed about, presumably preparing another spell.

My jaws closed around his torso before my weight bore us through the deck. Mage blood flooded my mouth. A thrill ran through me at the salty, metal taste. The sinuous length of my body encircled the vessel. Its boards creaked as I tightened my hold. I engulfed the other half of the sorcerer and the mage stones in his stomach. Power suffused me. Rearing back, I rammed the lower decks. The hull cracked. Water rushed in. My rills flattened as I sank into the water. Sailors swam toward shore. None reached its safe embrace. Lurid red human blood mingled with the silver-blue of my children.

Pain sharper than any blade cut deep. My children. Tears choked me.

I hooted dismay.

Rikka nudged their lifeless bodies as if unable to grasp the loss. I drew our children into the circle of my body as if I could shelter them from death. My heart bled. Lightning leaped over my scales. Coughing up one of the mage stones, I pushed it into the mouth of my oldest, Tella. Magic flared as I applied my will.

My daughter remained dead.

A deep keening rose from the center of my bones. I stretched to rub against Rikka, to find comfort in his presence and share my pain. His unblinking eyes met mine. Then he turned.

And swam away.

My gaze fell on the wreckage. I nudged my children into the twisted planks that had once formed the hull. Wrapping myself around the vessel again, I dragged it to the ocean floor and wandered until I found my trench. Wedging the funeral barge into a cave, I guarded it against all predators long after my children's bodies had returned to the earth.

From then on, no man sailing over my domain was safe. I crushed them all.

≈≈≈

I rose near the ship's bow. Stars dotted the night sky. A light breeze played over the waves as the ship skimmed over my domain. Low murmurs from the captain greeted my appearance. My eyes narrowed as I scanned for the pup. Earlier, I'd heard her piping voice reverberate through the hull as she talked with her father. Awe touched her voice as she spoke of petting me and how she hoped she'd see me again. Her father had muttered something consoling.

I didn't see her. She must still be below. With a disappointed click, I fell back and allowed the length of the ship to stream past me.

"Thank you," the captain said from where he stood midship. I nodded in acknowledgment. He rubbed his beard. "I don't understand why you spared us."

I looked aft toward the child sleeping in the captain's quarters. "Why did you bring a pup out on these treacherous waves?"

The man choked. "You talk?"

My neck rills flattened. "Of course, I talk."

"I apologize." He bowed formally. "Captain Shay Kyles at your service."

I wanted neither his name nor the connection that came with knowing it. Still, I found myself dipping my head in acknowledgment. "Ryu." After a moment, I prompted. "The pup?"

A ragged breath forced its way from his breast. His eyes shone strange and sad in the moonlight. "Cordelia. The cholera took her mother. I couldn't leave the wee one at home without any parent." In his eyes, I saw a loss that echoed my own. Then he chuckled softly. "I didn't expect to run into a sea serpent. Much less a talking one."

"Have men forgotten me?" My eyes went wide in curiosity.

"Aye, well, there's plenty of tales. In this enlightened time, men don't mind so much when a map says 'Here there be dragons,' figuring it was some grog-soaked sighting of a whale rather than a mon—"

My hoot was short and bright. I grinned. "Monster," I finished. "I am that."

"But not to us."

I shook my head.

"Why?" Need made his voice warble.

"I had pups. Once."

Perhaps he, too, saw the echo of loss, sensed a kindred soul. Instead of asking about my pups or murmuring distant consolations, he moved closer and stared into the night with me. A moment later, his hand reached up as if to touch my flank. The fingers curled into a loose paw, then his hand dropped.

I slid closer so my head was level with his own. "You may touch me."

The warmth of his hand pressed against my scales. "Next you'll be telling me the rest exist, unicorns and dragons and trolls under the bridge."

"Why wouldn't they?" I unfurled one gossamer wing. "I am a dragon, after all."

I thumped Captain Shay on the back as he choked. "Dr— dragon?"

"Sea serpents don't have limbs or wings."

"I thought dragons lived in caves in high mountains."

"Some do. I prefer the sea."

He shook his head and chuckled softly. "So do I."

"Does your pup—Cordie—swim? She could swim with me, if she wanted." Hope edged my voice.

"Water terrifies her." He paused. "A boy in our village went with some lads to the loch. When they didn't return, we looked for them. Cordie found the body." He shivered. "Is there ever an end to the things we can't protect our children from?"

I whistled in dismay. "Pain is part of living."

"Mayhap." He looked askance at me. "Are you planning to keep us company for long? Not that I'm eager to see you go. Cordie smiled for the first time since her mother died."

"I'll see you safely to the edge of my domain. After that …" I looked back over our wake. Each moment pulled me further from the trench and my children's bones. "We'll see. While they left me eons ago, I can't bear to leave my pups' resting grounds."

Shay's expression darkened. A moment later, his gaze drifted to his cabin door. "I understand."

We watched the stars travel across the sky in silence. Man and dragon, each wreathed in our own thoughts.

〰〰〰

It took a fortnight to convince Shay. Cordie was a more successful advocate than I. She'd wheedled and wailed until Shay's heart broke. I promised to keep her safe even though we'd left my territory a week ago. After all, what could threaten me?

Astride my back, Cordie giggled as the water ran through her fingers. We had no trouble pacing the *Selke's Siren*. The ship only had half its sails up. Seamen hooted and pointed as we frolicked in the wake. I'd have to teach them what their calls meant, and more appropriate phrases.

Emboldened, Cordie slid off my back. She splashed a few strokes. Panic made her motions jerky. A wave crashed over her head.

I cupped her belly in my clawed hand. "Breathe easy. I won't let anything happen to you. Slow and steady like I showed you." With my other hand, I showed her the stroke again.

Her fists clenched. After a few slow breaths, she pushed off my arm and started again. This time her strokes were steady. She swam.

Another loud hoot from the ship. "That's my girl," Shay said, his hands cupped around his mouth.

A cry of "Sea serpent!" rang out.

"Time to go, sweetling." I swam under her and came up so she was on my back.

"But I was swimming. Do we have to go? Papa won't mind."

Men scuttled across the deck. Lowering my head, I scented the water.

Another dragon? My heart leapt.

I tasted the waves again. My stomach rolled. A male. And it was sure that he'd scented me. The ship was in danger because of my presence. Just like my pod. I hooted softly.

Tiny fingers rubbed my scales.

"That's enough for your first time," I said. "Hold on."

My eyes met Shay's as I rose from the waves to deposit Cordie on the deck. Tight lines carved into his face.

The other dragon approached. The sun glinted off his orange and red scales.

"Kill it," I said.

"What?"

"That's a male. Either you kill him, or he destroys you." We turned to Cordie. "I'll keep him from you as long as possible. Raise those sails. Get out of his territory. Fast."

I bellowed a challenge as I dove under the boat.

The male roared.

"Shoot the orange one," Shay yelled. "Damn your souls. Get those sails out. Cordie, get below deck."

The boom of the cannons' discharge reverberated through the hull into the surrounding water. I couldn't focus on the chaos behind. The fight was before me.

My neck rills unfurled in challenge. The male rose. His fire-colored rills made an impressive ruff around his face. Long twisted horns curled back from his head. Shorter ones jutted straight out from his lower jaw. Fangs longer than the pup's arm hung from his upper jaw. He was twice my width. Twice my age. Death closed on me.

He lowered his head and rushed me. My claws slashed his eyes.

The clash of our scales thundered over the ocean. His fangs sank into my shoulder. Using his mass to push me under the waves, he repositioned himself over my back. Claws sought purchase but deflected off my scales. I twisted. Stomach to stomach, my claws slashed his underbelly. Bellowing, he loosened his hold.

We rose above the waves. Our blood, silver and orange, mixed in the water, leaving a trail behind us.

A cannon belched fire.

Oh, Shay. You damned fool.

The ship tacked toward us.

My teeth clamped on the male's tail. His lithe body thrashed. He turned, but I was quicker. I wrapped around his body, pinned his arms, and impeded his ability to swim. We sank.

Another cannonball hit the water next to us.

The dragon's hind claws scored my hide and tore into me. His jaws clamped down on my middle. With a shake, he ripped me from his side and tossed me away. Then he turned inexorably toward the ship.

Panting, I floated on the waves watching my lifeblood stream out. I should engage the male before he could harm the ship, but ice lodged in my gullet. Doubt crept into my thoughts. Fear weakened me.

The male roared, warning the ship from his mate.

Of course, Shay, ignorant of our tongue, didn't heed the warning. Two cannons belched fire and metal.

The male screamed as a ball slammed into his side. He dove and charged. If he hit the ship, its hull would crack.

A piping scream warbled on the breeze. My Cordelia.

She'd kissed me last night before going to bed. The warmth of that moment spread through my numb heart. The cold dread loosened its hold, and I breathed. Calling on the magic in my gullet, I pulled my body together. The dragon would not harm my pup. This one *would* live.

My teeth found his throat a mere longboat's-length away from the ship's hull. He reared. Our entwined bodies crashed onto the deck. Something soft snapped under me. Sailors scrambled. Swords flashed. The blades flicked off the male's hide.

"Damn your eyes. Hit him where she's ripped him open," Shay yelled. His sword stabbed into a rent I'd made at the male's shoulder.

The male writhed. I tightened my jaws around his windpipe. Our gyrations cleared the deck of barrels and men alike.

"Sharks!" a crewman shouted.

Shay withdrew. "Get those men out of the water."

My jaws clamped down another inch on the male's throat. His death throes increased. A thin scream filled my ears. Something splashed into the water.

My heart seized.

"Cordie!" Shay reached for a pup that was no longer there. His voice an echo of mine all those centuries ago when I'd known my children would die and I couldn't save them. Fear, both remembered and new, spiked through me.

The pup. I had to save my pup.

I released the male and dove into the water on the ship's starboard side.

A hulking striped shark charged Cordie. She grasped my horns as we rose from the water. Unable to stop or reverse its momentum, the tiger shark swam into my mouth. Its tough hide shredded on my teeth. I spit the carcass out. The other sharks fell upon it.

The male dragon splashed into the water. Cordie screamed. Bleeding from a dozen gashes and puncture wounds at his throat, the male rose. He would pursue me through death. I had to get the pup to the ship before the male had me.

"Hold your breath." The fighting had made my voice deep and rough.

The girl braced herself between my neck plates and gripped my horns. I dove. The water concussed around me as he followed. Seconds into the chase, Cordie floated up from my back, her grip weak.

Hold on, sweetling.

I lunged for the ship. Another crewman fell under my bulk as I slammed onto the deck. Shay ran forward and clasped his daughter to him. Orange blood slicked his sword.

Claws closed around my tail. It didn't matter. My Cordie was safe. I allowed the male to pull me into the water. His body twined around mine. Jaws clamped on my shoulder. He held my head under the waves as his claws gripped my sides. I twisted in his grip, but I was too weak, too tired. This was not the gentle lovemaking I'd shared with Rikka. Claws opened furrows in my sides.

Man's silver flashed. Shay had jumped on the back of the fire dragon, plunging his blade into the beast. Orange blood tinted the waves.

Passion-dazed, the monster didn't notice the assault. Didn't realize that each thrust propelled him closer to death. Shay screamed as he stabbed the male and widened the punctures I'd left in its neck. The dragon shuddered as the sword point went home again. Unable to ignore the annoyance, the male released my shoulder to snap at Shay, who dodged dozens of dagger-sharp teeth. The male loosened his coiled grip on me. Whipping around, I tore free. Bright pain flooded my sense. I pushed it aside. Shay needed me. Twining my body around the male, I pinned his limbs.

Memory flashed through me. A mage in scarlet robes lancing the water with blue fire. Fire designed to kill dragons. Power thrummed in my gullet where the stones lay. They knew what to do.

I unleashed the unholy fire.

Blue lightning crackled around us. Water sizzled where it touched us. The male went rigid. My teeth and claws found the wounds in the male's hide. I clamped down on his windpipe. Thin tissue shredded under my teeth. I ripped the breath from his body.

Waves kicked up by the male's death throes crashed over Shay and bore him under. The echoes of Shay's heartbeat pulsed irregularly. Sharks circled. Seeing my interest in the kill, the tiger sharks abandoned Shay and moved to gorge on the male's corpse, which glowed purple-blue in the dying light. The water foamed as the sharks reached frenzy.

My jaws closed around Shay. Rising for the last time, I lunged for the deck. Collapsed on it, I opened my mouth. Shay spilled out. A shuddered breath racked his lungs. He coughed up seawater and bile.

"Papa. Papa!" Cordie wailed.

His hand lifted and rested on her shoulder.

"He'll be all right," I said. "He killed the dragon."

Shaking, Shay staggered to his feet. His right hand moved to the top of Cordie's head, while his left caressed my face. A sea of my silver blood reflected in his eyes. Pain, almost as deep as when he spoke of his lost mate, etched his face.

"What can I do?" he asked.

"I'm dying."

"No. No, you'll get better." Cordie stroked my rills.

"You're not done swimming," Shay said.

"I don't know what your world remembers of magic, but power rests in the mage stones I carry. You need to cut them out of me. Cordelia must take them into her own body. I promised ..." My eyes rolled back in my head. His gentle caress called me back to my body. "She must take the stones."

"I don't understand." Tears streamed down his cheeks.

Cordie buried her face in my mane.

I took his sword in my hand. "Cut here." I drew a line under my scales.

"I—I can't."

"The stones' powers die with me unless they are removed before ..." I met his gaze. "You must do this to protect our Cordie."

His eyes flickered to his daughter. Resolve hardened his features. "I don't want to hurt you."

Under my instruction, Shay removed the half-hanging scales to expose my flesh. A quick cut. Silver blood slicked the stones he pulled from my gullet. Shay stared sightlessly at my blood on his hands.

"Put them in her hand. They will shrink to fit her. That's part of the magic."

"You can't go," Cordie cried. "You promised."

"Sweetling, put your hand out." Sniffling, the girl obeyed. "These stones are for you. They will keep you safe when I can't."

Shay placed the largest tiger's eye into her hand. Her wrist bent from the weight. A moment later, the stone shrank. When it was no bigger than a gold piece, Shay handed her an amethyst. The process was repeated until the obsidian, dragon's tear, and ruby were equally diminished.

My blood ran over the port side and left a trail the sharks followed. I couldn't outrun them. Soon they would grow bold enough to rip the flesh from my body.

Cordie couldn't see that.

Best to finish here quickly and slip below the waves.

"Swallow. Them." I panted between breaths.

The girl complied. An azure flicker surrounded her, then was gone.

"Let the magic teach you."

"I don't want you to die," Cordie said. "Not like Mama."

I rested my forehead against her chest. Her arms encircled my head. The warmth of her body against my face gave me strength to carry on a few more moments, enough time to bid Shay and her goodbye.

"I've lived a very long time. While I would have preferred to live a while longer yet, it isn't to be." I nudged her with my snout. Her arms fell away as she as staggered. "Go below and rest. Goodbye, my darling Cordelia."

She dragged a forearm under her nose. Sniffling, she said, "Goodbye, Ryu. I love you."

"And I you." I turned her toward the captain's quarters and nudged her forward.

She clung to Shay for a moment before he too sent her away.

When the cabin door closed, Shay bowed. His forelock brushed the oiled deck. "Thank you."

"Thank you as well."

His burst of laughter was ugly and dissonant. "For killing you?" He motioned to the blood flowing from me.

"Nay. For coming back for me, and giving me a reason to fight." Something deep inside, where the male had ravaged me, twinged. I winced. "There was only vengeance. I'd lost love. Even forgotten why we have pups. Why we'd die to save them. You gave that back to me. For however briefly."

"What do I do?"

I eased my bulk up. I wasn't designed to lie on a ship. The ocean called my name.

"Love your pup."

His fingers ran through my whiskers. A pang of longing washed through me for things that couldn't be.

"What are you going to do?"

"Try to go home. I'd like to die with the ship that once held my pups."

"Good journey," he said.

With a glance at the cabin doors, I slid into the water. The cool enveloped me. I listened to the sound of the hull cutting through the waves. Cordie's presence reached out from the cabin and enveloped me in a dusky jade glow. My heart swelled with the love and healing she sent.

Flicking my tail, I began the journey home.

～～～

The sharks that had hoped I'd be an easy meal filled my stomach. A giant octopus had moved into my lair. It, too, now nourished the life growing in me. I curled around the blood-red hull of the mage's ship. My children had died here once. It was only fitting they would now be born here. I closed my eyes to sleep.

My dreams were filled with visions of a sea captain and my Cordelia, her red hair streaming out behind her, borne over the waves on the backs of dragon pups.

～～～

Nancy DiMauro's alter ego, Nancy Greene, is a trial lawyer and woman-owned business advocate in the Washington, DC Metro Area. She's been published in two of the prior Superstars anthologies, *A Game of Horns* and *Dragon Writers*, and her nonfiction book, *Navigating Legal Landmines: A Practical Guide to Business Law for Real People*, is an Amazon best-seller. She lives on a horse-farm in Virginia with her three favorite guys (i.e., her husband and two boys), and likes the music of Jonathan Coulton whose song "I Crush Everything" was the inspiration for this story. For updates on Nancy's writing and what she's been doing lately, please visit www.attorneynancygreene.

IN THE GARDEN OF
THE CORAL KING

C. H. HUNG

The great reef lay dying, and the Coral King along with it.

A lament surged from the ocean, so quietly at first that it blended into the surf. With each wave, the threnody tumbled and rose higher, a chorus slowly amplifying the lull of the indigo sea until even the whales fell silent.

The song descended on the island that nestled within the reef like a pearl, one of a handful of nameless outposts scattered among the boundless seas. And within the variegated city sprouting from the island, its citizens trembled.

The Coral King is dying, the people babbled, *and he cannot hold up the reef.*

Our island will sink into its grave.

We are doomed.

The mystics blamed the stars; they diagrammed the astral misalignments and explained the resulting ripples in whispers. The scientists blamed the sewage spilling into the waterways; they hawked their proclamations like seagulls startling up into the sky. The villagers blamed everyone but themselves, because what role could they possibly have played? They were, after all, only simple villagers.

On her balcony overlooking the sea, Cleito buried her head under her mother's arm, the waves crashing against the cliffs below echoing like a hollow conch near her ear. The air vibrated with the throbbing of the sea, of her people, of everything clamoring in a dizzying rhythm that thrummed through her body to the edges of her nerves. She tried to hide, to burrow further into her mother's comforting embrace, but the melody persisted.

Cleito whimpered and pushed away from her mother. Her family's citadel had been carved from the walls of lava rock lining the northern shore of the island, and the craggy, dark bones of the balcony added to the oppression of the ocean's mourning. She clutched fistfuls of her golden hair in both hands and pulled. The pain along her scalp relieved the pressure between her ears until she released her grip. She moaned when the throbbing returned.

"Stop that." Her mother slapped at her hands. "We are princesses, and we do not act like wild children, even if you are only eleven."

Tears swam in Cleito's vision, and she blinked furiously to hold them back. "I don't care." She stamped her foot, ignoring the pain of striking unforgiving stone. "I'm sick of the ocean, and now I can't stop hearing it. I wish we lived somewhere else!"

"And how would you leave, little one?" Her mother smiled faintly. "You won't even go into the water."

Cleito turned away. Her greatest shame, that she couldn't bob along even in the shallows along the beach without nausea welling up in her throat, meant that she would never leave her island. She was as sea-locked as a land-bound snail.

"Don't worry." Her mother kissed Cleito's forehead. "Someday, we will find you a charming prince, and you will marry and bear many fine heirs to watch over our island."

But Cleito would have to cast her net for a prince from among the jetsam that passed through her city—unlike her mother, who had found her prince in the land of olives and honey across the seas. The music of the ocean continued to throb against Cleito's eardrums like the heartbeat of a dying serpent.

That night, Cleito dreamed she swam below the ocean, deep in the darkness where rumors and myth dwelled. Water, dark and cold and heavy, closed in around her as she drifted in the endless sea with nothing to anchor her. Bile rose in her throat. She kicked for the surface, but no matter how fast she scissored her legs, neither the gloom nor the weight eased. She opened her mouth to scream and choked on the briny sea.

Cleito jerked upright in her bed. Her heart thudded as she sucked in air with deep gasps, her body shaking with the effort of holding herself together.

Silvery moonlight filtered through the glass doors of her balcony. Bouncing off the sea, the light shimmered and danced across the walls, beckoning her to play. Cleito threw off her blankets and headed down the halls, her bare feet silent against the stone floors. A guard peeled silently from the wall to follow her at a discreet distance.

The ocean besieged her with its keening. She had to stop it or she would tear off her ears to end the torment. And what a fine princess she'd make then.

She left the citadel, heading east toward the beach. There, her toes sank into sand so pristine and fine that it gleamed under the midnight sky like vast plains of salt, reflecting the silver, gibbous moon. The grains, infinitely more numerous than the stars, dusted her soles in silicate. She wriggled her toes, imagining them like worms burrowing through the earth, wishing she could crawl through the world and come up the other side without braving open water.

Her steps dragged as earth gave way to water and the surf roared louder. The waves licked at the sand, foaming, the edges curling into themselves, hungry for her. The sand grew firmer and denser and colder the closer she came to the sea. Yawning endlessly into the distance, the dark water blended with the dark sky until the horizon disappeared. Only the stars marked the edge of the world.

Cleito sat down on the ground and tucked her knees to her chin, shivering. Moisture soaked through her nightdress from her bottom, the dampness creeping upward along her torso and back. She wasn't sure what she was looking for, but she knew, with the certainty and innocence of all eleven of her years, that she'd find it in the ocean.

Still, here at the edge of sand and tide was as close as she'd get.

The sea wailed and moaned with the wind. She buried her head under her arms, but the requiem continued, weeping with the tides.

If the pantheon of deities the priests believed in existed, she thought now would be a good time for them to manifest.

The waves crashed harder against the sand, their peaks frothing.

A column of water rose from the ocean, forming from the crest of the swells. She scrambled to her feet as it spiraled in a funnel, rising faster and higher with every revolution, until it stood as tall as she was. A gap opened toward the bottom of the column, where the foot met the ocean, and then split into two pillars that narrowed into legs. Smaller columns extended from the main trunk and shaped into arms. The top of the vortex shifted into a sphere, and features rippled across the surface of the water, forming the head and face of a boy about her age.

The boy made of water glided toward her on a pool that had suddenly stilled in front of her. Cleito glanced back at her ever-present guardsman, who raised a hand. His eye passed over the boy without a flicker of awareness.

She turned toward the boy.

He bowed. "Princess."

She curtsied as her mother had taught her, barely dipping her knees. Not many in the city merited deeper obeisance than that, and certainly not this boy. Not if he had addressed her first.

Nevertheless, her heart gave a little flutter. "Who are you?"

"Your people call me the Coral King."

Her eyes widened. "We hear the sea mourning you. We thought you were dying."

"I am always dying." He half-turned toward the ocean and tilted his head at her. "Reefs are made from the bones of dead coral. Your city is built upon an island that is formed from the bodies of *my* people."

"Then why this music—" She squeezed her eyes shut and clamped her hands over her ears. "Can't you make it stop?"

"No." He drifted closer. "But you can."

"How?"

He held out a hand. Currents flowed and shimmered through

his palms like fish flashing their scales.

She shrank from him. "I can't swim."

"I'll guide you."

"Where?" she asked, though the sinking feeling in her stomach already told her.

The boy gestured at the endless expanse of ocean. "My home, of course."

Her throat closed. "I can't."

"Trust me."

She shook her head and retreated a few steps.

His fingers quivered, then his hand dropped. His arm melded back into his body. With a sigh, the rest of him decayed with a crash of falling water into the tidal pool, the spray mingling with the salty trails streaking down Cleito's cheeks. The waves resumed licking their way across the wet sands, undaunted.

She wiped her nose on her sleeve and made her way back to her guardsman. "Did you see that?"

"See what, Princess?"

She headed back toward the city. "Nothing."

The next morning, the tides changed.

A ship coming into port ran aground on a sandbar—a quarter-league from where the maps had marked the bar. Divers plotted the changes in the shallows around the island. By early afternoon, the high tide still hadn't come in, hours overdue. Over the highest rooftop, the citadel raised a yellow flag emblazoned with the island's emblem of a twisted conch shell—a shell the citizens harvested to use as trumpets and bartering collateral—to alert ships of the changes in the sea. The lighthouses dotting the island's shores followed suit, and tripled their stockpiles of whale oil for the lanterns hanging in their towers.

Cleito drilled with her tutor on mathematics, writing solutions into her sand tablet before wiping the surface smooth and beginning anew with another problem, over and over. The rescue of the ship's refugees sank hooks of distraction into her mind. The tutor corrected her tablet while keeping one eye on the door, beyond which they both pretended not to hear the rustling of footsteps as visitors came and went.

At midnight, Cleito awoke to the sound of bells tolling, the brassy caroling keeping time with the ocean's ceaseless dirge. Her stomach fell.

Another shipwreck had been spotted. That would mean more lives to retrieve—*if* the ship had wrecked near enough to the shore to attempt rescue, like the last one had, and *if* survivors still clung to its bones.

"Apologies, Princess," the guardsman said when she tried to leave. He was the same one who had accompanied her to the beach. "Your father wants you to stay here."

"Why?"

"For your protection. We've taken in many refugees since the tides changed, and we can't be sure the premises are entirely secure."

"No one will notice me."

"Everyone notices royalty."

"Not unless you call attention to me."

"Princess—"

She ducked the guardsman, taking advantage of his reluctance to grab and possibly bruise her. He let out a startled exclamation, but she didn't stop. Her bare feet pattered against the stone as she ran down the hallway, and she quickly lost him in the crowd surging outside toward the beachhead and the shipwreck. In the distance, orange flames crackled hungrily skyward along the spines of broken masts, casting a burnt glow across the waters and the sky.

At the shoreline, she broke from the mob and veered south, picking her way among the rocks that grew in size and number the further she walked. She recited all the curses she knew, holding them fast in her temper so she wouldn't lose them when she confronted her target. When she found a quiet place out of sight and sound of the citizens, she perched on top of the biggest boulder—a black lump of lava rock with a dry spot atop its crown. She waited.

"Are you ready?"

She didn't stir at the boy's voice. "No."

The water slapped against the rocks, an impatient beating of immovable earth. "Then why are you here?"

"Why are you killing the ships?"

The sea ran down the crevices of the rocks, burbling protest before merging with the roar of the waves cresting against the shore. The boy's voice murmured in her ear as if he stood next to her, though she sat alone. "You weren't paying attention. Now you are."

"You don't have to hurt people to make your point."

"The reef is crumbling as it dies, Princess." His sigh shivered through the wind, stirring her hair. "Where it crumbles, it piles into mounds where none existed before. My coral garden is decaying underneath your feet."

She calculated how many of his people would have had to die for the sandbars to have formed and risen so high overnight. For the ships' keels to have found them and run aground. Her throat tightened, and she relinquished her litany without uttering it.

"I'm sorry," she whispered.

"Don't be. Come help us. Come help all of us."

"Why me?"

"Why not you? Someone has to watch over the island."

Surely it can't be me, she thought. *I'm not brave or worthy enough.*

No other citizen had failed to set sail before their tenth birthday, expanding the island's knowledge of every shoal and shallow and shelf in the oceans for thousands of leagues around them. It was that collected knowledge, tended so carefully in her family's archives at the citadel that had gained the island their status as the crossroads of the sea, nameless though they were.

And she, their princess, could not swim, could not venture further than knee-deep in the waters without drowning in vertigo. The guilt and shame she'd fought to bury bubbled to the surface.

What if she could go to a land where she could run and dance along the sand and not have to hide or learn to hold herself together through strength of will alone? She could be that wild child, laughing and crying without worrying about how she would be judged, how she might be found lacking.

It would be an easier life. The boulders of worries that lay at the bottom of her heart would dissolve into sand as fine as her beach, and she could blow them away, never to be anchored by them again.

Only, perhaps, to replace them with different, more numerous, concerns. She remembered the haggard lines etched across people's faces as they petitioned her father—the mystics and the scientists and especially the villagers. The worries may differ, but they existed all the same. No matter who they were, people tied themselves to obligations, like the ships lined up in their harbor. And she and her parents were tied to all of them, the piers that held them fast in the storm.

It was only when she was tied down that she felt safe.

A tingle raced down her spine. This was why she had come to the beach yesterday, what she had been waiting for. The gods had manifested after all.

She scrambled to her feet, balancing carefully as she brushed the gritty particles from her nightdress. Before her, water gushed in a small geyser and formed into the boy standing on a pillar, his eyes level with hers.

Her voice barely trembled as she spoke. "I'm ready."

He held out his hand.

Still, she hesitated. "Promise you won't let go?"

"Trust me."

Her hand closed around his, and it felt as solid and warm as a real boy's. She closed her eyes and jumped.

The shock of cold water enveloping her body took her breath away, air gurgled out of her lungs in a stream of bubbles. Dark spots splotched her vision and salt stung her eyes and sinuses. She thrashed her arms and legs, trying to hold her breath. Fire blossomed in her chest as her lungs shrieked for air.

The squeeze of the boy's hand brought her back to his promise: *Trust me.*

His touch brought her awareness back to him, and she fought the nausea swirling in her gut. Mentally, she solved arithmetic problems by rote, the routine giving her something to focus on besides the sickening sensation of floating adrift in the infinite seas.

Three and five is eight. Five and eight is thirteen …

Breathe.

She gasped. Water filled her nose and mouth and lungs, flooding her with the mossy, briny taste of the sea. The ocean roared in her ears.

And then she realized she *was* breathing. Breathing water. She blinked the sting away, and the spots faded.

The world had turned into shades of blue overlaid by algae green with undercurrents of violet beneath her, a vast emptiness yawning into the distance, sloping downward. Jagged rocks from the shore lay half-buried in the sand a few body-lengths below her feet, and colorful fish darted in and among the nooks and alcoves of their sparse shelter.

Above her, she could barely make out the last vestiges of the fires from the shipwreck, an orange glow that slowly faded with each heartbeat. She twisted around, reassured to see the sand shelf sloping upward toward the island and the lava rock boulders she'd jumped from.

The boy tugged her attention back to him.

Ready?

She clung to the lifeline of his touch, imagining him as the rope that held her in this world, that kept her from being swept out to sea, that lashed her to this boy like a sail to a mast. Her heart beat slowly, evenly. Bubbles no longer streamed from her nostrils.

She nodded. *Ready.*

He pulled her toward the bottom of the sea. Her body lengthened into the dive, one arm outstretched before her as it followed the downward pull of the boy. The gurgle of water rushing past and over her body rang in her ears, blending with the lament of the ocean that seemed to have taken on an expectant refrain, growing louder and picking up in tempo.

Che-tze, che-tze, che-tze, the song sang. And as the water changed the shape of the notes, Cleito understood the message, exultant and triumphant. *We live, we live, we live.*

Ambient violet light grew brighter both ahead and below them as they dived deeper into the ocean. The pressure at these depths should have been crushing her, never mind the otherworldliness of the purple, but she felt like an albatross soaring on the breeze. Even the chill had disappeared, the goose bumps along her flesh smoothing out. She gave up trying to make sense of this world.

Cleito couldn't see the boy anymore, his form blending into the watery depths, but every so often, she caught the faintest shimmer of an outline that hinted at where water moved against the current, where the figure of a boy might exist. Only the grip of his hand on hers told her that anyone guided her along at all.

She caught glimpses of shadows drawing near, taking on the outlines of fins and flippers or nebulous clouds of invertebrates suspended in the void. Crackling reverberated through the currents, the disembodied acoustic remnants of crustaceans, unseen and unconcerned.

Below, the seafloor rose to meet them. The boy led her across, skimming a foot above its surface until they arrived at the base of the coral reef.

The ebb and flow of the sea's elegy changed and shifted as she approached, becoming a quicker, excited rhythm. The chittering sound reminded her of bugs rather than music, even with the words humming in her consciousness.

We live, we live, we live.

The reef rose in whorls and spirals and curlicues dozens of feet above her head, draped with algae and seaweed and plants waving in the currents in a chaotic convulsion of colors awash in violet overtones. It stretched in a wall that curved slightly in both directions before disappearing from view. Crustaceans scampered across the ocean floor, raising puffs of sediment; neon fish peeked from behind anemone curtains; starfish crowned with thorns crept along the ribs of coral; and seahorses bobbed along, tails wrapped around living anchors, watching the world float on by.

Cleito's mouth opened and closed like a fish's as she spun, eyes wide. She let go of her fear—and the boy's hand. He reached for her, but she waved him off and took a tentative step forward. The familiar panic failed to hammer against her chest, and she moved toward the coral with her hands outstretched.

This was the loam-rich reef that protected her island and her city, that had given rise eons ago to the sand and rock and dirt that became her home. It would rise for eons more, growing as the kingdom grew—if it survived whatever was killing it.

What's wrong with the reef? she wondered.

Look closer. The boy's voice separated from the hum, lilting in her mind. *Find the pattern.*

She studied the coral city. Her mind catalogued the palette arrayed before her while she watched schools of fish playing their seafood games.

Schools and games. *Find the pattern.* The image of her sand tablet swam up to the surface of her memory.

Grabbing a rock with a sharp edge, Cleito began counting and making marks in the sand, then wiping the sand smooth and starting over again. When she reached the crowned starfish, she kept marking the sand until she could count no more. She stared at the pattern in the sand.

There were 367 starfish climbing over the coral that she could see, and multiplying quickly.

Six hundred ten now, the boy informed her. The throbbing threnody grew louder, affirming his assessment.

When did the ocean begin singing? she asked.

When my people began dying. When they couldn't fight back.

She propelled herself toward the nearest starfish. The chittering that had blended with the melody amplified, a rhythmic beat that pulsed with the flowing tide. She didn't dare touch the starfish's spiny thorns as she examined it.

The starfish boasted many arms, not the usual five. At least thirteen arms, all bristling outward. The sound of grinding recoiled through the water. She watched the starfish lift an arm and move higher up the coral, and during the moments that the slow, inexorable action took, the grinding stopped from the creature.

Combined, the sound of hundreds of starfish consuming coral created a symphony. The pauses each starfish took to move opened room for beats to emerge, to be swept up by the waves and carried out to the sea, to be carried above to the citizens of Cleito's island city.

This was what she'd been hearing. It was the crowned starfish who sang as they drained the coral of life.

Beside her, violet light condensed into the watery form of the boy, contained by a transparent membrane that emulated shape and skin. The light reflected off the contours of his outline, creating shadows for facial features to appear. His voice, when he spoke, echoed in her mind; his lips did not move.

There is no one left, he said. *No one to hunt the crowned starfish.*

But someone did before, she thought. *Who?*

The sea snails. The water boy shimmered as a convulsion shivered down his form. *They have been hunted into nothing by your people, princess,* he said, sadness diluting his voice with haunting emptiness.

She saw it then—the proud banners that flew above her home. The banners emblazoned with their trademark sigil, the twisted conch shell.

The conch, she realized. *Our trumpets and our currency.*

Buying and heralding our death. The violet light within the boy pulsed slower.

How do we stop it? She wanted to shout, but the water suffocated her voice.

The warm touch of the boy's fingers against her arm brought her gaze to his. His amethyst eyes dimmed with the gravitas of a messenger bearing bad news.

There are now 987 crowned starfish, he said, dry as a timekeeper.

The numbers marked a countdown to her island's doom. Cleito wrapped her arms around herself. *What do I do?*

Make a choice.

A whirlpool spun within the center of the boy—slowly, at first, then faster and faster until it became a maelstrom. In its nexus, the outline of her island appeared, growing and pulsing larger. It became the heart of the boy, throbbing in a rhythm as steady as the sea's currents.

Save the sea snail, the boy said. *Save my reef. And your island will prosper, for now.*

For now?

He flung out his arm, and the kingdom that was his heart launched outward with the movement. It broke into pieces before dissipating into the oceanic flow. *Your kingdom will someday sink into the ocean under the weight of its wealth. Other nations will come, drawn to the glitter of your city. War will destroy you, and the ocean will bury your bones.*

She frowned. *But we're a kingdom without a name, an outpost in the vast ocean. If we were not the crossroad of the seas, no one would care. None would stop to barter with us for the supplies they need on their journeys. Why war with us?*

Violet water shaped like coins trickled through the boy's fingers. *Because I will teach you to smelt orichalcum for currency, to replace your conch. You will be the only people in the world who know how, and others will war with you for the secret.*

And the other choice?

Purple deepened into a dark, pulsing miasma. Within the heart of the ocean, the boy took on the blackness of squid ink.

Let the reef die. Your island will crumble into the sea as it destroys the foundation your city sits upon. You will forever be lost in the obscurity of time, never earning a name or a place in mankind's history. But your island will live a longer, quieter, safer life. No one will bother you until the sea swallows you whole.

They *were* doomed. The mystics, the scientists, the villagers. All of her children and their children until the end. Cleito pushed her fist against her mouth, willing herself not to weep, but her body betrayed her. In the ocean, though, there was no sting to the tears that filled her eyes. It was small comfort to her that it didn't hurt to cry.

That isn't much of a choice.

Your island is lost either way, he admitted. *The question is, how will you live?*

We live, the starfish echoed. *We live, we live.*

She gazed at the starfish crowned with thorns. Deadly in its glory, designed to consume one thing only, even if it meant that when the reef died, the starfish would die with it. They would never know that in killing the reef, they would kill not just themselves, but an entire island.

And the sound of the starfish feeding—the lament she'd heard above—changed worlds the starfish would never know. Not in their small, limited existence.

Like her people's world—lost, already. Who knew what they could affect beyond their fate, if the ripples of their lives could spread farther than they'd ever dreamed?

Not far, if they remained the island with no name. An outpost at the service of sea traders. And she, their princess, tied to the island as surely as the island was tied to their reef.

She would never leave. Not because she was afraid of open water, but because she would never want to leave. The island was hers to watch over. As was this reef. As was this boy.

Why not give her people something greater than themselves to live for?

I choose to save the reef.

Violet rippled through the boy's figure. *Done.*

He opened his hand to reveal a small conch. He turned his palm, dropping the shell. It drifted down to the seafloor and settled into the sediment.

After a moment, the sea snail moved. It headed toward the reef, and the starfish.

〜〜〜

The boy deposited Cleito on the beach. She bent over and coughed up the sea before rolling onto her back on the damp sand, her arms flung to either side. The embers of the shipwreck had died completely; the beach was empty. Daybreak threatened to wash out the stars draped across the sky in celestial garlands.

The sea quieted to murmurs eddying in lazy pools. The boy sat next to Cleito, resting his chin on his knees and staring at the horizon.

"Are you leaving?" she asked.

"Soon."

Her heart pounded, but she said nothing. Princesses did not cry, and she was done crying.

"I'll come back when you're older," he said, softly. "I am more than your Coral King; I am the King of the Seas. But more than that, you are brave and worthy, and I would like to be the king of your heart."

Cleito thought for a moment, and found that she didn't mind the prospect very much at all. She would catch more than a prince on this island at the crossroads of the seas. She would catch a king.

More importantly, she would see the boy again.

"Yes," she said. "That would be all right."

His fingers laced through hers, the lifeline replaced by a handfast promise.

"What should I call you?" she asked.

"I have been called by many names and will be called by many more. Call me whatever you like; I will answer."

"Earth Shaker," she said. "For reshaping my world."

The boy smiled. "That is good."

Another name rose to mind, and she tested it, weighing the way it might carry the world. She knew she'd also give her kingdom a name to echo through the ages. Someday the island would fall, but not without making its mark upon history. Cleito could give her island that much, at least. She could give it the name of her future heir.

Atlantis.

The princess listened to the threnody dying as the dawn crowned her home in gold.

〜〜〜

C.H. Hung grew up among the musty book stacks of public libraries, once winning a reading competition by devouring more than three hundred books the summer after second grade. By the time she started third grade that fall, she had her picture in the local paper, beaming parents, a newfound love of good stories, and her first of many, many pairs of prescription glasses. After a brief, fifteen-year diversion in reality, C.H. Hung left the corporate world and reentered the world of myth and fantasy. She now lives among the majestic foothills of the Wasatch Front with her husband and too many paw kids, finally putting to paper the dreams and stories she's carried in her head since those long-ago summer days in the library. Visit her at www.chhung.com.

THE OLD MAN AND
THE SEA SIREN

STEVE PANTAZIS

The old man furiously bashed at the sea devils with his one remaining oar, but it wasn't enough to fend off the thieving monsters. The gray-green water bubbled and churned, sloshed and sprayed, a mix of fins and hungry mouths filled with daggered teeth. They tore into the carcass of the saberfish tied to the gunwale of his single-seat wood boat, the fish he'd pursued for days, his one last chance for salvation. The silver-bodied sea devils ripped out large chunks of flesh with their enormous mouths and whipped the water into a frenzy with their long-tipped tails. He cursed the gods for taking his sail, and now he cursed them again for taking his prize. They mocked him from behind a veil of angry clouds and battering wind. If they knew of mercy, they knew none this day.

"Be gone, be gone!" he yelled at the sea devils, as if they would heed him. They answered with the roil of seawater, the scent of blood and salt. His shoulders ached with every swing, his hands cramped from gripping the coarse wood handle of his oar, but he would not let them take his dignity. He would not!

The blade of his oar struck the bulk of one of the feasting creatures and snapped the shaft in twain. He jabbed with the broken handle, striking one body after another. The lather of sweat made his knotted forearms slick. His strength gave out finally, and he fell painfully to his knees, cursing the creatures while they devoured the remains of his treasured fish.

When they dove into the depths of the sea, he was left with bones and shreds of flesh, and a dreadful stillness that spanned the horizon. The head of the silver-skinned saberfish remained, its haunting obsidian eye looking at him as mocking as the gods themselves. The foot-long horn was gone, sheared clean off by the beasts below. The meat from the fish would have fed his village, and he could have bought a new mast, sail, and rigging, perhaps even a shirt and leggings to replace the tattered, sea-soaked ones that clung to his wasted frame, perhaps new sandals. But the horn ...

The horn!

He parted the strands of long white hair matted to his forehead and yelled at the darkening gray above. "You should have drowned me, that's what you should have done. Damn you all!" Thunder pealed among the storm clouds in the distance, the pitiless answer of the gods.

They had taken his wife, the light of his life, who died of the black pox, along with half his village. Now they threatened to take away his son, Liam, afflicted by the same illness and who clung to life by a breath.

I was a fool to leave him, to come here, to try to change his fate. What have I done?

The gods were to blame, he was sure of it. Had he offended them with his pride? Had he angered them with his japes and jests? Had he taunted them, dared them, blasphemed in their name?

Yes, old man, that and much more. The seer said you were cursed, didn't she? But she also said there was a way—one way!

He squeezed the last drops from his water skin onto his tongue, but they did little to ease his parched throat. Crumbs from the heel of bread he'd used as bait floated in the puddle beneath his sore knees. He had used all his food, and for naught.

Night fell without a star in the sky, and the murky sea spoke to him, an invitation to join the others who had taken one last plunge into the unforgiving waters. Instead, he rested his head against the rough wood deck and let sleep drift over his wearied mind.

~~~~

He awoke to the cry of gulls.

Several birds crowded the carcass of the fish and tore at the last morsels with their long, sinister, hooked bills while others hovered above them in a mad dance to find purchase. He swatted at them with his broken oar, but they only flapped their ash-white wings and screamed at him, knowing he'd grow tired eventually. And he did. He set down his oar and let them fight over the scraps until there was nothing left.

When they were gone, the chop of the sea settled until the water was smooth and turned the color of green shale. A mist with the slightest scent of brine swept over him, a moist coolness that teased the drought in this throat. The presence of gulls meant he was close to shore. He should have been heartened by the tiding, but he wasn't. The omen signified defeat. The boat drifted for a while, and then ...

He heard her song.

Sweet as the one his wife sang to him when they were newly in love, but with a lilting voice that carried a sadness like cloth over splintered wood. It brought tears to his eyes. It had to be her. It had to be! His beloved called to him from the afterlife. Glorious gods, the sacrifice of the horn of the great saberfish had made her whole again!

He wiped the sting of salt from his eyes, and in a raw voice, called back, "Isabel, is that you? Tell me it's you!" He willed himself to his feet. For a moment, the pain in his joints was gone, his thirst and hunger forgotten, the scrapes and bruises lost from his thoughts.

The water burbled ever so gently beyond the prow of his craft. It rippled as the water parted to reveal the face and body of a young, naked woman. Her glistening hair was the color of seaweed, her skin pale as blanched driftwood, her eyes as dark as pebbles along the shore, her lips full and moist with water. He saw only her smooth shoulders, the tops of her breasts, her long, willowy arms as she swam to him. She sang a sad song, a wistful tale of a dreamer lost at sea. Was this his beloved, or did his eyes deceive him?

He urged words from his dry throat. "Isabel, why are you in the water? Come to me, my love."

Her voice ran high, then low, like the tide under a full moon. His chest tightened as hope left him.

"You're not my Isabel, are you?"

Her singsong voice carried over the water, a drift of mist. "I'm the love you seek." Her fingertips brushed the hull, and he had to peer over the edge to see her press her palm to the wood. She pushed off and glided backward. Her hips lifted delicately above the water and then dipped below the surface.

He spoke softly. "My love is departed from this world. What I see before me is but a shade."

"Am I a shade?" Her breasts rose enticingly above the still glass water. "Am I not real? Am I just an illusion to elicit madness? What do you see? Tell me."

He saw his true love, young and sinuous, when time was his and fortune on his side. "I see ... No, it can't be. It can't be you."

Her voice carried through the fog, mellifluous and sweet. "It is me, my love. I've returned for you. Come swim. Strip away your rags and join me."

He pulled at his soaked, threadbare rags, ready to dive into the calm water, to swim up to his Isabel, kiss her full on the lips, say he was sorry, and pledge himself to her with undying love. Yet he hesitated. "I can't."

"Why not, my love?" She hummed a mariner's tune he knew, of the maiden who stood upon the misty shore, awaiting her captain's return.

The music was wrong. Isabel would never have hummed such a melody. The spell broke for a few heartbeats, enough for him to grab the haft of his broken oar and hold it out like a harpoon. "What do you want? Did the gods send you? Did they make a deal with you to play tricks on me?"

Her hair fanned out in the water behind her, the shape of a seashell. "Would you like me to sing to you instead? I could sing such words, my love. Words that would make your heart leap for joy, words that would make you cry, words that would make you love again."

"And what song is that? I have no ears for it. My ears were meant only for my wife, and she is gone. Can you bring her back with your song? Can you take back the empty winters and sleepless nights? Can you make me unsee the sickness that ravaged her? Can you heal my son, who hangs on to life by a thread? Can your song do that, siren?" Were his oar a spear, he would have pierced her with it.

She paddled closer, and her milk-smooth face glistened with water droplets. "Men want me to sing to them. Their loins stir, and their hearts burst to hear me. They love and lust and come to me to fulfill their desires. Let me sing to you. I can be your Isabel. I can be your beloved, my captain."

"I know what you do. I've seen the shattered ships you've lured upon the rocks. I've heard the cries of the mothers whose sons sank to their deaths. I've witnessed the wrecked homes born from your tragedy. Your honeyed words don't sway me, temptress."

She swam up to the skeleton of the saberfish. Although it no longer had its eyes, ghastly accusation remained in the empty sockets. "Even an old man like you has needs. Come, drink." She swam to the prow, where she dipped her hands into the water. She cupped them and lifted the small pool of water to her lips, where she blew. "Drink. This is clean."

"You would drown me, I know it."

"If I wanted to drown you, I would have done so already. Come, drink."

He stood his ground for a moment, but his thirst was too great, and he laid down his oar and kneeled before her. She smelled of sea-foam on a clear summer's morn. It brought back memories of his wife when she'd wait for him by the docks. The siren's water wasn't salty, but clean, cool, and sweet as the meltwater from the mountains. She let him drink his fill and sang until tears came to his eyes.

He wiped the water from his beard. "I shouldn't have drunk. I shouldn't have let you do this. I should have never come here. Your gift is poison."

"My gift is life."

"And what was it to the others who came before me? Death?"

"I harbor you no ill. Many a man came before me, and they all received their heart's desire. Look at me, and you'll see that."

"I see beauty and treachery. I see still and storm. I see clear skies, but I also see perilous waters. All I have to do is close my eyes for one instant, and I will break upon your rocks and descend to a watery grave. Is that what you want me to see?"

She floated on her back, water slipping over her skin. "I give men what they desire. All men have desires, even the old. Even you."

"And what do you desire, sorceress? To watch men lust after you and drown for it?"

"I am immortal. Perhaps I desire to become mortal, to know there is an end, not just to watch it happen to others."

"You say that, yet you cannot change your nature, just as the sea devils cannot change theirs. Others will die because of you, and you will always watch and never know. But I know of death. I've seen it, felt it, and soon enough, I will succumb to it myself. And if the gods are kind, they will see me pass before my son. Yet I fear that will not be possible. My desires are distant to me, daughter of Neptune. I had hope, just a glimmer of hope."

"Is that why you pursued the saberfish? Out of hope, not desire?"

He tossed the oar aside and stood as tall as a man half his age. "Perhaps I sought the saberfish out of pride. But it wasn't just that. It was for hope, a blind hope. And now that hope is at the bottom of the ocean, where I belong." His voice became quiet, as if asking the question to himself: "Why does anyone pursue the saberfish?"

Her hair twisted with the water, a beautiful rope of kelp green. It unfurled like a taut sail. "To answer one's prayers, of course."

"And did it answer mine?"

"Didn't it?"

It had cursed him, that's what it had done. It had brought him to this siren as punishment. He deserved to be here, to answer for his hubris. Yet his heart of hearts told him that his son, Liam, still drew breath.

Her dark eyes fell to his hands. "You've fought a terrible battle, my captain, and you've suffered for it." Rough, red furrows dug into his palms from where the rope he'd used to haul in the saberfish had cut his skin. For two days and two nights he had battled the monstrous fish; he had refused to let it win. In the end, the saberfish relented, and gave itself as a sacrifice before the gods. The ruts in his hands were all he had to show for it. "Come, dip your hands in the water." She reached up in offering. "Let me kiss your wounds. I will heal you."

He watched her for a long moment, the specter that was Isabel in all her ghostly beauty. "For six days and nights, I sailed the sea, casting hook and rope with bread smeared with the blood of minnows and tied with a silver coin the fishermen of my village promised would bring me luck. I had not gone out to catch any fish. I had gone out to catch *the* fish! The swordsman of the seas, the mighty saberfish. The mariners sing ballads of the great spiraled horn, of how it can make the old young, turn the poor rich, and even ..." He faltered, unable to say it.

The siren's singsong voice answered for him. "And even stay the hand of death."

He swallowed painfully, the rawness in his throat returned. "Yes."

"Was it worth it?"

The question erased the melancholy, like the tempest that had snapped his mast. "Was it worth it?" he echoed. The words rumbled angrily from his lips. "Is the dawn not deserving of the sun? Is a child not deserving of his mother's love? Is a man not deserving of his wife's happiness? Was it worth it, you ask? If you would have seen my Liam, you would have known. His voice is strong like the rising wind, his smile gentle as the dawn's first light, his heart warm and welcome as a campfire on a winter's night. He is the kindest of souls, but with a spirit that can withstand the mightiest of gales. He is loved by all in our village, and is betrothed to a sweet lass named Tessa who will be brokenhearted—but not as much as his father. No, his father shall weep and scrape at the ground and grovel for redemption. The gods saw fit to punish me, and they have!"

And they will torment me until my dying breath, he wanted to shout.

"Then you do have desires, old man. Even though the fire in your loins has long been extinguished, your heart burns pleadingly as a father must. You chased after the fabled saberfish for its horn, for the magic it holds, for your selfish wants."

He clenched his fists as viciously as if he still held the rope in the struggle with the blasted fish. "I would have fed my village with the bounty of my catch. I had them in mind, too!"

Her perfect lips curved across her face like a swirl in a pond. "Of course, you did, my brave captain of the sea. You would have filled their hungry bellies. Then you would have gone to the old seer, given her your potent offering, committed the sacred words, and burned the blessed horn to ash before the gods. And what then, my love?"

Tears wended down the wrinkled channels of his face. "Then I might have saved him. I would have seen him healed, held his hand until his strength returned, listened to his weakened heart until it galloped in his chest. I would have done that, and more." He rubbed the tears away with gnarled knuckles, but there were more, always more tears. "The gods scoff at me from above. I took what never should have been taken. All for pride. All for want. All for me." He saw the enchantress now, really saw her, and wept openly for her beauty and her deception and her brutality. "I have lost myself in an attempt to find myself. If this is the end, then let it be. Drown me. Take me to where you take the others. I am ready. I care no longer. If my son is to perish, then let me perish first."

Her black pearl eyes became sad, and it made his heart heavy. "If that is your wish. Swim with me."

The brooding, smooth water beckoned. He dipped into the cool sea and swam to her. Her loveliness drew him as a lodestone, and although there was no lust in it, his heart swelled with love long forgotten.

"Swim, my love, swim," she sang. The more he swam, the farther she went, until she was gone, and he was alone, and his boat lost in the shroud of fog.

She has left me to die. He only had to hold his breath, let himself sink, and join his ancestors at the bottom of the sea. He might tread water a little longer, but he was tired, so very tired. The muscles in his arms throbbed, and his thighs cramped. Although the worldly pain made his body suffer, his spirt was at peace, just as the ocean was quiet now, not a stir or ripple or sound. He could let go any moment, and it would be the right moment.

It won't be much longer, my sweet Isabel. I will see you soon, and our boy will follow.

Just as he thought he could tread no longer, a song cut through the fogbank, long and melodious, a haunting rhythm that called out to him. A shape emerged, supple and serene. The sea siren swam toward him. She carried a threaded, swirled dirk aloft, bleached as whalebone.

The horn. She had found it!

"But how? It was taken by the sea devils and lost in the deep. How did you find it?"

She sang, strong and clear. "I found it because you desired it, my love. I found it because you needed it. Take it. Go back to your village, conjure the spirits, and bend them to your will. Fulfill your desire. I give you your child's life back."

She opened her pale hand, the spiraled treasure upon her palm. All he had to do was take it from her, return to his ship, and let the current guide him home. The horn, with its magical properties, would bring back the son he loved. It would make him whole again.

"I would be a fool to refuse. You offer me this bounty, and yet …" He tried to find the words, but his mind was muddied from weariness and grief.

The lady of the sea floated before him, the blight of man, both beautiful beyond measure and venomous for the soul.

"And yet?"

"And yet I know you do not offer this freely. You would bind me with contract. It is what you have done to countless men before me. I am no different, I know that, feeble as I am, without manly appetites or temptation in my heart."

"You asked me to drown you, but I let you live. I do that freely."

"And my Liam? What of him?"

"Your son is fated to die. It is the will of the gods. This talisman is the only way to save him. But you already know that."

Her words bit into him, harder than the rope that had torn into his hands during his great battle with the saberfish. The horn was the key, his one chance. "Aye, of course I do. More than anything. But at what cost? What would you have of me?"

She drifted in the still sea, a buoy of hope hidden within an albatross of misery. Her voice was small and tender, a gentle but fell breeze upon the water. "It is but a small cost, my love."

≈≈≈

The fog broke, and he was greeted by the sound of waves breaking upon the shoreline.

He dragged the bow of his broken vessel upon the pebbled shore and staked it in the sand. Above, the haze began to clear. The village children played in the early morn, giggling and chasing each other into the surf. They had lost brothers and sisters, mothers and fathers, neighbors and friends to the black scourge, and yet they persevered, because that was what children did.

When he got to his sister's, he saw that Liam was still alive, although he was asleep, marked across face and body in black pustules and burning with fever. "The gods are kind to have waited for me," he said to himself, afraid if he spoke louder, the gods might change their mind.

That night, he and his sister, Agnes, took Liam to the seer. The seer was a half-blind crone, bent and withered, who chanted and spat over the campfire in the sand while Liam lay across a bed of dried reeds, shallow in breath, eyes closed, with his arms crossed over his chest. Agnes stood quietly behind them with Liam's betrothed, Tessa.

"He is but a whisper away from death," Tessa said with clasped hands. Locks of curly brown hair ran across her swollen eyes, shielding the tears. She was a good woman, a pretty lass. She'd make a noble wife and a loving mother.

"He holds on for you, his true love," the old man said. "You have stayed faithful to watch over him. I couldn't ask for a better daughter." *May fate be kinder to you than it was to me and my poor Isabel.* With a bitter tongue, the old man addressed the seer. "Go on, witch, do your magic. Show me what this mighty talisman has cost me."

The seer burned the horn of the saberfish. The old man expected the fire to flare into a towering pillar, the spirits to whip the smoky plume into a maelstrom, or the earth to quake, crack, and sunder before them, but the magic was more subtle. The horn glowed hot: scarlet, then indigo, then blue, until it became ash and nothing more, and the night became dawn.

The daylight brought with it mist and the scent of the sea, and his son's fever broke. Liam opened his eyes for the first time in weeks, and the old man wept for him.

"My boy, my courageous boy, look at you! The gods saw fit to bring you back to me. They are not as cruel as I have claimed. I am indebted to them this day." Tears ran down his face, and Agnes and Tessa cried as well.

Liam, a grown man in his own right, looked up and smiled weakly. The black sores were lessened now, and in a few days, would be gone. He was a handsome lad, and had all the looks from his mother, the red in his hair and beard, and her fierceness of spirit, too. It gladdened the old man to be reminded of her.

Liam's voice strained. "Papa."

"Rest and save your strength. You will need it soon enough." He knew what he had to say, and with a weighed-down heart, the old man took his son's hand in his. "I must go away now. Your aunt will look after you and your darling Tessa. I have already talked it over with them."

Liam tried to speak, but the old man stilled him with a gentle touch.

"You are my son, and you will live long and true. Someday, you will father your own children and look upon them, as I do upon you, and you will tell them how much joy they bring you and that you would do anything for them. Know that I love you with all my being, my son. You will always be with me." With that, he kissed Liam upon the brow, said his tearful goodbyes to Agnes and Tessa, and although they begged him to stay, he quickly made his way to shore before he had the chance to change his mind. There was no room for broken promises. He was a man of his word, and his word was as binding as the sorrow that ravaged his heart.

He borrowed oars from another vessel and took to the sea in his damaged craft. The gulls screeched noisily above the chop. He rowed long and hard until his muscles ached and his brow was soaked, and all the while comforting thoughts of his son lent him the strength to carry out his final task. The sea grew still and the water mirror smooth. He stowed his oars and waited.

It wasn't long before he saw her. She was a vision of beauty, young and lithe—his sweet Isabel, his siren of the sea. Her hair was spun of fire and gold, her skin fair and freckled, her smile as sweet as jasmine blossoms, just as he remembered her. She sang to him, as she had all those years ago, of their love, undying and true. It made him weep.

He stripped his rags and dipped into the cool of the ocean. Then, with his remaining strength, he swam out to meet her one last time.

≈≈≈

Steve Pantazis is an award-winning author of fantasy and science fiction. He won the prestigious Writers of the Future award in 2015, launching his career as a professional writer. Since then, he's gone on to publish a number of short stories in leading SF&F magazines, such as *Galaxy's Edge*. He is the author of the sci-fi novel *Godnet* and the fantasy novel *The Dark That Binds*. When not writing (a rare occasion!), Steve enjoys cooking extraordinary cuisine (earning the nickname "Love Chef"), exercises with vigor, and shares marvelous adventures with the love of his life. Originally from the Big Apple, he now calls Southern California home. Visit him at www.stevepantazis.com.

ALL YOURS

MELISSA KOONS

The storm raged against the ship. The wooden vessel creaked and groaned as the winds tossed its belly along the ferocious waves. Men shouted above, but their cries were drowned out by the screeching sleet that pounded the deck like stones. A gale blew against the ship, making the clipper pitch violently to the port side. It was a new vessel, the first of its kind having only been created two years prior, in 1843, but the storm made the wooden ship groan as if it had seen a thousand voyages.

I hit the hull as my body was flung with the momentum of the ship's rocking. I heard a muffled shout up top before it was sharply cut off and then drowned out by the howling storm. Regaining my footing, I gathered my irons and pressed oakum between the planks, fitting the caulking fiber into any gaps to ensure the seal between the wood remained watertight.

"Beckett! Get yer arse o'er here! We got another leak," the bosun, Ricky, shouted at me from across the hold.

I scrambled over the boxes of cargo and supplies, sliding across the slick floor.

Water seeped through a crack in the hull. Ricky pressed his hands against the wood, trying—and failing—to plug the leak with his thin fingers. Grabbing a wooden plug from my tool kit, I hammered it into the leak. Water spurted as the plug sank deeper into the planks.

"Get some blankets from the fo'c'sle! We need to pack them around the cargo. If the tea or opium gets wet you can say goodbye to ever eatin' again," Ricky shouted.

I dropped my tools and darted up the ladder to the galley. Just as I reached the forecastle, the ship rocked again, and then the violent pitching caused by the rough winds and turbulent ocean was suddenly over. Confused, I remained in the galley a moment, clutching the blankets in my arms, listening intently to the men shouting outside. The pounding sleet had lightened to a soft rain that pattered against the deck.

"Hey, Ricky, I think the storm's passing!" I shouted down to him. I expected to hear a gruff chuckle or a grunt of acknowledgment, but Ricky stayed silent.

Walking over to the ladder, I climbed down into the hold. "Ricky? Did ya hear me?" I asked, looking around the crates for the boatswain. I found him near the hull, hunched over with his ear pressed against the planks. "Ricky?" I asked, slowing my steps.

He looked up at me, his familiar unshakeable demeanor faltering slightly. His sun-weathered face blanched. "I think the storm was the least of our problems, kid," he said, his voice scratchy and hushed. He leaned closer to the hull and closed his eyes.

Overhead, I heard the pounding of the crew's boots stall for the briefest of moments.

"Captain! Starboard side!" the sailing master shouted.

"There, in the water!" another man shouted.

I looked to Ricky with a confused frown, but he just took a deep breath and kept his eyes closed. I mirrored Ricky and pressed my ear against the hull. I could hear splashing, but nothing seemed out of the ordinary considering the storm we'd just come through. But I was only fifteen, so I wasn't sure what was considered "ordinary" on the ship.

As soon as I'd come of age six months ago, I'd joined Captain Henderson's crew. We'd set out for China to get our cargo and made it there in ninety days. We expected the return journey to be about the same since our magnificent ship was one of the fastest clippers on the sea. We only had two weeks left to our journey before we would make port at home and claim our riches for the coveted teas and opium in our hold.

The crew's voices were muffled, but Ricky and I were still able to make out what the men up top were saying through the planks. "It—it can't be … it's just a legend …" the captain stammered.

"Ain't they good luck fer a sailor?" the sailing master asked.

"No," Ricky whispered beside me.

The ship pitched to starboard, and an inhuman growl echoed throughout the hold as something climbed aboard the ship. Panicked, I started to run toward the ladder, but Ricky grabbed my wrist and pulled me back. I stared up through the tiny gaps in the wood at the shadows crossing overhead.

"Lower the lifeboat!" the captain shouted.

Men shouted commands back and forth, but they were soon drowned out by ferocious growls. Their frantic shouts turned to screams.

Ricky's eyes focused on the planks above us, following the sounds of the men as they scrambled up top. Another growl reverberated through the ship. The rapid beating of boots against the planks was halted by a sinister scraping of leather against wood. The crew's terrible screams permeated the air before they were abruptly cut off. A thick stream of blood poured through the cracks in the planks above us, and the thin rays of surface light that had seeped into the hold were now blocked by heavy, fallen shadows.

I opened my mouth to scream, to ask what to do, to plead to God, but Ricky slapped his hand across my lips and shook his head at me, urging me to stay silent. We listened as the few remaining sailors on deck tried to escape the creature that had boarded our vessel.

After the longest and shortest minutes of my life, everything fell silent. The heavy shadows above us jerked, and then were ripped away, showering us with blood. I started, but remained silent. I listened to the crunching of bones and slurping of flesh as the creature devoured its meal.

Ricky let out a shuddering breath and closed his eyes. The main deck groaned as the creature slithered along the planks, dragging its engorged body across the ship, searching for any survivors. It seemed like an eternity before the ship swayed portside with the weight of the satiated creature. Ricky and I stumbled, reaching out to grab the hull to brace ourselves from falling and giving ourselves away. We held our breath and listened to the distinct *splash* as the creature returned to the depths of whatever hell it had emerged from.

After the creature hit the water, there were no other sounds except the lapping of waves against the ship and the caws of circling seagulls. Neither Ricky nor I spoke, we didn't move, and we barely breathed.

Ricky clapped his hand on my shoulder and covered his rough face with his other. The stream of blood had thinned to a drip above us, but it wasn't the only one. The entire ceiling seemed to be raining drops of blood into the cargo hold.

Following the drip lines, I noticed that our clothes were spotted with the horrific rain, the blood of our crew. My legs trembled. Ricky's hand on my shoulder tightened, holding me upright.

"No time fer that, kid," he said morosely. "Let's see if any of our men are still breathin'."

My head felt dizzy as I nodded in agreement. Ricky helped me regain my footing, and I followed closely behind him as we made our way up the ladder to the galley. Ricky paused. I wondered what he'd seen, and debated ducking back down into the protection of the hold. As if he knew my thoughts to flee, Ricky completed his climb and reached a hand down to help pull me up. As soon as my head poked over the edge of the hatch I saw the cause of Ricky's hesitation.

A severed arm stretched through the door, reaching toward the galley. There was no way to tell to whom the arm belonged, and I wasn't sure it mattered. A trail of smeared blood led through the fo'c'sle and out onto the main deck. My stomach churned. I heaved and vomited onto the floor, my muscles clenching and nearly lifting me out of my skin with the force of it.

Ricky patted me on the back and closed his eyes. "It's okay, kid. It's ov'r," he grunted.

Despite the attempt to calm me, I could hear the lie in his words. The tension of his shoulders and the sadness in his voice told me he didn't believe it was over at all. Whatever had done this to our crew—the monster that had devoured them and made strong men scream—wasn't far off.

Stepping over the severed arm, Ricky peeked around the corner. Identifying that everything was clear, he jerked his head, signaling for me to follow him.

I took a deep breath, swallowing down the rest of my dry heaves. I straightened and pulled myself together. I wasn't sure what Ricky was planning, but I knew I couldn't be a heaving mess in the galley if we were going to get through this. I followed his steps beyond the arm delicately, trying not to slip in the slimy blood congealed around the appendage.

Ricky led the way through the fo'c'sle, stopping short when he reached the main deck. "Ha'e mercy," he breathed out, his eyes wide while he scanned the carnage. The men—our men, our shipmates, our friends—were all gone. Well, not exactly *all* of them. Like the arm in the galley, there were fragments of the sailors scattered across the deck.

I closed my eyes and put all my strength into steadying my legs so I could move forward. Their remains told a story more horrifying than what I'd imagined. The deck was marred with scratch marks from the men clutching anything they could to avoid whatever terror devoured them. A pair of boots stood near the lifeboat—partially lowered at an awkward angle—with the owner's feet still inside them. The wooden planks were stained a rust color, the blood that had drenched them was drying and soaking deep into the woodgrain.

"Captain," Ricky whispered, walking toward the steering wheel. A fisted hand was wrapped around the spokes of the navigation wheel, a familiar tattoo on the severed wrist. Ricky's shoulders slumped, and he shook his head. "He was a good man."

I nodded. I'd spent five months with the captain and the crew. He had been a good man. They all had been.

"It never gets easier," Ricky muttered.

"What doesn't?" I asked, sidestepping a chunk of someone

that oozed near the railing. I cringed and looked toward Ricky.

"Losin' good men. I've lost crews like this before," he said, staring off into the calm waves that stretched before us. "I had no choice."

"No choice?" A shiver crawled up my spine and made the hairs on my neck stand on end. I backed away from the railing, my eyes scanning the ocean waves for the beast that had devastated our ship. There was no disturbance in the sparkling depths, but a tension started to build in my chest that I couldn't shake.

"I thought I was dead. There had been a storm—jus' like this one—decades ago. It nearly ripped our ship apart, the sails split from the ice and the wind. We were goners. Just when we all thought we were goin' down, it cleared." Ricky's shoulders slumped, and he held a spoke of the navigation wheel absentmindedly.

Listening to his story, I paced the main deck. The unsettling feeling in my chest tightened, but I couldn't explain why. The ocean was calm, and the skies were now clear. The seagulls circled overhead, their familiar caws echoing in the wisps of clouds. Such perfect conditions should have been a sailor's delight—but I was still on edge.

"I was in the sail locker gettin' a fresh sail when it came. I heard the growl—it shook the walls it was so loud."

The seagulls. Why were they just circling?

"My crew—I heard them scream. I heard them die. It wasn't a battle. There was no fight."

I looked at all the fresh meat around me and then back to the circling seagulls. Not one was making a dive for the deck. Not one seemed eager to fill its carrion gullet with the remains of the men. That could only mean the predator was still near. It hadn't finished its meal, yet.

"It was a feast," Ricky said, turning toward me. His brow was furrowed and his face drawn in anger. "I heard it all from the sail locker where I hid, like a coward. When their screams no longer echoed in my head, I came up top. It was ... this," he said, gesturing to the aftermath of the gruesome slaughter.

I heard a splash off the portside, and my fear spiked. I reached for the nearest weapon—a paddle that had fallen out of the dangling lifeboat.

"I saw it. The creature that ate 'em. I stared into its eyes as it filled its belly with my crew."

The splashing got closer, lapping at the hull below me. I crouched, readying myself for the monster to rear its head. I held the paddle out in front of me, unsure how to use it in battle but determined to fight the creature off.

"That's when she saved me. A beauty too good ter be true. She helped me reach port, helped me collect the pay for all my fallen crew," Ricky said, his anger fading into sadness.

The muscles in my back were so taut they hurt. I softened my battle stance. The splashing continued below at the water's edge, but nothing boarded the ship.

"I had to repay her for her kindness. Twenty years, I've been workin' my contract with her. She always saves me," he mumbled, releasing his hold on the navigation wheel and walking toward the railing on the port side. He looked down at the blue waters, and a soft smile curled his lips.

Frowning, I took a cautious step forward. Ricky leaned against the railing, relaxed and at ease. Still armed with the paddle, I peeked over the edge, and my breath caught in my throat.

I stared down at the most beautiful creature I'd ever seen. Her hair shimmered like starlight in the afternoon sun, and her alabaster skin had an unearthly glow to it. She turned her crystal green eyes away from Ricky and looked at me. My heart hammered in my chest, and I was filled with a sensation I couldn't name. She smiled at me, the sweetest smile I'd ever seen on a woman's face. I sighed, the dread melting away and replaced with a burning warmth that comforted me. I could see all my dreams in her eyes, and all my fears vanished on her voiceless, supple lips.

I dropped my weapon. I watched her splash in the waves, swimming carelessly with an air of delight and peace. "What is she?" I asked.

"Don't you know the legends, kid?" Ricky sneered. "She's a bloody mermaid."

I couldn't hear the seagulls above me anymore, but I didn't care. "I didn't think they were real," I said, unable to break my eyes away from hers.

"Aye, they are," Ricky said, the sadness returning to his voice. "Let me keep this one, please," he begged her. The mermaid turned her gaze away from mine and gave Ricky a charming smile. "He's just a boy," he said, shaking his head.

I blinked, my senses slowly returning to me. I looked toward the skies. The seagulls had flown away; I could spot their beating wings in the distance, but the breeze did not carry their familiar cries back to me. I looked down at the deck still untouched by their greedy beaks.

"Haven't you had yer fill?" Ricky asked, his tone sharp and biting.

The calmness that had settled within me trickled away as the tightness of dread and fear coiled within my breast. I backed away from the railing, my eyes locked on to Ricky's hunched shoulders. It wasn't relaxation that had softened his posture, it was defeat.

"You—you said she saved you?" I said, tripping backward and sprawling on the blood-soaked planks.

Ricky turned toward me, sadness in his eyes. "She did," he said. He walked toward me, his boots falling heavily on the wood. Each reverberation made my heart pound faster. Tears leaked from my eyes, and I scooted back, ignoring that my hands squished in the entrails of my friends.

"You said she saved you!" I shouted.

Ricky nodded, overcoming my weak escape in several strides. "She did save me." He scooped me up by my collar and dragged me back toward the railing.

I thrashed against him, clawing at his wrist. "H—how will you bring the ship to port? You can't do it by yourself." I wiggled out of his grasp and rolled away from him. "I—I can help! I'll help!" I bargained.

He paused, his eyes focused on the water beyond the railing. "It would be easier with two," he whispered.

I nodded, but he wasn't addressing me. There was a silent battle being waged, and my fate hung in the balance. I held my breath, waiting for the sword to slice and seal my life one way or the other.

Ricky shook his head. He stormed toward me, fisting his hand around my throat, stealing the breath from me.

Choking, I tried to yank his hand away, but he heaved me across the deck, tossing me at the base of the railing.

My heart plummeted, and I whimpered, shaking my head. "Please, no," I croaked. I tried to dart away from him again, but he was faster than me and caught me mid-lunge.

"Sorry, kid." He muttered, hoisting me over the railing.

I reached out, trying to grab hold of him, the railing—anything—but everything slipped through my fingers. Despair choked me as I hit the waters. Opening my eyes, I could see the sunlight twinkling above me, and the darkness of the deep ocean gaping below me. I turned, and there she was in all her splendor. Her perceived beauty from where I had stood on the ship turned to horror as I swam beneath the rippling surface.

Her piercing green eyes glowed in the blue currents, her pupils becoming vertical slits like a shark's. Her alabaster skin was luminescent, and the gills in her throat and ribs gaped with each breath she took. Her fin whipped through the waters like a blade and her webbed hands stretched toward me.

I jerked, trying to get away, but the ship was behind me, she was before me, and darkness loomed below me. There was no escape.

I looked up, seeing Ricky's distorted figure watching from the deck. I tried to swim to the surface, but her cold hand was on my cheek before I could breach. I couldn't comprehend how she moved through the water without disrupting the currents. Her nails dug into my temple, tearing the skin and making me scream in pain as she yanked me back down into the watery depths.

Air bubbles escaped my lips, and my lungs burned from lack of oxygen. She smiled—the most terrifying grin I'd ever seen. Her lips stretched back and revealed three rows of fang-like teeth. I closed my eyes. I didn't want her face to be the last thing I saw. My body shook, desperate for air. I tried to take in a gulp of water—wanting to drown before she ripped me apart with her fangs. I opened my mouth, ready for the rush of salt water and the blackness that would overtake me.

But it never came.

Her lips latched over mine, and oxygen flooded my lungs. She breathed air back into me, her nails digging into my throat to keep me anchored. I opened my eyes and was frozen by the lidless, green crystalline orbs that bore into my soul. Just when my lungs felt like they would burst, she let go.

A rope dropped into the water above my head. I grabbed it without hesitation. Ricky pulled me up the side of the ship. I hit the deck, gasping and sputtering seawater onto the wood. My body shook with shock, and my arms collapsed beneath my weight when I tried to push myself up.

"Take it easy there, kid," Ricky grunted, scooping me up under my arms and propping me against the railing.

"I—I don't understand," I gasped. I winced at the pain that shot through me and felt the tender, split skin of my throat.

"Twenty years is a long time, kid. Be thankful to her, it makes it easier," Ricky said, giving me a soft smile.

"Easier?" I choked out.

"To feed her, and repay yer debt." Ricky stood up from his crouch beside me, his face serious. His eyes held such pain in them, tears trickled down his cheeks. He turned so his back was against the railing and spread out his arms. "All yours, sweetheart."

He flung himself backward, face toward the clear sky and a grin on his lips.

I choked on a sob as an inhuman growl filled the air.

He screamed once, and then it was silent.

I lay against the railing, the ship drifting along the current toward port. I didn't have to look to know she was still there. I could hear her splashing alongside the ship. When the afternoon sun met the horizon, I finally found the strength to push myself up. I shuffled my way to the navigation wheel, peering over the bow to the rolling waves.

Her sparkling head was unmistakable. Unclasping the captain's severed hand, I rolled the wheel in the direction she was swimming. "All right, sweetheart. Take me home."

~~~

"Mermaids do that?" the incredulous young man in front of me gasped. His face was twisted in horror, and his head jerked from side to side, checking the waters around us for the terrifying creature. "*She* did *this*?"

I nodded. "She saved me, and I've been indebted to her—and Ricky—for the past fifteen years. It is my gift—and my curse," I said, looking up at the clear night sky. The full moon illuminated the glistening deck drenched in the blood of good men. A familiar splashing drew our attention to the starboard side, and a sad smile spread across my lips.

"No, no. You can't. I survived! You can't let her take me!" the young man shouted, backing away from me.

"Sorry, Willy. She only saves one." I grabbed him by his collar and flung him over the railing.

"All yours, sweetheart," I whispered, turning away.

His scream echoed in the crisp air long after it had been cut off, disturbing the stillness of the night.

~~~

Melissa Koons has always had a passion for books and creative writing. A former middle and high school English teacher, she now devotes her career to publishing, editing, writing, and tutoring with the hope to inspire and help writers everywhere achieve their goals. When she's not working, she's taking care of her two turtles and catching up on the latest comic book franchise. Learn more about her work at www.writeillusionllc.com.

TO BECOME

CJ ERICK

If I walk into the water, I will Become.

But will I be guardian or predator? Goddess or monster?

Lylea sat alone on the jagged rock, watching the waves rush over each other to toss themselves against the stone in a rhythmic cadence. The sun shifted from sunflower yellow to amber as it settled behind the stair-step clouds, skipping rays of light along the glistening ocean. The familiar scent of salty seaweed and shells and fish wafted to her on the landward breeze. Oblivious to the beauty, a sea otter floated on its back, hugging a squirming crab, nibbling at its writhing legs. Ivory seabirds wheeled and plunged into the surf, some coming up with mullet and smelt, others heavy with empty-beaked disappointment.

The sun hung just above the horizon. It seemed to pause, wavering and shimmering, and then split in two, a larger orange ball resting on top of a much smaller one, a common vision for the ocean sunset. The larger circle pressed the smaller one down into the waves and followed it, dragging the color from the sky with its ponderous gravity.

I am the little ball, and this life is the big one, pushing me down into the sea.

Hesstria, her grandmother, found her sitting on the rock hours later, when all the light had fled, and the birds had gone to roost in the rocks behind her. The breeze held steady from the water, keeping the insects away.

Hesstria came quiet as the fog, carrying an oil lamp in the crook of her arm. The light flickered behind the cloudy glass and played over her narrow, lined face and reflected from the waves of silver hair. She'd thrown a shawl the color of storm clouds over her pale night-robe, which she held closed in front of her. She stopped where the sand met the rock, well away from the water's edge. She shivered, but whether from cold or dread Lylea didn't know.

She gazed up at Lylea for the space of several waves before speaking. "Your mother is looking for you, child."

Lylea tried to hide her annoyance. "She's always looking for me."

"You've skipped supper again, and your studies."

"And the sun set all the same. If I skip bedtime, will the sun not rise tomorrow?"

Hesstria stood silently for a time. Lylea thought she heard her sigh. The old woman blew the lantern out, set it on the sand, and found a low shelf of rock to rest on. She joined Lylea in watching the waves wash in. She stayed well back from where the water caressed the stone and sand. A half-moon high in the sky lit the beach well enough to dazzle the tops of the waves and illuminate the expanse of ocean.

At last, she broke the silence. "The ocean calls you, Lylea."

"It called you, too, Grandmother," Lylea said, and immediately regretted it.

Five years earlier, at age thirteen, her life had changed. The Mark of the Seahorse had appeared behind her left ear, and she was known to be chosen. She was the New-ling, the one who would enter the sea and Become. But therein lay the mystery and the danger.

Generations ago, her ancestor Cedric had been called, and when he stepped into the sea, he had transformed into a mighty merman, fifty feet tall, with great arms and a tail like an orca, as depicted in the paintings in the Great Hall. Cedric the Sea King, he'd been called, a legend who not only protected the sea lanes from krakens and leviathans but also rescued countless sailors who had driven their ships onto the treacherous reefs around the Azure Islands.

Cedric's grandmother, Cybile, had blossomed into a beautiful sea maiden with flowing green hair like a garden of seaweed and skin like mother-of-pearl. Her song was said to be so beautiful and strong that she could tame schools of tiger sharks and crews of roguish seamen and guide ships safely through the islands' narrow channels.

But her great-great-grandmother, Hellenia, whose name was rarely spoken and still filled people's hearts with fear, had Become a monster, a giant hydra who turned on her people, plundered schools of fish, and dragged ships and men into the depths. In madness and rage, alone and unloved, she'd cast her bloated body on the Skeleton Rocks to die a terrible and agonizing death.

The people of Oceangate were all sea people, earning their livings as fishermen or whalers or as the crafts-people who supplied their ships and wares. When Lylea walked the streets of the city, the people she passed did not meet her eyes but sneaked sideways glances. She was the New-ling. When she entered the sea, would she follow the ways of Cedric the Sea King or the frightful beast Hellenia?

Lylea was brought back to her perch on the rock by the song of a whale. How far out in the water was the beast? Was it female or male, sad or happy? Would it grow to love her if she Became and fill its song with her praise? Or would it curse her in its whale-ish tongue?

The coarse rock cut into her backside and her palms. Her back ached, and the cool breeze sent ripples of a shiver along her spine. Her body urged her to return to the warmth and light of her parents' castle. But the warmth was like a fire slowly heating her to boiling; the light was an interrogation. Her parents expected her to take her place in the pantheon of those who were called and who answered. They did not want her to shame the family as her grandmother had done.

Hesstria's voice was tired, as though she had lived many lifetimes of regret and not just one. "Would you have a life like mine, child?"

Lylea let the thought lie. "Did you ever consider it later? After you met Grandfather?"

Hesstria fell silent. The waves counted—ten ... eleven ... twelve. "Yes, once or twice. But your grandfather loved me. And then our children were born—your mother and Uncle Silas. I could never have left them. But there were years when the sharks and giant polyps were numerous and the fish harvest suffered. Our people were starving and glared at me with anger and resentment."

Hesstria drew a deep breath, as if letting the salt air clear her head.

Lylea picked up her thoughts. "Perhaps you could have helped them. Did you fear Becoming something horrid? Or going mad?"

"Of course, child. But now, it feels only selfish."

"Will a good person Become a good thing, and a bad person a bad thing?"

"I don't know. How can any who are called? The best of them— the ones we sing about and honor with paintings and verse—we didn't really know them. We can guess they were strong people with strong character. I'm told Hellenia was a proud woman, strong and resourceful, but strong-willed. Was that her undoing?"

"You've had a good life, though. A man who loved you. A family."

"Yes. That is true." Hesstria hung her head for a time before speaking again, and Lylea feared her grandmother was crying. "But I was not truthful earlier. I have regretted not taking my place nearly every day. I let my people down to protect my own security. I let myself down for my fear. And I will never know what I would have Become."

Lylea said, "But why were we chosen? Why not your brother, Great-Uncle Drake, or Celinia?"

Lylea heard her grandmother's dry chuckle drifting through the moonlight. "Oh, yes, if your younger sister had been the one chosen, I would not be having this conversation with her. Your parents would have had to bind her in the castle to keep her from rushing into the surf at too young an age. I tremble to think what that bold little girl might have Become." She paused. "But you are not bold like your sister or proud like Hellenia. Even so, it is said that none were bolder or prouder than Cedric, and yet ... So how can one know unless one Becomes?"

"If I Become, I may never know Celinia or Roderick as they grow into adults. I might never see Mother and Father again. I would miss them terribly."

"That's true. As with all things in life, there can be no great glory without great sacrifice, or without risk."

"And I might never see you again."

"Hmm. That should be the last of your worries, child. I grow older just sitting here in the chill breeze, too close to the power of the water that still calls me. My life is almost at an end. Do not let my imminent passing cloud your thoughts or guide your decision."

Lylea let the waves come for several minutes. She felt guilty for pressing her grandmother with the worries that plagued her, but who else would understand?

"I'm afraid." It was the first time she'd named the terrible feeling in the pit of her stomach.

What would Becoming feel like? Would there be great pain, or pleasure, and which would be more terrifying? Would the change begin in her fingers and toes and consume her inwardly? Or would she fall asleep and awaken as a new thing?

Would she remember her past life, her family, her grandmother? Would she even remember herself?

Hesstria nurtured a respectful silence before answering. "Of course you're afraid. I'm sure Cedric was terrified. But his time was like ours. We have no champion. We have no one to master the sea. The sharks and squid are growing into great schools, and the storm clouds gather. Why are you called rather than another? None of us can say. What will you Become? None of us can know. But unless you step into the sea, you will never know. And then you will only know regret when you sit at the end of your life like I do."

They sat in silence while the air chilled Lylea to her bones and the waves whispered their ageless lullaby. The half-moon started its long dive into the western sea, and ghostly shadows stretched back from the stones across the water and sand.

Lylea pushed herself to her feet and climbed down from the rock. She stepped toward Hesstria and bent down to kiss the old woman on her wiry hair. And then she gazed out over the waves. She may be the little orange ball the sun pushed into the sea, but she was a little ball of fire.

"I know what I must do. I will walk into the sea and take my place. Right now, tonight, before my doubts bind me. I may Become a monster, but at least I will know."

Hesstria rose with an effort and joined her. "That is a brave decision, child. Know that your family will be proud of you, either way. And I will be most proud."

"But you must go with me."

Hesstria jerked. "But—"

"As you said, there's nothing keeping you here. Your husband has died and your children have grown. Your life is nearing its end. Why not choose the other life you denied?"

"I'm too old, child. My time has passed."

"By whose measure? Is it written that one must answer the call by a certain age? Besides, I won't go without you."

Hesstria took in a ragged breath and held it. Lylea could feel her trembling next to her.

She whispered, "But I'm afraid."

Lylea felt her own heart drumming in her chest. "Of course you are. But if you don't Become, how will you ever know?"

The old woman stood silently, gazing out over the sea to the sinking moon. Her hand rose to touch the place behind her left ear.

"Take my hand, Grandmother. Come with me."

The old woman slowly slipped her fingers into Lylea's hand.

Lylea gripped them firmly and swallowed down her own terror.

"Are you ready, Grandmother?"

They stepped forward into the sea, and flashes of light spread through the water, a thousand tiny creatures filling the surf with pink and blue and green fluorescence. The water licked at Lylea's toes, her heels, her ankles, enveloping her, warm as blood, sparking her skin with a thousand electric stings.

Grandmother whispered, "We all Become, whether we choose or not."

As she and Hesstria stepped into the water, the sea seemed not so dark nor so deep.

~~~

CJ Erick stumbled into Dallas in search of love, really good sushi, and easy access to big-box stores. Happily, he found all three and inhabits the city with his wife and their two ponderous, black-and-tan hounds. When tired of the reckless adventure of engineering, he pens tales of the space frontier, gothic horror, the odd steampunk mystery, and other unbalanced visions from deranged, caffeine-induced nightmares. Learn more at http://cjerickfiction.com.

HIGH SEAS BURNING

LEE FRENCH

C aptain." Nadya leaned through the door to her father's
quarters at the aft of the galleon she called home. Silk,
gold, and polished wood filled the spacious cabin. Light
streamed through two small-paned windows at the rear. She lived
with no such luxury. Like the rest of the crew, her bunk consisted
of a hammock in the hold.

The captain of the *Merriweather* sat at his desk, poring over his
precious nautical maps with a magnifying glass. He made notes
with white chalk on a slate. "Hmm?"

"Flyboat spotted. Coming on it fast. Looks like it's dead in the
water."

Captain Andre furrowed his brow as he set aside chalk, slate,
and magnifying glass. "A flyboat?" He tapped on his map. "We're
nowhere near shore."

"That's what I thought." Nadya opened the door wider.
"Orders?"

"Any flags?"

"Merchant's flag from Keryth."

The corner of his mouth curled up. "Bring us alongside and
prepare to board."

"Yes, sir." Nadya shut the door and climbed the ladder beside
it to reach the helm.

The first mate, Milo, stood at the wheel, peering at the ship in the distance through a brass spyglass. "No crew on the deck." He placed the spyglass in her hand, letting his fingers trail up her arm to her shoulder.

"Captain wants to raid it." Nadya resisted the urge to shrug his hand off as she raised the tube to her eye. Instead, she took a step to remove herself from his reach and checked the single mast. Loose canvas hung from the yard and gaff with signs of tearing.

Milo snorted. "Easiest raid ever. Even if anyone is on board, they'll expect a rescue."

Seeing nothing else of note, Nadya handed the spyglass back, dropping it into Milo's hand to avoid contact. She stepped to the railing and surveyed the *Merriweather*'s main deck. A dozen men lounged in the sunshine, sharing liquor and fish stories. They had little more than loose clothing, food, and alcohol, but they loved their jobs.

"Man the sails," she barked. To her satisfaction, every man snapped his head to give her their attention. She pointed to the other ship. "Make ready to board."

A chorus of gleeful "ayes" rose from the men as they jumped to their feet and swarmed over the masts. Captain Andre's men had raided enough ships to know what to do. Only the cabin boy had been on the ship less than three years, and even he raced below to do his job without being told.

"They never listen to me like that," Milo groused.

Nadya smirked. When she glanced at him, she noticed him eyeing her backside, something he did often. She faced him and leaned against the railing. The wind pushed locks of dark hair across her face, forcing her to brush them behind her ear. "You never give the fun orders."

Milo's gaze followed her hand, then flicked to her chest. The top four buttons of her collared shirt hung open as usual, exposing her tanned chest and a hint of cleavage.

"Yes," he said. "That must be it."

"My eyes are up here."

"I agree." He continued to stare at her chest.

She turned her back on him. He'd still stare, but at least she wouldn't see it. After a few moments of watching the crew wrangle the sails, she felt an unwanted hand at the small of her back. Before she could whirl and slap the first mate, the captain's door opened. Milo snatched his hand away.

Captain Andre stepped onto the main deck. A breezy wind rustled the blue and white feathers on his leather tricorn hat. His leather boots clacked on the deck. He wore his favorite faded red jacket over a brown shirt and pants—his raid-observing uniform. He surveyed the crew. "Good," he murmured. "Nadya, lead the boarding party."

"Yes, sir." Nadya climbed down the ladder, her movements stiff and stilted. Milo had that effect on her. The moment she set foot on the main deck, the cabin boy appeared at her elbow with her cutlass and leather belt. Buckling the belt around her waist, she crossed the deck to the railing closest to the other ship. Crewmen carrying grappling hooks hurried into position with her.

The *Merriweather* closed on the smaller ship from behind. Bright red lettering on the aft identified it as *Kerry's Corker*. The crew slowed the ship until it crawled alongside the smaller vessel. Nadya noted the good repair of the deck and the lack of a lifeboat. As she'd seen from afar, the sails hung in tatters. She thought a storm might have ripped them. From the broken loading arms, the storm might also have taken the lifeboat.

Crewmen tossed their grappling hooks, catching *Kerry's Corker*'s railing in eight places. Teams of two heaved on each rope, dragging the two ships together.

"May you find riches," Captain Andre said. He flicked his hand to spark the raid, then folded his arms across his chest.

Nadya nodded once and leaped across the gap to the lower, smaller ship. Crewmen followed her with enthusiastic shouts. By the time she reached the aft hatch into the ship's bowels, her men had already swarmed the two dozen barrels lashed to the deck.

"This one's full of wine!" a burly crewman shouted.

"Milo," Captain Andre boomed, "you should join them."

The first mate needed to help her lead the plunder of a crewless ship half the size of the *Merriweather*? Turning her back so no one could see her scowl, Nadya kicked open the unsecured hatch and climbed down the ladder. Her shoes splashed in a thin layer of dark seawater covering the floor. She wrinkled her nose at the thick stench of death in the stale air.

"Anyone here?" Her voice echoed in the gloom. No portholes lined the walls, giving her no way to let in more light or fresh air. The ship creaked as it bobbed in the water. "Anyone in need of rescue?"

Scratching noises deeper in the ship attracted her attention, though it didn't surprise her. Merchant ships often carried cats to control pests and amuse the sailors. The poor thing had probably been stuck down here with sloshing water for who knew how long. She nudged the hatch to the cargo hold with her shoe, but a twisted length of rusted metal through the locking loop kept it shut tight. Others would join her soon. They'd break the hatch open.

"Here, kitty, kitty." Nadya crouched and rubbed her fingers together, hoping to attract the animal.

Above, she heard Milo. His voice made her shiver, as it tended to in dark places. "Where's Nadya?"

Someone responded, his voice carried away by the wind.

"Secure these barrels. You two, get down there with her."

Nadya gave up on the cat and edged away from the ladder, her hand outstretched in the darkness. She found a pair of empty canvas hammocks, one above the other, mounted with hooks on wooden posts. The *Merriweather* had similar accommodations, though their ship boasted thirty crew. This one should support no more than ten. Most flyboat captains brought six to keep costs down and profits high.

"Phew! What died down here?" Griddy joined her on the crew deck. His bare feet splashed in the shallow water as he plunged into the darkness.

The other crewman, Lorca, snorted as he reached the bottom rung. One of their biggest men, he had to stoop to avoid hitting his head on the ceiling. "Probably the crew."

"There's something down here," Nadya said. "Maybe a cat."

Griddy giggled, his high-pitched voice filling the small space. "I hope it enjoyed the feast on its owners."

Nadya shrugged, though neither man saw it. She pressed closer to the aft, staying near the meager light. Four more hammocks lined the rear wall. Another two hung opposite the first pair she found. One on the back wall swayed with a heavy load, providing the stench. She dumped the body out into the light, curious how he'd died.

The dead man wore the gray pants common to merchant sailors and a torn, bloody shirt wrapped around his chest, but nothing else. His unnaturally purplish skin had tightened and puckered, and his eyes had shriveled into yellowish husks.

Lorca crouched beside the man and prodded the corpse with a dagger. "Take off the bandage?"

"Yes," Nadya said. "Let's see what they covered up."

Using his short blade, Lorca cut the shirt off the sailor's body. He paused at the sound of more scratching and looked around.

Wood cracked. Griddy shrieked behind her. Something big thumped on the floor with a splash. Nadya's breath caught. She'd guessed wrong about the cat.

"Griddy?" Lorca sprang to his feet and plunged into the darkness, his thin shoes clomping and sloshing with haste. "Where are you?"

Nadya drew her cutlass and braced for an attack. Grunts and moans filled the deck, mingling with shouts from above. More wood creaked. The ship groaned. Water gurgled. In the distance, she heard a muffled crash, like a barrel smashing open, but she couldn't tell which direction it came from.

She wondered if the ship was haunted, and if that led the crew to abandon it. In the darkness, she thought she saw unexpected movement. "Lorca?"

"I've got him," Lorca called out. He dragged Griddy into the light. The man was incoherent, but the dark stains on his clothes proved to be water, not blood.

Nadya flicked her gaze between him and the darkness over Lorca's shoulder.

"I don't see anything wrong with him," Lorca said. He prodded the back of Griddy's head. "Must've tripped and conked himself."

"Yes, he must have." Seeing nothing of concern, Nadya sheathed her cutlass. She hated to send him away, but more crew would funnel down here soon. "Get him back to the ship. Tell the first mate there's no light down here."

"Yes, ma'am." Lorca craned his neck back to shout at the hatch, "Need a little help down here!"

While men above assisted with removing Griddy, Nadya crouched over the dead body. Touching only the cleanest parts of the shirt, she peeled it away from the corpse to reveal three short, ragged cuts, each sewn shut with black thread and crusted with dried blood. They seemed oddly placed for knife wounds. Angry men with knives didn't make parallel lines. Holding her hand over it to get an idea of the distance between the cuts, she noticed they matched the space between her fingers.

Someone had clawed him.

She heard scratching again.

Nadya paled. Some*thing* had clawed him.

Boots hit the deck at the base of the ladder, startling her and sending her hand to the hilt of her cutlass again.

"What's this whining about light?" Milo asked.

Nadya debated releasing her weapon and waited for her pulse to slow. "Griddy almost killed himself tripping over something." She needed to calm down. Peeling her hands off the hilt, she stood and squared her shoulders.

Milo nudged the corpse with his boot. "Why do we care about this dead body?"

"Eyes look weird. Just checking in case he died of sickness." Nadya forced herself to shrug and appear aloof. "He didn't. Somebody killed him."

He tossed a sparker to her. "Good. They're long gone by now. Nothing to worry about."

Nadya caught the simple device. A set of tongs had been fitted with flint on one arm and steel on the other. Squeezing the arms together produced a spark to start a fire. "Did you bring a candle?"

"No. Find something and light it."

Refusing to show concern about whatever was scratching in the darkness, Nadya stalked around him. She stuck close to the port side, hoping to find a lantern. Her outstretched hand touched a shelf surrounded with a ledge. The first object on it was round and smooth like glass.

Pressure and weight on her hips came from behind her. She shrieked. More weight and blazing heat pressed against her back. She knocked down the thing on the shelf. Glass shattered on the wet floor. An iron grip on her wrist pinned her arm to her chest.

"Jumpy in the dark?" Milo breathed into her ear.

"Kemver's watery balls! Get off me." Nadya struggled, expecting him to let go. He'd always let go before.

"What for? Daddy's not here."

"This isn't funny, Milo. Let go."

"Stop wiggling. You know you want me. You're always strutting in front of me and pretending you don't like me." He took the sparker from her and held both of her hands. "But I know it's just an act for Daddy's benefit."

Nadya froze, not sure what to do. He was stronger and had her arms pinned. Struggling hadn't worked. The crew's chatter and the boat's walls would drown out a scream.

If she played along, he might let her go. Her father could set him straight later. She hated relying on her father for that, but Captain Andre's men respected him. When he laid down rules, they listened. Milo didn't command that kind of obedience.

But Milo wouldn't believe her if she suddenly melted in his arms. She had to use her head. "This isn't the time or place. There's a dead body over there, and the crew will come down here any minute." Her stomach churned. She clamped down on her discomfort to kill a tremble in her voice. "We're supposed to be working, not playing around."

The scratching echoed again.

"What's that noise?" Milo let go.

Nadya stepped aside and hugged herself to stop her hands shaking. Maybe the thing in the dark would snatch Milo and be satisfied. She could report the hold empty, shut the hatch, and claim Milo had gone to his cabin to nurse a bump to his head. Then she'd volunteer to man the helm, and no one would realize he'd been left behind until too late. When the crew failed to locate Milo, Nadya would become the first mate.

"Did you hear that?" Milo asked.

"Yes. I thought it came from the stern." Nadya edged toward the ladder and its promise of safety in the light. She heard Milo's boots shuffle across the deck, away from her.

Milo scraped the sparker to create tiny, fleeting lights. In the brief flashes, she tracked his outline as he moved deeper into the ship. He paused and rasped the sparker several times. Flame flared into life on a piece of cloth.

The sudden, bright light startled Nadya. She grabbed the ladder, ready to abandon him at the first sign of danger.

Tucking the sparker over his belt, Milo picked up a nearby lantern from a shelf. He lit it from the cloth, then dropped it into the water before plunging deeper into the deck. His sphere of light revealed trunks and floor-to-ceiling cupboards bolted to the frame and floor to form walkways. Milo ignored them. Moving farther from Nadya, he swept the lantern back and forth.

He disappeared behind the cupboards. After a few more steps, the glow of his lantern showed that he'd stopped. "There's another body, this one lying in the water. Not dead long—maybe a day or two. Hardly any bloating."

Nadya snapped her gaze to the hatch and the piece of metal holding it shut. Rust and dried blood sometimes looked the same. Wild theories about what had happened ran through her head. Anything could have ridden a wild wave in through a poorly secured hatch during a storm. She'd seen plenty of strange sea creatures in her twenty-two years of life, many with sharp teeth and even a few with claws.

She heard Milo sloshing again and saw his light move toward the center of the front wall. "What about the scratching?" she asked.

"There's nothing here. Probably a twitchy cat. Come check the captain's cabin with me."

Joining Milo in the captain's cabin held less appeal than chopping off her own thumbs. Nadya crouched to examine the hatch. "Go ahead." She poked the rust. Pieces flaked off and hit the brackish water. Instead of sinking to the floor like rust should, it dissolved into pinkish streaks.

"Fine," Milo snapped. Nadya heard hinges squeal.

Overhead, someone shouted, "Look out!"

A shadow blocked the light. Something heavy hit Nadya from above, knocking her onto the hatch. Wood cracked under her. She fell. More wood crashed. Nadya hit the floor again. Someone groaned nearby.

For several moments, Nadya lay in stunned shock. She heard splashing water. Afraid she might have punched a hole through the hull, she snapped her eyes open. Sparks of fear shot to her fingers and toes. Scrambling to her feet in the dim light, she stumbled over broken crates.

"Lorca," someone called from outside, "are you all right?"

Nadya blinked to clear her eyes. Her hand squished with something cool and slimy. She froze, her heart beating too fast. Chest heaving with short, frantic breaths, she raised her hand into the light. Blood covered it.

"Nadya?" Milo crouched on the edge of the hole above. "What happened?"

"I don't know," she whispered.

Next to her, Lorca gurgled. Nadya stared at him, unable to think straight. His bulk wobbled like something small had smacked into him. As she watched, frozen in confusion, a rounded shape rose above his chest. Two yellow eyes caught the light and met her gaze.

She screamed and scrambled for the ladder. But the ladder had shattered into a dozen pieces on the floor. "Milo, get me out of here!"

"What's wrong?" He sounded far too casual.

"There's something down here. It's eating Lorca!"

The creature dropped out of sight. Nadya heard shifting wood among the debris as it moved around him. She imagined it using clawed flippers to navigate around the broken pieces of wood and unknown number of corpses scattered in its makeshift lair.

"Sure there is. But yes, I'll get you out." Though she only saw him in silhouette, she heard a dark grin in his voice. "If you agree to bed me."

"What?" Nadya moved out of the light, desperate to put her back against something solid. She drew her cutlass and hoped the creature's eyes gave it away before it reached her.

"I don't think I'm asking much. Just a reward for rescuing you after I've put up with all your teasing for the past few years."

"And this is your idea of being romantic?" She wondered if the creature would take so long to reach her that her men would reach her first. A flash of blue-green on the edge of the light doused her hope.

"No. Practical."

She wanted to kill him. When she told her father about this, he'd let her. "Get me out of here, then we'll talk."

Milo *tsked*. "No, I don't think so. Last chance, Nadya."

She saw a fresh ripple in the water on her side of the pool of light. The creature had circled her. Nadya took a deep breath and thought about her dreams. She wanted to have a ship of her own, one like *Kerry's Corker* that only needed a few sailors. She'd share it with someone who respected her as an equal. Someone who'd see her as more than body parts.

Giving in to Milo now might work. She could always deal with him later. Except she'd given in before and now he wanted more. Edging along the port wall, she scanned the darkness and failed to answer.

"So be it." Milo straightened and climbed the ladder to the main deck. "He broke through the hull," she heard him shout. "He's dead, and the ship is sinking!"

The uppermost hatch slammed shut, cutting off all sunshine. Nadya squinted while her eyes adjusted to the dim light from the lantern Milo had left behind. He'd abandoned her and Lorca. She'd thought he would leave without a word, expecting others to find her when they came for Lorca.

Hissing came from nearby. The sound reminded her of a cat, but bigger.

She considered trying to saw through the hull. If she swam out, the crew would fish her out of the water. The ship heaved astern. They'd already cut it loose to keep it from dragging down the *Merriweather*. Above, she thought she heard the glass lantern fall over and roll. The creature splashed and screeched.

Aiming for the noise, she slashed her cutlass through the air. The stupid creature wouldn't get the best of her, and even if the ship caught fire, she had no intention of dying here. Milo didn't deserve to win.

Her blade caught something. Fire whoomphed overhead. Light flared, letting her see the three-foot-long blue creature with smooth skin, spiny frills, a mouthful of fangs, and floppy tail fins. Three sets of claws lined numerous webbed, hand-like parts on short, stubby legs. One webbed hand flopped on the floor and spewed inky blood, severed by her strike.

She held her sword out, recoiling from the strange, monstrous creature. It hissed at her, gaze flicking between the shiny metal, its hand, and its new stump.

"That's right," she growled. "You mess with me, you get parts chopped off." She should have told Milo that the first time he trailed his fingertips down her arm. Ignoring him had never solved anything.

The creature darted its head in and snapped its jaws at her. She hopped back and slashed with her cutlass. Her blade scraped along the creature's jaw, shearing off a fang. It hissed again and skittered away, circling behind Lorca's corpse.

Nadya waited for it to leap over the body and rush her. When her limbs began to shake, she noticed the light had grown brighter, dancing and flickering. Defeating the creature meant nothing if she burned to death. She needed to reach the gaping hole above.

Even using her cutlass to augment her reach, she only scraped the wood of the deck above. She scanned the hold, sparing a moment to lament Lorca's horrific death. Later, she'd give him the send-off he deserved. First, she had to escape this death trap. Three intact crates sat on the fringes of the light. With the creature afraid of the sword, she kept it in her hand as she shoved a crate across the floor to the hole.

She climbed atop the crate and discovered her sword reached halfway past the deck. Another few feet would get her a better handhold, but thick, black smoke crept across the ceiling of the hold. Flames licked the edge farthest from the ladder.

With no time to do better, she hacked her blade into the broken planks of the deck. She jumped and pulled. Swinging her body, she caught the ledge with her foot, then her fingers, then her knee and elbow. Her body half on the ledge, she yanked her sword free and rolled onto the deck. Coughing in the smoke, she jumped to the ladder and climbed as fast as she could.

At the top, she braced her shoulder against the outer hatch and shoved with all her flagging strength. The thick wood flew up and open. Heaving herself and her cutlass out, she sucked in lungfuls of fresh air between hacking coughs while plumes of black smoke pumped out of the hatch. She wanted to savor this moment in the sunshine but knew she had little time before the flames engulfed the ship. Scrambling onto the deck, she strained to find the *Merriweather*. It hadn't gone far.

She jumped to her feet and waved her arms in the air. "Hey! Come back!" Shading her eyes, she saw someone notice her. He returned her wave and shouted to Captain Andre. Her father barked orders to his crew.

Assured she'd be rescued, Nadya sheathed her sword and sagged against the railing. The rush of fear, battle, and escape drained away, leaving aches and stinging scrapes behind. She watched the crew work frantically to bring the ship around. Milo stood at the helm. Even from a distance, she could see his scowl.

By the time someone threw a rope to her, she wanted nothing more than to lie down and sleep for days. She caught the rope, wound it under her foot and around her arm, and swung over the water to the *Merriweather*'s sidewall. Men hauled the rope up and helped her on deck.

Captain Andre draped his arm around her shoulders. "Milo said you'd gone below. I didn't realize he meant on the other ship."

Nadya's eyes narrowed as she noted the first mate still at the helm, glaring at her. He touched his neck in a subtle, easily misunderstood gesture to suggest he'd kill her if she said anything against him. She hesitated, uncertain how her father would react to hearing about Milo's treachery. Captain Andre would believe Milo had gotten too familiar with her, but leaving her to die seemed a harder sell.

She glanced back at *Kerry's Corker*. In its hold, she'd faced a horrifying creature and won. As her aching body attested, it hadn't been without cost, but she'd won. The stakes for this battle were lower—or were they? Death versus the rest of her life boiled down to the same thing. Maybe she needed to take a stand and wage the war instead of delaying it again and again.

Locking her gaze with Milo, she said to her father, "He left me behind. On purpose." She used a low voice so Milo wouldn't overhear.

Captain Andre regarded her with a raised eyebrow. "Why would he do that?" His tone, warning yet curious, made her tear her gaze away from Milo to look her father in the eye. There, she found surprise. He'd never noticed. Milo had been so careful and her father so oblivious that he'd missed everything.

"Because I said no."

Realization crept across his face. Anger chased it and settled in the weathered lines. "I trusted him." He glared at the deck, then looked back at her with a dark, dangerous grin. "You handle it. Do whatever seems right."

Nadya raised her brow. "Are you sure?"

"The crew needs to respect you, not just me." Without turning his head toward the helm, he called out in a conversational tone, "Milo, report."

Milo slid down the ladder and swaggered to the captain's side. "Yes, Captain?"

Nadya punched him in his smug face. While he reeled, she kneed him in the groin and shoved him to the deck. After all the uncomfortable moments, all the times he'd let his hand linger a moment too long, all the staring at her body, she reveled in the glory of paying him back. This should have happened years ago, but she'd never said a word.

Half-formed fears about losing her father's respect, being left behind because she was causing problems, and the crew never trusting her had always stopped her before.

Milo rubbed his face. "You little—" He stopped when he discovered the captain's sword at his throat. "Captain, whatever she said, she's lying."

"I've known you for five years, and I've never had cause to doubt the trust I placed in you." He paused, leaving Nadya to wonder if he might consider this punishment enough. "But, you see, I've known Nadya for twenty-two years. Her whole life. And I know how men can be around pretty girls. My Nadya is pretty, and I know it, which is why I've been very clear, many times, that no one on my ship touches her *without her permission.*"

The crew, now gathered around the spectacle, murmured their agreement. Nadya, focused on Milo and her father, had forgotten about them. Tension drained from her shoulders as she realized they all had her back. All of them deserved the trust she placed in them every night when she climbed into her hammock to sleep. Everyone supported her over the first mate.

Milo gulped and looked to Nadya. "I didn't do anything. Tell him the truth!"

"The truth?" Nadya touched her father's hand, making him lower his sword. She addressed the crew. "The truth is, he made me think no one would believe me over him. He made me fear your judgment for his actions. And when I decided I'd had enough, he tried to kill me and left Lorca's body behind. That's the truth."

Anger rumbled through the crew.

"You're a liar," Milo spat.

"They all heard you say Lorca was dead. And they all heard you *not* say anything about me. Griddy knows I was down there."

"Aye, she was." Griddy sat on the deck, a bandage wrapped around his head. "And Lorca deserved better than being left behind."

"I believe Nadya, and I believe Griddy. Take Milo to the hold," Captain Andre snapped. "Does anyone object to Nadya taking his place as first mate?"

Men leaped at the chance to tie up Milo. None spoke against Nadya.

"Very well. Nadya, set a course for port. We have a mutineer to hang. As we sail away, we salute Lorca, who gave his life in service to his brothers—and sister. His pyre isn't good enough, but nothing ever can be for our fallen."

Nadya turned and saluted the plume of black smoke with the rest of the crew. Then she faced forward. Into the future. With the knowledge she had the support of a family on her father's ship.

Lee French lives in Olympia, Washington, with two kids, two bicycles, and too much stuff. She has published more than a dozen fantasy and science fiction titles, including the bestselling Spirit Knights young adult urban fantasy series. She is an active member of the Northwest Independent Writers Association, the Science Fiction and Fantasy Writers of America, and the Olympia Area Writers Co-op, as well as being one of two Municipal Liaisons for the NaNoWriMo Olympia region and a founding member of Clockwork Dragon Books. Find out more about her work at authorleefrench.com.

HEROES OF THE RUSSIAN FEDERATION

CHRIS BARILI

AUGUST 12, 2000, 0600 HOURS

Captain First Rank Gennady Petrovich Lyachin stood atop the conning tower and took one last look at the drab shoreline behind him. They'd left Murmansk two days ago, a bittersweet departure as always, and skirted the coastline north. Even in mid-August, when Moscow danced with greenery and warmth, Murmansk shivered with rock and snow.

Gennady closed his eyes and listened to the faint hum of the submarine's engines, tasted the salt in the air, and felt the cold breeze wash over his cheeks.

With a sigh, he patted the envelope tucked in the inside pocket of his uniform jacket. Irina had given him the letter as he left, turning from his offered kiss. He would read it later, once they were submerged—surfaced was no time for distraction. The paper felt heavy as an anchor around his neck. For once, he feared leaving home.

After twenty-eight years, salt water ran in his veins. Yet perhaps it was time to bid the sea farewell. Retire with his wife.

Below him, the sleek, black cigar that was K-141 slid through the water with ease, its nuclear-powered screws pushing it forward with so little noise American subs would struggle to find it. That made him grin, that something the size of two jet liners would be almost silent.

Called *Kursk* after the city in Russia, K-141 was a Project 949A ANTEY cruise missile submarine. An OSCAR II, in NATO terms. Gennady had been the Executive Officer on its predecessor, and had commanded the *Kursk* for four years. Just last year, he'd commanded the sub in one of Russia's most successful clandestine missions, surveilling American defenses along Turkey's coastline for weeks without being detected.

Now he set out for an exercise in the Barents Sea where American subs were supposedly watching.

He would evade them, too.

Taking in one last breath of briny sea air, Gennady descended the ladder down through the lookout room, ordering a young seaman there to close the hatch. Then he continued down into the bridge.

American movies depicted submarine bridges as dark, but the cramped bridge of the *Kursk* was a bright beehive of activity. Crewmen in blue jumpsuits fussed over workstations, while overhead light reflected off steel bulkheads and glass gauges. At the front of the space, the periscope stood like a sentry.

The air smelled of sweat and bleach.

"Captain on deck!" First Officer Sergei Dudko, a handsome man with dark hair and eyes as gray as Murmansk's shoreline, announced Gennady's arrival. All crewmen not actively driving the boat snapped to attention.

Except one.

Captain Second Rank Dimitriy Raschenko leaned against a steel bulkhead, arms crossed over his chest, tiny eyes regarding Gennady like a parent might observe a petulant child. Like Gennady, he wore his dress uniform, separating them from the crew in their sky-blue jumpsuits.

But for all his posing, Raschenko's face betrayed him. His

forehead furrowed, and he studied Gennady's name tag instead of meeting his gaze.

Gennady turned to the navigation officer, a blade-faced man with slits for eyes. "Captain-Lieutenant Safonov, set heading two-nine-five degrees, engines at one-third."

"Aye, Captain. Setting two-nine-five degrees at one-third throttle." Safonov relayed the command to a petty officer at the helm.

Gennady nodded and turned to Raschenko.

"Dimitry, a word?" He strode to a corner near Dudko. Raschenko hesitated, so Gennady gave him a stern glare. "I insist."

Raschenko flinched at the sudden authority in his voice. Gennady's natural leadership style was more personal, inclusive. Upon taking command, he had written to each sailor's family and promised to protect their son. Their crew had won the award for "Best in Northern Fleet," so Gennady knew his leadership style worked.

Yet when Raschenko joined them, Gennady forced himself to remain stern and cold.

"As much as we appreciate the contributions a *zampolit* offers, why is a political officer suddenly aboard my vessel after all these years?"

A little of Raschenko's arrogance returned. "Command thought it best that someone … guide you, Gennady. They're concerned following your mistreatment of those Moscow officers."

"That situation has been resolved," Dudko interjected. "Command realizes Captain Lyachin did no—"

"And yet Command issued a reprimand." Raschenko crossed his arms over his chest. Unfazed, Dudko met his glare.

Gennady kept his voice low. "Why are you really here, Dimitry? If it was about my manners toward some stuffed shirts, you would have addressed it long ago."

Raschenko dropped his arms to his sides, and again refused to meet Gennady's gaze.

"I don't know what you're talking about, Gennady."

"Captain."

The zampolit shrugged. "What?"

Gennady straightened. "I am in command of the *Kursk*, and you are a military guest onboard. I am, therefore, your captain, and you will refer to me as such." Raschenko tried to argue, but Gennady cut him off. "And what I'm talking about is the fact that we're going to an alleged 'exercise zone' to work with a dozen other ships, but we're getting there more than six hours before them. Other than a missile firing on day one, we've done no exercising. Further, we're making this journey with a full operational loadout of torpedoes and cruise missiles. Very few practice weapons."

His voice had risen enough that the bridge crew watched in tense silence. Gennady ignored them and went on.

"So tell me again, Captain Second Rank, why are you here?"

The interior of the control room always stayed at twenty degrees centigrade, but sweat beaded on Raschenko's forehead.

"Fine, if you must know." Irritation tightened his voice, but something else lurked there, too. Fear? "Our job is to clear the Americans out and make the area safe for our fleet."

Gennady studied the zampolit's expression, and Raschenko blinked. A tiny gesture, but one that spoke volumes. Yet Gennady would not figure it out here.

"First Officer Dudko, you have the conn. I'll be in my quarters."

"Captain leaving the bridge!" Dudko's voice snapped.

As Gennady stepped through the hatch and into the corridor, he thought again of the letter in his pocket. As good a time as any, he supposed.

≈≈≈≈

Gennady poured himself another vodka, letting the clear liquid cascade over the ice like spring water over a glacier. On the table beside his tumbler sat the letter, refolded, as if he'd never opened it. Maybe he shouldn't have.

His quarters were spacious for a submarine, but at that moment, with the letter sitting before him accusingly, he felt the bulkheads pressing in, threatening to crush him. Even his cabin's dim lights seared his eyes.

You're never home, and he is. I don't know how much longer I can stay like this.

Gennady downed the vodka in one gulp and slammed the tumbler on the table.

Yes, he would retire as soon as they docked. He needed to be home. To see Irina.

"Bridge to Captain Lyachin." Dudko's voice over the intercom cut through Gennady's fog. "Captain to the bridge immediately."

Gennady closed the bottle, straightened his uniform, and picked up the letter. He held it to his forehead, then stuffed it in his pocket.

"On my way."

≈≈≈

Gennady strode into the control room, ducking through the hatch and waving off Dudko before he could call the deck to attention.

"First Officer, report."

Dudko appeared at his side. "Sir, passive sonar reports an unidentified ... vessel in the area."

"You sound unsure."

Dudko shifted his weight from one foot to the other. "Sir, the propulsion signature didn't match anything in the database. And then it just disappeared."

Gennady paced the tiny space of the control room, scratching his chin.

"The OHIO-class is almost silent," he said. "Are you certain—"

"Yes, Captain."

Gennady touched the letter in his jacket pocket and paced some more. Something wasn't right.

He thought again of Irina, and his gut clenched. The irrational thought that he'd never see her again nagged at him, persistent and unfounded.

"Do we know what direction it ..." He let the question trail off.

In a corner, away from all but the young steersman, stood Raschenko, shoulders slumped, eyes locked on his feet.

"Captain Second Rank," Gennady demanded, "what do you know of this?"

Raschenko straightened and cleared his throat.

"We knew the Americans might be operating here. They could be testing a new boat. Surely your crew can handle it."

Gennady ignored the jibe. "We don't know what we're up against. Perhaps you could fill us in?"

Raschenko fussed with the hem of his jacket. "I cannot divulge that information at this time."

Dudko's granite eyes darkened, and he took a step toward the zampolit.

Gennady put a hand on Dudko's elbow. "Captain Raschenko, the lives of my crew may be at stake. Any intelligence you may have …"

Raschenko stared a moment, then marched from the bridge.

Gennady turned to Dudko. "Are we in the exercise zone yet?"

Safonov answered from the navigator's station. "We're still thirty minutes away, Captain. We—"

A sound like nails on a chalkboard screeched through the submarine, echoing into the bridge. Something had scraped across the sub's outer shell. The proximity klaxon melded with the shriek, making Gennady shiver. The crew froze, but the sound ended as suddenly as it had begun.

"Sonar! Track whatever that was." Gennady moved to the captain's chair, skin tingling with adrenaline, as Dudko relayed his order to the sonar room. "Safonov, stay on sonar's track. Follow that thing."

"Aye, Captain."

A moment later, a voice crackled over the intercom. "Sonar to bridge. Passive sonar is tracking a vessel approximately a half kilometer off our bow, moving northwest rapidly. It's just like before. Propulsion signature doesn't match anything in our database."

Gennady shifted in his chair, another rush of adrenaline making him antsy. "Aye, sonar, keep track of it. Captain Safonov, adjust course and match speed with it. We don't know what we're dealing with."

"Aye, Captain."

A moment later, the sonar room piped up again. "Captain, whatever it is, it's gone."

Gennady puffed out his breath. "Keep searching. Use active sonar, if needed." He turned to Safonov. "Where was it headed?"

Safonov studied his on-screen chart for a moment. "Straight for the exercise area, Captain."

Dudko whispered in Gennady's ear. "Could be a trap."

"Understood. And it's our job to spring that trap before the rest of our fleet arrives."

He thought again of Irina, and suddenly the bridge seemed smaller than ever; a casket filled with the living.

~~~~

Gennady stood behind his captain's chair thirty minutes later, glaring at the political officer sandwiched between Dudko and a petty officer with arms the size of tree trunks. Raschenko stuck his chin out, like he was daring Dudko to punch it.

Safanov turned halfway around in his yellow navigator's chair. "Crossing into the exercise area, Captain."

"Any sign of other vessels—ours or theirs?" Gennady knew the answer, but had to ask.

"Negative, Captain. The rest of the fleet reports they're still six hours away. And we've heard nothing on passive or active sonar to indicate any American vessels are nearby."

Gennady leveled a withering glare at Raschenko. The man flinched, his confidence eroding.

"Start talking. Where are the Americans you warned us about?"

Rashcenko shrugged. "There could be three OHIO-class subs here, and you wouldn't know it until they fired on you. Look at your crew. They're sloppy and undisciplined, hardly—"

"Silence!" Gennady's voice cracked like a whip, and Raschenko's jaw clamped shut. "Stop trying to change the subject. Why are we here?"

Raschenko swallowed hard. "All I know is that we're supposed to clear the area so it's safe for the fleet's exercise."

Gennady strode forward until he stood toe-to-toe with the smaller officer. "You're lying. And I hate—"

Something rocked the boat, making sailors grab for anything to stay upright. Gennady managed to stumble back to his command chair. Lights flashed, alarms shrieked, and the submarine listed heavily to port before righting itself.

"Sound collision!" Gennady shouted from his chair. "All hands to battle stations! Sonar, what hit us?"

The voice over the intercom quaked with fear. "It's the same thing, Captain. We picked it up on passive sonar just before it hit us. Now we have it on active sonar, and Captain, it's ... huge. Bigger than we are."

Gennady wasn't sure what to say. Something underwater that was larger than his sub seemed impossible.

"Is it a submarine?"

"Not sure, sir, but the propulsion sounds wrong."

"Track it, Lieutenant. Don't let it out of your sight."

"Captain Lyachin!" This time the voice came from the lookout room above them. "It's right above us!"

Gennady and Dudko exchanged a glance, and both ran for the ladder. Gennady made it up first into the dark, window-lined chamber of the lookout. A frightened petty officer trembled at the nearest window.

Dudko joined them and put a hand on the sailor's shoulder. "Steady."

At first, Gennady saw nothing, but as his eyes adjusted to the dim exterior light, he caught a glimpse of something sliding through the sea above them. It gleamed a ghostly gray, its surface shiny. Sleek. It pulsed through the water, faint light glinting off something metallic.

Then the thing banked to starboard and disappeared into the ocean's shadows. Just before it vanished, Gennady swore he saw a tentacle.

≈≈≈

Back in the control room, Raschenko yelled at the burly petty officer, who had moved to block the exit.

"I'll have your head, sailor! I am a Captain Second Rank, and—"

"And his orders come directly from me, Dimitry. Why the hurry to leave? Afraid to explain what I just saw?"

Raschenko paled. "Y-you saw it?"

"I'm not exactly sure what *it* is, but it was not an American submarine. Start talking. Now."

Raschenko looked down his nose at them. "I have not received authorization to release that information."

"Captain!" The sonar room's voice crackled with panic. "It's inbound off our stern, sir. Fast. Collision in twenty seconds."

Gennady dropped into his chair, heart thudding in his chest. "Sound collision. Helm, hard to starboard. Two-thirds throttle. Evasive maneuvers!"

"Aye, Captain."

His crew responded with the precision he'd come to expect from them, masking whatever fear they felt for the time being. The *Kursk* banked right, and Raschenko staggered into the wall.

Sonar shouted through the speaker. "It's still on us, Captain! Impact in ten seconds. Nine. Eight. Seven."

"Brace for impact." Gennady ground his teeth. A rear collision would cripple their propellers, leaving them dead in the water.

"It's gone, Captain." The sonar man sounded perplexed. "It just … vanished. We can't hear it. Active sonar has nothing."

A tense silence gripped the control room. No one dared make a sound.

"It's ahead of us, Captain!"

A buzz filled the bridge, and Gennady rapped a forefinger against his temple. "Helm, what's our speed?"

"Twenty-five knots, Captain."

How did something that large pass them?

"It's coming for us again, Captain. Closing rate fifty-five knots. Impact in thirty seconds!"

"Hard to port, all engines three-quarters. Outrun them, helm!"

"Aye, Captain."

The sub leaned again, and the engine thrum reverberated through the bridge as they picked up speed.

Fear rippled in the sonar man's voice. "Torpedo in the water! Closing fast!"

"Evasive maneuvers, helm! Deploy decoys!" Gennady didn't like this. He needed Raschenko to talk.

Three loud *clunks* echoed as the decoys shot out from their tubes. An instant later, the *Kursk* shook, but only a little.

"Decoys worked, Captain. No damage. Sonar signature matched an old Russian torpedo."

Gennady strode to Raschenko, grabbed him by the front of his coat, and slammed him against a bulkhead. "I saw a living creature out there, and now it's shooting torpedoes at us!"

"I am not at liberty—"

Gennady flung the man to the floor at Dudko's feet. "First Officer, put Captain Raschenko into missile tube four and launch him."

Raschenko's eyes widened as Dudko and the petty officer hauled him to his feet.

"No, please, Gennady! We've known each other for years!"

Gennady held his stance and waited.

"It was an experiment!" Raschenko finally blurted. "We called it Boris."

≈≈≈

AUGUST 12, 2000, 1115 HOURS

"Torpedo inbound!"

Gennady's stomach clenched as he shouted orders. "Hard to port, evasive maneuvers! Decoys out!"

The voice from sonar crackled. "This one is newer, Captain. Not quite modern, but newer."

Tension wrapped the control room like ropes of electricity, and as the torpedo exploded—again, behind them—Safonov twitched in his chair. Gennady loosened his tie, as the control room had turned claustrophobic. He wished for the open space around his home in Murmansk.

"Weapons officer." Gennady's voice broke. "Can we send this thing some real torpedoes?"

Lieutenant Ivanov shook his blond head, blue eyes focused on the screens in front of him. "We can't get a lock on it long enough to fire."

The lookout came sliding down the ladder. "I-it's out there," he stammered.

Gennady picked up the microphone. "Weapons and sonar, this thing is close. Engage and destroy it!" He turned to Dudko. "With me."

The two officers climbed to the lookout tower, and what Gennady saw made his throat tighten until he could barely breathe.

The largest octopus Gennady had ever seen slid through the water, keeping pace with the *Kursk* like they were standing still. Its bulbous, gray head rippled as it moved ahead in busts, and plates of armor gave rigidity to its nebulous body. Elsewhere, ridges of scar marred its otherwise smooth skin.

Dudko whistled, eyes wide.

Easily as long as the *Kursk*, most of the creature's tentacles extended back, beyond the tower, out of sight. One, however, reached for the sub's starboard side, the tip scraping at the cover of a missile tube. Its eye glowed an eerie green. A BOFORS forty-millimeter cannon sprouted from the top of its head, and several tentacles looked to have been repaired with flexible steel tubing.

"Project Boris started in 1995." Raschenko's voice startled both men. "Our scientists discovered the DNA of cephalopods was different than anything they'd seen before. Almost alien. So we played God, and made them better. Most died, but Boris lived. And adapted."

"Learned," he sighed.

"He was supposed to become a covert weapon to attack American warships without warning or detection. Our program supplied the laser range finder in its eye, the gun turret, and some of the armor. We engineered the size, and worked with the creature's incredible intelligence to teach weapons use.

"But it was too smart, and escaped. Added its own modifications. The ink sac now holds and fires torpedoes, and the beast has begun armor-plating its body. It's a most formidable foe."

The creature snapped its head to look at them, then disappeared. An instant later, it appeared at the window, making all three men jump. Its eye pressed to the glass, and a beam of green light swept the room, locking on to Gennady for a moment before winking out. As Boris wheeled and pulsed away, one thick tentacle slid across the lookout windows, producing the same scraping sound they'd heard before.

A warning. No, a threat.

"And now Boris is out here doing what, exactly?" Dudko asked.

"Gathering." Raschenko's voice dropped to a whisper. "The beast has been attacking warships, taking their weapons, and making itself better for years. It has even integrated sonar into its brain and uses an old UHF radio to communicate with us. Threats, mostly.

"Boris wants revenge for the pain we caused. It fights here because, according to our intelligence, its weapons cache is hidden somewhere in the exercise area. Boris can fight a long battle here."

"And what does Boris want from the *Kursk*?" Dudko asked, grabbing the political officer by the collar.

Raschenko's gaze slid from Dudko to Gennady to the floor. "Torpedoes. Missiles."

Gennady's throat tightened. The *Kursk* was equipped with advanced torpedoes and twenty-four cruise missiles, capable of carrying nuclear warheads.

"If that thing gets ahold of our weapons ..." Dudko let the sentence trail off.

Raschenko looked up, eyes glistening. "We must destroy it before the fleet arrives, or they'll have no warning."

Gennady paced the lookout room, curling his fingers into fists to keep his hands from shaking. And from touching the letter again. "If we attack and lose, it will have our missiles. The fleet won't stand a chance."

Raschenko touched Gennady's arm. "Our orders are—"

"Our orders are no longer relevant. I have to think of the

safety of my crew and the homeland. We will escape and warn the fleet, then bring all the vessels against it."

"They'll never believe you," Raschenko said. "And Command will make sure you end up in Siberia if you leak this."

The lookout room seemed to close in around him, spinning like a whirlpool. Images flashed before his eyes. His crewmen. Their parents.

Irina.

He had to get home to Irina. He thought only an instant more before sliding down the ladder into the control room. The other two men followed.

"Captain Safonov, set course for the quickest exit from the exercise area. Helm, as soon as you have that heading, all ahead flank. We'll see how fast this thing is."

Raschenko rushed forward, grabbing Gennady's elbow. "You can't run. You cannot allow the fleet to sail into this trap."

Gennady pushed him back, again hiding the tremors in his hands. "The fleet has more firepower than we do. I must think of my crew."

"We have to try."

"No. That's final." Gennady turned to the helmsman. "All ahead flank!"

"Ahead flank, aye."

Gennady felt the *Kursk* surge forward, the vibration of its engines, tuned nearly to musical perfection.

"Sonar to Captain." The speaker crackled with static. "It's in front of us again, sir. We're sailing right toward it." He paused, then shouted, "Torpedo inbound!"

Before Gennady could order evasive maneuvers, the sub rocked with a massive explosion. Its nose dove, and for a moment, he fought to remain in his chair.

He checked his watch. Eleven-eighteen.

"Damage report!" he barked.

The intercom crackled again, and a man's voice shouted over the noise of men yelling. Screaming. Gennady fought to not retch as his stomach roiled.

"Captain, this is Seaman Nefedkov in the torpedo room. We

took a direct hit. Outer hull is breached. Inner hull remains intact. All torpedo tubes damaged. But sir, we have a bigger problem."

He hesitated.

"Go on, Seaman."

"Two of our torpedoes were damaged. They're both leaking HTP. We're trying to clean it up, but it's too much for us."

Gennady put his head in his hands. HTP. The high-test peroxide was used as propellant for the torpedoes. Highly unstable and combustible with iron and copper—two elements abundant in the torpedo room.

If left alone, the HTP would come in contact with a warhead and then …

"How long do we have, Seaman Nefedkov?"

After a short delay, the seaman answered, "Maybe two minutes, sir."

The defeat in the young man's voice told Gennady all he needed to know.

"Helm, prepare to surface."

At least he could get some of his men off before explosions tore his boat apart.

"Sonar to Captain, it's coming for us. It's—"

The boat rocked again, and the lookout shouted from above.

"It's wrapped around our midsection, Captain! It's trying to open missile tube four!"

The hull creaked and groaned with the strain, and the whole boat shuddered, knocking two men to the bridge floor.

"Fire missile four," Gennady commanded the weapons officer. "If it wants a missile, let's give it one."

"Sir, we're not at firing depth."

"Acknowledged. Fire, and self-destruct the missile as soon as it's clear."

The lieutenant hammered a button, and the sound of the missile firing slugged the boat. With a crash, the groaning stopped. A few seconds later, he flipped a switch, and a distant explosion rumbled through their hull.

"Missile self-destructed," the weapons officer reported.

"It let go, Captain!" shouted the lookout.

"Surface! Now! Get us up there!"

Raschenko appeared in Gennady's face. "You cannot do this. You're an easy target on the surface. The creature will win. It will have your missiles, and your crew will still die. And Irina will remember you as a coward."

Gennady blinked, confusion clouding his thoughts. How did Raschenko know Irina?

"Irina." Tears clouded his sight. "My crew. Home."

Raschenko shook Gennady by the shoulders until their gazes met. "There is no going home. That thing will kill us all before it lets us escape."

Gennady's heart thundered in his chest, and his breaths came in ragged wheezes.

"Irina," he muttered.

Dudko put his hand on Gennady's shoulder. "We cannot return home as cowards, Captain. Let us die as heroes."

Closing his eyes, Gennady touched the letter one last time, allowing his fingertip to slide along the paper's smooth surface. Then he opened his eyes and glanced around the bridge. Every man, even Raschenko, stood at attention. They knew what needed done, and were willing to do it. The shield of their courage blunted the bite of his fear.

He'd never retire with Irina, but she'd remember him as a hero, not a coward.

Gennady nodded and took a deep breath. "Helm, new course. Dive as fast as possible. Take us to the floor."

The control room snapped back into action, every man focused on their individual tasks. Gennady signaled to the young seaman in the lookout above them.

"Seaman, once that thing grabs us, you tell me if it lets go."

The young man nodded and disappeared back into the lookout.

"Captain, if I might suggest?" Dudko's brow furrowed in thought.

"Go ahead."

"Every other time, this creature has gotten ahead of us and then fired. I suspect it will do so again."

Raschenko nodded. "It is intelligent, but not creative."

Gennady picked up the microphone. "Captain to torpedo room."

"Torpedo room, sir. Seaman Shug'lin."

"Where is Nefedkov?"

"Sir, he … didn't make it."

Gennady ground his teeth. "Seaman, how long before that HTP ignites something?"

"It's just me and Zubov now, Captain. We're not enough to stop it. The compartment is sealed, but we might have thirty seconds."

Gennady summoned the courage he'd need to give the next order. "Seaman, keep that HTP contained until I give the order. Then allow it make contact with those warheads."

"Sir?"

"We're engaging the enemy. And we're all going to be heroes of the Russian Federation."

"Sonar to Captain, it's ahead of us again!"

Of course, it was.

"Helm, ahead flank. Give it everything we've got. Let's send this thing back to hell where it belongs."

The *Kursk* picked up another knot or two, and then a shock wave ripped through the boat.

"It's latched onto the nose, Captain!" The lookout didn't even poke his head down. He just yelled. "It's wrapped around compartment one."

The torpedo room. It was trying to steal the torpedoes. Which gave Gennady an idea.

"Torpedo room, be ready. On my mark."

"Aye, Captain."

Gennady turned to Safonov. "What's our depth?"

"Seventy, Captain, and dropping."

The boat's steel shrieked as the giant monster squeezed, trying to crush the nose.

"And the floor?"

"One hundred and eight, Captain."

Perfect. They could pin the beast like a Russian wrestler pins an American. Then kill it.

"Count down."

Safonov's voice cracked as he obeyed. "Eighty meters. Eighty-five."

"Gentlemen," Gennady announced to the entire vessel, "it has been a privilege and an honor to serve with you."

"Eighty-five. Ninety. We're going to strike bottom, sir."

"Count down!"

"Ninety-five. One hundred meters!"

Gennady gave the command. "Now, torpedo room! Now!"

He touched the letter in his pocket, took one last look at his crew as they pinned Boris against the ocean floor, then he closed his eyes and pictured the rocky shores of Murmansk. As the explosions began, he lost himself in the scene, seeing only his beautiful red-haired woman standing on the shore, waving to him.

Irina.

His remaining fear washed away in the flames.

〰〰〰

EXCERPT, RUSSIAN TOP SECRET REPORT

AUGUST 2002

At eleven-eighteen hours on August 12, 2000, during a torpedo handling exercise, a faulty weld on a practice torpedo failed, leaking HTP, which ignited the torpedo's kerosene. The initial explosion destroyed the torpedo room, killed the bridge crew, and started a fire, causing the submarine to sink. At eleven-thirty hours, the fire detonated several live warheads after the boat struck bottom, causing a secondary explosion that killed everyone forward of the reactor.

These explosions left twenty-three men trapped in compartment nine, but rescue attempts were unjustifiably delayed, and all 118 crewmen perished.

Conclusion: This accident was the result of stunning breaches of discipline, shoddy, obsolete, and poorly maintained equipment, as well as leadership's negligence, incompetence, and mismanagement. However, we do not recommend revoking the award of "Hero of the Russian Federation" for Captain Gennady Petrovich Lyachin, nor the "Order of Courage" for the remaining crewmen, as it would reflect poorly on Mother Russia. Finally, it is crucial to keep the fact that Captain Second Rank Dimitry Raschenko was onboard classified, and leave the death toll at 118.

∿∿∿

Chris Barili's short fiction has appeared in the anthology *Temporally Out of Order* by Zombies Need Brains Press, and in three anthologies by Sky Warrior Books. His stories have also appeared online on *The Western Online*, on *Quantum Fairy Tales*, on *Evil Girlfriend Media*, and on *Zetetic: A Journal of Unusual Inquiry*. In 2016, he published his first novel, *Smothered*, through Winlock Press under his pseudonym, B.T. Clearwater. He holds an MFA in Creative Writing (Popular Genre Fiction) from Western State Colorado University, and a bachelor's degree in English from University of Nebraska at Omaha. Learn more about Chris at https://authorchrisbarili.com.

FOUR BILLION YEARS
OF SOLITUDE

ALEX P. BERG

Sharna stared through the porthole at the barren, lifeless surface before her, an endless pockmarked field of gray silicate rock and dirty ice, a mixture of water and carbon dioxide frozen hard as granite in Callisto's balmy afternoon highs of a hundred and ten below zero. For billions of years, the dust had sat there, unmoving except for when rearranged by a wayward meteor strike. Billions of years of nothingness, until they'd arrived in their rovers and put up their bunker and deposited a half meter of regolith over the top to protect themselves from radiation. Callisto might be the most suitable spot for humanity among the Jovian moons, but that wasn't saying much.

Sharna shifted her eyes to the swirling mass of Jupiter above, its tans and reds vibrant against the black of night. Even now, almost two million kilometers away, the gas giant appeared ten times larger than the moon did on Earth. And it would appear even closer. In a few weeks, perhaps ...

Sharna heard the slow *clop-clop* of low-g footsteps and turned to see Lieutenant Commander Bill Bales approaching her from the dining hall, his freshly-shaved head gleaming under the LEDs.

"Kaz," he said, nodding. "Get the message?"

"What message?" She glanced at her wrist and tapped her watch. Sure enough, there was an unread alert.

Bill clapped her on the shoulder, his grip strong even after years of minimal gravity. "Save you the effort of tapping through. Captain said she wanted to see us."

"She say why?"

"Nope. Just to get our asses to her office."

"Think it's about Europa?"

Bill smiled. "Has to be, right?"

The big man bounded down the hallway in the loping gait that worked so well on Callisto, leaving Sharna to follow. The bunker wasn't big, two and a half times the square footage of the *Osprey*, even after accounting for the inflatable laboratory on the moon's surface. With a literal hop, skip, and a jump, Sharna rounded the corner of the hall and pulled herself through the hatch into Commander Shipley's compartment.

Bales spoke up. "You asked to meet with us, Captain?"

Lauren Shipley looked up from her computer terminal, a tall Amazon of a woman with long blonde hair that never left its ponytail, the former captain of her volleyball team at UW as compared to Bill, who'd never risen beyond backup point guard at Georgia Tech. In the place of those two, NASA could've easily sent three people Sharna's size, but the pair had proven their worth many times over since leaving Earth, so apparently the directors knew best.

"Lieutenant Bales. Doctor Kazmeier. Have a seat." Shipley nodded to a pair of collapsible fabric and aluminum chairs.

Sharna hopped over the chair back and settled into the cloth. "So, what's up, Captain?"

Ship flicked off her computer. "I received the daily status report from the driller platform on Europa. Something unexpected happened."

Bill's face fell. "It's not the heaters, is it? Please tell me it didn't freeze."

Sharna's stomach lurched. Two and a half years in transit. A lifetime in waiting—for what? A mechanical failure? *Oh please, no.*

Shipley smiled. "Quite the opposite. We broke through."

Sharna blinked. "Already?"

The captain nodded. "Ice thickness of six point two kilometers, a fair bit less than the eight to ten we were expecting. And you can forget that warm convecting ice theory. There's water underneath. *Liquid* water."

Sharna heard the words as if they echoed from a mile away. Her heart soared and fluttered at the same time. She wanted to dance and scream and punch her fist in the air, but mixed with the elation was the same familiar, lingering dread, always one step slower to arrive. Suddenly her skin felt clammy, and the air she drew into her lungs couldn't quite fill them.

Bill clapped his hands together. "Bam! That's what I'm talking about. So much for the satellite radiography, am I right, Kaz?"

Sharna took a deep breath, forcing away the physical symptoms like someone else might shrug out of a jacket. She'd grown experienced over the years.

Commander Shipley eyed her with concern. "Are you all right, Doctor Kazmeier?"

Sharna forced a smile onto her face. "Are you kidding? I'm better than all right. I'm *ecstatic*. I thought we'd have to wait another month at least."

"As did I," said Shipley. "Which is why you're here. Obviously, the driller was designed with Europa in mind, as were the *Deepsea Voyager* and the docking platform, and so far, all the instrument readings coming back show no signs of degradation. But between the cold and the five sieverts of radiation slamming into the equipment every day, who knows how long that'll last."

"You want to move up the launch date?" said Bales.

Shipley nodded. "I do. The report indicated the heaters are in place at the bottom of the ice shaft. The driller is crawling out to allow entry for the docking platform as we speak. I think we can authorize takeoff within a week."

Sharna felt another flutter but managed to suppress anything more. "I'm in. Let's do it."

Shipley held up a hand. "Hold on. I'll need your approval to move forward, but not before we go over the risks. A change in timing affects mission parameters. We need to be in agreement before we proceed."

Bales nodded. "Understood. You've got our full attention, Captain."

Shipley glanced at Sharna to make sure she agreed. Like Bales, she nodded, but the commander's gaze lingered longer on her than on the lieutenant—maybe because she knew Bales better, or maybe Sharna hadn't hidden her dread as well as she'd thought.

"Most of the operational details will remain the same," said Shipley. "We'll have to pack more fuel onto the ship than we'd planned given Europa's position around Jupiter, but we'll still fly in roughly the same trajectory—at perpendicular inclination to the orbit of the moons to keep you out of the magnetosphere's charged plasma for as long as possible. The change in trajectory will also mean a slightly longer transit, so you'll have to keep an eye on the ship's electrostatic shield."

"So we don't fry like bacon and die agonizing deaths," said Bales.

Shipley cocked an eyebrow. "Exactly. If all goes to plan, you'll land square on the docking platform. If, for whatever, reason you don't, you're to immediately blast off on a return trip. You can't risk overland surface radiation traveling to the sub, and you won't have enough fuel to take off and try again. Are we understood?"

Sharna nodded, as did Bales.

"Good. From there, you know what to do. Launch the *Deepsea Voyager* and search for signs of life. Our most recent surveillance suggests the ocean floor is a hundred kilometers down, so you should be able to make it all the way."

Sharna had a hard time wrapping her head around that. On Earth, the pressure at a hundred kilometers, if such a depth even existed in the oceans, would crush their best sub like a grape, but thanks to Europa's skimpy gravity, the *Deepsea Voyager* should only experience about a hundred and ten megapascals at that depth.

"One last thing," said Shipley. "We've stocked supplies for seven surface-to-floor voyages, but for safety reasons, you're only to conduct a maximum of three. Are we clear?"

Two echoing voices. "Yes, Captain."

"Good," said Shipley. "I'll clear everything with mission control. They're stodgy and might need convincing, but I'll make it happen. In the meantime, I want both of you to rerun every simulation we've been practicing for the past few months. I'm expecting perfect scores, otherwise we'll have to delay. Got it?"

"Absolutely, Captain." Sharna popped out of her seat and bounded toward the hatch.

"Oh, and Kazmeier? Bales?"

Sharna turned, her body already halfway out the office. "Yes?"

"When you touch down on Europa, our base will be almost a million kilometers away. That's not enough to produce a significant signal delay, but for all intents and purposes, you'll be on your own. This mission is not without risk. Remember that."

Shipley wasn't the sort to scare people straight. Likely she meant the statement as inspiration, but in either case, it didn't work. Sharna had never been more motivated—or more terrified.

≈≈≈

Sharna stared at the panel of instruments in front of her, her muscles stiff and in need of a stretch. At least the lack of gravity made it so sitting in a chair for three days wasn't the chore it would've been on Earth.

She unclipped herself. Unfolding, she reached up, using her feet to keep herself from floating away. Sharna emitted a catlike moan as her fingers scraped the top of the pod. One of her many advantages over Bill.

Bales looked at her over his shoulder. "You're alive."

"Of course I am."

"Could've fooled me."

Sharna settled into her seat and clipped back in. "What's that supposed to mean?"

"Just that you've been quiet for the past two days."

"I'm always quiet."

"True. It's one of the qualities that makes you such a good travel companion. I'm not sure I could've stood your company in the various tin cans we've shared over the years if not for that."

Sharna snorted. *"Thanks."*

"You're welcome. But my point is you've been *unnaturally* quiet since we took off from Callisto, even by your standards."

"I've had a lot on my mind."

"You're excited?"

Sharna glanced back. "To be the first people ever to set foot on Europa? The first people to explore *two* of the Jovian moons? To search an alien world for signs of life? What do you think, BB?"

"Just making sure. It's hard to tell with you sometimes." He paused, tapping his fingers. "But you're nervous, too."

"Shouldn't I be? If anything goes wrong, we freeze to death, or explode, or vaporize, or get crushed into pancakes under a hundred kilometers of water."

"Well, sure," said Bill, "but that's been the case ever since we left Earth—except for that last one; that'll be new—but you've been fine, more or less, the whole voyage. Until now."

Sharna swallowed hard. With a day of travel left to Europa, the fear came in waves. Even after years of hiding it, it manifested into physical symptoms despite her best efforts. Thankfully, she hadn't developed any nausea or dizziness, but she'd had her moments. Mild shaking. Sweating. An elevated heart rate. And apparently she hadn't been as *chatty* as normal. What else had Bill noticed? How much did he know? He had the authority to abort the mission if he thought she wasn't in a condition to complete it.

Sharna tried to distract herself with the trajectory data on her console. "I'm fine. Honest. Just tense. Nerves, I guess."

Bill grunted. "You're sure your name isn't really Sharna Levine?"

"What?"

"I'm guessing you don't read a lot of classic science fiction."

Sharna shot Bill a raised eyebrow—not that he could see it with his back to her.

"Levine was the marine biologist in that novel *Sphere* by Michael Crichton. He didn't make it to the crashed spaceship in the middle of the ocean because he got claustrophobic."

"And since I'm a marine biologist, I'm liable to get claustrophobic, too? Give me a break, BB. I've been in space with you for years. I've never had any problem with enclosed spaces."

"But we've never been in a space this enclosed. Not since our launch from Earth, and that was only for an hour. If it's a mild case ... Well, you'd be the sort of person to be able to hide that from the mission evaluators is all I'm saying."

Another twinge of fear. He *did* know, didn't he? "I'm *not* claustrophobic. And what do you mean I'd be able to hide it?"

"I know your resume, Kaz. PhD in marine biology. Masters in microbiology. It's that dual bachelors—biology and behavioral psychology? Kind of a giveaway. Plus, I know you. You may look small and innocent, but beneath that pixie exterior of yours lies a shrewd, calculating little chinchilla."

"A chinchilla?"

"The first small animal that came to mind. Replace it with your favorite marine mammal, if you prefer."

Sharna felt the fear pooling at the edges of her psyche, threatening to darken her vision and force sweat through her pores. Fear of Bill aborting the mission, fear of the mission itself, of failing and all its implications. A pervasive fear, but surprisingly, a known quantity. She'd thought it would've surged inside her like a tide, brought on by the threat of Bill's knowledge. But there it was. The same as ever.

It made sense. She didn't fear Bill, fear his knowledge. He was one of her best friends, one of the few people left to her in this universe, one of the few with whom laughter and jokes weren't transmitted through millions of kilometers on the wings of electrons. She could trust him—*couldn't she?*

Sharna took a deep breath. "BB, what if we don't find anything?"

Bill laughed, striking daggers into her heart. "Seriously? That's what you're afraid of? Of our mission ending in failure?"

So close, but yet so far.

Sharna shook her head, keeping an eye on the control screen. "We've been looking on Mars for thirty years. It had far better conditions for life, at least in the past. If nobody's been successful there, what chance do we have?"

"As good a chance as any, I suppose," said Bill. "If there's warm water, liquid water? We know there's sulfur from Io, plus free oxygen, and tons of ionizing radiation creating more all the time. If there's any kind of convection, any movement between the frozen surface and the water underneath, there's a chance at life that oxidizes hydrogen sulfide, especially if the tidal forces from Jupiter are enough to cause heating in Europa's core. And with emissions from a vent? You bet."

"I'm familiar with the science, BB. But just because the conditions make it possible, the chances ..." Her heart fluttered, and she felt a chill. "They're not good."

"Well, we'll look. Maybe we'll get lucky. And if not here, elsewhere. There's a few dozen billion other exoplanets and moons in our galaxy that might harbor life. Some of them are even close. Proxima Centauri b, Tau Ceti e, Kapteyn's star, Wolf, all the Glieses. There's life out there, Kaz. It's only a matter of time until we find it."

Sharna wanted to respond that until they procured incontrovertible evidence, all the planets and moons in the galaxy represented nothing more than ten to the thirty-fifth kilos of lifeless rock and gas, a trillion yottakilos of death. But she couldn't get the words through her suddenly constricted airway, past the rising tide of bile that clenched her stomach and inched its way up her windpipe.

Sharna closed her eyes and breathed deeply, fighting off the darkness and physical revulsion, hoping Bill hadn't noticed. He'd meant well, with his numbers. For him, the light years between Earth and Proxima Centauri and Tau Ceti were an engineering problem waiting to be solved, the central question of life nothing more than an exercise in statistics.

Not for Sharna. Bill might be satisfied with future possibilities, but her? Interstellar flight wouldn't happen in her lifetime, not unless that ridiculous propulsionless drive broke physics and finally worked. No. This was it. And as she sat there, fighting off the shakes and the dizziness and the screaming panic inside her, her body as taut as a driller's winch cable, it occurred to her it might be the only chance she'd ever get.

~~~~

The descent to Europa was oddly uneventful, almost quiet. There was the muted bellow of the ship's engines, firing as they had been for the past two hours to slow their approach, but it was nothing compared to the violent shaking and all-consuming roar of an aerobraking maneuver into Mars or Earth.

Jupiter filled their field of view, taking up an incomprehensible twenty-four degrees of arc in the sky, Europa at their back as they hurtled toward her in reverse. Then a mighty burst from the engines and a slight jostle and they were there. When the rush of deceleration faded, Sharna could feel the moon's slight pull, indistinguishable from that of Callisto, like the embrace of an acquaintance who wasn't quite a friend. In front of her, blinking, the panels read exactly as they'd hoped. A perfect landing, square on the pad.

Bill unclipped, clapped her on the shoulder, and with their pressure suits already donned and checked and rechecked, they headed out. Through the hatch at their feet, into the lock, down the rungs. So many rungs, even for the small *Goshawk Mark IV*, which served their deep-space needs fine, but paled in comparison to the hundred-and-fifty-meter behemoths that had gotten them out of Earth's gravity well.

As she descended past the end of the *Goshawk*, she saw the brilliant surface of Europa, cracked and cragged and brutal, like a glacier that reached to the horizon, dirty with streaks of yellow and brown from billions of years of Io's spitting. But there was no time to gawk. The chill already seeped through the suit's insulation into her bones, and though she couldn't feel it, she knew all too acutely the destructive power of the sulfur and oxygen ions crashing into her every second.

So she stuck to the rungs, dropping five or six at a time thanks to the low gravity, and upon reaching the landing platform, bounded over to the descent platform where the *Deepsea Voyager* waited for them, painted a bright lime green like its predecessor, the *Deepsea Challenger*, that had once carried man to the lowest point of Earth's oceans.

In the top she went, ahead of Bill. Closed the hatch. Settled into the beast's belly. Then came the whoosh of pressurizing air, followed by the whirr of the winch cable lowering them through the ice and out of striking range of the ionizing plasma, and somehow through it all Sharna kept her cool. Kept the creeping darkness locked inside, kept her mind clear. Perhaps her palms were sweating, but the suit wicked those dry.

She wormed her way into her chair, this one situated directly beside the other instead of back-to-back like in the *Goshawk*. The interior of the *Voyager* closely resembled the home she'd known for the past three days, perhaps even more cramped, but filled with the same battery of panels and readouts, oxygen gauges and carbon dioxide scrubbers, depth gauges and battery monitors.

Bill settled in next to her. The whoosh of air circulating inside the capsule slowed to a trickle, then nothing. A beep rang through the interior, and the display showed full pressure—a hundred and one kilopascals.

Bill's hand flicked to his neck, undoing the latch on his helmet. He tucked it underneath his chair and leaned forward, staring out the small porthole in front of them. The light from above had already dimmed to near total darkness, obscuring the ice into a dark blur.

Sharna undid the clasp holding her own helmet in place and tucked it away, breathing in a lungful of cool, sterile air. The last ten minutes had passed in a blur, yet here they were. Aboard the *Voyager*, on their way down.

Bill shot her a look. "Feeling all right? Any headaches or light-headedness?"

"For the last time, I'm *not* claustrophobic."

"You seem to be very aware of the symptoms for someone who isn't. But I was describing acute radiation poisoning. I was going to suggest fluids if you were."

Sharna tucked her scowl away. "Sorry, BB. I guess I'm a little—"

"In disbelief?"

She searched for the right words. "Yeah. That about sums it up."

"Imagine how you'll feel when we hit the water."

They didn't have to wait long. The winch let them drop, accelerating to fifteen kilometers per hour while Sharna and Bill flicked through the sensor reports, checking to make sure the system diagnostics were all reporting full functionality.

If not for the deceleration of the winch, followed by the warm glow of the tunnel heaters at the bottom of the shaft, Sharna might've missed it. She looked up in time to see the heating elements whip past them. A fraction of a second later, the submarine jostled, and she heard a distinctive *sploosh*.

The porthole was too small to get a good view, so she flicked on the exterior floodlights and tapped over to the external camera on her screen.

Water—as far as the lights could illuminate. Unfathomable amounts, capped by an endless sky of pale-blue ice as smooth as glass.

Bill smiled. "Feeling pretty real now, I'd wager."

"Yeah." Sharna was fairly sure she'd spoken out loud, but maybe the breath escaping her lips had been a sigh of relief.

She'd made it. She'd *really made it*. After months of drilling, years in transit, decades spent in preparation, training, and education, and after a monumental combination of hard work, ability, and luck, she'd made it. Breached Europa's liquid core. The first to descend into an ocean beyond Earth's shores.

And then it hit her, washing through her like a wave of the saltiest brine. The fear. The unbridled, inexplicable terror. The nausea and dizziness and shortness of breath that had afflicted her throughout her life, every night when she'd stared into the infinite, starry expanse of the universe. But it couldn't overwhelm her this time, even without her actively fighting it, because her body was waging a war of its own, excitement versus terror, possibilities versus disappointments, death versus life.

The ice above them faded as the *Voyager* sank. Bill tapped on his panel. "I'm going to engage the descent motors, assuming you're in agreement."

Sharna nodded, too conflicted to speak.

"Great. Here we go." Bill's fingers danced. A muted hum sounded from above. "Diagnostics looking good. Seafloor ETA is about twelve hours. I'll turn on the temperature gradient controls. I doubt we'll see any changes laterally until we're much closer to the floor, but should they appear, we might as well start moving toward them during the descent. We'll want to maximize every hour we have in this thing."

Sharna swallowed, pushing the frothing mass of emotions back. "Agreed."

She forced herself to focus on her control panel, swiping through measurements so Bill wouldn't suspect anything. Silence stretched as the exterior pressure gauge ticked up.

"It's going to be a long descent," said Bill. "Mind if I put on some music?"

Sharna cast a disapproving glance Bill's way. "We're completely alone on a Jovian moon, one no other human has ever set foot on, descending into a liquid ocean the volume of all the bodies of water on Earth combined, the likes of which no other explorer has ever encountered, and you want to *listen to music?*"

"It's twelve hours to the bottom, Kaz. Some tunes aren't going to sully the experience any more than me snacking, sleeping, or relieving myself in my suit is."

Sharna sighed. "Whatever."

Bill tapped his watch. A few seconds later, a tinny sound blared through the sub's interior speakers. Crunchy guitars and thumping drumbeats, though higher pitched than they should be.

Bill grunted. "Figures. Thirty million dollars spent on a state-of-the-art sub, untold billions more getting the thing and all the support equipment to Europa, and NASA can't bother to install decent speakers."

Sharna squinted as the music played. "What is this, anyway?"

"So you don't like classic science fiction *or* classic metal."

"Apparently not."

"These are the godfathers of the genre. Metallica. 'Trapped Under Ice.'"

Sharna suppressed a groan. "You've been waiting for years to spring that on me, haven't you?"

Bill grinned. "If you'd said no, I would've put it on anyway."

Sharna shook her head and turned back to her instruments.

Both fear and excitement coursed through her, keeping her wired like the world's strongest coffee, but as the conflicting emotions faded, they left behind a tingling void, one even Bill's ancient metal music couldn't fill.

After a few hours of monotony, with yawns striking her in bursts, she matched her alarm to the ship's pressure sensor and told Bill to wake her should anything come up.

≈≈≈

Bill's iron grip shook her from her slumber. "Hey. Kaz. Check this out."

Sharna blinked, feeling as if she'd just closed her eyes. She glanced at her watch. Six hours she'd slept, the slumber of the dead, but the depth gauge still indicated they were fifteen kilometers from the floor. They had well over an hour's descent left.

She rubbed her eyes, noticing the music had been silenced. "You've been at the controls this whole time? You should've woken me."

Bill's eyes remained glued to his screen, his brow a mass of creases. "Can swap later. Sonar picked something up. Two kilometers away. Something big."

Sharna shot upright, instantly awake. "A volcanic ridge?"

Bill shook his head. "Density's all wrong. This is only barely showing. That's why the sensors didn't spot it until now."

"Thermocouples picking anything up?"

"A slow rise during the descent. No lateral gradient yet."

Sharna tapped into her console. "Two kilometers you said?"

Bill nodded.

"Well, let's check it out."

Sharna brought up the sonar display as she engaged the lateral motors. She felt a surge as they kicked in, and she flicked through to the data.

She blinked—her emotional core a gaping void. That wasn't right.

It can't be.

"How long till we arrive?"

"If I push her up to seven knots? A few minutes."

"Do it."

Sharna felt the craft accelerate as she switched her display to the external cameras. Darkness filled the screen. She reactivated the floodlights that she and Bill had turned off to conserve power, turning the sea of black into one of uniform deep blue.

Sharna brought the sonar up side by side with the external camera view. One kilometer to go. Seven hundred fifty meters. Five hundred.

Bill stared at his screen, the furrows in his brow becoming canyons. "Uh, Kaz?"

"There."

She pointed to her screen. There was something beyond the inky sea of blue. A reflective spec, still blue but paler than the rest. Then more than a spec. A mound. A mountain, rising from the deep.

Bill gaped. "Oh … my … *God.*"

Sharna shot out of her seat and pressed her face to the porthole, unable to believe what she was seeing, but it wasn't a mirage. The porthole confirmed it.

A massive column rose from the depths, a branched structure with fingers sprouting from arms like a giant fractal. They hung there, glowing eerily in the light of their sub, perfectly still except for at the tips of the smallest branches where there were flickers of movement. A vascular plume.

Sharna had seen similar mechanisms before in the depths of the Pacific, near hydrothermal vents. Never so calm. Never so massive. But she'd seen them.

Bill let out a *whoop.* "Holy crap, Kaz! Can you believe it? Tube worms! Europan tube worms! What did I tell you about the hydrogen sulfide oxidation? *What did I tell you?*"

He sprang from his seat and pulled her into a bear hug, going on about thermal updrafts and metabolic rates, how many hundreds of millions of years it must've taken to grow such a colony, bouncing up and down as best he could in the tiny craft.

Sharna barely heard it, barely felt his embrace, barely noticed anything except the light that shone within her, burning away every trace of fear and hesitation and doubt, banishing it to the dark expanse of night from which it had come.

Her voice cracked. "You were right, Bill."

"What? About the chemosynthesis? I know!"

The words poured out. No need to fear them anymore. "No. About me. I lied. To you. To the evaluators."

"What are you talking about?"

Sharna smiled, reveling in an internal warmth she'd never before felt. "Most call it autophobia. Some monophobia, isolophobia, eremophobia. A fear of isolation. It was easy to hide, not because of my degree, but because I didn't have it. Not precisely. My case was different. More exoisolophobia, a fear of being alone in the universe. But we never were alone, were we? We've merely spent the last four billion years in solitude. Until today."

≈≈≈

Alex P. Berg is a mystery, fantasy, and science fiction writer and the author of the best-selling Daggers & Steele mystery series. As a scientist with a PhD in Nuclear Engineering, he knows way too much about the ill-effects of radiation and what the word "critical" really means. He's also a discerning heavy metal aficionado and would be happy to debate the merits of his favorite bands ad nauseum. Connect with him on Facebook, Twitter, or at his website alexpberg.com.

SONGS TO SING AND STORIES TO TELL

L.D. COLTER

Tansy pushed the floating bits around in her half-eaten bowl of cereal and wished her foster mom would buy the O-kind instead of the flake-kind that always got soggy. Miss Judy's baby didn't like her breakfast either; she turned her head away from the spoon and slapped her hand into a puddle of strained peaches on the high-chair tray, sending gobs arcing onto the floor.

Miss Judy sighed and headed for the sink. Her toddler, Alyssa, tried to follow her but slipped on the peach goo, fell, and started to cry. The twins, Carlos and Miguel—eight years old to Tansy's seven, and only in foster care five weeks to Tansy's five months—shot wet cereal at each other through their orange juice straws. Miss Judy lifted Alyssa to one hip and turned back to the sink. The phone rang.

"Oh, for Pete's sake," she said.

She pulled a wet cloth off the faucet, answered the phone, stuck it under her chin, and returned to the table to wipe the baby's hand. "Yes, that's me." There was a long pause and she straightened, the dishrag dangling from her fingers. She glanced at Tansy. "I see. Okay. Should I tell her or should I wait?" Another pause. "Sure. Friday would be fine. What time? All right, we'll expect them then."

The other children had fallen as motionless as Tansy—even the baby stared at Miss Judy. Still holding Alyssa, Miss Judy hung up and pulled her chair close to Tansy's.

"Do you remember a lady named Hannah Yoshida?"

Tansy shook her head.

"Well, she remembers you. She was a friend of your mother's. It sounds like she's been going through the steps to get a foster license, and she and her husband want to fly out from California and take you back to Sacramento to live with them. Doesn't that sound wonderful?"

"I guess," Tansy said. She had no idea if it was wonderful or not because she didn't remember anyone named Hannah. She looked at the stuffed dog sitting on the table by her bowl and wished she could ask Cowboy if he remembered her. He'd lived with Tansy in Bakersfield before the car accident that sent her parents to heaven, and he'd moved with her to her grandparents' house here in Maine two years ago, and then into the foster home after Grandpa Kelly died, all of a sudden, in March.

The twins, realizing the phone call had nothing to do with them, pushed away from the table with a clatter and ran for the living room.

"Get back here and clean up your dishes," Miss Judy shouted. The boys returned to the kitchen like a fast-moving hurricane—grabbing cereal bowls and glasses, sloshing leftover milk and juice, competing to see who could get to the sink first. The baby swatted at her tiny, plastic bowl, flipping it over.

Miss Judy cleaned up after the baby again, and Tansy waited until the twins cycloned away before dumping the rest of her cereal in the sink. Plucking Cowboy from the table, she opened the patio door and headed for the sandbox Mr. Dennis had built in the backyard at the beginning of summer.

When Miss Judy vanished from the kitchen, shouting something to the boys, Tansy ran down the narrow side yard to the back gate that led to the street and the beach beyond. She'd snuck out twice before—both times soon after she'd moved into the foster home, when she had especially missed going to the ocean with Grandpa

Kelly—but she'd gotten in such trouble when she was caught the second time that she hadn't tried again.

She ran the first block, hoping the twins wouldn't tumble out into the front yard and see her, then slowed and walked the last couple of blocks to the beach. On the way, she told Cowboy about the pigeon she'd seen from her bedroom window that morning because she wasn't ready to talk about the lady coming to take her somewhere new. She reached the beach and trudged through the deep sand, glad there were no people to see her and make her go home. Eastport was tiny, almost an island, and hardly anybody came to this part of the beach except on the weekend.

Tansy plunked down near the tide line and watched the clouds. They drifted so close to the ocean it looked as if they wanted to dip down and ride the waves like cowboys on bucking horses. Her grandmother had said that Tansy's parents taking her to rodeos was why she'd named her stuffed dog Cowboy, though Tansy didn't remember naming him and only sort of remembered rodeos.

"I'll bet Grandpa would've gone swimming today," she said, "even with Old Sow so close."

She'd once asked Grandpa Kelly how an ocean could have a whirlpool, and he'd told her it had to do with tides and a canyon under the water. Her Grandma Natalia told her that it wasn't a whirlpool at all, but a water monster. She said it was one of the many children of a monster named Charybdis who ate sailors, and her babies had spread out around the world to lure human children out to drown. Grandpa Kelly said they were silly tales from her old country and she shouldn't say scary things to a little girl. Her grandma never said it again, but she never took it back either.

Tansy brushed beach sand from Cowboy's face, but her fingers spread more fine grains across the bulbous brown muzzle and triangular black felt nose than they removed. She inspected the base of his floppy left ear where her grandmother's large stitches were pulling loose. Her grandmother had insisted on washing Cowboy weekly when Tansy first moved in, though it made his bandanna fray and fall off and tore one ear. She'd sewn the ear back on, and then she got sick and died, and Cowboy didn't get washed anymore.

"I beat Emily Waters in a race across the pool in Seahorse swim class on Saturday. Her name even has 'water' in it, and I still beat her. I'll bet I could swim by myself in the ocean if I wanted to, like Grandpa did."

Cowboy would believe anything she said, but listening to the eerie moans coming from Old Sow, Tansy wasn't as confident as Cowboy might think. The water monster story still scared her, and she didn't like the cold water, but she'd often walked in the surf holding hands with her grandpa. He'd let her swim a couple of times, too, though he held onto her around the middle.

Tansy listened to the distant grunts and burps that had given Old Sow its name. People said you couldn't hear it from shore, but Tansy had heard it all three times she'd been here since Grandpa Kelly died. Today she not only heard the piggy noises, but for the first time, she also heard a soft rise and fall beneath the gurgles and splashes—the comforting lilt of a woman's voice. Listening harder, she thought she heard words beneath the noises, almost but not quite words she could understand.

"Do you hear it?" Tansy asked Cowboy. The sounds came and went—sometimes splashes and moans, sometimes a voice, and sometimes the waves drowned it out altogether. Each time the voice returned it seemed more clear until, suddenly, in a quiet lull between waves, she recognized actual words.

"Goodnight room," it said. It was a line from a favorite bedtime story Tansy had almost forgotten.

"I think it's Mommy's voice," she whispered, though she didn't actually remember her mother's voice. She leaned forward until she squished Cowboy, eyes wide, mouth open, listening. "Mommy, is that you? It's me, Tansy."

The words came again, snatches from favorite stories and bits of barely remembered lullabies, alternating off and on, off and on, with the sounds of the ocean.

The sun peeked through the clouds for a moment, like a light from a lighthouse beacon, there and then gone as it rotated away, but the sudden brightness had pulled Tansy back to the present. Old Sow gurgled with no hint of her mother's voice. A moment longer, and even the sucking noises faded away. She wasn't sure how long she'd sat at the beach, but the angle of the sun told her it had been longer than she'd meant to stay. Clenching Cowboy in one hand, she pushed to her feet. Sand rained off her as she ran up the beach to the rows of nearby houses.

~~~

Tansy slipped through the gate to the backyard. She sifted a handful of Legos out of the un-mown grass so she could plunk down at a moment's notice and pretend to have been playing there all along. A crash came from inside the house, and Carlos and Miguel tumbled out the patio door, plastic lightsabers in hand.

"*Pssshewww, pssshewww,*" Carlos yelled, striking furiously.

"*Pssshewww,*" Miguel yelled back. "*Zumm, zumm, zumm,*" he hummed, holding his lightsaber at one shoulder for another strike.

"Get in here now," Miss Judy shouted from the door, Alyssa still on her hip. The baby was crying inside. "Give me those toys. You woke the baby, and you could have broken that bowl."

She sounded cross, but the boys seemed unfazed. They ran past her, relinquishing their lightsabers as they jostled through the door. Tansy heard a thump as the heavy candy dish was set back on the side table. Miss Judy stepped out onto the narrow row of boards outside the patio door and spotted Tansy. "There you are," she said in a scolding tone. "I called for you earlier." Footsteps pounded up the stairs as the twins ran to their room to find some new game to play. "You stay close, you hear?" Miss Judy headed for the baby's crib.

Tansy began playing with the Legos for real, snapping them together, unsure what she was making until the *L* shape reminded her of the largest pier on the beach, the one where the boats tied up. She outlined a section of the coast and added the other little piers.

"I'm sure it was her," she told Cowboy, who sat next to her in the grass. Even if she didn't remember her mother's voice, the songs and stories were ones her mother had recited to her when Tansy was little. She traced the edge of her coastline with a finger, stopping where Old Sow lived. What if it wasn't just her mother's voice? What if her mother wasn't really in heaven but out there in the ocean? Grandpa Kelly told her that Old Sow was farther away than it looked but it moved sometimes—up to half a mile, he'd said.

She imagined the swirling funnel of water walking to and fro beneath the surface on long watery legs and hoped that Old Sow would walk closer to shore, so she could talk to her mother and tell her that she didn't want to live with foster parents or go away with the new lady.

~~~

The next morning, Miss Judy bundled everyone into the car to go to Calais, about half an hour away, to shop for back-to-school things and run errands. The baby cried most of the time except when she was asleep, and Alyssa spilled her sippy cup of juice on the backseat of the car. Carlos and Miguel got lost in the Walmart, and Miss Judy had to have their names called over the loudspeaker. Tansy followed Miss Judy up and down the long aisles, first in the Walmart then in the grocery store, more anxious with each row of canned goods and pasta and cereal that the whirlpool would shrink away like it sometimes did, or walk farther out to sea before she could get back to the ocean. She might never hear her mother's voice again.

After they got home and had lunch, Miss Judy put out warm milk and cookies and popcorn and played one of the *Ice Age* movies. She liked to make warm milk when she wanted everyone to take a nap, but it was Miss Judy who fell asleep on the couch while the twins ate all the popcorn *and* all the cookies except the ones Miss Judy handed out first. As soon as Miss Judy was asleep, Tansy grabbed Cowboy and slipped outside.

Old Sow hadn't moved away; if anything, she thought, the whirlpool had come *closer*. She clutched Cowboy to her chest and listened as hard as she could for her mother's voice. There were gurgles and sloshes, but no words or songs.

"I'm here, Mommy," she called to the whirlpool. "It's Tansy. I came back."

There was no answer.

She thought maybe having her feet in the water would help, and she sat down to take off her socks and shoes, then picked Cowboy up again and waded into the surf. The tide was gentle, and she walked out until the cold waves lapped at her knees.

"I think I *do* hear better," she told Cowboy.

Tansy wished she had her swimsuit and goggles. She was a good swimmer—Mr. Ivins who taught Seahorse swim class said so. She'd earned her 100-meter swim badge the week before Grandpa Kelly died but hadn't gotten to swim again until last month, and Miss Judy didn't take her as often as Grandpa Kelly had. She waded out a little farther, clutching Cowboy under her chin to keep the waves from hitting him.

Tansy felt certain she heard singing buried beneath the sound of the ocean and the distant slurp and gurgle of the whirlpool. She was up to her chest, the farthest she'd ever gone out into the ocean. The cold water pushed her off balance and made her shiver, but the waves seemed to rise and fall in time to the distant singing, though the language sounded like what Grandma Natalia used to speak on the phone sometimes. She felt a humming vibration of the song in the soles of her feet as the sand shifted and slipped under her. The words became English, and Tansy recognized "Twinkle, Twinkle, Little Star." She sang it to Cowboy in case he couldn't hear it.

When a small wave splashed at her neck and trickled down her back, she realized she'd walked out deeper into the ocean. The bottom half of Cowboy was soaked. She looked toward the beach, finding it farther away than she expected.

Tansy thought about turning back, but she felt more certain by the moment that she would be able to see or touch or talk with her mother if she could only get a little closer. Emotions welled up inside her, tightening her chest and burning her throat. She wondered if heaven had fallen into the center of the whirlpool, and she began to cry without knowing exactly why.

Clutching Cowboy with one hand, she pushed off the sand and tried to dog-paddle to keep her head above water, but the salt water splashed into her eyes and stung. It was awkward swimming with

Cowboy, and the swells and the salt water made it much harder than swimming in the pool.

The voice coming from Old Sow got louder, and the song became a story, the one she'd heard yesterday. "Goodnight room. Goodnight moon," Tansy heard the voice recite. "Goodnight cow jumping over the moon."

A wave splashed in her face and went into her mouth. She choked, and her arms flailed as she coughed, struggling to lift her head up high enough not to inhale more water. Remembering to tread water like Mr. Ivins taught her to do when she was in trouble or got tired, she bicycled with her legs and made figure eights with her hands until she coughed the rest of the water out.

She realized she no longer held Cowboy. Desperate, she twisted around and saw him floating toward the beach. When she turned her back on the whirlpool, the songs and stories stopped, like Miss Judy putting a movie on pause when she went to the kitchen. Or like her mother might be mad at her or would go away if she chose Cowboy instead of her. Old Sow was hard to see beyond the waves, but it looked at least as far away as it had before.

She glanced back again for Cowboy but saw nothing for a horrifying second before his tail and butt bobbed to the surface. In another moment he'd vanish altogether. Tansy dog-paddled furiously toward him. It was hard to see with drops of water in her eyes, but swimming toward shore was easier than swimming into the waves. A triangular black nose and beady brown eye showed below a foamy crest of water near her. She kicked hard and reached forward, holding her breath and breathing out through her nose as her head went underwater. Her hand closed around the soft felt and stuffing. One of her toes brushed the sand, and after dog-paddling a few more strokes, she was able to stand on the bottom again.

She hugged Cowboy to her neck and told him how sorry she was, and that she'd never let him go again. Tansy's body shook with cold as she stood knee-deep in the water and stared toward the swirling hole, more frightened now at what she'd done than when she'd been doing it. Old Sow had gone back to water talk, and Tansy didn't know if the whirlpool was her mother or a bit of heaven or a monster, but she ran, shivering, all the way back to the house.

She didn't think she'd been gone long, but it'd been long enough that Carlos and Miguel had lost interest in the movie and were running around the front yard pretending to be Diego the saber-toothed lion and Sid the ... whatever he was. Going in through the back gate, she avoided the boys seeing her, and Miss Judy and Alyssa and the baby were still asleep with the TV on when Tansy slipped upstairs to dry off and change clothes and get warm.

She had never been so disobedient before or done anything so dangerous ever. And yet, the whirlpool still called to her. She couldn't hear the star lullaby or the *Goodnight Moon* story anymore, but not hearing it was a little like her parents dying all over again, and, though she hadn't gotten over being scared, it made her want more than ever to go back to the ocean and hear it again.

That night she heard the ocean from her bedroom window, something she could rarely do unless the wind was just right and the tide coming in. Sounds floated to her as if carried on shafts of light from the full moon sailing over the sea—over Old Sow. There were snatches of *Where the Wild Things Are* and "Itsy Bitsy Spider" and a dozen other stories and songs she'd forgotten, so soft they sounded as far away as Bakersfield.

Tansy squirmed her head under the covers and hugged Cowboy, still ocean-damp, trying not to hear the voice. She thought about running into the waves and swimming as hard as she could out to Old Sow until it seemed she could feel the cold ocean close around her, feel the pull of the whirlpool as she got closer. She imagined spinning down into the mouth of it like water down her bathtub drain and popping out somewhere dry and warm and being with her parents again.

But she knew that Cowboy would tell her that oceans weren't dry and warm, and Tansy remembered her grandmother's warning about the monster whirlpools that stole little girls away and drowned them. She tried to remember how serious and scared her

Grandma Natalia had looked, but all she could think about was the urge to open her door and run to the ocean. And then she thought about nearly losing Cowboy, and that maybe she would get lost the same way in the ocean but there'd be no one to save her.

≈≈≈

"You need to wear something nice today to meet Miss Hannah and Mister Troy," her foster mother said the next morning, setting a dress and stockings out for her.

Tansy was putting on her second shoe when the doorbell rang, and Miss Judy took her downstairs. Tansy thought the couple on the doorstep looked a lot like she felt. The woman clasped her fingers tightly together at her waist, and the man stood close to her with one hand on her shoulder. He gave her a little pat, and she stepped inside and walked straight to Tansy, hardly saying hello to Miss Judy, who was still holding the door.

The lady squatted down. "Hello, Tansy. I haven't seen you in a very long time, not since you were very little. About her age." The lady pointed to Alyssa hanging onto Miss Judy's leg. "My name is Hannah, and I knew your mother. My mommy died, too, when I was about as old as you are now, and my daddy wasn't around, so your grandparents took me in. I grew up like a sister to your mommy."

Tansy didn't know what to say, so she said nothing. Miss Judy led them all to the couches and chairs in the living room, muttering about the boys and their mess as she picked up a few stray toys, gesturing to Carlos and Miguel, who had been sent outside to play. Tansy sat at one end of the couch, Hannah sat next to her, and the man sat next to Hannah, holding her hand.

Hannah turned to her again. "Troy and I have been in Japan, teaching school. We flew back for the funeral when your parents died, and again when your grandma Natalia died, but Papa Kelly passed so suddenly, I never heard about it. Papa Kelly wrote and called sometimes, but he had our old address in his will and since they hadn't adopted me formally, nobody knew to call me. I didn't know about any of this until we moved back and I tried to contact him."

Tansy didn't understand it all, except that this lady had grown up with her mother.

"Your mother's family took very good care of me when I needed it, and I'd like to do the same thing for you. I know this is all very sudden, but we'd like to take you home to California to live with us."

It *was* sudden, too sudden, and it was frightening. Tansy squeezed Cowboy so hard his middle squished to the size of her fist.

Hannah looked down, noticing him. "Is that Cowboy?"

Tansy looked up at her, surprised. "Yes."

"What happened to his bandanna?"

"Grandma used to wash him in the washer and it came off."

Hannah laughed—she had a nice laugh. "She used to wash my favorite stuffed horse when we visited. I had to hide him on wash days because his tail unraveled and started to fall out."

Tansy smiled. "Was he a bucking horse?"

"No, he was my pony and I pretended to ride him. But your grandparents used to live in California a long time ago, and your mommy and I grew up going to rodeos in Bakersfield and watching bucking horses. We have rodeos where we live, too. Would you like to go to one?"

Tansy nodded. She liked that Hannah knew about Cowboy and rodeos.

"We have some appointments we have to go to this afternoon so we won't be leaving until tomorrow, but I promise we'll be back for you soon."

~~~

The visit had been short and confusing, and Tansy couldn't sleep that night. Miss Judy had packed all her things except her clothes for tomorrow, and the suitcase and box of toys and clothes made strange shapes in the twilight glow coming through her gauzy curtains.

She heard Old Sow again, calling her—first in her grandma's language, then in English, then telling her stories and singing songs. If it was her mother, then Tansy wanted to swim out to the whirlpool and stay with her, but her mother had never spoken Greek. Her mother had died and gone to heaven. And the whirlpool had nearly made her lose Cowboy. Even the new lady, Hannah, understood how much Cowboy meant.

Still in her Toy Story pajamas and cat slippers, she left her bedroom with Cowboy in hand. Miss Judy and Mr. Dennis were sitting on the front porch, talking. Tansy unlocked the sliding patio door in the kitchen and ran down to the beach.

The first stars were getting bright, and the full moon was rising over the sea. Old Sow had moved so close to shore that Tansy could see the circle of white caps glinting in the moonlight, closer than she'd ever seen it before. It read *Goodnight Moon* to her so loudly she could hear every word in the gurgling sloshes. The voice soothed her and eroded her resolve—until she looked down at Cowboy. Her mother would never have let her lose him.

She spoke loudly so she wouldn't have to go in the ocean. "I think Grandma Natalia told the truth," she said. "I think you want a little girl of your own. But I can't be your little girl, and I think if I tried, you would drown me. I like to swim better than almost anything, but I can't live in the water and I don't think I can turn into a mermaid or something. I don't think my mommy and daddy can live in the ocean either, and I don't think heaven fell from the sky. I have to stay on land, and I have to stay with Cowboy, and I have to go away with the new lady, Hannah. Stop singing and telling me stories, please. I have to go now. 'Bye."

~~~~

Tansy had been unable to eat breakfast, no matter how many times Miss Judy told her she needed something before traveling. Her things had been moved downstairs, and the twins were playing with toy cars in the living room. The shouting and squealing of brakes and loud "bam" and "ksshew" of pretend car crashes made Tansy feel more sick to her tummy. She wondered if she'd dreamed last night, or if she'd sent her real mother away and lost her only chance to be with her again.

The doorbell rang, seeming twice as loud as the twins.

Hannah and Troy came in, and Troy started carrying Tansy's things out to their car. Hannah carried a book in one hand, and when she saw Tansy looking at it, she held it out to her. "Have you read *Charlotte's Web*?" she asked.

Tansy thought she might have and nodded. "Do you know *Goodnight Moon* and 'Itsy Bitsy Spider' and 'Twinkle, Twinkle, Little Star'?" she asked.

"I do," Hannah said. "I know all of those and more. I teach school for children about your age, and I know lots of stories and songs. Do you like to sing songs and read books?"

"I like it a lot."

"Will you read with me on the plane?" Hannah asked.

Tansy nodded again. She thought she might like reading and singing songs with Hannah very much. She took Hannah's hand and said goodbye to Miss Judy. Troy came back in, and the three of them left together for the car and the plane and California.

Due to a varied work background, Liz has harnessed, hitched, and worked draft horses, as well as worked in medicine and canoe expeditioning, and as a roller-skating waitress. She also knows more about concrete than you might suspect. Her published work includes her debut novel, *A Borrowed Hell*, from Shirtsleeve Press, along with short stories in a variety of magazines and anthologies. A complete list of published works and her blog can be found at her website lizcolter.com.

Underwater Cats

Mary Pletsch

Closing the cabin was a lot of work at the best of times, but it was even more so now that he wouldn't be coming back. Mark Adams knew he ought to be doing what he could, or at least packing the things he wanted to take with him. Instead he ignored the voice of wisdom in favor of stumbling down the slope from his front porch to the lake.

He'd made the path himself over the course of fourteen years, hiking back and forth between his dock and his cabin. He knew every rock, every upraised root. He had worn the bark off those roots and polished the bare wood with the soles of his shoes. Now he half-walked, half-slid from tree to tree, angling his shoulders to catch himself against their sturdy trunks so he wouldn't tumble down the slope. He'd have bruises tomorrow, but that didn't matter, he'd always believed in toughing things out.

His ankles wobbled inside his untied boots. He'd not been able to tie the laces with his left hand numb and clumsy, and, frustrated, he'd given up. It was an unwanted reminder that sheer force of will could not put feeling back into his face, his fingers, his leg.

Mark staggered onto the narrow strip of rocky ground between the bottom of the slope and the lake. A boat with an outboard motor bobbed on the right side of his dock. The left side was empty. The Cessna Caravan C-FDXP was gone, assigned to his successor, and Jane's floatplane had not yet arrived.

Mark raised his head, lifting his right hand to blot out the sun as he scanned the brilliant blue sky, even though he knew he'd hear the plane long before he saw it. He heard birdsong and the soft burble of waves against the dock, nothing more. He dropped his gaze to the trees and saw a touch of yellow, a suggestion of orange, all the little hints of incipient autumn and the inevitable decline into winter.

Mark kicked off his boots on impulse. He undid his belt, then unbuttoned his jeans and let them fall to the dirt. He stepped out with his right foot, hoping he could shake the clothing free. He stumbled a few times, fell to his knee once, and finally managed to drag his left leg out of the pants. He pulled off his flannel shirt, the one he hadn't bothered to try to button, and tossed it onto the jeans. Clad in his boxers, he limped to the water's edge.

He ordinarily swam naked—no reason not to; nobody else lived on his lake—but he wouldn't want his friend and former coworker to see him without his underwear on. He and Jane had never had that sort of relationship. On some level, he knew she was going to have to fish his sorry ass out of the lake.

Mark lurched forward into the cool water, driving ripples ahead of him. Submerged pebbles bit into the sole of his right foot. He guessed they were doing the same to his left, he just couldn't feel them. He made a note to check his left foot for cuts when he was done.

A large rock turned over beneath his right sole and he staggered, dropping to one knee with a thunderous splash. Scattered droplets soaked his hair. Water climbed up the leg of his boxers, chilling as it spread. Mark struggled, making three attempts to rise before he finally got his feet under him again.

If he fell like that in deeper water, he might drown. From now on he ought to respect the difference between what he wanted to do and what he could safely accomplish. He wasn't what he used to be, would never be again, and it was time to accept his situation for what it was and start making wise decisions.

But when he looked over his shoulder back up at the cabin

Jane had helped him build, he admitted he probably wouldn't be able to climb the slope without assistance. He'd passed the point of no return some time ago, and now there was nothing for it but to go forward.

He gazed down into waist-deep water as its surface grew still around him, marred only by the wind's gentle waves, and what he saw looking back at him was the face of a man he recognized, an athletic man with broad shoulders and a strong jaw and the kind of beard a man could grow up here where there was no one to judge him. The lake told a truth the mirror in his cabin never could. The lake knew who he was.

The mirror in his cabin insisted on telling him other truths. Things like the droop in the corner of his mouth and the tears that leaked, unbidden, from the corner of his left eye. The mirror showed him a stranger, a man cut down by a stroke days after the spring equinox. A man who couldn't live alone in a cabin in the wilderness; a man who'd barely managed to convince Jane to bring him back here long enough to put his affairs in order.

He'd be better off living with his brother in the city. He *would*. The doctors said there was no reason he couldn't get his own apartment in time; the city had condominiums with associations that handled snow removal in the winter and maintenance year-round. It had cleaning services he could hire to tidy his place for him and restaurants that could bring food to his door. And it wasn't as though he'd never lived in an urban center before.

He'd survived four years of university in the city, and he could survive again—never mind that living in the city had felt like four long years of suffocation. Four years of desperate escape into the sky, earning his commercial pilot's license, dividing his time between the schooling his parents insisted he take and the foundation he knew he needed for the future he wanted. When the weather was poor or the money was tight, he turned to his sketchbook, drawing planes and forests and lakes and counting down the days until he could *get out*.

Never mind that his professors had told him he was throwing away his *potential*. He hadn't cared about postgraduate scholarships or internships or marriage; he didn't value what most people thought was important. He'd just wanted his bush pilot's wings and his wild horizons and his solitude.

Those dreams were ashes now. He'd never fly again. The life he'd worked so hard for had slipped through his fingers. He'd come down to the lake to say goodbye.

As he raised his eyes from his reflection in the water to the far-off horizon, Mark wondered if maybe it might be better if he just kept walking until the waters of his lake closed over his head and swallowed him down into their depths.

It was a fanciful idea, of course—he'd float, unless he weighed himself down with something heavier than the boots he'd left on the shore. But it would be possible to make his way out to a place where the water went over his head, requiring swimming ability he no longer possessed to keep his nose and mouth above water. The problem would be in those terrible minutes when his lungs would cry for air and his right leg would kick furiously and his left leg would move so feebly in the water—when the animal imperative toward survival overcame the philosophical understanding that his life, as he knew it, was already over.

I should be grateful, Mark told himself as he tried to shake away his morbid thoughts. He was lucky to have a brother who was willing to take him in. He should be thankful that he wasn't left-handed, that he could still *draw.* It was the only thing that had kept him sane in the hospital—pretending that he was sketching in his cabin while the winter winds howled outside.

Potential, his teachers had said, and he wondered now if that potential sat waiting in a cobwebbed corner of his soul, if he could pick it up and dust it off and continue where he'd left off, or whether, in the long years he'd left it fallow, it had gone to rot.

He'd never been afraid of dying out here. It didn't seem right that he hadn't. He'd trusted caution and skill to preserve him from accidents, both in and out of the floatplanes, and he'd accepted what risks remained and let the chips fall where they may.

And he'd never been afraid of monsters.

Wet fur slid over the back of his right calf. Maybe the left, too, and he just couldn't feel it. There was no feeling quite like the caress of a thick pelt under water, and Mark smiled a lopsided grin.

A few moments later, two paws breached the water near the end of his dock. Huge black claws grated over the weathered wood, finding anchor spots in chinks and crannies. Next came the horned head, the line of triangular spikes down its back, and finally the spiny tail as the creature clambered up onto the dock and flopped onto its side. Its fur dribbled moisture onto the faded boards. It rolled onto its back, paws tucked to its chest, and gazed at Mark through slitted eyes in an upside-down head.

"Hello," Mark said quietly, and the mishipizhiw purred.

He suspected this one was a kitten. It had been the size of a Labrador retriever pup when he'd first built the cabin, and now it was closer in height to a Great Dane. Mark could only guess how long they lived, or how big they got. He'd seen huge spines breaking the surface farther out in the lake, out where Jane had told him the water ran half a kilometer deep. Jane had also taught him the word *mishipizhiw*, which meant "Great Underwater Cat," and at the time he'd laughed because who ever heard of a cat that liked water, let alone lived *under* it?

But to Jane—who went home to a husband and a daughter and a house in town—the mishipizhiw were myths from a bygone era. To Mark, alone when the winter dark howled outside his cabin walls, the line between truth and story often grew hazy, and sometimes vanished altogether.

Mark had learned to accept the mishipizhiw the way he'd come to accept the peculiar shapes of the snowdrifts as they furled around his woodpile, his trees, his cabin. He knew that in a few months' time the drifts would return and take forms similar to those they had taken last year, and the year before that, and the year before that. His language had no words to describe their particular qualities, but he knew the shape of their curves and the changing textures of the snow. He knew that they were real even in the summer when they existed only in his mind. Presence was not the same as reality, and things could be real and unreal at the same time.

The mishipizhiw was far from the only thing here in the North that defied explanation. There were other things he couldn't talk about with his brother, like the peculiar and perfect shade of black of pine trees silhouetted against the setting sun, or the soundless voice that called to him from over the horizon, calling him to come and see what lay beyond. His brother did not understand, and Mark had given up after his best attempts implied either madness or dreams.

Mark doubted there were mishipizhiw in the city.

He stumbled sideways in the waist-deep water until his good hand touched the dock. Then, leaning on the sun-warmed wood, he lurched along, leaning against it, ignoring the splinters and the scrapes against his side, until he was next to the mishipizhiw. The underwater cat rolled upright and raised its tail in a gesture of welcome, and Mark wished with everything in him that he did not have to leave his home and his lake and his friend the mishipizhiw.

Mark could not describe the mishipizhiw's communication: speech implied sound, sign language required gestures. The mishipizhiw conveyed meaning in *impressions* of images and knowledge, and from the way it responded to his thoughts, Mark was certain the communication was two-way.

Mark held out his hand. The mishipizhiw bunted its moist cheek into his palm, and as it did so, Mark received a sensation of how it would feel to be taken down into the lake forever.

The mishipizhiw told him that he would not be the first. The water plants far below cradled bones beyond counting in the center of the lake where the water was deep. There had been other people who had thought themselves a burden to the world, people who had given themselves to the lake and lost themselves within it. Mark understood that he did not need an anchor to weigh his body down. The mishipizhiw could pull him under, and it would be quick.

Mark had never been afraid of monsters, and he'd never been afraid of dying. By all rights, he should have died on the floor of his cabin. Instead Jane had found him, soon enough to save his life but not nearly soon enough to reverse the damage done.

He was about to tell the mishipizhiw *yes* when the cat rose to its feet and rubbed its wet fur against his arm. Another image swam into Mark's mind, moving soundlessly, like a silent film.

A young woman dressed in deer hide slouched on a fallen log, the left side of her face drooping down, her left arm withered at her side—but the children at her feet listened in rapt fascination to her words. A fire burned in front of her, and behind her, Mark saw massive spines breach the still waters of the lake and then slide back under the surface.

The scene changed, became a man with a bushy blond beard reclining in a canoe paddled by two other men. A memory from an elementary school history class supplied Mark with a name: *voyageurs*. The white wake fanned out from the stern of the canoe and in the ripples, a spiked tail rose, lashing, from the water.

The blond man's face was pale, and his right arm ended in a swath of cloth tied tightly with rope. In the way of dreams, Mark knew the canoe was taking this man home to a wife and children, and though the man feared what they would think of a crippled husband and father, still he dared to return to them and be the best partner, the best parent, that he could. The man set his jaw resolutely, and the mishipizhiw behind his canoe dived deep, vanishing into the lake.

Mark was not sure if it was intuition or the mishipizhiw speaking to him directly, but in that moment, he knew that just as the mishipizhiw guarded the bones of the men and women who had given themselves to the lake, so too were there men and women who had declined the mishipizhiw's gift.

The distant drone of an aircraft engine reached his ears from somewhere far away in the late summer sky.

His mishipizhiw had heard his wish, but maybe he could yet find, if not somewhere else to truly call home, at least some way to add a little more goodness to the world before he left it. Or maybe he couldn't. But he would never know if the lake took him to its heart today. The courage he would need to survive in the city was of a very different order than the courage it had taken to make a life here in the North, but Mark had never been one to back down from a challenge, and surely he had not changed that much.

"Thank you," Mark said as he rubbed the mishipizhiw behind its horns, "but no."

The mishipizhiw licked him, just once, and then it slid from beneath his fingers.

Mark took a deep breath and started to turn himself around. If he leaned on the dock, he might be able to make it out of the water before Jane arrived.

Partway through the turn, he hesitated. He looked back over his shoulder, half-expecting the mishipizhiw to be gone, but the underwater cat was still there, standing at the edge of the dock.

"You could have taken me," he said hesitantly, "but you showed me another way. Why?"

The mishipizhiw tilted its head and sent Mark one more image: a felinoid, like a lynx or a cougar, yet not quite either, planting its forepaws into the cool waters of the lake. It looked back over its shoulder, and though Mark could not see what pursued it, he could sense hunger in the shadows, menace in the rustling leaves, and a looming despair like the one he'd felt during the long nights in the hospital. The cat took a deep breath, as if bracing itself, and then plunged into the lake, where it—

Let go of itself were the only words Mark could think to use. It released its old nature and embraced the potential of becoming something other. It clung to life and possibility and let everything else go, and in doing so, began its metamorphosis.

The mishipizhiw winked at Mark, and for the first time, he perceived its communication as words.

Did you think we were always underwater cats? it asked, and Mark recognized the good humor in its tone. And then the mishipizhiw slipped off the end of the dock and down into the water and vanished beneath the surface, as if it had never been.

Mary Pletsch attended Superstars Writing Seminars in 2010 and has since published short stories and novellas in a variety of genres including science fiction, steampunk, fantasy, and horror. She is now working on her second novel. She lives in New Brunswick with Dylan Blacquiere and their four cats. Visit her online at fictorians.com.

LURE

Joy Dawn Johnson

The barrel of the revolver pressed against Landon's temple. "You ain't no crab fisherman." Trent's deep Southern drawl was unmistakable.

Landon held up his hands. His palms weren't calloused like the rest of the boat's crew—something he hoped Trent wouldn't notice. "I'm not here to cause trouble."

With the deck empty of crab pots, the two men were alone up top. The clouds parted briefly, and the moon cast a swath of light across six-foot ocean waves before darkness overtook them again. If it wasn't for the overhead lights, it'd be impossible to see.

"You've got thirty seconds before your brains become tomorrow's bait." Trent twisted the hood of Landon's rain slicker with his free hand. The wet plastic felt like wire across his throat.

Landon swallowed. "Or what? You'll take me to the captain?"

Trent cocked the gun.

Landon closed his eyes. It couldn't happen this way. Not yet. He needed answers. A strong gust blew through his short-cropped hair. An ocean swell rocked the boat forward. Landon caught himself on the railing.

"You're a dead man." Trent's voice shook.

"You don't need to do this. I can explain." Landon took several deep breaths to think, but the freezing drizzle and onslaught of salt water blending with the distinct stench of fish tacos made it difficult to tamp down his rising panic. He reminded himself why he was there. "What do you know about the *Arctic Siren*?"

Harrowing moments crept by until Trent finally loosened his grip. Swearing, he removed the revolver from Landon's temple and scrounged in his pocket for a newspaper clipping that he shoved into Landon's face. "Found this gem in your bag." His voice thickened with each word. "Start talking."

In bold type on page one was the headline "Bering Strait Legend Claims Third Crew in Five Years." Another wave crashed over the railing, soaking the bottom corner of the paper. Printed just above the fold was a photo of the *Arctic Siren*'s crew. On the far right stood a man who was the reflection of Landon, only with a full beard.

With the front sight of the gun, Trent pointed to one of the other men. "See this guy?" Clearly in his element, the man had a furrowed brow that appeared to be about as permanent as the hook-shaped scar along his jaw. "Boyd's been my buddy since we were kids." There was more than salt water at the corner of his eyes. "You were on that boat. Tell me—" He raised the gun then coughed into his sleeve to gather himself. "How are you alive? What do you know?"

Not a hell of a lot, unfortunately, Landon thought. *And that's not me. It's my brother.*

But he figured right now wouldn't be the best time to contradict the twitchy fisherman.

Five weeks ago, he had shaved his face and hit up the local Alaskan drinking holes to find a captain crazy enough to head far west. The legend of the Bering Sea Behemoth kept most boats from dropping their string of pots out this far, but for the last two years, Mother Nature had followed her own plans.

Landon wasn't sure he'd find a boat willing to take the chance after another crew had vanished, but with the seismic shift in the water temperature, most of the crab population closer to shore had disappeared. After a few rounds of Duck Fart shots, it turned out that the *Crawler Troller*'s captain planned to take the risk. Just the idea of being on a boat for weeks made Landon want to dive overboard. He hadn't even known anyone who fished until his reckless brother sold his bike, jumped on the first boat, and was never heard from again. Landon feared the worst but would do whatever it took to find his brother.

"I don't know where your friend is." Landon pointed to the newspaper clipping that had been liberated from his pack. "*That* is my brother, Brandon."

The crew wanted to make quota.

Landon wanted to find his missing twin. He could still feel his brother out there. Half of him was missing, and he feared he'd never feel whole again.

Trent's eyes lost their burning focus on Landon. Slowly, ever so slowly, he lowered the gun.

"You've heard of the Behemoth, right?"

Trent nodded. "An enormous creature that yanks the crew right off the boat, one by one, with its tentacles—or tongue—depending on who tells it." They both wanted answers, but all they had was the legend of some horrible sea monster that everyone knew from hearsay and speculation. No one who'd truly seen it had survived.

"I found a connection between a few of the boats, including the *Arctic Siren*."

"Are you serious?" Trent leaned in conspiratorially, seemingly oblivious to the fact that he'd just threatened Landon's life, and was, in fact, still pointing a loaded gun in his direction.

Landon regretted saying anything. Apparently, Trent hadn't searched his bag thoroughly enough to find his notes. Eyes on the gun, Landon figured he better tell him something. "In every ship log I've seen, the last recording reported spotting a dead body."

Trent shivered. "Don't tell me—"

"Put that thing away!" The chief engineer bellowed at Trent as he came onto deck.

Trent dropped the paper. A wave crashed over the side, the water reaching their knees, and swept away the one photo Landon had brought of his brother. Trent hadn't seemed to notice as the chief engineer continued to drill into him.

"You've hazed the greenhorn enough."

Trent looked at the gun as though the boogeyman had slipped it into his hand. He disappeared below to stow it.

"And greenhorn," Chief began, "you better follow him and prep the bait before we throw you over."

Landon wished he could take another look at the logs. No one had mentioned a tongue before—though any part of the legend seemed too unreal to be true. Since he'd boarded the boat, Landon had been up to his elbows in herring guts. Tongues and eating hadn't exactly been on his mind.

≈≈≈

"We've got a floater." Chief's voice crackled on the radio well past midnight. "Not a buoy, Cap. Life preserver, and it ain't empty."

"Haul 'er in."

The words had Landon on his feet and up the stairs, hands still dripping with fish innards. Trent followed. With the moon covered by the clouds, the main light served as their guide on deck. It shone across the preserver, giving them a clear view of the initials *A.S.* printed on the back.

Trent swallowed and finally managed to say, "*Arctic Siren.*"

Exactly what Landon had been thinking. His greatest fear had been never knowing his brother's fate. He did a mental scan of the boats he'd researched for the same initials and came up empty.

The other deckhand used the smaller crane to hoist the body onto the boat. It wasn't easy for Landon to stay still. The chances it was Brandon were slim, but ...

Landon held a hand against his forehead and squinted, but looking into the main light did little more than put spots in his vision. The deckhand lowered the body onto the deck. Heart pounding, fearing the worst, Landon stepped forward to get a better look.

The lights flickered.

Everything went black.

"What the—? Chief!" The captain called from his chair, but the emergency siren drowned out his three-pack-a-day deep voice.

"I'm on it," Chief yelled back. "Trent, follow me below."

"But—" The siren drowned out his plea to stay. Crestfallen, Trent disappeared below.

Under the faint glow of the cabin's emergency light, Landon could barely make out the silhouettes of the deckhand and the body on deck.

The boat hit a swell. Water surged over the railing, flooding the deck. The wave slammed into the back of Landon's legs. He reached for the base of the crane. The metal had iced over, and the cold bit into his hands. He clenched his teeth and held on.

The siren cut off mid-wail and the backup generator flared to life, powering up the main light.

The body was not on the deck.

Landon sprang to the railing and scoured the dark, frothing waters for the faintest hint of orange ...

Nothing.

The body was gone.

He ran his hands through his wet hair and turned to tell the deckhand.

Gone.

"Cap! Man overboard!"

The captain cleared his throat over the speaker. "Get Trent and Chief up here."

"Cap, I—"

"Now."

Landon raced to the engine room and brought the two men back up. He cupped his hands to yell to the captain. The main light clearly illuminated the empty wheelhouse. No trace of the captain remained.

"What the hell?" Chief leaned against the railing and wiped his face. "Where—" His eyes bulged as an unseen force yanked him backward over the edge.

"Oh, god!" Trent and Landon yelled. They dashed across the deck to where Chief had gone overboard.

Nothing.

"Wh—where'd he go?" Trent yelled out over the crashing waves.

"Where'd they *all* go?" Landon held onto the railing and

shuffled around the boat. He caught his breath. "Get your gun." Leaning over the bow, he was sure he'd seen something enormous beneath the surface of the water. The more he stared, the more it seemed the moon had appeared just long enough to cast the boat's shadow before disappearing back into the clouds. He almost hoped the Behemoth *did* exist so he'd have some explanation.

The boards behind him creaked. "That was fast, but I don't think—"

Something grabbed him, shredding his slicker from his shoulders and peeling his flesh away like an orange. He screamed.

The claws raked like lightning across his skin. His vision blurred. His body tingled and grew numb. The world tilted, and he snatched a quick glance at the creature. It hunched on all fours, but with an unexpected human quality to it.

"Hey! Get away! Get back!" Trent pointed the gun at the creature's back.

"Don't shoooot it," Landon slurred, sagging to the deck. He opened his mouth again, to tell Trent who the creature was, but the words came out in a garbled mess.

Trent pulled the trigger, and the shot cracked into the night.

The creature spun around. Seeing the threat, it crouched low. Thick saliva mixed with bits of flesh streamed to the deck.

Trent took several steps backward, dropping the gun. Eyes wide, his chin began to shake. *"Boyd?"* The distinctly hook-shaped scar across the creature's jaw was unmistakable.

In a streak of orange life preserver, the creature pounced on Trent.

Landon tried to push himself up to help, but his limbs were wet noodles. A wave crashed onto the deck, and the gun washed up against Landon's arm. Whatever the creature had done had left him paralyzed, but conscious enough to know what was happening.

The creature casually ripped Trent's arm from its socket with a gut-wrenching snap, and Trent's bestial scream tore through the night. The rain slicker slid onto the deck like the intestine casing peeling from a sausage. The creature that had once been Trent's friend held the limb by the wrist and lapped the marrow from the bone.

With a trembling hand, Landon reached for the gun and felt the reassuring grip slide into his palm. He held the revolver up a few inches above the deck and willed his mouth to form the words. "Where is—"

The creature raised its head from its meal. A tendon stretched taut, then snapped against the creature's chin. Without warning, it picked up the dying Trent and casually tossed him overboard like a fish too small to keep. Landon had begun to think the legends were wrong, and there was no Behemoth. But why else would this creature take so few bites and throw the rest over? Landon shivered with the thought and forced himself to focus. He cocked the gun. "Tell me ..." He'd feared never knowing the truth, but this was worse. "Where is my brother?"

The creature paused, seeming to consider Landon, before a long tongue emerged to lick its decayed lips.

"No, please no." He refused to believe it. This thing couldn't be the Behemoth of legend, swallowing men and ships as quick as a breath, but this creature knew what had happened. He was sure of it. "What did you do?"

The creature cocked its head as though studying him, then its black eyes flashed. "Same, same," it hissed.

It took Landon a moment to understand. "Yes. My brother looked like me."

"Do you want the same fate?"

Everything screamed at Landon to say no, but he was about to die anyway. He needed to know what had happened. "Yes."

A hideous smile crossed the creature's face, and it lunged forward, biting Landon on the shoulder.

Landon fired the gun, hitting the creature twice in the chest, staggering it. His next shot put a hole in its forehead. With a phlegm-filled scream, the creature spun around and slumped to the deck. Impossibly, the thing lifted its partially shattered head, looked directly into Landon's soul, and said, "He's coming for you." Then it scuttled over the railing, dropping into the frothing water.

Landon rested his temple against the deck. The tingles changed

to a constant, burning sting, and his body stopped responding. The gun slipped from his fingers.

A wave crashed over the bow. Landon wanted to reach out to grab something, but the water carried him over the side. He plunged into the ocean. In his mind, he kicked and moved his arms, but the signals didn't transmit to his limbs.

All he could do was wait for the Behemoth to swallow him whole.

Deep.

Deeper.

His body twitched as he sank. He felt the hunger growing in his belly, in his chest and arms and throughout his body. He realized death wasn't the worst thing that could happen to him.

Through the depths, a dark silhouette swam toward him. He tensed, ready for the end. As the moonlight shone through the water, he saw someone reaching out for him. His own reflection—except for the long, tangled beard.

"Come, brother."

They rose to the surface of the waves, floating. Thinking … Hungering … Waiting …

There was no Behemoth to fear.

Only them.

〜〜〜

Joy Dawn Johnson has a BFA, an MBA, and ghostwrites novels for a *USA Today* bestselling author. She was the 2015 recipient of the Superstars Writing scholarship funded by the *One Horn to Rule Them All* anthology, and since then, her stories have been selected for three other anthologies.

Visit her at joydawnjohnson.com.

EAT ME

LAUREN LANG

There's a nervous energy in the air. A hiss. A crackle. A hum of electricity, and not just from the generator attached to our truck. There's something about going live, about being on television in front of millions of people, that adds urgency to everything.

Minute details become suddenly important. The cut of a bathing suit, for example. Most women worry how they'll appear in front of, at most, a few hundred people at the beach. In a moment, I'll be entering millions of living rooms and bedrooms wearing a swimsuit picked out by my boss's boss.

Is the two-piece too revealing? Not revealing enough? Is white the right color? Will the audience still be able to see me in the dark water? We'll all find out together in minutes.

"I'll do anything to have this done. Anything," I intone silently to myself.

This isn't your average news story, and it certainly isn't a normal live shot, as much as I would like to pretend that it is. I'm the consummate professional, however. The viewers don't need to know that I'm secretly eating my heart because I'm about to have some toothy competition for my flesh.

"Angela, audio check?"

I jump imperceptibly at the intrusion into my thoughts as my earpiece crackles to life.

"One, two, three, four, five," I answer into the microphone in my hands. The shaft feels slick with the sweat on my palms, but I hold it and my gaze firm as I stare into the camera.

"Thanks, Angela. We're good. Ask Rick to pan right a little bit, would you?"

"Rick, Jordan wants you to pan right a little." My cameraman makes a last second, micromillimeter adjustment to the camera until my producer is happy.

"Stand by for the live tease," Jordan warns.

Over-the-air audio begins filtering through my earpiece as Jordan goes silent, replaced by the voice of lead anchor, Marcela Anthony.

"And coming up on KWQB at ten—snow hits the Western United States causing this thirty-car pileup. The incredible story of how one woman survived."

"And that same storm is headed our way. I'm meteorologist Greg Dalton, and I'll tell you when you need to break out the boots."

"You're live," Jordan tells me.

"And later," I jump in right on cue, but falter for a split second as the over-the-air monitor in front of me changes to my shot, and all 250 pounds of me appears on television clad in a white beach towel. "A new health trend is sweeping the US. Can a recent deep-sea discovery really help you lose weight? I'm Angela Ioane, and tonight I'll be undergoing the procedure live to see if the dramatic claims made about Octosuction hold water."

I hold the most serious facial expression I can manage tight on my face until I get the all clear.

"We're in commercial," Jordan assures me. "You're eight minutes out."

I'm one B-block of national news stories and weather away from taking off this towel and climbing into a tank full of sea creatures no one really understands. I wonder if I look as crazy as I feel.

Rick is already frantically moving equipment out of the lobby into the interior of the building in preparation for my dramatic entrance into the room that houses the Antipods.

Looking up, I catch the eye of Dr. Stewart. He's standing behind Rick, grinning ear to ear.

"Angela, I can't wait for you to share this procedure with your viewers. It's absolutely going to change your life, and theirs," he says, walking toward me.

I blink furiously, trying to clear the spots from my eyes left by the lights. "And you're sure this is safe?"

Grasping my shoulder firmly in what I assume is meant to be a reassuring gesture, he reiterates what he told me over the telephone a few days ago. "Clinical trials have showed Octosuction has virtually no ill effects on patient health. Of course, we'll have to wait for studies on the long-term impact of the procedure, but as far as I'm concerned, this is as close to a miracle cure for obesity as science is ever going to get."

"I guess I'll just have to see for myself," I say with a smile, trying to keep the nervousness out of my voice.

"Angela, let's run through your standup once more," Rick calls from down the hall.

"Shall we?" Dr. Stewart motions for me to lead the way.

Reluctantly, I follow Rick's voice down the hallway until Dr. Stewart and I reach the procedure room. I practice the moves the three of us planned earlier one more time. The minutes pass quickly, and before I know it, Jordan is in my ear with a thirty-second warning.

I take a long, deep breath.

"Fifteen seconds."

Marcela's voice once again fills my ear as I hear the over-the-air audio. "Tonight on Health Check. It's being called a miracle cure for obesity. The company behind Octosuction says the procedure is safe and effective, but some who've undergone the treatment say they're now suffering serious complications."

"You're in double box," Jordan tells me as my oval face appears on the screen next to Marcela's slender one.

"Tonight, KWQB's own Angela Ioane is live at Octosuction company headquarters to try the procedure for herself."

"Stand by," Jordan whispers as I nod on screen.

"Angela," Marcela's voice says in my earpiece, "you volunteered for this assignment. The results are staggering, but the long-term risks are still unknown. Why are you willing to take this chance with your health?"

"And cue." Jordan points to me. The screen cuts to a tight shot of my face, and the camera starts to pull out as I begin reading my script.

"Marcela, the long-term health effects of obesity are well understood. I've struggled with my weight since childhood, which means I'm at a higher risk for heart disease, diabetes, high blood pressure, liver disease, and stroke, to name a few. And I'm far from alone. Today two out of three adults are overweight, and one in three are obese. And like many of my fellow Americans, I've tried diet and exercise to lose weight, without success."

I can see in the monitor that the camera has fully widened to reveal me head to toe, a white beach towel covering my white two-piece.

"More extreme weight loss measures, such as gastric bypass surgery, carry their own health risks and expenses and have never been the right option for me. However, I'm desperate to shed the weight. So tonight, I am taking off the towel in search of a lasting way to lose the weight and improve my overall health, which is what researchers say Octosuction can do for me."

With that sentence, a prerecorded story about the tiny sea creature involved in the procedure—Octopus Antipodi—begins to play. I listen breathlessly through the earpiece to my own voice reading the lines I wrote earlier today.

"Octopus Antipodi were discovered nearly five years ago in the bodies of dead sperm whales that began washing up on the shores of Australia and New Zealand.

"Researchers investigating the cause of the animals' deaths performed necropsies, or animal autopsies, of the whales, which revealed the half-inch-long mollusks, more commonly known as Antipodi.

"The researchers found up to one hundred healed wounds per whale, which they theorized were caused when the Octopus

Antipodi used their beak-shaped mouths and tentacles to bore holes deep within the whale's blubber.

"There they developed a commensalism relationship where the Antipodi fed on and bred within the whale's fat—"

"Hey, you okay?" Jordan's question intrudes on my thoughts. Momentarily jarred back to reality, I motion for Dr. Stewart to join me in front of the camera. "Yeah, I'm fine. We're good to go."

"All right, thirty seconds out."

I listen to my own voice finish telling viewers about the discovery of the Antipodi.

"This phosphorescent mollusk emits a blue glow, which researchers believe the creature may have developed in response to its deep-sea habitat."

"Stand by," Jordan warns me. "Cue is, 'still much to be learned.'"

"However, researchers still don't know exactly where in the Mariana Trench the animal originates from or why they have just recently begun appearing in the fatty tissue of whales. They reiterate there is still much to be learned."

With that line, the camera cuts back to me live.

"Dr. David Stewart is the world's leading expert on Octopus Antipodi, and it's his research that has led to what millions of Americans are calling a weight-loss breakthrough. Dr. Stewart joins me now to discuss what the Octosuction procedure entails."

"Angela, the Antipodi will enter your body through tiny holes they bore in your skin. Once inside, they will begin to eat excess body fat, beginning with your midsection and spreading slowly to the rest of your body over the course of a few days. Within a few weeks, they'll begin to reproduce, ensuring that you remain slender for the rest of your life."

"Before we proceed, Doctor, I want to show viewers what I look like at my current weight."

With a small flourish, I unfold the tuck in the towel I've made above my left breast and allow the terry cloth to fall to the floor. I stand in front of the camera, silent, for what feels like hours but is really only seconds, clad in nothing but a white bikini.

I smile at Dr. Stewart. "I'm ready to begin my transformation."

"This way." Dr. Stewart gestures gallantly toward the procedure room. He walks and talks, explaining the next steps as we draw closer to the doorway. "The Antipodi live deep in the Mariana Trench, meaning that very little light penetrates the water. As you've already told your viewers, that's why we believe they glow. However, to keep them alive in captivity, we have to replicate their natural habitat as closely as possible, which means keeping them in almost complete darkness at all times."

Rick is close behind us, his camera mounted firmly on his shoulder. He catches every miniscule twinge of terror in my expression as I turn to face the camera and prepare to head into the room.

"So, viewers at home, that means this procedure will take place in almost complete darkness. There will be a slight glow from the Antipodi, but I will mostly be describing what I'm feeling to Dr. Stewart, who will keep this microphone with him. You'll be able to hear what I'm saying the entire time I'm in the tank with the Antipodi."

"Are you ready to begin, Angela?"

"I've been waiting for this my entire life."

I remove my earpiece and hand it and the microphone to Dr. Stewart before crossing the threshold into the room. Rick follows with the camera.

It's pitch-black, and I walk slowly, careful not to lose my footing on the cold tile lining the floor.

"This is a wet room, so it doesn't matter if you splash water on the floor," Dr. Stewart says. "The tank is directly ahead of you. It's sunk into the floor like a swimming pool, so I want you to walk carefully and slowly until your eyes begin to adjust."

My pupils, already wide with anxiety and a healthy dose of fear, expand even further. It's not completely dark. There, within the floor, I can see the Antipodi glowing faintly. As I move closer, I can see them writhing in the tank. It's a small, almost imperceptible wriggling motion as they bob under the surface.

"This is the side of the tank. I want you to sit down slowly on the floor and, when you're ready, move forward until you can comfortably place your legs in the water."

I do as I'm told, knowing I should be saying something about the experience to the viewers at home, but I'm too anxious to utter a word. Finally, I feel the tips of my toes come in contact with the water. I keep moving forward, millimeter by millimeter, until the water reaches mid-calf. I try to avoid making direct contact with any of the floating Antipodi. I can hear some of the liquid being displaced as it overflows the tank.

"It's cold!" I exclaim.

"You may experience some slight discomfort due to the water temperature, but I assure you, it's necessary to keep the Antipodi alive. Just keep moving forward. Go at your own pace. I want you to stand fully upright within the tank."

Ignoring my own hatred of the cold, I keep moving forward, faster now, trying to ease the initial shock. I stop avoiding the increasingly active Antipodi and ignore the sound of water flowing onto the floor as I slide my thighs and finally my hips fully into the water. My feet make contact with the bottom of the tank.

"All right, Doctor, I'm standing upright. The tank is quite shallow. It must only be three feet deep," I say, trying to keep my teeth from chattering.

"Good, Angela. Now I want you to sit down and immerse yourself in the water up to your neck, but be careful not to allow your head to go underwater."

I'm glad the viewers at home can't see my face in the dark as I grimace and begin to sit. I feel the Antipodi bump into my body as I sink further into the tank. One of the floating organisms makes contact with my thigh, and I feel tiny tentacles tickle my leg, almost as if it's exploring my flesh, though it's becoming harder to tell as I'm beginning to lose sensation.

"The Antipodi are beginning to touch me, Doctor. I think I feel tentacles. It almost tickles."

"That's normal. Now, the Antipodi are going to be attracted to your body heat. They're going to gravitate toward you. Do not be alarmed."

Even as he says it, I can see more glowing blue organisms moving toward me. Unable to clamp my jaw shut any longer, my teeth begin to chatter loudly and I start to shiver violently. The movement of the water seems to excite the Antipodi, and I can see as well as feel tiny glowing tentacles probing my flesh. The tentacles are attached to short, cylindrical bodies.

Suddenly, I feel a sharp pinch on the left side of my abdomen.

"Doctor," I say, trying to keep my voice steady, "I believe the first one has bitten me."

"Good, good," Dr. Stewart says in soothing tone. "It's going to work its way into your body now. Don't be frightened. The procedure is going quite well."

Despite the cold, I feel several sharper pinches where the Antipodi have attached to my side. It takes everything I have not to cry out. Desperately, I scan the room for Rick, looking for any kind of reassurance, but in the darkness, I can only make out his outline a few feet from the tank.

More sharp pinches follow on my thighs, my breasts, and the right side of my buttock as additional Antipodi begin attaching themselves to me.

"There's multiple Antipodi on me now. I'm in some pain, Doctor, is this normal?"

I don't hear his answer. The first Antipodi that attached to my torso must have eaten its way through the skin because suddenly there's a writhing feeling about a quarter-inch *inside* of me. I can feel it moving, digging into my side. It's cold and disgusting, unlike anything I've ever felt before.

"Doctor, it's inside me!" I cry out, the panic in my voice obvious.

"Just stay still. You're doing well," he tells me.

Everything doesn't feel well. There's more Antipodi entering me now. They're freezing cold, like living, squirming icicles. I can no longer feel my skin, but internally I can feel them inching inside. The deepest one feels as if it has reached the center of my abdomen. I imagine their tentacles grabbing onto my muscle fibers and pulling themselves further into my body.

I scream, completely forgetting the audience observing the procedure live on television.

I begin to thrash within the tank, violently splashing water onto the floor in a desperate effort to escape. Suddenly, I catch sight of a glowing Antipodi in my thigh, half of its body sticking out of my leg. I grab it and pull, screaming as its beaklike teeth tear at the middle of my quadriceps.

"Angela, stop! Calm down!" Doctor Stewart yells frantically. "It's normal! This is normal!"

I'm panting, screaming, and thrashing uncontrollably when suddenly I feel hands on my shoulders. They're Rick's, strong and familiar, and they're pushing me back down into the water.

"Hold still, Angela," Doctor Stewart's voice says from somewhere near my ear.

I feel a sharp pinch in my neck. The faint blue glow of the room begins to fade as I sink into the true blackness of unconsciousness.

〰〰〰

Even through closed eyelids, I can sense the light. I don't want to wake up, but in the back of my mind, something silently whispers that it's morning. Late morning. I jerk my eyelids open in a panic. I'm late for work.

But this isn't my bedroom. I'm momentarily confused by the strange artwork on the walls and the odd sounds in the distance. I pause to listen as the sound of feet approaching the room grows louder. I see a man in blue scrubs pass the doorway, continuing down the hall. Nothing makes sense.

Frantically I search for the last thing I can remember. Octosuction. The Antipodi. Oh, God, the Antipodi!

I bolt upright, surprised at my speed. It's oddly easy to move. Glancing down, I expect to see the tops of my breasts but instead find myself looking squarely at the center of my stomach.

Slowly I pull back the bedding to reveal a hospital gown. It's several sizes too large. In fact, I'm nearly swimming in it.

I pull the bottom of the gown up until I can see my left thigh. There's a large white bandage over the spot where I remember the Antipodi entering my body, but the gauze isn't the shocking part. My leg itself makes me gasp. It's half its normal size.

Slowly I take my hands and wrap them around the muscle, forming a circle. For the first time in my life, my fingertips can almost touch.

Frantically I begin patting my hands all over my body. My breasts, my stomach, my arms—everything is smaller, thinner. I encounter extra flaps of skin under my arms and across my rib cage, but I ignore them for the time being.

"It worked! I'm thin!" I scream to the empty room, tears of joy streaming down my face.

My shout draws attention to the fact I'm awake, and a second later, the male nurse I spotted earlier enters the room followed closely by my boss.

"How are you feeling?" the nurse asks me.

"I'm thin!" I scream without thinking.

"The doctor is making his rounds. He'll be in shortly to update you on your condition. Do you need anything for the time being?" he asks me, a slight smile on his face.

Desperate to see my face, I gasp, "A mirror. Is there a mirror in here?"

"Let's hold off on that," my boss chimes in. "I'd like to save the big reveal for the viewers, if you don't mind."

I turn my attention to him for the first time and feel dread replace my excitement.

"Oh, God, how much of it did you air?" I ask him.

"We cut away right before you started screaming." He makes air quotes as he says, "We had 'technical difficulties.' We missed the worst of it. You're a celebrity though. The story went national. Over the last twelve hours, the newsroom has been flooded with calls from all over the country asking about your condition. We'd like to get you back on air with an update as soon as possible."

"Of course, of course," I say. "Just as soon as I get something to eat. I'm starting to feel light-headed from all the excitement."

My boss leaves to grab a cup of coffee, and I order a hearty breakfast of waffles and eggs as I wait for the doctor. I can feel a slight shifting in my stomach, but I write it off as hunger pangs. It only takes a few minutes for food to arrive, but by the time the orderly brings in the steaming tray I'm famished.

The doctor catches me in the middle of devouring my food.

"You're healing. The hunger is normal." The doctor reviews my chart. "I can start the release paperwork."

"I want you live at five," my boss says, holding his coffee in one hand and a breakfast burrito in the other. The smell is intoxicating. Despite finishing my own food just seconds ago, my stomach rumbles.

"But what do I wear? I don't think I have anything that fits anymore," I say, glancing down at my slender frame.

"The station has taken care of it. Don't worry, considering the unique circumstances, we'll wait until you have some overtime on a check to worry about reimbursement."

It's hard to focus on what he's saying. I greedily watch him brush the crumbs from his shirt as he finishes his burrito and stands to leave. "Head over to the station once you're done here."

"Yes, sir," I say with a mock salute. "I may be half the reporter I once was, but I still expect my full salary."

He laughs as he walks to the door. "Oh, I wouldn't worry about that."

Processing the paperwork feels like it takes forever, and my stomach is churning with anxiety. Slight muscle spasms shoot through my biceps and legs, but since it only happens once in a while, I ignore it.

Once everything is signed, Rick meets me at the hospital entrance. He doesn't even comment on my messy hair or hospital-issue sweats as he scoops me up in a huge hug.

"Look at you! There's hardly any of you left! You look amazing. But you nearly scared me to death last night. I thought we were going to lose you there for a second."

I laugh. "Hey, I'm not that easy to get rid of. Look, I don't want to be a pain, but do you mind if we stop for a snack along the way? The doctor said it was normal to be hungry as I healed, but, man, I'm starving!"

"No problem. What do you want?"

"Danishes. I want cherry Danishes."

"You got it."

We pull up to a pastry shop down the road, and I grab several to eat in the car. My leg twitches with pleasure as I chow down. I don't think anything has ever tasted so good. Three servings per pastry be damned. For the first time in my life, I'm unconcerned about calories. Nothing is going to stick to these thighs ever again.

A sea of emotions greets us as we walk into the newsroom. It isn't necessarily unexpected, but the mixture of concerned glances and horror on the faces of my coworkers catches me somewhat by surprise. Even Rick's face is starting to tighten with fear.

"Hey, you're starting to look a little pale. You sure you're feeling okay?" he asks me quietly.

"Yeah, yeah. I'm fine." In truth, I'm feeling a little peaked, and the muscle spasms are getting stronger. It almost feels as if the Antipodi are still moving inside of me, but that can't be. "Let me just get something from the vending machine. The procedure must have taken more out of me than I thought."

I grab a bag of pretzels and munch away as I start writing up my live shot. A package of Pop Tarts and a couple of candy bars keep me going through the afternoon. By the glances my coworkers toss my direction, I can tell I look better, but the vending machine is worse for wear.

The station has brought in a hair and makeup artist for my big reveal. I get all dolled up before they present me with a stunning blue blouse and black skirt they've purchased for me to wear. The skirt is a little loose, and out of curiosity, I peek at the size. It's an eight, just large enough to cover the extra skin on my abdomen while still giving me a slender profile. I smile, elated. I've never worn anything in the single digits, and once I get the extra skin removed, I'll actually be much smaller.

When five o'clock rolls around, I'm more than ready to show off for the viewers. The studio has placed a full-size mirror for me and covered it with the same white towel I wore last night. What a difference twenty-four hours can make.

I hear the open roll through my earpiece as the show starts.

"Good evening. I'm Marcela Anthony. Our top story tonight, one of KWQB's own undergoes the popular weight-loss procedure, Octosuction. It's being called a miracle by those struggling to shed pounds, but others say it's dangerous. We wanted to show it to you live and let you, the viewer, decide. Due to technical difficulties, we were unable to air the procedure in its entirety last night, leaving people around the country concerned about reporter Angela

Ioane's condition. Tonight, she joins us to reveal her amazing transformation. Angela?"

The camera cuts to me in a different part of the studio, standing in front of the covered mirror.

"Thank you, Marcela. And I want to thank each and every one of you who has called and emailed the station for your concern. I'm recovering, but I wanted to take this opportunity to share the results of Octosuction with you."

I slowly spin for the camera, showing off my slender new physique.

"As you can see, I have lost over one hundred pounds in just under twenty-four hours. And while I know I'm thinner, I have yet to see myself in a mirror. So, without further ado ..." I pull aside the towel and stare myself in the eyes for the first time.

I'm horrified by what I see. It's obvious that even with heavy makeup, I'm extremely pale. Dark circles ring my eyes.

Glancing down, I stare at my body. Under the form-fitting blouse, there is a lump on my abdomen. Without warning, it starts to move, simulating the muscle contractions I've been having all day.

They aren't muscle contractions. It's the Antipodi moving inside me.

My scream is bloodcurdling.

The station cuts to commercial.

~~~~

SIX MONTHS LATER

"Due to this procedure, I now face a life-threatening health condition," I tell the half-circle of men and women seated on the dais in front of me.

"Antipodism is a condition in which the Antipodi used in the Octosuction procedure reproduce faster and more frequently in individuals with certain body chemistry than they do in others. I am one such patient, and as a result, I am forced to eat upwards of eight thousand calories a day or risk death by starvation. To consume that many calories, I need to eat every few minutes. Hundreds of other women like me who were desperate to lose weight are now similarly incapacitated. Like so many of them I have lost my career, and I find myself unable to do anything but eat."

Tears spring to my eyes as I describe my new relationship with food to the assembled group. It's just like my old relationship: dysfunctional.

"Doctor Stewart's faulty research and the negligence of Octosuction executives have made me thin, as promised, but they have also caused this irreversible and devastating condition. That is why I came here to testify today. I urge you all to vote to move P.L.10002-5589 forward and ban Octosuction in the United States. Thank you."

Following my testimony in front of Congress, I walk down the steps of the Capitol, surrounded by reporters. A chorus of voices calls out to me.

"Miss Ioane, how are you feeling?"

"Angela, do you believe the bill will pass?"

"Angela, is there anything you'd like to say?"

I pause, digging through my purse for something to eat. My standard array of sandwiches greets me. Pulling one out and unwrapping it, I take a giant bite. Crumbs tumble down the front of my blouse as I look up to find the faces of my former colleagues staring at me, expectantly, cameras pointed directly at my face.

"Yeah. Eat me."

≈≈≈

Lauren Lang is a freelance photographer and videographer living and working in Denver, CO. She has loved telling stories since a young age, dictating her first piece of fiction to her mother before she was old enough to write. She has worked as a broadcast journalist in her quest to tell compelling, true narratives. She has crossed three states in seven years working as a video editor, producer, and writer at several local television stations. "Eat Me" is loosely based on her professional experience in the industry. Learn more about Lauren and her photography at http://jacobinphotography.zenfolio.com/about.html.

BOOKEND

CHRIS MANDEVILLE

R uth Levinstein picked at one of the chips on the Formica table, prolonging her morning coffee. She glanced sideways at the rain boots and coat by her door. They were taunting her.

Begrudgingly she pushed back from the table, the dread building in her chest. As she washed her cereal bowl, she could almost hear him.

"Ruth, you must go. The time, the time!"

She stared past the mismatched salt and pepper shakers on the windowsill to the neighborhood outside. The pink house with its year-round plastic Halloween pumpkins, the immaculate lemon-yellow Victorian, the drab monolith whose backside held the most vibrant mural in the Mission. Like most days, the street was coated in wet. Ruth wished the rain could make San Francisco feel clean.

"Ruuuth."

He wanted her to go out there. She clutched her sweater against her chest to slow the pounding of her heart as she imagined drug deals in the alleys, gangers in every car, sirens announcing yet another crime.

No, it was too dangerous outside. Why couldn't she stay where it was safe? Just one day, safe and cozy. She could read a book or watch the TV. Just one day.

"You have to go."

She poured out the cold remains of her coffee and squeezed Palmolive into the mug. She'd tried before to ignore him, tried until his wails built and her eardrums ached worse than the dread in her chest. But maybe today he'd give her some peace. It was just one day.

A car went by, smooth and slow, like a great white shark tracking its prey. Her knees quaked, and she tried to focus on the business of washing, but the rain boots grew in her peripheral vision and she couldn't keep her hand from shaking. The mug clanked against the bowl as she placed it in the drainer.

"It's out there, Ruth. It's all alone. You must go find it."

Sometimes he reminded her of her dear, nagging Avner. But Avner had always told her *not* to go. *Stop collecting junk, Ruth,* he'd always said. Funny to think she was finally willing to oblige ten years after he'd passed.

"Ruuuth!"

"Can't you just leave me be?" she called, storming into the living room to face him. "I don't want to go. Not today."

He glowered at her from the bookshelf, yellow eyes sunken deep in his scaly head, his fang-filled mouth as frothy as the frozen ocean waves he rested on. She could see beyond his rage to the desperation and loss, the fear in his eyes.

"I'm sorry," she told him. "I'll go tomorrow." She reached out, but stopped just shy of touching his fin.

She turned and went to the television, feeling hope flutter in her breast. Perhaps today would be different.

She pushed the button on the set. As soon as the picture came into focus, she changed the station. She couldn't stomach the news with the gangs and the robberies and the hit-and-runs, or the cop-show fictions of the very same stories.

She stopped on a program that would soothe her—a woman cooking—and backed up until she felt the couch behind her. She didn't dare look at him on the bookshelf while she sank into the cushions, though she could feel his gaze on her.

"Stir it by hand," the woman on TV said. "Don't try to get the lumps out. The lumps are what make the cake tender."

Ruth was about to put her feet up on the hassock when she heard him. It built in volume like the hum of a vacuum getting closer.

"Ruth. Ruuuth. Ruuuth."

Cursing the broken remote, she heaved herself from the sofa and turned up the volume by hand. She stood a foot from the blaring set, but it didn't help. She could still hear him crying out for his other half, lost long before she'd met him.

She looked at the front door, and her heart bucked against her ribs. She knew what was out there. She turned back to the television, willing herself to focus on the woman filling the Bundt pan.

"Ruuuth!"

≈≈≈

Ruth slogged through the drizzle, her two-wheeled cart clattering along the sidewalk behind her. At her next stop, there would be hot tea. She flinched as a truck splashed through a puddle beside her, but she tried not to let her fear get to her. If she let it, it would seep into her bones like the wet chill. Instead, she focused on putting one foot in front of the other, humming that tired tune while she imagined the smell of Earl Grey wafting up from a steaming mug.

The bells on the wooden door jangled, announcing her arrival to old Mr. Wilson behind the counter. He looked up and nodded. She nodded back, stamping her feet on the rubber doormat. He went back to his crossword while she parked her cart, then peeled off her jacket and hung it on a rickety coat-tree that was likely as old as the shop itself.

"Water's hot," Wilson said around the pencil in his mouth. "Help yourself."

Ruth headed to the "bookstore" section and filled two mugs with water from an electric kettle. She unwrapped a bag of chamomile and dropped it in one, Earl Grey in the other. After squeezing honey in both, she took them to the front counter, bags still steeping.

"What's an eight-letter word for a bulbous oven?"

Ruth shrugged and handed him his mug.

Wilson tapped his pencil on the counter three times, then laid it on the newspaper.

Ruth dunked her tea bag by the string. He didn't have what she was here for. If he did, he would have said so by now.

"Mr. Pemberton is ill again."

Ruth raised her eyebrows. "Is it serious?"

Wilson shrugged. "He and Mrs. Crawley got into the trash again. It's probably just indigestion. Or a hair ball."

Ruth blew across the top of her mug, then took a tentative sip.

"You hungry?" Wilson asked. "I have some crackers here someplace." He opened a drawer.

"No, thank you." Talk of trash and hair balls wasn't the most appetizing.

She blew on her tea again and drank.

"You know, you really should get yourself a cat. Or why not two! They're such good company. I hate to think of you going back to your quiet house all alone."

Ruth choked on her tea. If he only knew.

"Supposed to rain all week," he said, his gaze slipping to the picture window that framed the wet street and cars and shops and shoppers outside.

Ruth shivered, but not from the cold. She looked down at her mug, half empty now. It was almost time to go back out there.

"Ol' Monty got a big estate in."

Her ears perked up.

"A big estate," Wilson repeated. "Been going through stuff all week. You never know—maybe he'll have what you're looking for."

"You never know." Ruth didn't want to get her hopes up. Three times now Monty had told her he'd found it. "Guess I'd better go see." She stood.

"Oh, I almost forgot." Wilson reached for something under the counter. "I wondered if you had the match to this." He held out a little Dutch girl salt shaker, complete with red frock, curved bonnet, and clogs.

Ruth sighed. "I'm afraid I don't." Her heart clenched at the sadness of it all, the little Dutch girl without her pepper shaker mate.

"That's too bad." Wilson shook his head. "She's destined for the wastebasket … unless you take her."

Ruth gritted her teeth, thinking how full her windowsill was, not to mention the pantry shelves. But she couldn't bear to see the little thing thrown out and forgotten about, forever alone. She plucked it from Wilson's palm and dropped it in her pocket.

Wilson gave her a half-smile before he picked up his pencil and hunched over the newspaper. "A bulbous oven," he mused, then said, "chiminea" and filled in the small squares.

Ruth shrugged into her jacket. "Thank you for the tea, Mr. Wilson."

Wilson looked up. "You *will* come see me next week, won't you, Mrs. Levinstein? Even if you find it?"

"Of course, Mr. Wilson. See you next week."

The bells clanged as she pulled her cart out onto the sidewalk, leaving the warmth and safety of Mr. Wilson and his shop. Her next stop wasn't nearly as inviting, but she had her routine. She kept to her routine. That's what gave her the courage to cross each street, to keep going.

Five blocks later, she arrived at Johanssen's Junk with its hodgepodge window displays framed by peeling turquoise paint. She pulled open the door and was about to drag her cart over the threshold when a shrill cry rang out.

"We don't have it, Mrs. Levinstein. Come back next week."

Harriet Johanssen had no use for pleasantries, but that was nothing new.

"Thank you just the same," Ruth called, stepping back onto the sidewalk. In truth, she was glad to not spend any time there. The dank smell of the resident clutter cloaked in Harriet's gardenia perfume was enough to gag a garbage man. Besides, despite herself, she was excited about the prospect of Monty's latest haul. Sure, it was a long shot, but it always had been. Maybe today would be the day.

~~~

Monty's warehouse was just the other side of the busiest street on her Thursday route. She took a deep breath, pulled back her shoulders, and stepped into the breach. Despite a blaring horn that nearly made her leap out of her galoshes, she crossed safely to the other side. She smiled at the victory, despite her racing heart.

As she stood outside Monty's place, a forlorn saltbox adorned with equal parts mural and graffiti, she thought how rich Monty would be if he finally sold it to one of those developers who wanted to turn it into lofts. But then what would he do? Where would he go? Who would he be?

She stomped the rain from her boots, wincing as they pinched her now-swollen feet. She heaved open the door and went inside, too tired to pull her cart in with her. "Monty? It's me—Ruth Levinstein."

From the depths of the dim building, she heard footfalls. They approached more rapidly than usual, if she wasn't mistaken.

"Mrs. Levinstein, I found it!" Monty came into view, carrying a cardboard box. "I really found it this time."

Her heart skipped a beat. They'd lived this scene several times before, always with the same disappointing end. Still, this time could be different.

"Take a look." Monty placed the box on a folding table piled with mail. "I could hardly believe it when I came across it." He beamed as he opened the cardboard flaps. "This has got to be the one."

Ruth held her breath. She didn't move. She didn't want the moment to end. That perfect moment of possibility when the box could actually contain what she'd been seeking all these years. Once she looked, she would know what was in the box one way or the other, and the moment would be gone.

But Monty had no sense of the moment. He reached into the box and lifted out the object.

~~~

Ruth arrived home more exhausted than usual. She sat on the bench inside the front door and struggled to shuck the boots from her sausage-like feet. The effort had her breathing hard.

Reaching up to hang her coat on the hook, pain shot through her shoulder, and she staggered, hugging her arm to her chest. What had she done? Pulled a muscle? The cart wasn't that heavy.

The cart.

How could she have forgotten it on the porch? She was so tired she wasn't thinking clearly.

"Ruuuth, did you find it?"

"Hold your horses, you old codger."

She opened the front door again and grasped the cart by the handle. It took all her strength to pull it inside. Gasping for breath, she closed the door and leaned against it. Her shoulder felt like it was being squeezed in a vise.

"Ruuuth!"

She straightened and wiped her brow, then lifted the cardboard box from the cart. She set it on the bench, pausing to massage her shoulder.

"A box? A box!"

With her back to him, she opened the flaps and removed the object. She couldn't help but smile as she turned to show him.

"You found it!"

She held it up. The emerald-green scales matched exactly. The frothy frozen waves were the same. Even the aged brown bases were identical. She eyed the failures on the bottom shelf of the bookcase—eight bookends, the tails of other creatures whose heads she could only imagine. For a second, she thought she could hear them calling to her, but of course that was silly. They had no mouths. And thank goodness for that because she was too tired to go hunting for anything else.

"Ruuuth!"

She walked toward him, hands outstretched despite the pain in her shoulder. He would finally be reunited with his other half, and she would have some peace.

〜〜〜

Shouting and pounding interrupted a perfectly quiet morning. Finally, it stopped.

Then a loud *thwak*, a splintering of wood, and the door opened.

"Police department. Anyone here?"

"Mrs. Levinstein? We're coming in."

Two strangers invaded the sanctuary, breaking the reverie.

The male looked down at Ruth on the floor. "Looks like that shop owner was right to be worried."

"Clearing the house." The female passed through the room, her weapon extended.

"Poor lady," the male said, kneeling and touching Ruth's wrist. His brown eyes were liquid, and his lined face held genuine emotion. "Didn't you have anyone?" he whispered.

"All clear." The female came back. "Cruz, you call it in?"

"Nah, you go ahead."

"Natural causes?"

He shrugged. "Above my pay grade. Call investigations."

"Roger that." The female rubbed her nose. "I'm going outside."

Cruz nodded. "I'll stay with her."

~~~~

The house was cold. So many people coming in and out, the door hanging open. Finally, most had left. But one, Cruz, had stayed as he said he would.

Gloved hands lifted Ruth and placed her inside a black bag. The bag was zipped shut, put on a gurney, and wheeled to the door.

"Come back!"

Cruz turned. "Did you hear that?"

"Hear what?"

"I thought I heard something."

"The old lady have a cat, maybe?"

"No sign of one," Cruz said. "But I'll make one more sweep. You go on."

Cruz crossed the room and disappeared into the back of the house.

The gurney with Ruth in the bag bumped over the threshold. Then it was gone.

"No!"

Cruz dashed into the room, his weapon panning from corner to corner.

He stood for a long moment, his head cocked. Then he closed his eyes and let out a breath. "Get a grip," he muttered.

"It's so close."

Cruz turned. His eyes lit on it. He put away his weapon and walked over to the bookshelf.

He picked it up off the floor and turned it over in his hands.

"Yes! Yes, that's it."

Then Cruz bent down and placed it on the bottom shelf.

He exited the house, pulling the broken door closed behind him.

"No! Come back. Cruuuz!"

~~~~

Chris Mandeville writes science fiction and fantasy, as well as nonfiction for writers. Her books include *SeedsA: A Post-apocalyptic Adventure* and *52 Ways to Get Unstuck: Exercises to Break Through Writer's Block*. She contributes regularly to the Kobo Writing Life blog with her column Tools for Writers, and she loves to teach writing workshops. She lives in the Rocky Mountains of Colorado with her family and service dog, Finn. Learn more at chrismandeville.com.

TEENS TEACH TECH

TERRY MADDEN

I knock on the door of my assigned room in the Sunset Gardens retirement home. When I get no answer, I open the door and walk in. I take one look at Ms. Ness and walk right back out.

"Excuse me," I call to the lady who showed me in. Her name tag says *Claire*. She's fussing with some paperwork at the nurse's station. When she looks up at me over the top of her glasses, I say, "There's a mistake in my assignment. I'm supposed to help with technology, but I don't think Ms. Ness could even use an iPhone." I motion to the room I just left.

Claire is wearing scrubs covered in pink hippos. She tips her head back so she's looking at me through the glass part of her glasses, and says, "Marcus, was it?"

"Yes, ma'am. I signed up for the Teens Teach Tech program, and this is my first time. I thought I'd get something easy."

She laughs. "Ms. Ness is easy. She doesn't talk much, but she's a sweetheart. Says here you're good with that virtual reality stuff. A *gamer* or some such? They're testing some new kind of headset on her, for dementia patients. Remembering their past is the first step to remembering the now." She leads me past a team of old people in wheelchairs, back to room 552. "But the doctor says it will be more helpful if someone is in there with her, asking her questions. Wherever *there* is."

"Ms. Ness? In VR?"

"Sure. You'd be surprised what a change it can make. It brings all the memories back in full color."

She knocks on the door and *yoo-hoos* loudly as she leads the way in. The room has a fluorescent light that hums louder than the TV. The old woman by the window isn't watching it anyway; she's staring out the window at the beach in the distance.

"You have a visitor, Ms. Ness," Claire says loudly and fusses with the blanket that's fallen off Ms. Ness's lap.

My eyes are drawn to the single sketch hanging on the white wall in a simple frame. The paper is yellowed, and one corner is torn. It looks like it had been crumpled and laid flat again in the glass frame. A sea creature of some kind floats in green water. It's human-ish, sort of. The colored pencil strokes are delicate enough that I can tell the skin isn't covered in fish scales, but more like feathers, like this thing might swim and fly at the same time. In one eye shines the sun, and in the other, the moon. Fins grow from the spine and hands, flowing, feathery, rippling like a Spanish dancer's skirt, like a fancy goldfish. And the hair …

Claire's hand on my shoulder brings me back to the room. She firmly guides me toward the open seat beside Ms. Ness. I can't help wondering why the old woman just has that one drawing on her wall. The other walls are stained and spattered with holes from previous hangings, but bare, all around. Maybe her grandchild drew the picture, or maybe it was left by the person who lived in the room before.

The old woman by the window turns dark, watery eyes on me. They are vacant, just like *mi abuelo*, my grandfather. Lights barely on in there anymore. He just sits in front of the TV, too, staring. It freaks me out.

Ms. Ness is so tiny she looks like the recliner has started to eat her.

I want to run. The disinfectant can't cover up the smell of someone just waiting to die. If I didn't need the extra credit in calculus, I'd be long gone.

"Hi," I say. "I'm Marcus."

Her eyebrows lift and her lips tremble. There are words hanging behind them, and I know they will dribble away even before she opens her mouth. Lost and pointless.

Claire slips an electrode-studded shower cap on Ms. Ness. Next come the VR goggles. Ms. Ness's gnarled fingers shake, and she looks scared, like she wants to push the goggles away. I don't want to scare her.

"Maybe she doesn't want to," I say.

"She doesn't know what she wants. She'll be happy once she's in there, don't you worry."

Claire indicates a matching cap and headset for me. I find some haptic gloves with it, too. This is some sweet VR gear her doctor ordered; makes my setup look cheap.

I slip the equipment on and boot my system, create my avatar name: Marcus. Clever. The world comes into first-person view.

I'm standing in the middle of a village square. Old times. There's only one car in sight and it's the old kind, like the ones they drive in black-and-white movies. But this place is far from black and white. Shops crowd against whitewashed stone buildings that fly brightly colored flags, and the window boxes are full of blooming flowers. England, maybe?

The program this thing is running must take Ms. Ness's memories and render them in virtual. Sweet. I'm trying to figure out how I can save up for one of these myself when a bell rings and the doors of what looks like a school open, spilling uniformed teenagers onto the cobbled street. They wear navy blue jackets with crests on their left shoulder that say, "Saints by the Sea Academy."

Without even looking at the name tag hovering over her head, I know it's her—or her avatar at least—Lily Ness. The girl staring back at me is no older than I am, light brown hair in wavy curls and lipstick that's faded to bare pink. There's fear in her dark eyes. The same fear I saw in the eyes of the old woman sitting by the window. She clutches her books to her chest, takes one look at me, and walks the other way.

"Ms. Ness!" I call, but she doesn't turn.

I follow. "I know you don't want to be here. I saw you trying to stop Claire from putting the headset on you, but the doctor says it helps."

"Helps? He's a fool. Why would anyone want to remember these days, this time?"

She talks just fine here, remembers just fine. This is some kind of miracle. A program that can read a person's memories and make them real. The possibilities are endless. I have to force myself back to what's going on here.

"Well, it looks like high school," I say. "Why not remember?"

She stops walking and glares at me. "You don't understand, young man."

"I'm Marcus." I stick out my hand.

She ignores it and walks on.

"Where are we going?" I ask.

"I'm going to the library until that … that woman agrees to remove this thing from my head. And if you really want to help me, Marcus, then you'll convince the doctor that this charade does absolutely nothing for me."

I have a hard time understanding her through the thick Scottish accent. But I get the idea. She's here against her will. That seems crazy. Why would she want to sit in that dark room and stare at game shows when she could be here instead?

"You're talking to me," I say. "You even remembered my name. I think it's working for you. Hey, where is this place anyway?" Questions. I was here to ask questions.

"Ardminish. Now run along." She struggles with the door of an ancient building, and it takes all my strength to hold it open for her.

Okay. I get it. It's like a quest. Like a dungeon. And Ms. Ness is the boss. The only problem is, I can't figure out exactly what it is I'm supposed to get her to remember. This place … she is rendering it somehow from her memories. The town where she grew up, probably. Ardminish. No more than two streets with stone houses and a few shops. The library looks like a converted medieval church. The floor is stone and has ruts in it where people have walked for centuries.

Ms. Ness takes a desk and opens her math book.

"You need help with that?" I ask.

She glares at me.

"I'm pretty good at calculus," I say. "It's why I'm here actually. Well, not *here*, but doing the Teens Teach Tech thing. Extra credit if I spend two weekends helping you. I'm this close to an A." I indicate the space with my fingers.

Ms. Ness looks back at her book. "Bully for you."

"Lily," a girl whispers from the rows of books.

Ms. Ness glances over her shoulder then turns back to her book.

"The choosing's tonight. We're building a bonfire," the girl says. "You must come, you know." With that, the girl winks at Ms. Ness. Secrets.

"Choosing?" I ask. "What are you choosing?"

Ms. Ness slams her math book so loudly it sounds like a gunshot.

"It could be fun," I say. "Let's go and ... choose."

"You go," Ms. Ness tells me. She stands and tucks the book under her arm.

I extend my hand to the girl who has stepped from the book stacks. "I'm Marcus."

She takes my hand, saying, "A pleasure, Marcus. I'm Muriel."

"You don't belong in my memories," Ms. Ness says to me. "You're changing them. I'm going to tell Dr. Fischer."

"Tell him after we go to the choosing," I say. "Come on, it will be fun, I think."

It takes Muriel's pestering to get Ms. Ness to agree to go. It's at a beach somewhere. The day doesn't seem like beach weather to me, but I'm a spoiled San Diego kid. I suppose people in cold climates still enjoy the water.

"Why is it so important for me to remember?" Ms. Ness asks as the three of us make our way down a sandy trail toward a headland. It looks like spring, all the grass and flowers, but the wind is icy cold.

"Remembering the past helps to remember the now," I say. "That's what Claire told me."

"My past is complete. Long gone. And the now ... that's so lifeless it's best if I forget."

"You have family?" I ask.

She looks off toward the headland, and I realize the landscape is unrendered here. It's all wireframe, some flat-shading of green and blue hexagons. Not even the sea is there. She's refusing to remember this place, and the program can't fill it in. Interesting.

"Muriel," Ms. Ness says, halting in the middle of the trail, her back to the disjointed horizon, "I can't. You go on."

Then she vanishes. Logs out.

"Sorry, Muriel," I say, and log out right behind her.

After peeling off my VR headset, I see Ms. Ness in her recliner struggling with her own equipment, her quaking hands battling with the straps. She's figured out how to exit the program herself. That's got to be a step in the right direction, or maybe not. I help her out of the thing and gently pull the cap from her head. An alarm must have sounded because Claire is there in an instant.

"That was a short trip," she says.

But Ms. Ness is making sounds, trying to speak as if there was something important she needed to get out. "Thy kingdom come," she says. Then her face folds up in confusion and she shakes her head. "Thy kingdom come ..."

I pull my chair closer.

"The brain gets stuck sometimes," Claire says, "and can't come up with the right words."

"I'm listening," I tell Ms. Ness.

She stops struggling to speak and takes my hand, becoming instantly serene. Her skin is like cool plastic, and she turns wide eyes to me. Her mouth gapes and works for words. The smooth, flushed cheeks sag into wrinkles and her yellowing eyes fill with tears.

At last she says, "You're a strong swimmer, Muriel. You should go."

≈≈≈

"I'm perfectly happy the way I am," Lily explains, brushing a lock of brown hair over her ear.

"I'm sure you are," I say. "But Dr. Fischer—"

"Blast Dr. Fischer!" Lily yells. "He doesn't know anything

except the workings of blood and bone. That's nothing. It means nothing." She stops in the middle of the trail to the headland, the wind blowing her skirt and her hair wildly so she looks like a girl on the cover of one of those Jane Austen novels my sister likes to read. It had taken us three Saturdays to get this far down the trail. Today the sun is so bright it hurts my eyes.

She stands straight as a soldier and indicates herself. "This body of ours," she says. "It's like the stem that shoots forth from the earth, but everything that engenders the flower comes from below, from the dark. We're like that. Marcus—it is Marcus, isn't it?—let me tell you something, Marcus, I'm not even supposed to be in that retirement home with the smelly dining hall."

She's caught me off guard. "Then where are you supposed to be?"

She plops down. Right there in the middle of the trail, she pulls her knees to her chest, and I notice her white socks have a ruffle around the edge and she's wearing those orthopedic-like black-and-white shoes. I sit down beside her, draw my knees to my chest to mimic her pose. I follow her gaze. Her forehead is furrowed with concentration.

She looks out to where the sea should be, and … there it is. What was nothing but wireframe and flat-shading has taken form, and the breeze suddenly smells of the fresh, salty sea. I don't think I've ever seen anything as surreal as this place or been in any VR so realistic. The water is a paintpot of blue and green. On the horizon, I can make out the barest hint of a rocky island. Fog hangs over it as if we're not supposed to see what's there. Maybe Lily doesn't want me to see.

I look down at the cove far below. About a dozen people are there, and a fire is roaring.

I stand, reach a hand to Lily, and to my surprise, she takes it. I say, "Let's go down."

We reach the cove, hand in hand. The kids stop talking and run toward us as if to welcome us.

"No," Lily says, backing away as they close in. "I can't choose. I can't leave."

Then she's gone.

Muriel gives me a questioning look.

"She's afraid of something," I tell her. "Something happened here that she doesn't want to remember."

Muriel nods. "The choosing." She fades away as Lily shuts down the program from her room in the retirement home. The image of Muriel's bright red hair burns in my retina after I open my eyes to find Ms. Ness weeping in her recliner.

"It's the choosing, isn't it?" I say.

"I should have gone. Muriel stayed with me because I didn't want to go. She stayed and she never complained, but I knew she always wanted the salt, not the soil. I should have gone."

"Gone where?"

"Thy kingdom come," she mutters. "Thy kingdom come."

~~~~

I'd completed my extra-credit assignment for math two Saturdays earlier. We're so close to facing the "choosing," it's all I can think of. I didn't know if the girls and guys were choosing partners or what, but whatever it was, it mattered to Lily. And she was afraid of it.

The week drags, but finally Saturday arrives. Claire waves and stops me in the hall of Sunset Gardens, saying, "Dr. Fischer is impressed with your progress. He even had a conversation with Ms. Ness yesterday. Wherever you two are going with those headsets, it must be something."

"Thanks. Ms. Ness is really something, that's for sure." But I'm unsure about the whole thing. I only know I have to see it through, for Lily. But she's resisting, and I don't know why. "Who's Muriel?" I ask Claire.

"Oh, the two were best friends." Her face folds into a frown. "Inseparable. Ms. Ness took a turn for the worse after Muriel passed. It's when she moved into Sunset Gardens, in fact—about three years ago."

I find Ms. Ness pushing some peas around on a plate with meat loaf and pale gravy. She smiles when she sees me and points to the drawing on the wall, the one of the sea creature with the sun and moon in its eyes.

"Sure you're finished with dinner?" I ask.

She calls me closer, then whispers in my ear, "I miss Muriel."

"Did she do this drawing? It's really cool."

She points at herself, her quaking fingers curled one around the other. "I can't draw anymore." She holds up her gnarled hands, and there are tears in her eyes.

I feel my own tears burn, but I can't let them out. I sniff them back, and say, "It's a beautiful drawing."

She gives me a thankful smile.

"Okay. Let's get geared up."

I help her get the cap and the gloves on, then I put on my own. We land, not in the village by the school like we normally do, but on the headland. The seabirds greet us, and Lily walks ahead of me, her arms in the air as the birds crowd around her. It looks like they might lift her from the bluff to soar with them. I wish she never had to take the headset off, never had to leave her childhood, and simply spend the rest of her days here in Ardminish.

She turns to me suddenly, reaches her hand out, and says, "I have something to show you, Marcus."

The trail narrows, and the grasses are mounded around us. My eye is drawn to the island, half-hidden by fog. There are buildings there, ruins, maybe.

"What is that place?" I ask her.

She follows my pointing finger then gives me an impish grin. "The Nixie's home."

"The Nixie? Who's that?"

She ignores my question because, on the beach before us, her friends have seen her. Muriel is the first to reach her this time. She swings Lily around until their uniform skirts billow like parachutes.

"You came!" Muriel cries.

There are about a dozen kids here, all about my age, and they have built the biggest bonfire I've ever seen. I can't tell the difference between the roar of the blaze and the hiss of the waves on the sand. When the kids see Lily, a cheer erupts, and two girls take her hand and mine and we're drawn into a dance. Muriel is at the front of the line, leading us in a twisting spiral around the blaze that's so hot I feel fevered.

She guides us in an endless, twisting snake while two guys play a drum and a whistle. The simple instruments make the most incredible music, like nothing I've ever heard. It takes me a bit to figure out the steps of the dance, but Lily exaggerates her own so I can follow. They're all singing a tune, but I can't understand the words. Some kind of Gaelic or something.

I finally get the chorus and join in, *"Salt nan Deur, sweet an t-uisge."*

Were Lily and Muriel going to choose one of these guys?

Between choruses, there's laughter. The next time I look up from my feet, Muriel is leading us into the surf. Two girls break the chain and run back to shore. Lily tries to do the same, but I won't let go of her hand. There's fear in her eyes again.

"I must stay," Lily says. "I haven't been in the water since the night of the Nixie moon, since we all came here to learn the ways of men."

"What do you mean? What's a Nixie moon?"

She just says, "The land feels good beneath my feet."

"But Muriel is a strong swimmer," I say. I have no idea what it means, but I know it has something to do with this choosing. It has something to do with Lily's fear, with the reason she sits by the window and watches the ocean from Sunset Gardens.

Lily breaks the chain when we get knee-deep in the small surf. The sun is setting behind the island, and the rays of light pierce the empty windows of the ruined castle there. I think I see someone high on the walls, a figure. With the distance, I can't make it out. But it's moving, pacing along the upper walls.

"She calls!" a boy cries. "What shall it be, children of the Nix? Salt or soil?"

What is he talking about? "Who calls?" I ask Lily.

"The Nix." She points to the island.

Most of the kids wade deeper into the water, Muriel leading them.

"Come, Lily," she says. "Come with me. I can't leave you. We'll live in the deep."

Lily takes Muriel in a long embrace. She says, "We know the land, we know the bloom of flower and the creations of man. How can we forget it all?"

"There are other wonders," Muriel says. "Those we've left behind in the palace of the sea. Come." Muriel leads Lily deeper into the water. "The earth is dry and smells of worms."

"But it grows flowers," Lily says.

"We're the Nixie's fry, you and I."

"And we've seen too much," Lily says. "She should never have sent us to shore."

Their fingers part, and Muriel lifts her arms into the last rays of sunlight. She sheds her uniform, and from her fingertips, feathery fins grow, sprouting from her spine and her hips. White foam from the waves—no, they are tiny beings that are formed *from* the foam—cover her skin like feathery fish scales, iridescent like a hummingbird's wings. And her hair ...

"You're afraid," I say to Lily. "That old woman sitting by the window in that room that smells. She's forgotten the world below the waves."

"I have the right to choose."

I nod in agreement as everything begins to make sense. "You chose the soil. Back then. But you left something here in the waves, or we wouldn't be here now. Muriel stayed with you. And now, she's gone back to the sea and left you in the room in Sunset Gardens."

I look back at the empty beach, knowing Lily has the chance to change her mind now.

"Was your life what you wanted it to be?" I ask.

"How could it ever be?" she whispers. "Does anyone lead the life they wish for? You shan't either, Marcus, and one day you'll wonder ... what if I'd taken the other path?"

"Maybe you should find out."

I reach a hand out to her, and we step into the icy water. She clutches my hand tightly, but as her body begins to change, I feel her release her soul to the gentle tugging of the waves. Her hand becomes cold, her fingers webbed, and she lets go of me. The creature she has become breaks the surface of the water in a spiral dance, her scales reflecting the light in blinding glints of color. She gazes back at me, a silver moon in one eye and a golden sun in the other.

I'm suddenly aware of the waves around me. The foam is made of a thousand tiny creatures, silver fish, and some of them, a few dozen, wash up on the sand. They *are* fish, like grunion, but in the next instant, they shed their fins and scales. They grow legs and become children. They walk in the direction of the bonfire. They start up the trail, naked boys and girls laughing and chattering. There's a man coming down to meet them.

"Come, come, my little fry!" he calls to them. "The learning waits. You've got the ways of land to know, the ciphering of books and machines. The art and music of mankind."

As I watch, they vanish up the trail, and I'm alone in the surf. Lily has gone with Muriel to find the palace of the sea.

I manage to log out of the program and slip off my headset. I'm sitting in room 552, but there's no one here. The bed is stripped to the mattress and all of Lily's things are gone.

Claire steps into the room and asks, "Can I help you, young man?"

"I was working with Ms. Ness. You know, Teens Teach Tech, and—"

"Oh, you must be looking for Mr. Fillory. He's in 553. His son just bought him an iPhone, and he doesn't even know how to turn the dang thing on."

"But Ms. Ness …"

"Who?"

I stand to leave and see the picture on the wall. It's still here. A pencil sketch of a shimmering creature with the sun and moon in her eyes. I lift it from the wall, tuck it under my arm, and take it with me.

〜〜〜

Terry Madden is a Writers of the Future winner and author of the fantasy series, Three Wells of the Sea. When not writing or hiking, she teaches high school chemistry and astronomy. The idea for this story came from a student who participates in a local "Teens Teach Tech" program. Visit Terry at www.ThreeWellsoftheSea.com.

GUARDIAN OF THE SEA

KRISTIN LUNA

G rab those buckets, *mijo*," Andrés Diaz instructed his sixteen-year-old son, Michael.

Michael picked them up without complaint, but regretted staying up until one o'clock leveling up his troll mage. If he would've known his father wanted to ship off by four in the morning when it was still pitch-black outside, he would've ended his gaming time much earlier.

As he set the buckets inside his father's sport fishing boat, Michael scolded himself for not remembering vapor rub to smear under his nose. He knew his father liked a deal, but Michael couldn't figure why his father kept his boat in Gables by the Sea, the cheapest marina in Miami, when it always smelled like seagull poop and hot, rotting fish guts. But to his father's credit, he kept his boat, which he'd named after Michael's mother, Lucía, sparkling clean.

Michael stepped onto the *Lucía* and steadied his balance. He walked mostly by memory, as the marina lights only shined on the docks and very little light spilled onto the *Lucía*.

"We'll get you some sea legs yet," his father said, his dark eyes squinting as he laughed.

"I don't know about that," Michael grumbled.

"Hey, open mind, remember?" Andrés hopped over the side to

the dock, spry for his fifty-two years, and grabbed the fishing poles. "You promised you'd go into this with an open mind, *mijo.*"

"I am!" Michael argued. He ran his fingers through his black hair. He willed himself to put on a brave face. He hoped he could make his father proud.

"Well, just give it a chance. Remember our deal: if you don't fall in love with fishing by the end of the day, then we can talk about you going to college for game ... something."

"Video game design," Michael finished for his father with a sigh.

"Yes, video game design. But if you can work with me, then that's more money we bring in for our family."

Michael bit his lip. He wished fishing appealed to him. Even just a little.

"You know we could really use the extra money. Theresa is heading into high school, and Ruiz is already working full-time and going to community college."

"Video game design could make us a lot of money, too," Michael countered. "Besides, don't you want me to do something a little more legitimate?"

Andrés's brow furrowed. "This is legitimate! My father did this. And his father, too. I catch fish and sell them at the market the same day. There is nothing fresher than that. It's the way we've done it for years."

Michael sighed. "I know, Dad. I'll do my best."

"That's all I ask," Andrés said. "Now, get that rope and let's get going."

Michael fussed with the thick rope knotted around the cleat hitch that kept their boat tied to the dock.

After a minute, Andrés threw up his hands. "Didn't I teach you knots when you were little?"

Michael rolled his eyes as his father clomped over and pulled a section of the knot, untying the whole thing like a magic trick.

"Maybe you were too busy with your video games," Andrés grumbled.

Michael swallowed and looked away.

Andrés gathered the rope and tucked it inside the boat. He

turned to the steering console and started the motor. "Hold on or sit down," he said.

Michael sat on the seat next to his father as he steered them out of the Gables by the Sea marina.

Just before hitting open water, his father slowed the boat. He looked up to the northern sky and then closed his eyes.

"What are you doing?" Michael asked.

His father opened his eyes and looked to his son. "Don't tell your mother, okay?"

"Don't tell her what?"

"Do you see those stars?" Andrés pointed to the north.

"I see lots of stars."

"Follow my finger. See that one? It connects to that other one, and this one." Andrés traced his finger along more stars to form a constellation. "It's called Draco. Draco is the guardian of the sea. Some people even say he created the sea. He governs the waters and watches over us."

"So you pray to it?" Michael asked, wrinkling his brow. "But we're Catholic."

"*Mijo*, when you're on the water, you pray to any god that listens." His father laughed, drawing a smile from his reluctant son. Andrés revved the motor and turned right, taking them south. Ocean spray salted their faces, and the faint rotting smell of the marina faded.

Michael glanced behind him at the constellation. He traced the crude outline of a head and long tail. It was funny, Michael thought, that his father followed the dragon each day, while he chased dragons each night in video games.

The sun crested in the east, illuminating the choppy ocean waves. The faintest hints of Key West emerged to their right.

A wave of nausea hit Michael, and he sat still, breathing deeply.

"Oh, Michael. Seasick?" His father shook his head. "Keep your eyes on the horizon."

Michael's stomach made squishing sounds. "I'm not feeling so good."

"It's best to think about something else. Have I told you why I come to this spot to fish? It's good luck." Andrés babbled on, explaining the importance of a good spot and the best weather conditions for deep-sea fishing. He said on a good day, he could reel in a mackerel or grouper, which sold for eight to ten dollars per pound at the market. He was just starting to get into the importance of bait when Michael casually turned his head to the starboard side and vomited into the ocean.

"¡*Dios Mío!*" Andrés shouted. "Where is your Diaz fishing blood?"

"I might've just thrown it up," Michael mumbled. He wiped his mouth with the sleeve of his sweatshirt, wishing more than anything he was coding the video game he started three days ago. He'd created the game using 8-bit graphics, but Michael felt great pride in his senior programming project.

"Did I tell you about the video game I've been working on?" Michael said to his father, trying to distract himself from his queasiness.

"In a moment, *mijo*, we're almost there."

Michael looked down and picked at his fingernails, trying to hide his disappointment.

His father slowed the boat. "Okay, let me show you how to drop anchor. If the wind is overtaking the ocean, we head into the wind. If the waves are overtaking the wind, we head into the ocean."

Michael nodded, trying to make it look like he understood what his father had just said.

Andrés slowed the boat to a crawl, then hopped over to the line and anchor. "Now we make sure the anchor is clear. You don't want to get this rope tangled with anything, like your foot. Help me lower it over."

Michael helped his father pick up the anchor, startled by the weight of it. He tried not to notice the disapproval on his father's face. Michael's own face flushed as he regretted not taking weight-lifting classes as electives.

The metal anchor slid into the water, and the rope fluttered as it sunk deeper and deeper.

"Now we just tie the line off to the cleat," Andrés narrated as Michael watched helplessly. Andrés tied the line, then hopped back to the control, where he shifted the gear into reverse.

"We pull the anchor to make sure it's set on the bottom. If it drags, then we have to do it all over again." When the boat buzzed with effort but didn't move, Andrés gave a nod of approval and cut the motor.

"Now, the fun part!" Andrés reached down to one of the coolers and flipped it open, revealing a Ziploc bag of red and silver fish parts. "We fish!"

Andrés busied himself placing four fishing poles onto the secured holders on both sides of the boat while Michael watched. He finished in less than fifteen minutes.

"See? Easy," his father said, motioning to the poles.

"Uh, yeah." Michael looked at them, baffled. "Easy peasy."

For the rest of the morning, the two sat on the boat, tending to their lines. Andrés's line bent, then broke. He told Michael that it might've been a shark, so it was better that the line snapped. Not twenty minutes later, Andrés's line pulled taut. He carefully reeled in the fish, fighting against the fish's weight. Coral-red scales caught the light as it broke the surface of the water.

"Snapper!" Andrés yelled proudly, pulling the line closer to the boat. "Grab the net, *mijo*! Let's get her into the boat."

They brought the snapper up from the water and hauled it over the side.

"They love the squid bait," Andrés said, beaming. "She feels like a twelve-pounder. That'll sell for about a hundred dollars at the market. She doesn't look too old. When we clean her, we'll be able to tell."

Michael watched as his father put the fish in one of the coolers. He felt a pang of pity.

"How can you tell her age? By her color?" Michael asked.

"By her ear bone. Snappers grow rings on them each year, like a tree trunk."

Michael's stomach churned again thinking about taking out the fish's ear bone just to count her rings.

Andrés shut the cooler and stretched. "Well, *mijo*, are you hungry?"

"Not really."

"We should get some food into you. You lost most of it on the way here."

They had a lunch of sandwiches that Lucía had made for them that morning—shredded spiced chicken from last night's dinner, *queso fresco*, and lettuce on a *torta*. Andrés snapped open two cans of soda and handed one to his son.

"Isn't this the life?" he said, smiling as he looked out over the sea.

Michael could barely hold down what little he ate of his *torta*.

"Well," Andrés said as they finished, "it's time to get back to fishing."

Michael sighed. He didn't know how to break it to his father that the trip so far hadn't engendered any appreciation for fishing. He bit his lip. Maybe he shouldn't tell him at all. Maybe he should lie and say that he loved fishing. His family needed him to work; they needed the money.

As he looked out over the water, considering his options, something shiny caught his eye. He squinted, putting his hand on his forehead to shade his eyes, and walked to the starboard side.

"What do you see, *mijo*?"

"I don't know," Michael said. "It's coming a little closer. It's moving."

Andrés grabbed his black binoculars. "Looks like something caught up in a net." He sighed and slammed the binoculars down near the control panel. "Damn it. These boats—they just throw their old nets overboard. And then this happens. The ghost nets trap dolphins and sharks and turtles. We have to go to it and see if we can cut it loose."

Michael forgot his seasickness and watched his father pull up anchor, then take them closer to the net. Admiration for his father washed over his ambivalence toward his father's profession. His father not only felt an obligation to this animal, but a moral obligation to help it as well.

When they came upon the net, Andrés stopped the boat and dropped anchor about ten feet away.

"Sometimes the creature is hurt and panicking. We'll try to help him from here," Andrés explained.

Michael studied the trapped fish—it was about the size of his pet pit bull, Chewy—but he couldn't see it clearly because of the massive net wrapped around it.

"How do we free it?"

His father looked around the boat, then grabbed a pole with a hook on the end. He opened a drawer next to the control panel and produced a multi-tool with a six-inch blade.

"This will have to do," his father said. Maneuvering over the side of the boat, Andrés angled the pole to hook around the net. Michael went to his father's side, helping him secure the net. The fish thrashed, splashing water onto their shirts.

"Feels heavy," Michael said.

His father grunted. "Yes. Our friend here has some fight left in him."

Together, they pulled the animal closer to the side of the boat. Through the netting, Michael noted the bright aquamarine color and teal stripes on the scales of the fish.

"Whatever he is, he's beautiful," Andrés said. "Hold the pole steady. Wedge the end into that corner. I'm going to try to cut him loose."

Michael all but sat on the pole to keep it steady, the animal thrashed so violently. Concern lined his features. "Careful, Dad."

Andrés's head moved back and forth as he searched for an opening. His arm darted into the water and caught a hold of some netting. As Andrés flipped open the blade of the multi-tool, Michael saw the flash of a golden eye the size of his fist from between two slots of netting. Even more violently than before, the animal tore away from Andrés's grip, nearly taking a finger with it.

Andrés clenched his fist, rubbing the finger.

"Are you okay?" Michael asked.

"I can't get a good grip. I'll need your help to get this thing onto the boat."

Andrés helped Michael attach the pole to the side of the boat and wedge the end into a corner.

"Just like fishing nets, *mijo*. We're going to grab opposite sides on three. Ready?"

The fish's tail whacked the water, splashing them both. Michael shuffled toward the bow while his father went to the stern.

Andrés looked at his son, his own hands out and ready. "One, two, three!"

Both Michael and his father plunged their hands into the water, hooking their fingers into the net.

"Pull!" Andrés yelled over the splashing.

As his biceps pulsed, Michael cursed himself again for not taking more weight-lifting classes.

The seconds seemed to stretch on like minutes. He and his father used their feet to push into the side of the boat as they pulled the fish over the edge. Just when Michael's legs began to shake and threatened to give up, he felt the weight tip in their favor. The fish fell into the boat, taking both father and son down with it.

Michael noted the unusual length of the fish, and how the scales seemed to shimmer through the netting like diamonds in the sun.

Andrés stood up in a flash, ready with the multi-tool. "We have to cut! There's another knife under the controls." His weathered hands quickly unraveled the parts of the net he cut through.

Michael found the knife under the panel and turned back to the thrashing fish. He froze when he saw just how long the thing was. It looked like a sea snake with a long, muscular tail and fins like arms tangled helplessly in the net.

"Hurry!" Andrés yelled, pulling Michael out of his shock.

Michael took a deep breath and fell to his knees, quickly cutting into any piece of the net he could grip. For two tense minutes, they cut furiously, pulling up pieces of the net and throwing them to the corners of the boat.

The fish squirmed and bucked; this time its tail was free enough to whip at a wider angle, and it hit Andrés's right leg. The man fell to his knees, gripping his thigh.

"Dad!" Michael yelled.

"I'm fine! Keep going!" Andrés yelled. "Pull the net, it's nearly out."

Michael ignored his father's orders and rushed to his side. "We have to keep you out of striking distance, Dad." He ushered his father to the captain's seat, then rushed back and pulled up on the netting his father had cut, using the fish's momentum to unroll the fish.

As he threw the netting aside, Michael heard his father curse in Spanish.

In front of them was not a fish or sea snake. With its brilliant blue and green scales, bone-like external spine, and golden eyes, Michael knew the creature before them was a sea dragon.

"This can't be real," Michael said. He shook his head in an effort to clear his vision.

"Draco," Andrés whispered, clutching the armrests of his chair.

The sea dragon's head snapped toward Andrés. Michael put his body directly in front of his father. The dragon's front fins propped up its body, then helped it slither closer to Michael. Michael clutched his father's hand and watched the dragon come closer, its tongue darting out and in.

Michael gulped. "I love you, Dad."

Andrés gripped his son's hand tighter. "I love you, too, *mijo*."

Michael closed his eyes as the dragon's face came within inches of his own. He waited for death.

And waited.

Shaking, Michael opened one eye to see the dragon's face in front of his own. Its eye, like rings of varying shades of gold, studied his face, the slit pupil darting.

Michael stayed still, watching as the dragon regarded him.

"*Mijo?*" his father asked cautiously.

The dragon's head glided down to Andrés's face.

"Draco," Andrés said again. The dragon's head tilted to the side. "This is the god of the sea, *mijo*."

The dragon let out a small moan and angled its long neck toward its fin.

Michael followed its gaze and saw angry, dark blue net imprints on the dragon's fin.

"It's hurt," Michael said. Cautiously, he held out his hands, palms up.

The dragon's eyes darted to Michael, watching him as he slowly went to his knees and looked closer at the dragon's fin.

Andrés appeared behind him, leaning over his shoulder. "Do you see the gash there?"

The dragon let out another moan and slumped onto the deck.

"I think I have something for it. It's not much, but maybe it'll help." Andrés hobbled to the front of the boat and grabbed a bottle of water and a tube of antibiotic ointment.

Michael looked at him quizzically, though he also kept his attention on the dragon.

"It's waterproof. It'll stop the wound from bleeding," Andrés explained.

"I guess it's worth a try," Michael said. "But how do we put it on without it lashing out at us?"

"I don't know," Andrés said, then sighed. "But if we can help, then we should try."

Andrés unscrewed the cap from the water bottle, then held it up for the dragon to see. Then he poured the fresh water over the wound.

Then, Andrés went for the ointment, but Michael snatched it from his hands.

"*Mijo*, no. Give that back. Don't be foolish."

"I'm not letting you do this. Besides, if it kills me, you can still get home. If it kills you, I don't know how to get this damn boat to work."

Andrés snorted and shook his head, some tension visibly leaving his body. He sighed when Michael showed no signs of giving in.

"Be careful," Andrés instructed.

"I will," Michael said, then squirted a thick glob of ointment on his finger. He hesitantly held the ointment up to show the dragon, and to his shock, the dragon's head came close, sniffing his finger. Michael tried not to shake under its inspecting eye or move his finger away. When the dragon pulled back its head, Michael took it as its blessing to continue.

Michael took a deep breath, moving closer to the dragon's fin. The dragon remained steady, letting its fin hang loose at its side. Very gently, Michael pressed his finger onto the fin then let up. The dragon didn't move or react, so Michael pressed the antibiotic to the fin again, smearing the goo into the scales. The scales felt cool and hard under his fingers. When he'd sufficiently covered the wound, Michael slowly pulled back his hand.

The dragon looked at him with his golden eye, then down to the fin. It tested the fin then sniffed at it.

Andrés threw his arm around his son. "Good work, *mijo!*"

The boat suddenly began to turn. A small whirlpool formed under the boat, then increased in speed, pulling them around in a circle.

The sea dragon seemed calm, still assessing its covered wound.

Michael felt his stomach flip-flop, nausea gripping him. He looked over the side of the boat, readying himself to be sick, and saw what was making them turn.

Just under the surface of the water was a thick, dark shadow reaching as far as he could see. When Michael squinted and leaned closer, a golden eye the size of the boat motor blinked at him. The color matched the sea dragon's eyes.

Michael flew back to the middle of the boat. "Dad!"

"I see it, *mijo.*" His dad stood on his feet, favoring his right leg, watching the shadow surrounding their boat. Andrés rubbed his thigh, watching as they hopelessly spun in the middle of the ocean. "Draco of the sky has come to the ocean."

The giant creature sparkled as the sunlight hit the water, its green body gliding under the surface, sucking the boat further below the waterline like a funnel.

Michael looked at the sea dragon still in the boat, seemingly oblivious to what was happening around them. He thought back to a quest he had completed a few days ago as a troll mage. He licked his lips and turned to his father.

"I have an idea."

Andrés's alarm showed on every feature of his face. "I don't know what you're thinking, *mijo*, but Draco is in command of the sea, and there is nothing we can do to control the boat."

"I think I know what it wants."

Michael approached the young sea dragon, waiting to see if it would react. The sea dragon looked at Michael and tilted its head to the side. Michael put out his arm and slowly began moving forward to corral it.

"Help me, Dad. Just move it to the side of the boat," Michael said.

Andrés hobbled to his son's side and mirrored his outstretched arms. "This is crazy."

"But it just might work. Move forward again."

As the two moved forward, the dragon's back ridges straightened, pointing in the air. Its fins fluttered in warning. It opened its mouth, showing a row of translucent, pointed teeth. But it didn't strike.

"Just keep moving forward, nice and slow," Michael instructed.

The two took small steps until they had the sea dragon cornered on the side of the boat.

"We need to get it out of the boat," Michael said.

"How?" Andrés asked.

"I don't know." Michael looked around the boat. Finally, he spotted the cooler that contained his father's catch. Following his son's gaze, Andrés hobbled to the cooler and brought it to his son.

Andrés pulled the snapper out of the cooler so the sea dragon could see it. Immediately, the sea dragon's golden eyes flickered with attention. When Andrés moved the fish, the sea dragon's eyes followed.

"¡Dios Mío! I'm throwing a hundred dollars overboard," Andrés muttered. Michael gave his father a look, and Andrés took a deep breath and reluctantly threw the fish back into the ocean.

The sea dragon didn't hesitate. It jumped out of the boat, following the fish with an open mouth, slithering in the air until it met the cold water.

A bone-rattling screech filled the air. The pull of the whirlpool slowed.

Michael and Andrés looked over the side of the boat as the giant sea dragon slowed its body, its fins gently gliding around the smaller sea dragon. The two bodies twisted together playfully.

The whirlpool settled until the boat drifted lazily in a slight circle.

Andrés looked at his son in disbelief. Michael stared back with just as much surprise. They turned back to the sea dragons and watched as they dove into the deep.

"How did you … How did you know to do something like that?" Andrés clapped his son on the back, enveloping him in a hug.

Michael hugged his father and smiled. "Video games. I was playing this quest where I rescued a baby mammoth. When the mother came, you had to give the baby back to its mother or she would kill you. I died three times trying to figure that out."

Andrés pulled his son back to look at him and laughed. They hugged, tears of joy streaming from their eyes.

A splash tore them away from each other.

Their smiles vanished as the giant sea dragon's head and long neck loomed over them, shadowing them. Michael swallowed; it could eat their boat whole with one bite. Its two golden eyes beamed down at them, its scaled and horned face ominously close to their humble seacraft.

The dragon's mouth opened, revealing green-stained, spear-like teeth. Andrés's grip on Michael's shoulder tightened.

The dragon's face came closer, its eyes widening. The dragon made a retching noise, then moved slightly to their left and threw up, heavy contents pounding onto the deck with a thud.

"Gross," Michael said, unable to help himself.

The dragon had thrown up a king marlin and an enormous tuna, both still alive.

Andrés gawked at the fish while Michael looked up at the sea dragon, unsure. Its head turned to the side, its golden eye watching them both as it slid back into the ocean. Its shadow dissolved as it dove deep into the sea. The smaller sea dragon's head crested the waterline in the distance, and Michael nudged his father. They both watched as the dragon studied them for a moment longer, then disappeared into the deep, following its mother.

Michael's father looked down at the fish, then at his son, then back at the fish.

"*Mijo*, the tuna alone is enough to pay our bills for the next five years!"

Michael beamed with happiness as he watched his father assess the marlin and tuna, securing them in the boat. His father seemed to all but forget the ache in his leg as he cheered and hopped around the fish, yelling in Spanish how Draco had blessed them for saving the sea dragon. His father's joy permeated Michael's very core.

Andrés finally stopped celebrating and pulled up anchor, turning them toward Gables by the Sea.

"So. What did you think? Have I made a fisherman out of you?" Andrés yelled over the boat motor, winking at his son.

Michael laughed. "I think you have a crazy, dangerous, fun, and honorable job." He took a deep breath. "But I'd rather meet sea dragons from the safety of my computer."

Andrés smiled at his son. "Then that's what you'll do. We'll sell these fish at the market, and then you can tell me about that video game you're making."

Michael beamed the whole ride back to the marina.

Kristin Luna has been making up stories and getting in trouble for them since elementary school. She especially loves magical realism, fantasy, Nic Cage, literary fiction, action movies from the '80s and '90s, and Taco Bell. She has written book reviews for *Urban Fantasy Magazine*, writes for the blog *The Fictorians* (fictorians.com), and her short stories have appeared on *Pseudopod* and in other anthologies published by WordFire Press. She lives in San Diego with her husband, Nic, and is currently writing a novel.

IN THE WATER

JESSICA GUERNSEY

Peering out the small window at nearly 30,000 feet in the air, I can see the ocean. I imagine flashes of dark shapes in the water, and my chest freezes. I automatically reach for the inhaler in my jacket, but then leave it in my pocket and try taking soft, slow breaths until the moment passes. Just bad memories. I close the shade.

As the plane taxies to the gate, I look through my notes again. So many names and stories: Kelpie. Pooka. Nykur. Each-uisge.

Which one? I wonder. I'm here to find out.

Moments later, I walk up to the rail-thin woman by the baggage claim holding the sign with my name.

"I'm Kendra Lowry," I say and brace myself.

Sure enough, the onslaught begins. "Ms. Lowry, I'm Tabby Longwith. I'm such a big fan of *Changeling*. That book changed my life. It's a huge honor to show you around Cape Breton."

I let her gush as she leads me to the waiting car, but my smile already feels tight. Her voice is as thin and sharp as her nose, and I'm done listening before we reach the main road. I explain that I'm tired and lean my head back against the seat, closing my eyes. Helps that I can't see the sea any more.

This isn't my first time in Nova Scotia. I'm told I was too young to remember being here before. But I do remember. And that memory makes me grip my inhaler a little harder.

Over a chunky clam chowder, the thin woman—I really ought to call her Tabby—reviews my itinerary.

"After lunch, we'll visit the An Drochaid museum," she said, her food untouched. "They're having a special exhibit of local art inspired by all the fairy folklore, so your timing is perfect. After that, we'll tour the island with a historian who can show you the sights and give more details to the stories."

I half-listen. I already know this. My insides feel quivery, and I can't really bring myself to eat. I'm so close. *But which one?*

"The historian was quite excited that a famous author such as yourself would want to use our legends as the inspiration for your next book."

Finally, she stops talking. I breathe a sigh of relief but then I look up. She was just waiting for me to make eye contact.

"I have to ask," she says, and by the way she's starting to blush, I know what's coming next. "Is Artur real?"

I look at her, demanding that my eyes not roll in their sockets.

"Because he's so perfect, so ... lovely," she says, finally moving her spoon through her chowder. "He has to be based on a real person, right?"

I wink, but say nothing. She giggles and winks back.

Just outside the small house that serves as the museum, I make the mistake of catching a glimpse of the sea again. My inhaler saves the day. There's nothing in the water. I am able to follow tiny Tabby inside.

The museum looks more like someone emptied several attics and spewed the contents all over the house. We move up narrow stairs to the art exhibit. I wander through the pictures, skimming descriptions. Nothing strikes me. There's images of selkies galore, fairy-born seals that can shed their skin and become human. But I've already done selkies. Tabby's Artur is a selkie, seeking his betrothed, Cassandra, who was sent away as a changeling, a fairy-born child switched for a mortal baby, hence the title of my book-turned-blockbuster-movie. He helped her discover her true self, and they lived happily ever after. Or so Tabby would believe.

I turn away from a painting of a screaming banshee and am immediately taken in by a picture of a horse and rider. This one is all crude lines, nearly childlike in its rendering, but the emotion is there. The terror in the rider's too-wide eyes, the power in the horse's legs. And the water, shown in rough wavy lines as the horse's destination.

The horse and the sea. I scramble for my inhaler, squeeze and breathe.

In an instant, Tabby is at my elbow.

"Are you okay?" Her narrow face is crinkled in concern.

"I'm fine." I wave her back. "Just not seeing what I had in mind. I thought these were supposed to be based on local legends, but there doesn't seem to be any connection."

Tabby glances around at the art. "Well, we are a Scottish community with plenty of history. Our ancestors brought their tales and beliefs with them. There are a lot of stories to tell."

I'm frowning. I can feel my mouth pulling down, and I do nothing to change that.

"Maybe if I knew what you're looking for?" Tabby peeks up at me.

"I'm looking for a monster," I say, my eyes straying to the horse again. "One that lives in the sea."

Tabby follows my eye. "But that's a picture of a kelpie. They appear as horses, only to make it impossible for the rider to dismount until they are drowned. They live in rivers."

"Maybe your historian can help me." I pull my gaze away from the kelpie painting. That's not the right story. I can mark one off my list.

"Oh, yes." Tabby immediately perks up, her smile turning up the wattage. "I'm sure of it."

≈≈≈

We wait at a pier for the historian. I don't see him until he's a few feet away because I'm trying desperately not to look at the water, lest I need my inhaler again. But I can see why Tabby is suddenly so much more animated. He might be a respected academic, but physically, he's an Adonis, with the bronzed abs to match. Low-slung swimming trunks and an unbuttoned, fluttering shirt. He must know the effect he has on women. And that's even before he smiles. His teeth are perfectly white and wide. I'm a sucker for good teeth. But the flutter in my stomach isn't attraction. There's something about him that doesn't seem to fit.

Tabby is on him faster than I could say "Artur is real."

"Dr. Noggle." She grew giddy as she took his hand. "I'm so glad you could meet us today. May I introduce you to the famous Kendra Lowry?"

They both turn toward me.

"Miss Lowry." His voice rumbles deeper than I expect.

I take his hand. "Please, call me Kendra."

He tilts his head to one side, lanky curls skimming his shoulder. "Then I insist you call me Ethan."

Ethan is a much better fit. Because a "noggle" is a fairy horse that traps travelers. They hunt exclusively on land, not in water like the kelpies. Considering I'm technically a traveler, the name makes me a little nervous.

"Were you swimming?" Tabby asks.

But Ethan doesn't take his large dark eyes from my face as he answers, "Why do you ask? Am I still wet?"

"A little." Tabby runs a hand down his arm to test or just to be able to touch him. "And I think there's seaweed in your hair."

"Aye, it's for good luck." He gives her a wink.

She simpers through some response. But already his attention is back to me. I try not to flinch.

"Where would you like to start, Miss Lowry?" he asks.

"She's looking for a monster," Tabby blurts, nearly squeezing herself between us. And as thin as she is, she might make it. "A sea monster."

"Monsters, eh?" he asks, his lips turning up at one end. Is he smirking? "Why's that?"

Tabby doesn't have the answer so she has no choice but to fall silent.

"Every good story has a monster," I say and attempt a smile.

A slight twitch at the corner of his eye. Ethan can tell I am lying.

"And a fairy one at that?" he asks.

"Haven't you seen *Changeling?*" Tabby asks and begins to repeat her previous gushing at the airport.

"Aye," Ethan says, cutting Tabby off as she was describing Artur's tall blondness in exact detail. "But a selkie is not the sort of monster you seek, eh, Kendra?"

"No, it's not."

We stare at each other a moment longer. He seems to be waiting for me to say more. When I press my lips together and keep silent, he nods.

"Good then," he said. "And we're off. Plenty of stories to tell out on the water."

He takes my hand and starts down toward the pier. My heels dig in. Ethan looks back at me, his face in profile.

"No water." My clenched teeth refuse to separate.

"But that's where the monsters are," he says, not letting go.

"No water," I repeat.

With the one eye I can see, he studies my face for a second longer.

"Land it is," he says and changes direction. Just like he'd intended to go that way all along. He still has hold of my hand, and I can hear Tabby tapping along on her heels behind us.

"Now why Cape Breton?" Ethan asks. "Inverness is said to be built right over a fairy mound. All sorts of tales of people going missing there." We walk along the main street as Ethan talks. "But Cape Breton mostly has tales of fairy-born horses. That's not your typical sea monster."

No, definitely not typical. But every name on my list is a kind of horse. Every last one.

I shrug. "I have my reasons," I say and try to look like a wise, best-selling author, when really I can feel my heart galloping in my chest at the mere mention of horses. My fingers grasp the familiar plastic tube in my pocket, but I don't bring it out, focusing on my breathing.

"Have you looked into the Formorians?" Ethan offers. "Nasty buggers. They were driven into the sea."

"Yes, definitely sea monsters," I say, then turn to look at him. "Found only around Ireland."

He grins. Is he testing me? Well, I can play that game.

"Nykur?" I lift one eyebrow.

He shakes his head. "Iceland. Not cold enough here."

"Pooka, then," I say. "Any of those around?"

He strokes his chin, narrowing his eyes at me, but then shrugs. "Not nearly cruel enough in these parts. Mostly, they're helpful. And not always in the water."

Two more off my list, then.

After a few minutes of silence, I break it. "Tell me about your sea monsters here in Cape Breton."

"Bochain," he replies, using the Scottish pronunciation that makes it sound more like "buckin."

"Those are in swamps, not the ocean." I look away. Now I know he's just playing with me. But why?

"What about Ogogpogo?" Tabby teeters on her heels as she hurries to keep pace with us, and I'm tempted to nudge her so she falls over. Just as I lean toward her, the good doctor places a hand on her arm. She'd probably enjoy falling into him if I go through with it, so instead, I bite my lip and try my best to swallow my irritation.

"Ogogpogo is a lake monster," I say, proud that I don't have to speak through clenched teeth. "I'm looking for something in the sea."

She tilts her head to one side. "Like Nessie in Scotland?"

My smile feels tight, but Tabby doesn't seem to notice. "No. That's also a lake. Sea monsters live in the sea. Salt water. The ocean. Open waters."

She doesn't get it.

"And I'd also like to find an area that has a lighthouse."

They both look at me now.

"Why a lighthouse?" Tabby asks, her features shifting from befuddled to glowing. "Is the love interest a lonely lighthouse keeper? That would be super romantic."

"There are several lighthouses." Ethan is looking at me from the side again. "We're a peninsula so we have plenty."

I've seen the pictures. I know exactly which lighthouse. "Oh, you know." I loosen my stance and let my hands fall. "Something tall and white. With a light on top."

He nods and looks off toward the water. Tabby is looking at her nails. If we're not talking about a man, she's not interested, apparently.

"A sea monster that can be seen from a lighthouse, eh? I think I know the one," Ethan says, rubbing that long jaw of his. How does a man instinctively know the right amount of stubble that will make a woman swoon?

Tabby swivels her pencil neck to look at him. "Which one? Kidston Island lighthouse is cool."

"Nah," he says, and a grin starts to spread. "We're going to Enragee Point."

Tabby groans. "That road is awful. I'll get car sick."

I'm about to offer to leave her behind when Ethan keeps talking.

"Can't see much from the road, anyway. They don't let us lay folk get close, what with the iron fence and all. Best to approach it from the water."

My mouth goes dry.

"That way you get the sight of it that your monster might see." He smiles at me, teeth showing and everything. I want to break those teeth out.

"No water." I might actually be growling but don't care.

"Can't be helped, love," he says. At least his grin slips enough and his eyes show me sincerity. "Best option."

"Then it has to be a large boat." I try to relax my jaw but the urge to punch someone is growing so I keep it clenched. "No little dinghy or sloop or whatever. I want something with a life raft."

"No worries, love." He pulls out his cell phone. "My nephew Doonie has just the thing."

While he turns away from us to talk on the phone, Tabby starts bouncing again. "I could get used to being called 'love' all day if it's someone like him saying it."

She giggles and nudges me with her elbow. I consider shoving her into oncoming traffic, but there aren't any cars. So I just make sure my back is facing the ocean.

I should have brought my spare inhaler.

"Are you all right?" Ethan asks. He steers us back toward the pier, and I'm trying not to notice the water.

"Fine, just fine," I say. "How many miles away is this lighthouse?"

"Miles?" Tabby rolls her eyes far too dramatically. "Don't you mean kilometers?" She giggles again and says, "Americans."

"I'm Canadian, actually," I say. "I was born here, adopted by an American couple."

"Wow," she says on an exhale. She is standing too close to me. "Did you ever look for your birth mother?"

"No," I say. Because I know my birth mother is dead. Murdered even as I was drowning. Before the dark images and terror can take control, I stuff my inhaler in my mouth and breathe deep. To get their eyes off me, I point to some random item in a nearby shop window and pretend to coo over the details. "That's lovely."

Ethan steps forward to look at the object of my apparent admiration. "You're interested in knives?"

I blink. The shop has a large display of knives. Hunting. Fishing. Even a few ornamental ones. I shudder. I don't like knives.

"I, uh, meant the wooden box there," I say, wondering why I feel the need to explain.

Ethan nods but keeps his eyes on me. Tabby is already prattling on about something else as she walks beside me.

"There's something I wanted to know about your work." Tabby loops her arm through mine, and I try to repress a shudder. "Why write about changelings?"

"Fairies have always fascinated me." I try to tug my arm loose by pretending to look in another window but Tabby holds on and looks with me.

"But why changelings?" she asked, her nose wrinkling. "Don't you think it's rather awful? Fairies that steal babies only to leave theirs behind?"

I don't answer because I agree. It is awful.

She keeps talking. "Do you think all changelings have to find out what they are? Like Cassandra did? She had no idea until she went to the ocean."

"I wouldn't know," I say.

It's not the answer she wanted so Tabby tries a different route. "Do you think fairies still steal babies?"

"Oh, I imagine they wouldn't need to steal a child anymore," I say, fiddling with my inhaler in my pocket.

"True," Ethan chimes in from my other side. "They wouldn't want the FBI tracking them back to their fairy rings. They'd adapt. Modernize."

Tabby flutters her eyelashes at him. "So you don't think there are changelings anymore?"

"Of course there are," he says, his broad grin returning. "But the fair folk wouldn't need to kidnap kids. They'd just put the changelings up for adoption. Plenty of couples want a baby."

Tabby's smile isn't nearly as nice. Her teeth are too little and yellow, like she drinks too much coffee. "A grown man who believes in fairies."

"I've made a name studying folklore." He shrugs. "There are stranger things to believe in."

I want to ask him more about that, but we've arrived back at the pier. And the nephew's boat is pulling in. It's not what I expected.

"A pirate ship?" I nearly stop walking again, but Tabby still has hold of my arm.

Ethan flashes his grin and turns his eyes to the boat. I catch a glimpse of something green in his hair. Must be more seaweed, but something in my memory clicks. The last name on my list comes to mind.

"My nephew takes out a lot of tourists," he says. "Fairies aren't the only good stories on our little peninsula."

The crew slides out a gangplank. Honestly. Just a plain board barely shoulder-width. No railing. The crew reaches their hands out to help us onboard. Tabby nearly skips across and hops on to the deck, her heels *thunking* on the wood. My feet refuse to move.

"Just three feet," Ethan says right next to my ear. "Then you're safe on the boat."

I want to laugh in his face. Safe? Not remotely. We are heading into the den of a monster. But they don't know what I've seen.

They still think I'm chasing stories.

I let out my breath. It's more ragged than I would like. I can't let the fear keep me away from the answers. I take a step.

Don't look down, I think. But my already overactive imagination gives me views of the water beneath my shaking knees. Dark shapes swirl, tentacles trailing.

I stop moving.

Ethan is behind me on the plank. I can feel his hand on the small of my back, pushing gently forward. He seems to be whispering soothingly to me, but my racing mind can't hear the words.

I look down. Wood. Only wood. I made it across the water. If I'm so safe now, then why is my heart still pounding at my chest like it's bent on escaping?

Tabby is pestering a crewman almost as scrawny as she is as he attaches orange balls to a net. At least she's not bothering me. I move to the center of the boat. It probably has some official name, but to me it's just a solid wall with ladders on either end. I press my back to the wall, using both hands to grip the wooden railing that runs all around the boat. This way I can see what is coming. Nothing to sneak up on me from here.

Ethan talks to what looks like a younger version of himself. Ethan might have twenty years on the other one but they are nearly identical. Same jawline, same broad smile. The younger man even has a strand of seaweed tucked behind his ear. Must be the nephew, Doonie. Another tickle of my memory reminds me that a "doonie" is also a type of fairy. Another horse. I study their faces. Strong jaw, broad cheekbones, and a long nose. Not to mention Ethan's tendency to turn his face to the side, showing his flawless profile, with one eye on me.

I want to ask. I want to say I know what he is, to use the old name for his kind, say the name of the beast I thought existed only in my nightmares.

Once you've met one fairy, the others are easier to spot. Poor Artur and Cassandra. They were doomed from the moment they met. Our last Spring Break before college, spending time at the beach with friends. But I couldn't get close to the water without seeing gnashing jaws and darkness swirling through my memories.

No sooner had the waves wrapped themselves around Cassandra's ankles than my childhood friend turned into a seal before my very eyes. At that moment, I knew the monster I'd seen in the water all those years ago was real.

Noggle. Doonie. Both types of fairy horses. They aren't on my list because neither are found near the water. But there is another fairy horse. One that lives in the sea, occasionally taking human form. One that might be recognized by the seaweed in their hair. One that haunts my memories and drives the oxygen from my lungs at the very thought of it. It's the last name on my list—the one I fear the most and the one I am looking for: each-uisge.

When Ethan joins me against the railing, I try not to look at him directly.

"Lots of stories in these waters," he says. "Rumors of a sea monster, eight meters long. Could wrap itself around a small boat. There's even photos of that one."

I can barely hear him. Surrounded by the ocean, no way to escape. I can almost feel the shapes under the water, the monster lurking there just as it had decades ago. Waiting for me.

A squeeze from my inhaler brings no relief. I try again, holding harder, longer. Nothing. I shake it. Empty.

"Let me see that." Ethan takes the inhaler from my weak fingers and studies the label. "Saline solution? That seems a little odd for an inhaler."

"Saline is the only thing that soothes my lungs."

"You breathe the sea."

I glare at him and snatch back the useless plastic thing. I try not to breathe.

A thin cry erupts from behind me. I turn in time to see a tangle of fishing nets and Tabby slide over the railing and out of sight.

Shouts sound all around me. I think I might have made some of the noise. I rush to the rail where she went over. Dread grips my chest and holds tight. I look down.

I can't see anything but the swirls and froth of the water below. Ethan appears at the edge of my sight. He's not looking down.

"Why are you so afraid of the ocean, Kendra?" he asks.

My breathing is shallow, and I repeat his question in my head, attempting to understand the words.

"You don't understand," I try to say, but my jaw feels heavy and my words thick. "I saw something in the water."

"In the water," he says, but it's not a question. "What was it, love?"

"A m-m-monster," I stammer and hate myself for it. "Something that shouldn't be there."

"Tell me."

"It looked like an enormous horse, larger than any I've ever seen but ... *wrong*. It was all wrong. The jaw split all the way down the head, and the teeth ... I've never seen such teeth. Like they were broken from spears of coral and jammed into an impossibly long jaw."

I can almost see it now, a dark shape rearing below the surface. Mouth of horrors opening to eat me whole. The mane flowing out behind but whipping back toward me, like tentacles wanting to tear off pieces of me.

"I saw it," I say. "It killed my mother. I remember drowning."

"No, love," he says, and he's right there beside me.

"What?" I sputter and wipe at the saltwater spray hitting my face, making my skin feel thicker and rougher, like it isn't mine any more.

"You don't remember drowning."

"I *do*. I remember the water in my lungs and a monster in the water."

"You don't remember drowning," he repeats, and I feel his hands on my shoulders. "You remember being born."

He shoves me hard, toppling me over the side of the boat.

I hit the water with my mouth open, screaming. Immediately, I suck in the sea. My lungs stop burning.

I flail in the dark cold. My hair floats and fuses, forming tentacles. My jaw aches. My arms feel too long, too thin, as I reach for the light above me with hooves instead of hands.

I break the surface but don't take in air. Instead, I see Ethan smiling over the railing. He calls to me.

"Welcome home, daughter."

~~~

Jessica Guernsey writes urban fantasy novels and short stories. She received her degree in journalism from Brigham Young University, and her work has been published in magazines and anthologies. She is a manuscript evaluator for two publishers, along with providing freelance feedback. Frequently, she can be found at writing conferences. She isn't difficult to spot; just look for the extrovert with purple hair.

While she spent her teenage angst in Texas, she now lives on a mountain in Utah with her husband, three kids, and a codependent mini schnauzer. Connect with her on Twitter @JessGuernsey.

COLD, SILENT, AND DARK

KARY ENGLISH

I t is an hour past midnight, and I cannot sleep. Have not slept for a year of nights.

Dim light filters in through the blinds. The moon is thinner than a child's fingernail, and the stars are pinpricks on the expanse of the velvet night. Their twinkling should be calming, but it isn't. They stick out like slubs in silk, each one a tiny, itching annoyance.

Jason sleeps soundly beside me. He is not snoring, not snuffling or moaning. He does not toss or call out in his sleep. He is only breathing, but each draw and crash of it grates like sand against my skin. A streetlight buzzes on the corner, and in the distance, an occasional car passes. I bury my head under the pillow, but it does not lessen the assault of light and sound that steals away my sleep.

My only relief is in knowing that this is my last sleepless night.

〜〜〜

Jason and I met a year ago at the marina. I was sunning myself on the deck of the *Lorelei*, earbuds in, singing along with my favorite opera.

He was the captain of a sculling crew, shuttling back and forth to the boathouse with armloads of oars and life jackets. He'd set the oars down, leaning on one of them and watching me until I looked up.

"Shouldn't you be combing your hair on a rock?" he'd said. "Care for a drink?"

"Shouldn't you be tied to a mast?" I answered back.

He held up the oar. "It's a very small boat. No mast."

"Then it will have to be a very small drink."

We both smiled. One month and several drinks later, we moved in together. I learned to scull; he let me drag him to *Lucia di Lammermoor* and *Madame Butterfly*. He asked me once how long I planned to stay.

"A year and a day," I'd answered. "Maybe longer if the tide turns."

That was eleven months ago. Three hundred thirty-four moon rises, twenty-two neap tides, and not a single hour of sleep.

~~~

The year passed at midnight, and the day begins at dawn.

In the morning, Jason will take me to the marina. He will surprise me with a chartered boat, lilies, and crystal champagne flutes. After we leave the harbor, we will stand near the rail, feeling the spray on our faces and cool, sea air filling our lungs. The wind will lift my hair and whip tendrils across my face and throat.

Jason will move closer, tucking a strand behind my ear and telling me how alive I seem when I'm on the water. He will take the hidden ring box from his pocket.

I will gasp, cover my mouth, let salt tears run down my cheeks. I will wrap my arms around him and whisper "Yes" against his ear.

He will slide the ring on my finger. His eyes will laugh, and he will ask me if the tide has turned.

I will laugh back, bubbling with true joy when I kiss him.

The boat will lurch, and I will hold him tight, tighter, tightest. I will arch my back toward the cresting waves and pull him with me into the blue-green sea.

He will struggle, and when he does, he will finally understand that I am most alive *in* the water, not on it.

He will try to scream, but the green depths swallow all sound.

We will drift ever downward until kelp surrounds us, and the last green light from above fades to a liquid, velvety black.

When we come to rest, he will be mine forever, down where it is cold, silent, and dark.

Only then I will sleep.

≈≈≈

Kary English grew up in the snowy Midwest where she avoided siblings and frostbite by reading book after book in a warm corner behind a recliner chair. She blames her only high school detention on Douglas Adams, whose *The Hitchhiker's Guide to the Galaxy* made her laugh out loud while reading it behind her geometry textbook.

Today, Kary still spends most of her time with her head in the clouds and her nose in a book. To the great relief of her parents, she seems to be making a living at it. Her greatest ambition is to make her own work detention-worthy.

A Hugo and Campbell finalist, Kary is a Writers of the Future winner whose work has appeared in *Daily Science Fiction, Grantville Gazette's Universe Annex, Writers of the Future, Vol. 31,* and *Galaxy's Edge.* Her website is www.KaryEnglish.com.

SEA DREAMS

REBECCA MOESTA AND KEVIN J. ANDERSON

Julia called me tonight as she has so many times before. Not on the telephone, but in that eerie, undeniable way she used since we met as little girls, strangers and best friends at once. It usually meant she needed me, had something urgent or personal to say.

But this time I needed her, in a desperate, throw-common-sense-to-the-wind way ... and she knew it. Julia always knew.

And she had something to tell me.

Alone in the tiny bedroom of my comfortably conservative Florida apartment, I felt it as surely as I felt the cool sheets beneath me and the humid, moon-warm September air that flowed through my half-opened window. At such times, common sense goes completely to sleep, leaving imagination wide awake and open to possibilities. And she called out to me.

Julia had been gone for five years, gone to the sea. Others might have said "drowned," might have used "gone" as a euphemism for "dead." I never did. The only thing I knew—that anyone could know for certain—was this: Julia was gone.

~~~

It had begun when we were eleven. That year, my parents and I left our Wisconsin home behind to spend our vacation at my grandmother's oceanside cottage in Cocoa Beach, Florida.

I had grown up in the Midwest, familiar with green hills and sprawling fields, but nothing had prepared me for my first sight of the Atlantic: an infinite force of blue-green mystery, its churning waves a magnet for my sensibilities, a sleeping power I had never suspected might exist.

Excited by the journey and the strange place, I was unable to sleep that first night in grandmother's cottage. The rumble of the waves, the insistent shushing whisper of the surf muttering a white-noise of secrets, vibrated even through the glass ... and grew louder still when I got up and nudged open the window to smell the salt air.

There, in the moonlight, a young girl stood on the beach— someone other than Grandmother, her friends, and my parents, talking about grown-up things while I patiently played the role of well-behaved daughter.

It was another girl unable to sleep.

I put on a bikini (my first) and a pair of jeans, tiptoed down the stairs, and let myself out the sliding glass door onto the sand. As I walked toward the ocean, reprimanding myself for the foolhardiness of going out alone at night, I saw her standing there, staring out into the waves.

She seemed statuesque in the moonlight, fragile, ethereal. She had waist-length hair the color of sun-washed sand, wide green eyes—I couldn't see them in the dark, but I knew they were green—and a smile that matched the warmth and gentleness of the evening breeze.

"Thank you for coming," she said. She paused for a few moments, perhaps waiting for a response. As I carefully weighed the advisability of speaking to a stranger, even one who looked as delicate as a princess from a fairy tale, she added, "My name is Julia."

"I'm Elizabeth," I replied after another ten seconds of agonized deliberation. I shook her outstretched hand as gravely as she had extended it, thinking what an odd gesture this was for someone who had probably just completed the sixth grade. Which, I discovered once we started to talk, was exactly the case—as it was for me.

We spoke to each other as if I had been there all along and often came out for a chat instead of strangers who had just met on the beach after midnight. Within half an hour, we were sitting and talking like old friends, laughing at spontaneous jokes, sharing confidences, even finishing each other's sentences as though we somehow knew what the other meant to say.

"Do you like secrets? And stories?" Julia asked during a brief lull in our conversation. When I hastened to assure her that I did—though I had never given it much thought—she fell silent for a long moment and then began to weave me a tale as she looked out upon the waves, like an astronomer gazing toward a distant galaxy.

"I have seen the Princes of the Seven Seas," she said in a soft, dreamy voice, "and each of their kingdoms is filled with more magic and wonder than the next. The two mightiest princes are the handsome twins, Ammeron and Ariston, who rule the kingdoms of the North."

She had found a large seashell on the beach and held it up to her ear, as if listening. "They tell me secrets. They tell me stories. Listen."

Julia half-closed her green eyes and talked in a whispery, hypnotic voice, as if reciting from memory—or repeating words she heard in the convolutions of the seashell.

"They have exquisite underwater homes, soaring castles made of coral, whose spires reach so close to the surface that they can climb to the topmost turrets when the waves are calm and catch a glimpse of the sky."

I giggled. Julia's voice was so earnest, so breathless. She frowned at me for my moment of disrespect, and I fell silent, listening with growing wonder as her story caught us both in a web of fantasy and carried us to a land of blues and greens, lights and shadows, beneath the shushing waves.

"Each kingdom is enchanted, filled with light and warmth, and the princes rarely stay long in their castles. They prefer instead to ride across the brilliant landscapes of the underwater world, watching over their realms.

"Their loyal steeds are sleek narwhals that carry Ammeron and Ariston to all—"

"What's a narwhal?" I asked, betraying my Midwestern ignorance of the sea and its mysteries.

Julia blinked at me. "They're a sort of whale—like unicorns of the sea. Strong swimmers with a single horn. Ancient sailors used to think they were monsters capable of sinking ships."

She cocked her head, listening to the shell. Her face fell into deep sadness for the next part of her story, and I wondered how she could make it all up so fast.

"The sea princes enjoy a charmed existence, full of adventure. They live forever, you know. One of their favorite quests is to hunt the kraken, hideous creatures that ruled the oceans in the time before the Seven Princes, but the defeated monsters hide now, brooding over their lost empires. They hate Ammeron and Ariston most of all, and lurk in dark sea caves, dreaming of their chance to murder the princes and take back what they believe is rightfully theirs.

"On one such hunt, when Ammeron and Ariston rode their beloved narwhal steeds into a deep cavern, armed with abalone-tipped spears, they flushed out the kraken king, an enormous tentacled beast twice the size of any monster the two brothers had fought before.

"Their battle churned the waves for days—we called it a hurricane here above the surface—until finally, in one terrible moment, the kraken managed to capture Ammeron with a tentacle and drew the prince toward its sharp beak, to slice him to pieces!"

I let out an unwilling gasp, but Julia didn't seem to notice.

"But at the last moment, Ammeron's brave narwhal, seeing his beloved prince about to die, charged in without regard for his own safety, and gouged out the kraken's eye with his single long horn! In agony, the monster released Ammeron and, thrashing about in the throes of death, caught the faithful narwhal in its powerful tentacles and crushed the noble steed an instant before the kraken, too, died."

A single tear slipped down Julia's cheek.

"And though the prince now rides a new steed, his loyal narwhal companion is lost forever. He realizes how lonely he is, despite the friendship of his brother. Very lonely. Ammeron longs for another companion to ease the pain, a princess he can love forever.

"Ariston also yearns for a mate, but the princes are wise and powerful. They will accept none other than the perfect partner. And they can wait. They live forever. They can wait."

We watched the moon disappear behind us and gradually the darkness over the ocean blossomed into petals of peach and pink and gold. I was awed by the swollen red sphere of the sun as it first bulged over the flat horizon, then rose higher, raining dawn across the waves like a firestorm. I had never seen such a sunrise before, and I would never see one as beautiful again.

But with the dawn came the realization that I had been up all night, talking with Julia. My parents never got up early, especially not on vacation. Still, I was anxious to get back to my grandmother's house, partly to snatch an hour or two of sleep, but mostly to avoid any chance of being caught.

I knew exactly what my parents would say if they knew I had gone out alone and spent the quiet, dark hours of the night talking to a total stranger. And I wouldn't be able to argue with them. It did sound crazy, completely unlike anything I had ever done before. Irresponsible. Even thinking the terrible word brought a hot flush of embarrassment to my cheeks.

But I wouldn't have traded that night for anything. Though I had resisted such silliness for most of my life, that was the first time I ever experienced magic.

≈≈≈

The vacation to Cocoa Beach became an annual event. Even when I went back to Wisconsin, Julia and I were rarely out of touch. My parents taught me to be practical and realistic, to think of the future and set long-term goals. Julia, however, remained carefree and unconcerned, as comfortable with her fantasies as with her real life.

We wrote long letters filled with plans for the future, and the hopes and hurts of growing up. We weren't allowed to call each other often, but whenever something important happened to me, the phone would ring and I would know it was Julia. She knew, somehow. Julia always knew.

During our summer weeks together, Julia spent endless hours telling me her daydreams about life in the enchanted realms beneath the sea. She had taught herself to sketch, and she drew marvelous, sweeping pictures of the undersea kingdoms. After listening to her for so long, I gradually learned to tell a passable story, though never with the ring of truth that she could give to her imaginings.

From Julia, I learned about the color of sunlight shining down from above, filtered through layers of rippling water. In my mind, I saw plankton blooms that made a stained-glass effect, especially at sunset. I learned how storms churned the surface of the sea, while the depths remained calm, though with a "mistiness" caused by the foamy wave tops above.

I learned about hidden canyons filled with huge mollusks, shells as big and as old as the giant redwood trees, which patiently collected all the information brought to them by the fish.

Julia told me about secret meeting places in kelp forests, where Ammeron and Ariston spent carefree hours in their unending lives playing hide-and-seek with porpoises. But the lush green kelp groves now seemed empty to them, empty as the places in their hearts that waited for true love.

One day we found a short chain of round metal links at the water's edge. What its original purpose was or who had left it there, I could not fathom. Julia picked it up with a look that was even more unfathomable. She touched each of the loops again and again, moving them through her fingers as if saying some magical rosary. We kept walking, splashing up to our ankles in the low waves, until Julia gave a small cry. One of the links had come loose in her hand. She stared at it for a moment in consternation, then gave a delighted laugh. She slid the circlet from one finger to the next until it came to rest on the ring finger of her right hand, a perfect fit.

"There. I always knew he'd ask." Julia sent me a sidelong glance, a twinkle lurking in the green of her irises. She loosened another link and slipped it quickly onto my hand.

"All right," I sighed, feeling suddenly apprehensive, but knowing it was no use trying to ignore her once she got started. "Who is 'he,' and what did he ask?"

"I am betrothed to Ammeron, heir to the Kingdom of the Seventh Sea," she said proudly.

"Sure, and I'm betrothed to his brother, Ariston." I held up the cheap metal ring on my finger. "Aren't we a bit young to get engaged, Jule?"

Julia was unruffled. "Time means nothing in the kingdoms beneath the sea. While a year passes here, it's no more than a day to them. Time is infinite there. Our princes will wait for us."

"You really think we're worth it? Besides, how do they know whether or not we accept?" I challenged, adding a completely out-of-place practicality to Julia's fairy tales. But my sarcasm sailed as far over Julia's head as a shooting star.

"Wait," she said, grasping my arm as she swept the ocean with her intense gaze. Suddenly, she drew in a sharp breath. "Look!" Her eyes lit up as a dolphin leapt twice, not far from where we stood on the shore. "There," she sighed, "do we need any more proof than that?"

Even in the face of her excitement, I couldn't keep the slight edge out of my voice. "I'll admit that I've never seen dolphins leap so close to shore, but what does that have to do with—"

"Dolphins are the messengers of the royal families beneath the sea," she replied in her patient way. Always patient. "One leap is a greeting. Two leaps ask a question. Three leaps give an answer." She flashed a smile at me. There was certainty in her voice that sent a shiver down my back. "And now they're waiting for us to respond!"

I struggled for a moment with impatience but couldn't bring myself to answer with more of my cynicism. I tried my most soothing voice. "Well, I'm sure Ammeron will understand that you—"

But she wasn't listening. Before I could finish my thought, she was running at top speed along the damp, packed sand. I looked after her, and as I watched in amazement, she executed three of the most graceful leaps I had ever seen, strong and clean and confident. I knew I would look foolish if I even tried something like that. I'd probably fall flat on my face in the sand.

By the time I caught up to her, Julia was looking seaward, ankle-deep in waves, with tears sparkling on her lashes—or perhaps it was only the sea spray.

In her hand, she held two more of the metal links from the chain she had found. Silently she handed me one of the links, then closed her eyes and threw the remaining one as far into the water as she could. I did the same, imitating her gesture but without the same conviction.

"Elizabeth," Julia said after a long moment, startling me with her quiet voice, "you are a very sensible person." It sounded like an accusation—and coming from Julia, it probably was.

We moved to dryer sand and sat for a long time watching the waves, letting the bright sun dazzle our eyes. Perhaps too long. But Julia's hand on my arm let me know that she saw it, too.

Far out in the water a dolphin leapt. Three times.

≈≈≈

Our lives were divided each year into reality and imagination, north and south, school and vacation, rationality and magic, until we finished high school.

I planned my life as carefully and sensibly as I could. My parents had taught me that a woman had to be practical—and I believed it. I chose my college courses with an eye toward the job market, avoiding "frivolous" art and history classes, no matter how much fun they sounded. After all, what good would they do me later in life?

My one concession to the lifelong pull the ocean had exerted on me was my choice to go to school at Florida State. Luckily, it was a perfectly acceptable school for the business management and accounting classes I intended to take, so I wasn't forced to define my reasons more precisely.

And it allowed me to see Julia more often.

Julia, on the other hand, always lived on the edge of reality. My parents disapproved of her, and I grew tired of defending her choices, so we came to the unspoken agreement that we would avoid the subject entirely, though even I couldn't help being a bit disappointed in my friend. To me, it seemed Julia was wasting her life at the seaside.

I tried to help her make some sensible choices as well. She wasn't interested in college, preferring to spend her days hanging out near the ocean, making sketches that she sold for a pittance in local gift shops, doing odd jobs.

I convinced her to learn scuba diving. With her love of the sea, I knew she would be a natural, and in less than a year she was a certified instructor with a small, steady business. I even took lessons from her, as did one of my boyfriends, though that ended in disaster.

As for romance, I occasionally went out on dates with men I met in classes, since I felt our mutual interests should form a solid basis for long-term partnership, but my dating resulted only in passionless short-term relationships that usually ended with an agreement to be "just friends." I never let on how much these breakups really hurt me, except to Julia.

After each one, I would call Julia and she would meet me at the Original Fat Boy's Bar-B-Que, waiting patiently while I drowned my sorrows in beer and brisket. Then we would drive to the beach, where I'd cry for a while, tell her the whole miserable tale, and vow never to make the same mistake again. Sometimes she drew tiny caricatures of my stories, turning them into comical melodramas as I spoke, until I was forced to acknowledge how silly or inconsequential each romance seemed as I dissolved into laughter and tears.

Julia dated often, drifting through each relationship with little thought for the future, until the inevitable stormy end—usually, I suspected, sparked by Julia's spur-of-the-moment nature and consequent unreliability that frequently frustrated men. Somehow on those nights, she would call to me and, no matter where I was, I would feel the need to go walking on our beach. And she would be there.

Once, burned at the end of a particularly tempestuous relationship, she asked what she was doing wrong—a rhetorical question, perhaps, but I answered her, despite my own poor track record in love. "You're spending too much time in a fairy tale, Jule. I used to really love your stories about the princes and the sea kingdoms, but we're not kids any more. Be a little more practical."

The ocean breeze lifted her pale hair in waves about her face as her sea-green eyes widened. "Practical? I could say you're living in just as much of a fairy tale, Elizabeth. The American Dream ... following all the rules, taking the right classes, expecting to find treasure in your career and a prince in some accountant or lawyer or doctor. Doesn't sound any more realistic to me."

It stung, but she just sighed and looked out to sea, getting that lost expression on her face again. "I'm sorry. I didn't mean to dump on you like that. Don't worry. I guess I shouldn't be so upset either. It doesn't really matter, you know. After all, I'm betrothed to the Prince of the Seventh Sea."

And I managed to laugh, which made me feel better. But Julia had a disturbing certainty in her voice.

≋≋≋

The last time I ever saw Julia, her call was very strong. I was studying late on campus, preparing for a final exam when for no apparent reason, I felt an overpowering need to get away from my books and talk to Julia. It had been months since I'd seen her.

But she needed to talk to me.

Even though there was a storm warning in effect, I ran out the door without even stopping to pick up a jacket, got into my car, and sped all the way to Cocoa Beach. As I sprinted down to the beach behind Julia's house, I saw her standing on the sand. Dimly silhouetted against the cloudy sky, wearing nothing but a white bathing suit, her long hair blew wildly in the wind as she stared out to sea. It reminded me of the first time I had seen Julia as a little girl, standing in the moonlight.

When I came to stand beside her and saw her startled

expression, I realized that something was very wrong: Julia hadn't expected me.

"You called me, Jule," I said. "What's going on?"

"I ... didn't mean to." She seemed to hesitate. "I'm going diving."

Then I noticed the pile of scuba gear close by, near the water. I understood Julia's subtle stubbornness enough to realize that she placed more weight on her feelings than on simple common sense, so I stifled the impulse to launch into a safety lecture and kept my voice neutral. "I know you have plenty of night-diving experience, but you shouldn't dive alone. Not tonight. The weather's not good. Look at the surf."

For a while, I thought she wouldn't answer. At last she said softly, "David's gone."

"The artist?" I asked, momentarily at a loss before successfully placing the name of the current man in her life.

She nodded. "It doesn't really matter, you know. He fell head-over-heels for a pharmacist. It hit him so hard, I almost felt sorry for him. Don't worry; I don't feel hurt. After all ..." Her voice trailed off. Her fingers toyed with the plain metal ring that hung from a silver chain around her neck. She had kept it all these years.

Her face was calm, but the storm in her sea-swept eyes rivaled the one brewing over the ocean. "After all," she finished with an enigmatic quirk of her lips, "I think tonight is my wedding night."

Uneasy, I tried for humor, hoping to stall her. "Don't you need a bridesmaid, then? I'll just go get my formal scuba tanks and my dress fins and meet you back here, okay?"

After a minute or so, she looked straight at me, clear-eyed and smiling. "Thank you for coming. I really did need to see you again, but right now I think I need to be alone for a while."

"I'm not sure I should leave," I said, reluctant to let her go, unable to force her to stay. "Friends don't let friends dive alone, you know."

"Don't worry, Elizabeth," she said, barely above a whisper. "Remember, no matter what happens, I'll call you." She put on her diving gear, letting me help her adjust the tanks, kissed me on the cheek, and waded into the turbulent water. "I'll call you in a week—probably less. I promise."

As I left the beach, I looked back every few seconds to watch her until I saw her head disappear beneath the waves.

≈≈≈

Later, Julia's tanks and her buoyancy compensator vest were found in perfect condition on the shore a few miles away. And a plain silver chain for a necklace. That was all.

≈≈≈

That was five years ago. And tonight, when I needed her the most, I heard her call again.

Sitting on the damp sands, I listened to the hushed purr of the waves and stared at the Atlantic Ocean under the moonlight.

At times like this, here on the beach where Julia and I used to sit together, I wondered if I really was the sensible one. Yes, I made all the "right" choices, earned my degree, found a suitable job, got a comfortable apartment—though no dashing prince (accountant, lawyer, or otherwise) seemed to notice. I had been supremely confident that it would only be a matter of time.

But then, with a simple blood test, I ran out of time. Next came more tests, then a biopsy, then a brief stay in the hospital. And behind it all loomed the specter of more and more time spent among the other cancer patients, other walking cadavers with the ticking of the death watch growing louder and louder inside their heads.

I would rather listen to the ocean.

It wasn't fair!

I raged at the universe. Hadn't I done everything right? Then why had I fallen under a medical curse, with no prince to kiss my cold lips and dislodge the bit of poisoned apple from my throat?

I needed to hear Julia's stories again. I longed to know more about the princes and their sea-unicorns, the defeated kraken, and the tall spires of coral castles in that enchanted undersea world where everyone lived forever.

I found a seashell on the shore, washed up by the tide, as if deposited there for me alone. I picked it up, brushing loose grains of sand from the edge. I held it to my ear ... and listened.

Far out in the water, I saw a dolphin make a double jump, two graceful silver arcs under the bright light of the moon.

My heart leapt with it, and I stood, blinking for a moment in disbelief. Then, feeling surprisingly restless and full of energy, I decided to go for a run along the beach.

And if I happened to leap once, twice, or three times ... who was there to know?

≈≈≈

Kevin J. Anderson is the author of 140 novels, fifty-six of which have appeared on national or international bestseller lists; he has over twenty-three million books in print in thirty languages. Anderson has coauthored fourteen books in the Dune saga with Brian Herbert; he and Herbert have also written an original SF trilogy, Hellhole. Anderson's popular epic SF series, The Saga of Seven Suns, as well as its sequel trilogy, The Saga of Shadows, are among his most ambitious works. He has also written a sweeping nautical fantasy trilogy, Terra Incognita, accompanied by two rock CDs (which he wrote and produced). He has written two steampunk novels, *Clockwork Angels* and *Clockwork Lives*, with legendary Rush drummer and lyricist Neil Peart. He also created the popular humorous horror series featuring Dan Shamble, Zombie P.I., and has written eight high-tech thrillers with Colonel Doug Beason.

He holds a physics/astronomy degree and spent fourteen years working as a technical writer for the Lawrence Livermore National Laboratory. He is now the publisher of Colorado-based WordFire Press. He and his wife, bestselling author Rebecca Moesta, have lived in Colorado for twenty years. Anderson has climbed all of the mountains over 14,000 feet in the state, and he has also hiked the 500-mile Colorado Trail.

Rebecca Moesta (pronounced MESS-tuh) is the author of many science fiction and fantasy young-adult books, both solo and in collaboration with her husband, Kevin J. Anderson—including the Star Wars: Young Jedi Knights series, Buffy the Vampire Slayer: Little Things, *Star Trek: TNG, The Gorn Crisis* graphic novel, the original Crystal Doors trilogy, *Grumpy Old Monsters,* and the Star Challengers trilogy. She is also the co-publisher of WordFire Press, which has released 300 titles so far.

MANDALA

JODY LYNN NYE

Manami, Aoki thought dreamily, wriggling his way along the smooth, silver sand. Ever since he had come to maturity, he had believed that she was the only female whose eggs would produce perfect offspring—his offspring. If only she felt the same way!

Aoki swam up from the design to survey it from above with one bulging eye. He had completed one more ray of his creation. The carved pattern in the sand of the riverbed looked like a sea anemone. Its white spokes jutted outward from the center platform, and small cuplike depressions had been filled with lighter particles and bits of shell and seaweed that danced in the current. The small, brown-and-white puffer fish had incised his design within a perfect circle, not a line or a single element beyond that ring.

Satisfying to behold, but not nearly strong or appealing enough, he thought, flitting to and fro in his impatience. *More. I must do more. She is choosy, and she deserves the best. I am the best.*

So many males vied for Manami, including a score from his own school, brothers and cousins spawned in nests like this one, in riverbeds all around the coast of the tropical island off the huge mainland. Unlike fish from lesser species like lionfish, puffers did not descend to fighting to the death to gain the female of their choice. Rather, they threw their passion into art to entice the mates

...., ,ought. Aoki had seen some of the efforts of his siblings. He had not been impressed. He was a far better artist than they.

When he had gone hunting for the ideal place to design his nest, this estuary beckoned to the very depths of his soul. None of his brothers had sought out this particular riverbed. Not long ago, there had been a gaping hole that everyone believed was haunted by the spirits of the deep. It had disappeared under the shifting sands, leaving behind an open expanse where he could create the great art that would bring females from all over the eastern seas, but especially Manami. Besides, Aoki didn't believe in spirits.

"When you mate, it is not just for life," his father had told his swarm of sons. "It is for the life of all existence. Creativity begets creation. You'll feel the urgency of the body, but that is the basest impulse. You will entice your mate to lay eggs that you fertilize, then you have to protect the young with all the power and art that is in you, for a year at the least. We are tied to the rest of the world, to things that you will never see, lives you will never live. Wisdom such as this requires you to relinquish the self and to find unity with all being. Dig deeply, and you will find wonders beyond wonders. Art puts things where they belong. Great art keeps them there."

Aoki did his best to keep his father's lessons in mind, but he found it difficult, picturing Manami's flawless fins, nearly translucent as they beat against the current, the bulge of her head, the flirtatious curve of her tail, the way her brown-spotted back curved so enticingly into the smooth creaminess of her belly.

Focus! he ordered himself. *All of creation! Not just one beautiful female.*

A Diadema spine in the midst of the heap of materials he had gathered caught his eye. Its deep blue coloration would add contrast and sharpness to the mandala, but not symmetry. Hadn't he gathered at least five? He attacked the pile. Coral sand flew up in a cloud, blinding him, but he knew the smells of everything. In moments, he had extracted the handsome spines, and swam to the edge of his pattern to survey where they might go.

Are you not finished yet, my friend?

The words came from within Aoki's mind. Alarmed, he scooted into a hollow in the sand, burying himself deeply. The mind-voice laughed.

A hand pushed aside the sand, and a huge, round, human face peered down at him. Aoki's heart beat with panic, then calmed. He feared the fishermen who came from inland of the Nansei islands, who had captured and consumed so many of his family despite the poison in his spines and organs. Oromani only looked like a land-being in her upper half. The rest of the *ningyo* was as much a fish as he.

"What do you want?" Aoki asked. "Manami said she would come to see my art at the evening tides."

"There is no need to finish this sad spectacle," Oromani said, swishing her blue-scaled tail playfully near the circular design. "By tomorrow, all will be laid waste, and you will not have to be concerned with mates and children."

"What do you mean?" Aoki asked, alarmed. "Don't touch that! I have spent days perfecting it!"

The ningyo scooped up a handful of coral fragments from the center of the mandala. Aoki puffed himself up and flew at her. She dodged the deadly spines easily.

"You are so focused on yourself," Oromani complained, dropping the bits from her hand. They floated haphazardly in the current. "It is sterile, plain—without power. Certainly not perfect. Have you not felt the juddering of the seafloor?"

"Of course!" Aoki said with indignation, gathering up the pieces in his mouth. He spat them back into the center of the design. "You are interrupting me. Manami said she would come to see it before the evening tides. I do not want to disappoint her."

Oromani laughed again, her mouth lined with pointed teeth like an eel's.

"You would do well to concentrate on saving yourself," she said, "and not so much on winning a mate. Manami will be very disappointed. There is nothing of your soul in what you are doing, only your ego. That way lies the death of us all. You are opening a window to destruction. You see only what is on the surface, not the whole."

Aoki felt his temper rise.

"How dare you say that?" he said. "This is a great work of art!"
Oromani flitted to and fro. She made a disdainful face.

"I like you, but if you do not listen, you will die in ignorance.
This is my last warning."

She slashed the mandala with her tail, leaving a deep gash in
the white sands. The riverbed began to dance and heave. Alarmed,
Aoki swam back and forth, furious at her carelessness.

"Leave me alone!" he snapped.

"Stop wasting your time!" she called back as she glided away
through the muddied waters.

Time? he thought. How could mating be a waste of time? His
whole being ached with the yearning to raise young. He surveyed
the ruin of his pattern. Only hours remained before the evening
tides began, and Manami's promised visit. He had to start all over!

Yet, the riverbed continued to buck and shift. He had felt
such disturbances in his youth. The seafloor and the islands rested
unsteadily upon the breast of the world. When its heart heaved,
all the inhabitants of the deep felt it. He dithered, his small fins
vibrating in the water. Should he flee and come back another day?

No, I should not, he thought. Earthquakes happened frequently
on the rim of the great ocean. Even in the ultramarine depths, where
his kind lived after hatching, the seafloor jumped and juddered at
times. His father never showed alarm at the movement. No reason
to cease his efforts. With the rise of the moon, his beloved would
find her way to this lonely spot, and their future would be ensured.

Grumbling to himself over Oromani's mistreatment of his
pattern, he began to rebuild.

It took time to reassemble the collection of artifacts from
where she had scattered them. Aoki pressed his smooth side
into the cushiony sand, carving out the complicated rays he had
envisioned.

No soul? He felt insulted at Oromani's careless remark. Still,
the ningyo had lived many centuries. She had seen countless puffers
like himself recreating the designs of desire and protection. He
had listened to his father and grandsires and other senior males

describing the passion that drove them. Their mandalas had surely been wonders to behold. Was he being too shallow?

Aoki held still for a moment, held in place by the flutter of the tiny winglike fins on his sides. He let the fast-moving current flow over his back, sensing the elements around him. Water held such power, as did the hot white sun that beat down through the shimmering surface. The bed below only commanded his interest when he sought food or, as now, the perfect place to raise his young.

The riverbed did seem unusually restive. He had combed it smooth before Oromani had upset it. If he wanted the perfect nest, he had to concentrate his efforts, and not let anything, especially a playful ningyo, distract him. He set to work.

Conscious of every sensation, he enjoyed the smooth flow of the sand against his sides, like a caress from a loved one. In his mind, he pictured the ideal circle, gleaming like the pearl of an oyster, clean, round and shining. With every movement, he did his best to bring that perfection into being. At the end of every ripple, he turned upward and dove back toward the center as if his body turned on an invisible sphere. All his movements described circles within circles, the most perfect shape in creation. Eggs were round. Eyes were round. The world was round. He felt a deep oneness with all of existence.

Aoki completed etching the preliminary design into the sand, the template he intended to follow, and rose above it to take a look. As much as he hated to admit it, Oromani had been right. The difference between a nest made mindfully and one into which he poured his whole being was the same as between a starfish and the daystar. How brightly the design seemed to gleam! It held its shape against the flow of water. A tiny orange worm creeping along the riverbed changed direction to avoid it. The circle held an almost hypnotic beauty. Shapes seemed to shift within its confines, like the phantoms of a dream. Aoki swam closer to have a look.

Suddenly, a massive, green-scaled hand shot upward from the center.

Terrified, Aoki backfinned and shot away from the circle. He took shelter behind the nearest outcropping, a boulder slimy with green moss. Cautiously, he peered around its bulk.

The hand flailed around, feeling for the edge, though not seeming to grasp it. Aoki's small heart pounded in fear. Had he created this monstrosity? Never in his wildest imaginings had such a thing ever appeared. It looked like one of the horrors his eldest grandsire told in a cautionary nighttime tale, guaranteed to make the feeble-stomached among them excrete in fear. A *ningen*, Grandsire had called it, giant kin to the ningyo, but far larger and without mercy. It tore young fish to quivering gobbets of flesh and devoured them by the thousand.

Aoki twitched back and forth in the water, his gills flapping. That must be the source of the hole in the riverbed that they had all seen!

He wanted to flee and never return to the spot, but his father's voice came back to him. If he was ready to be a parent, he took on the forces of creation. If he had been responsible for conjuring such a terror, he had to drive it back again. Manami could arrive at any moment.

He spotted a drift of large stones in the nearest bend. Aoki snatched up the biggest one he could fit in his mouth. He swam above the hand and let it drop. To his astonishment, the rock fell *through* the hand. It struck the mandala, sending up a spray of sand and coral bits. The fingers splayed outward in alarm. Then the hand vanished. It was insubstantial, but would it remain so?

What have I done? Aoki thought, in a panic. He zipped back and forth over his ruined design. His effort to create a nest to attract his ladylove had turned into a portal for a monster from the depths to ascend. He swam around and around the circle, but there was no sign of the creature. The translucency he had seen before had also vanished when the perfection of the circle was smashed by his rock. He nudged frantically at the edges, urging them back into line. With his nose, he pressed sand into a rim to surround the design, hoping to hold it in place.

Instead of the lyrical shapes of courtship that he had been drawing, he dragged forth memories of strong forms that his father had shown him. In a thousand lifetimes, he never would have imagined that he would have to use them in a mating nest. Instead of the endless loops that invited a female to stay, he began to incise a spiral, working from the outermost edge inward, all too keenly aware of the monster lurking just below the surface. The fear made it harder to concentrate, but he had to focus.

The purpose of a mandala, as his father had said, was that the image and the creation of the image brought all thoughts to bear upon one goal. Normally, his nest would be a comfortable and soothing place to bring up young to maturity of a year or more, granting protection from other creatures that would eat the tender young fry. Aoki knew that other mandalas lay upon the seabed. He had seen the colorful circles here and there, but never thought to ask why they existed, and he cursed himself for his incuriosity. Monsters could come up through those empty portals if no one drew a protective symbol upon them. The midnight tales his grandsire had told were true! That had been the meaning of Oromani's warning. Why hadn't she told him what to do?

Perhaps she wanted him to fail, Aoki thought sulkily, as he came to the center and planted the purple-rimmed shell of a poisonous sea snail deep in its heart.

No, she had been a friend. The fear of the monster was a poison working on his mind, in the way that a creature stung by the puffer venom would suffer paralysis and death. All things were circular. Life and death were part of the cycle. He consumed smaller fish and krill to live. Their death fed his life.

Is that the cost of safety, then? Aoki wondered. He looked around at the flowing river full of life in its many colors and shapes: plants, insects, fish, shellfish, even the dauntless humans sailing on the surface. Should the monster crawl out of its dark realm, it might snuff out all life here, or so his grandsire's tales said.

Aoki blew himself up to his greatest size. Very well, then. If it meant protecting this place from the ningen, he would give his own life. Alas for the young who would never come to be, but the living deserved to continue. Aoki concentrated on the love he had for his family and the rest of his kind, for the other undersea life that teemed around him, and even for those who walked upon dry land surrounded by the sea. He had the power and the responsibility to stop the monster from coming up here if he could.

Once he was resolved, calm settled over him like a cloak of sunshine. He began to draw protective patterns along the spiral path, strengthening its endless form with bold lines, squares, interlocking loops and curves.

Crash! The sea snail shell bobbed at the center. Aoki peered into the depths of his design. The monster retreated a length or two, then rushed forward, smashing against the portal again and again. Aoki could not help but be fascinated. The more clearly he drew the mandala, the more visible that which lay underneath it became.

He saw a fantastic landscape, a sea of many colors, pearlescent, electric, jagged, smooth, beautiful, and terrifying, populated by creatures beyond his imagination. The ningen was not even the most frightening of those who lived there and wanted to creep out into the upper reality. Things with countless eyes in the middle of a mass of tentacles opened huge red maws at him. A fish whose sawlike proboscis was three times the length of its dull green body swam back and forth as if waiting for the way to be open. Aoki thought he saw a jellyfish whose body flashed disturbing colored lights intended to drive him mad.

Aoki fought against even the tiniest illusion that tried to peep through unfinished circles. Whenever the ningen attempted to thrust a finger between the tight lines, Aoki darted over with a stone or a chunk of coral. His movements were slowing down, and he knew it. He was tired and growing hungry. During the days in which he was planning the first design, he had the leisure to stop and eat a passing shrimp or worm, even to gnaw upon moss, but now he could not stop until the pattern was fully drawn.

Overhead, the daystar began to set, casting reds and deep blues upon the water. A small boat drifted overhead. The shifting current disturbed the edge of the mandala, and instantly, a gnarled green finger began to scratch at the pattern, upsetting stones. Aoki seized a mouthful of stones and dropped them onto the ningen's hand. To his horror, some of them bounced off. The ningen was beginning to solidify. Aoki stacked more and more pebbles until the finger vanished again, but the pattern pulsed upward again and again, like an eggshell whose inhabitant was ready to hatch.

This monster must not be birthed into the world.

The puffer dove back into the lines on the sand, deepening them and adding bits of shell and coral to make them even stronger. He felt his strength began to flag with the dying of the day. How he regretted choosing a site so far away from his brothers! He could have called upon them for help.

Aoki had a sudden inspiration. He hurried back to his pile of found objects and dragged an urchin spine upon the heaving mound. Where it touched, the fingers recoiled as if stung. Aoki flapped his fins in triumph. The blue spikes had the power to repel. He needed as many as he could find.

But he had only five, not nearly enough to cover the mandala with a protective pattern. He knew where the rest of them lay, though he feared that if he left the nest to retrieve them, the ningen would find a way to batter through in his absence. What to do?

"Aoki, where are you?"

To his horror, he looked toward the sky and realized the hour. Manami had come to see his offering.

"Go away!" he shouted. "Go back! Don't come here!"

The soft, pale body fluttered down from the current. Her protuberant eyes looked sad.

"You asked me to come," she said. "I thought you wished me to be your mate."

"More than anything," Aoki said. Despite his worry, he was enchanted by her beauty. He wanted to rub along her side and feel the smoothness of her scales, but he had to keep building. "But I cannot. There is danger here! Please go, Manami—and remember me."

"Remember you?" she asked, following him as he dragged yet another branch of coral into his pattern. "Why, what is wrong?"

At the sound of her voice, the clawed hand shot through the mandala.

Aoki thrust himself between her and the ningen, urging her upward toward the surface of the river. He dropped a pebble on the hand. It recoiled, but only a little.

"This place," he said, "is a portal to the underworld. I brought power here, and it attracted the ningen. Manami, it is my mistake, and my responsibility. The monster must not break through. I have to stop it. Go back and warn the others, in case I fail."

Even as he spoke, he heard the weakness in his voice. Manami's eyes softened. She swam forward to touch lips with him. He felt a surge of love and worry.

"You are so brave, much braver than your brothers," she said. "Of course I will not leave. I am glad I came. How can I help?"

Aoki felt torn between terror for her safety and relief. "Are you certain?"

"I am," Manami said. "I will not desert you."

"Do you see these spines?" he asked, swimming down to rearrange the urchin needles. "I took these from a hollow near the river mouth. I cannot leave, so you must bring all that you can carry. Hurry!"

"I fly, my love," Manami said. Her tail flicked, and she vanished into the twilight. Soon, she returned, and dropped three of the precious spears at the edge of the mandala. A baleful eye so large that its lids lay beyond the circle glared up at them. Aoki took the spines into the center of the design, and she left to bring more.

"That is all there is," Manami said, spitting out four small blue-black spines. She helped Aoki arrange them in a hexagonal pattern near the center.

Once those were placed, the two puffers retreated upward. Aoki's gills fluttered, trying to bring in as much life-giving oxygen as possible. He had never felt so tired.

"Thank you," he said.

"My pleasure," Manami said. "It is very beautiful."

Aoki looked down at his work. The lines etched in the sand formed the most complicated of designs, even more than he had realized he was constructing. It formed a lacelike net with the stones and coral and other items studding it like jewels. The cup at the center held nothing but hope to hold back the constant battering it received from below. In a short time, the fierce efforts of the ningen would set it free, to wreak havoc in the upper world.

"It's not enough," he said, in resignation. "I have given it all the power I have within me, and more. The ningen will break through."

"Not all," Manami said, with a shy look. "You have not yet given it the power of life."

Aoki regarded her with wonder. "You would … mate with me? Despite the danger?"

"That is why you asked me to come here, isn't it?"

"Well …" He dithered, wishing her far away and safe, but desperate enough to grasp at any possibility. "The strength of our mating might be enough to make the mandala permanent and protect this place. I see how much stronger it is just from your help."

Manami gave a coy flick of her tail. "If I hadn't seen the monster, I would say it was an attempt to get me to accept you. The world is ending. The monster is coming."

Aoki flustered. "Then go," he said, puffing himself up. "I would not coerce you. Tell the others to prepare."

Manami laughed.

"Don't be silly," she said. She flitted to the center of the mandala. "It is very beautiful."

Aoki followed, feeling silly. "It is not what I intended to have for you."

"What female would not be impressed by a male who could harness danger on her behalf?" Manami said. She settled into the heaving sands and bent her body. First one at a time, then in small clusters, small round gray eggs, as perfect as pearls, began to settle into the depression that was made to hold them. Aoki felt a surge of joy. He rose above her and released his seed onto the eggs.

The riverbed below them bucked like a shark caught in a net. Beneath the mandala, the immense eye pressed against the transparent surface. Aoki did his best to ignore it. When he had finished fertilizing Manami's eggs, he nestled beside her in the sandy cup.

"The mandala will either hold or it won't," he said, enjoying the closeness, but unwilling to sacrifice her. "Your part is finished. You do not need to stay if you fear the monster."

"It will hold," she insisted, her round dark eye fixed upon him. "I trust you. You are my chosen, and these will be our children."

"Then all is perfect," Aoki said. He hoped it was true.

Though the circle heaved and tossed beneath him, he kept his energy focused upon her and thought of the thousands of young who would hatch from the eggs around them, the new guardians of the river. Circles within circles, as his father would say.

Knives of green fire burst like lightning between the lines drawn in the sand. Aoki put himself between them and Manami. Talons poked at them from underneath as the ningen's claws tried to break through the barrier. The whole circle bucked and quivered like the worst seaquake ever. A howl burst forth. Aoki and Manami looked at each other with concern. In a heartbeat, they were surrounded by dancing demons of green fire. Aoki felt his scales seem to crisp in the heat. He puffed himself out. He vowed to withstand it all, for the sake of his young yet to come, and the female to whom he had given his life and his heart.

"I will not be beaten by you!" he cried.

The demons rushed at him. Aoki turned and turned again, striking them with the spines in his side, willing that his venom would destroy his enemy. He rammed the demons. The pain made him gasp, but he would not stop until the last fire was out. They would not win, not while there was life in his body to triumph over death.

Suddenly, the last demon flickered and disappeared. All was still. Aoki and Manami remained hovering a short distance above the cup, wary of another attack, but none came. The hand and the baleful eye were gone.

The translucence faded, leaving the circle beneath him spent and drained of color. He flitted out of the small enclosure to check the eggs. They were intact. Several had begun clouding slightly, meaning that they were fertile. Aoki felt his heart swell with relief and joy. They had beaten the monster back and sealed the way against it.

Manami laughed. She flicked her ventral fin and rose upward. "What tales we will have to tell these young," she said. "You are exhausted, my love. Let me bring you food."

Resting in the heart of the mandala, Aoki felt it to be a living thing, a protection and a bulwark, a true third member of their family.

"What tales, indeed?" he said, and waited for his mate to return.

≈≈≈

Jody Lynn Nye lists her main career activity as "spoiling cats." When not engaged upon this worthy occupation, she writes fantasy and science fiction books and short stories.

Since 1987, she has published more than fifty books and 160 short stories, including epic fantasies, contemporary humorous fantasy, humorous military science fiction, and edited three anthologies. She collaborated with Anne McCaffrey on a number of books, including the *New York Times* bestseller *Crisis on Doona*. She also wrote eight books with Robert Asprin, and continues both Asprin's Myth-Adventures series and Dragons series. Her newest series is the Lord Thomas Kinago adventures, the most recent of which is *Rhythm of the Imperium* (Baen Books), a humorous military SF novel.

Her other recent books are *Myth-Fits* (Ace Books); *Wishing on a Star* (Arc Manor Press); an e-collection of cat stories; *Pros and Cons*, a collection of essays for new writers co-written with her husband, Bill Fawcett; and *Moon Beam*, a young adult science fiction novel coauthored with scientist Travis S. Taylor. Jody runs the two-day intensive writers' workshop at DragonCon, and she and Bill Fawcett are the book reviewers for *Galaxy's Edge Magazine*. Learn more about Jody at jodylynnye.com.

ABOUT THE EDITOR

Lisa Mangum has worked in the publishing industry since 1997. She is currently the Managing Editor for Shadow Mountain Publishing. She is also the author of four national best-selling YA novels (The Hourglass Door trilogy and *After Hello*) as well as several short stories and novellas. She edited *One Horn to Rule Them All: A Purple Unicorn Anthology*, *A Game of Horns: A Red Unicorn Anthology*, and *Dragon Writers: An Anthology*, also published by WordFire Press. She graduated with honors from the University of Utah, and currently lives in Taylorsville, Utah, with her husband, Tracy. Visit her at facebook.com/lisamangum or on Twitter @LisaMangum.

IF YOU LIKED ...

If you liked *Undercurrents*, you might also enjoy these other
WordFire Press Anthologies:

Dragon Writers

Maximum Velocity

Avatar Dreams

OTHER WORDFIRE PRESS ANTHOLOGIES EDITED BY LISA MANGUM

One Horn to Rule Them All

A Game of Horns

Dragon Writers

Our list of other WordFire Press authors and titles is always growing. To find out more and to see our selection of titles, visit us at:

wordfirepress.com